Missing Pieces

David and Debbie Paton

We would like to dedicate this book in memory of our grandparents. For the short time we had them with us, it was priceless.

To our parents for their support and encouragement to follow our dreams. These people have all enriched our lives and for that we would like to say thank you.

Appreciation

Once again I must say thank you to my wife, Debbie, for editing this book and working with me on it. It is so much fun sharing ideas on the many different parts of the book. Wait until you see what we have in store for you in the next book.

To Don Wyatt, my friend, who helped me on my first book. He was very willing to help again with this book. He has given many suggestions and has given much time.

Thank you both so very much!

Missing Pieces

Table of Contents

Chapter 1

Dashing Into Darkness

I had waited for this night for a long time making prepa-
rations for my trip to the city. Some of the men in the
settlement had talked about going to the city to bring back
more loved ones, but no one had. I told them once that I
would like to go back and find my Grandma Ramona and
Grandpa Russell. They just laughed at me and said, "Carl
Wilson, you are too young to make such a trip." I stood up
and told them that I was not too young and that some day I
would go to the city and find my grandma and grandpa. You
just wait and see!

Tonight is that night. I had carefully planned my exit.
Most of my supplies I had carried to the cave behind the
waterfall, only taking a few things at a time so no one would
get suspicious of what I was planning.

I could tell Kayla was starting to drift off to sleep. She
liked to sing her little songs that she had learned in school
or some of the silly ones that she made up. It was funny
to listen to her sing; she had stopped and started that same
song four times now. It wouldn't be long now until she'd be
sleeping. I would miss her and her silly little songs. There
went mom and dad's light in their bedroom. It would not be
long until dad was snoring. Mom said that his snoring was

loud enough to wake the dead. Dad, of course, says it's not him that is snoring but that it's mom; and then he winks at Kayla and me. Then mom would mess up dad's hair-what little he had left. I'd miss those fun times at the kitchen table. Oh my! There goes dad and his snoring.

I would wait a little longer before I left the house. I would have to make my bed to make it look like I was still sleeping, just in case mom looked in. I had dad's old backpack mostly loaded. There were just a few more things to put in there. That could be done while I made sure all in the house were sleeping. I would leave them this note to tell them what I was doing: Dear Mom and Dad, Don't be mad. I have gone to get Grandma Ramona and Grandpa Russell and bring them home to us where they belong. I will be careful; and I will trust in God to bring us all home safe and soon. Love, your son, Carl

P.S. Tell Kayla not to cry.

Now, where to put this note so that they would find it, but not too soon that they would catch up to me and stop me from my mission of bringing back grandma and grandpa. I'd place the note under my blankets so when they came to wake me up to have breakfast, I would have been gone a good eight hours or more.

It was time to go now, so I slung my backpack on and walked down the hallway trying not to hit too many of the squeaky floorboards. I looked in on Kayla and said goodbye to her while she slept. I gently grabbed the partially opened door to her room. The moon was shining through her bedroom window giving her face an angelic glow as she slept with the blanket tucked in and around her chin.

"Goodbye, Kayla, and don't cry too much. I will be home soon with grandma and grandpa. Then we all can be one big family again."

Carefully I shut the door and checked to see if mom and dad were sleeping. Dad's snoring had quieted down some.

The one true test to see if your mom is sleeping is to stand outside her bedroom and softly say, "Mom, mom, mom" three times and then wait a little. If you hear nothing, it is then time to go. I heard nothing stirring, so it was time to go.

I walked through the house in the dark making sure I didn't bump into anything on my way to the back door. As I entered the kitchen, I could feel the butterflies in my stomach. I walked around the table with my hand touching each of the chairs. The first chair was Kayla's. She had always sat across from me at the table; and when we were little, we would sometimes kick each other. To Kayla's right was mom's chair, and to her left was dad's chair. The last chair was mine. I sat the closest to the door because mom always said I was in a hurry to go outside and play. Tonight I was no longer playing. I was no longer little Carl, the son of Mark and Maggie Wilson.

As I walked through the door, I could feel the cool, late August night air lightly blowing across my face. The moon was peeking in and out of the clouds. That may make getting out of the settlement a little bit harder, but I did plan for that. I dressed in my darkest clothes. I darkened my face with some of the dirt from mom's flowerbed so that the moonlight would not shine on my white skin. The leather hat would hide my blonde hair. Now all I had to do was wait until the night guard made his checks at this end of the settlement, and I would be on my way. Even though the settlement had been here for many years, they still had someone stand guard just in case the state police would happen to find us. The guard would be able to sound the alarm, and some of us could make it to another backup settlement deeper into the wilderness, but only the elders knew where that was.

The guard was coming now. It shouldn't be long. Last night I counted to 85, and then he was out of sight. What was he doing? No! Don't sit down now to take a rest. I need you to move along. I need all the time I can get to get going! I must have made a noise because the guard was looking right towards me. I couldn't move a muscle or he would see me. He was starting to walk this way. I must stay calm.

I heard a window opening on the side of the house. "Hello, Pastor Mark, can't sleep tonight?" the guard asked.

"No, I have this strange feeling that something isn't right. Maybe it's something I ate. Maybe I'll have to get a cup of milk to settle my stomach down so I can get some rest. Just knowing you're out there on duty, Peter, will help me get rid of that feeling that something is not right."

"Good night, Pastor Mark. Sleep well. Nothing gets past old Peter."

"Thanks, Peter."

I heard dad shut the window, and Peter continued the rest of his rounds. When he got past Brad's house, I headed to the path leading to the waterfall and the tunnel back to the city. The light was on in the kitchen, and I saw dad getting more than a cup of milk out of the icebox. It looked like he was going for some of the leftover chicken from supper. Oh, mom just caught dad. That was not good for dad or me. If mom decided to check my room on her way back to her bedroom, my trip to the city would be very short. I had to drop my backpack by the tree outside the window of my room and get inside. I rushed to the partly opened window and opened it as wide as I could and slipped into bed.

I heard mom and dad coming down the hall. They were at Kayla's room. Then I heard them come down the hall and whisper something outside my door. The hinges on my door began to squeak. Dad said, "Just open the door fast and it won't squeak as much."

"Or maybe if you would put a little oil on it, that would stop the squeak altogether," Mom said with a hint of sarcasm.

"There, Carl's sleeping like a log. Now can we go to bed?"

I heard the door squeak shut. I reached up and put my hand on top of my head and gave a sigh of relief. I found I still had my hat on. I grabbed my hat and pulled it under the blankets hoping that they didn't notice that I had it on in bed. Oooops! There was the door squeaking again. I was caught for sure.

"See Maggie, Carl isn't sleeping with a hat on. You say that my eyes are bad."

As the door went shut, I could feel my heart beating about a hundred beats per minute, and my hands were all sweaty. I had to move quickly and remake the bed. I stood by the window looking to see where Peter was. Hopefully he was still on the other side of the settlement. As I crawled out the window, I remembered that I hadn't put my note back under the blanket. I found the note on the floor next to my bed. It was a little wrinkled from jumping into bed when mom and dad were coming down the hall. I smoothed the note out the best I could. There, everything was back the way it was. I must get moving because I had a long night ahead of me. I slipped out the window and over to my backpack. I took a couple quick looks to see if anyone was around. The path that would lead me to the waterfall and tunnel was about 100 yards away. I ran a short distance and then stopped behind some of the big oak trees. Then I could see if anybody was coming. I had 20 yards to go between here and the edge of the woods and no place to stop and hide if someone would happen to come out and see me running. I was just about to make one last dash into the darkness when something grabbed my backpack. It seemed like my heart stopped forever. I tried turning to see who it was. I found that when I stood up, I had hooked my backpack on a birdhouse that someone had hung on the tree.

"Halt! Who goes there?"

It was Peter. He must have seen me struggling to unhook the birdhouse from my backpack. Well, I better say it's me or he'd start blowing his whistle and wake up the whole settlement. I opened my mouth to say something.

Another voice said, "Peter, you old fool. You don't know your own wife? I've come to bring you something to eat and drink."

Peter tried to cover up his embarrassment and said, "Why, of course I do, dear. I was just having a little fun with you. Let's sit over here while I eat and drink what you have brought me tonight."

They walked over to sit down on a stump of an oak tree that had been cut down after that big storm earlier this spring. The stump made a great bench for sitting. It was also far enough away so that I could make my last dash into the darkness of the woods. I ran quietly and as fast as I could, only slowing down to turn to see if Peter and his wife had noticed me running. As I reached the edge of the woods, I stopped and looked back at the settlement one last time before I journeyed into the city where dad grew up. He said all he remembered was the cold grayness of everything and no one ever smiled, unless it was the state police and they had just caught you doing something wrong. I walked down the path to the cave opening where I had been putting things for the past few weeks. I could hear the animals of the night moving about.

I reached the open, grassy field where dad said he first saw some kids from the settlement wave to him many years ago. Now I was going to cross the same grassy field. The clouds had broken up and the sky was mostly clear. The moon was lighting the way. The tall, dry grass had taken on the white from the moonlight making it seem a little like snow. The path that I needed to follow was dark and wound its way to the other side where it was then swallowed up by the dark forest. I started across the field. The grass was waist high and it was as if I was floating. I heard nothing but the rustling of the grass in the light breeze; and before I knew it, I was at the other edge of the grassy field heading back into the darkness of the forest.

I could now hear the sound of the waterfall in front of the cave where I would rest for a short time only to scratch a short note to those that may come looking for me. What I would say to them I didn't know. I still had a ways to go before I got there. Maybe then I would have something figured out to say, and then again maybe not. I walked along the path trying not to trip on the rocks and roots that littered it. Kids were not permitted to come this far unless they were on an outing with adults, usually to go fishing. When I came up over a rise, I could see the waterfall sparkling through the trees because of the moonlight shining on the water. As I got closer to the waterfall, it seemed to grow taller; or was it the moonlight playing tricks on me? I stood at the base of the waterfall. The moonlight was shining through the mist of the falling water and producing a rainbow. I knew what to scratch on the wall to those that may come looking for me once I saw the rainbow. I walked into the cave and headed to the pond's edge. The moonlight was illuminating the water and giving me enough light to walk about the room to find the rest of my supplies that I had put there for my journey. I placed as many of my supplies in my backpack as I could cram in there. The rest I put in a smaller sack made from deer hide and tied that to my poles that would be used as a ladder. I grabbed my things and headed up to the upper room where I would leave a note to those that would come looking for me. Dad would most likely be the first one to come looking, so I would write my note next to the words he left when he came to the settlement many years ago. There wasn't enough moonlight to see the writings on the wall, so I took out my flint and knife and a piece of old cotton. With just a few strikes of my knife against the flint, sparks started the cotton on fire so I could light a candle. The candlelight filled the room with a soft yellow glow. Slowly walking around the room, I read many of the writings of the others that had traveled this way before. I came across dad's words he scratched in the wall. There was a clear spot next to his words.

The lid of an old food can that I found worked great for scratching my words: "I must make this journey back to the city that is so gray and has little hope. I will be like the rainbow I have seen tonight made by the moonlight and the mist from the waterfall. Though it is small, it is a light into the darkness. Don't follow but only pray. Each time you see a rainbow, think of me and pray." When I finished my note, I stood back to read it and hoped that I hadn't misspelled any words. After reading it one more time, I signed it Carl W. "Time is a wasting" as Great Grandpa Roy would say. I needed to start into the tunnel and get as much distance between me and those that would come looking for me in the morning when they found out that the lump under the blankets in my bed was not me. Because I'd heard the story of the trip through the tunnel from dad, it would take a lot of the guesswork away as to whether I go left or right.

I carefully worked my way through the tunnel getting the feel for where I may be for the next few days. I needed to pace myself as dad did. One hand I kept on the wall as I walked the winding path through the cave. At times I had to crawl and drag my backpack and other supplies behind me. I stopped to rest and drink a little water whenever I needed to; that helped me keep a steady pace through the tunnel. The tunnel was starting to drop down, and the steepness was forcing me to slow down my pace even more. My backpack, other supplies, and poles got caught on rocks sticking out and in cracks in the floor or walls along the way. I had to stop several times to unhook them. My legs were starting to get a burning feeling from the steep climb. I needed to rest.

Just then, my poles that I was dragging got wedged between some rocks and that gave me an idea. If I would wedge the four poles between this group of rocks and place the other end of the poles on the other side, it would be long enough and wide enough for me to lie down and rest and stretch out. I secured the poles in position and carefully removed my pack and put it on the one end of my new bed and stretched out using my pack as a pillow as lumpy as it was. It felt good to stretch out and rest, but I must not fall asleep. I couldn't sleep until after I got up the shaft; and not knowing how far I had yet to go, I could only rest a short time. I'd make a mark on the side of my candle, and when it melted down to that point, then I would pack up my things and move toward the shaft.

I thought about many things as I lay there. What did the people in the settlement think of me taking off without telling anybody? Would they be mad at mom and dad for not keeping me in control? I hoped they would not worry. What could I expect on the other side when I got to the city? So much could have changed since the time dad left the city. I remembered talking with dad about what he thought the city would be like now, and he just hung his head and said he wouldn't want to be a boy my age. Some of the boys in his school would do anything possible to get on the state police force at the junior level, so when they got out of school, they wouldn't have to work in the state-run factories. He always said he was glad that I wouldn't ever have to go through that. I remember dad talking about this old guy named Ernie. Dad would sometimes say he wondered what good old Ernie was up to. Lately dad had changed the words and wondered if good old Ernie was still alive. Then I would see a tear sneak out the corner of his eye, and he would try to hide the fact that he was crying. It would be nice if Ernie or someone else would be on the other side to help me find Grandma Ramona and Grandpa Russell. Now I was starting to get tears in my eyes, and I hadn't even met them.

Well, that was enough rest. The candle was just about burnt down to the mark that I made. The rest had refreshed my legs so I should be good for a long time without having to take another break. Slowly I bumped my way down the steep tunnel until I noticed that there were fewer rocks for me to trip on and the steepness was getting less. Could that mean that I was getting to the room where the shaft was? I remembered dad saying that he had to crawl on his belly. I felt the ceiling getting closer to the floor. I would have to tie my pack and other supplies to one leg and drag them through the tunnel. That would slow my progress down. Constantly I was reaching back and unhooking my pack and supplies because they kept getting caught on the rocks. This went on for what seemed like hours until my head popped out into a good size room. I wriggled myself through the opening and then pulled my pack and other things into the room with me.

I held the candle off to one side and got a good look at the room. I was filled with excitement to see the pile of rocks that my dad had left to mark the two tunnels not to take. Looking up the shaft, I could see that I would have to climb to get to the next part of the tunnel. I rested for a short bit, and at the same time started to build my ladder so I could reach the first set of hand and footholds. I untied the poles and laid them out as I had back at the settlement when I came up with the plan. I knew I would need help getting started because dad said that the ceiling was one foot higher than his head, and I'm not as tall as he was. Taking hold of the sack that I had been dragging behind me, I untied the straps and pulled out the crosspieces of the ladder and the bundle of leather straps that I would use to tie the ladder together. The pieces I put in their proper places and began wrapping the leather straps as tight as I could. The five rungs of the ladder would have to be in the right place in order to make it strong enough to hold as much weight as possible for when I climbed up the shaft. It was also for when Grandma and Grandpa Wilson would have to climb down. They would not be able to make a drop from that high up at their age without breaking something. The work on the ladder made my hands sore with the combination of the cold, damp air in the tunnel and the rough texture of the leather. As I wrapped it around the rungs, the leather would slap against my hands. Blood was starting to seep from where the leather had rubbed my skin raw. I would have to fight through the pain because there were only two rungs left.

I thought I heard someone talking, and my breathing quickened. I listened for a time and the breathing slowed down. Quietly I continued working on the ladder until I finished it, and then I laid back to rest more. My hands were red and raw from my work. The pain wasn't as bad. I must have gotten past the worst part. I would take some of the bandages I brought with me and wrap my hands to stop the bleeding. Mom would be proud of me if she could see me wash out my cuts first before I wrapped them up.

After my short rest I set the ladder up to see if I had to make any modifications to it to make it work. From what I could see, it would be plenty long enough to reach well up into the shaft. I heard some more noise. I froze in place to listen. It was my stomach wanting to be fed, but there was no time for that. I couldn't rest until I got up the shaft. That was the point at which I think the people looking for me would stop and say that I had crossed the point of no return. The time had come for me to raise the ladder up into the shaft. As I lifted the ladder up over my head to put it into position, sand fell into my eyes and I couldn't see. I tried to blindly place the ladder into position, but I couldn't do it. I dropped the ladder as softly as I could. My arms and hands were sore, so it landed with a thud. I blinked and blinked to work up some tears to wash the sand from my eyes. When I did that, I could see a little clearer to look at the ladder to see if there was any damage done when I dropped it. Then I was ready to try to put the ladder up again, but this time I placed the ladder on its side and kicked off as much sand as I could before raising it back up into the shaft.

It was a perfect fit. Now I had to try it out. I placed one foot on the bottom rung. The legs of the ladder sunk into the sand more than I thought they would. The top part of the ladder moved closer to the edge of the shaft. If it would sink much more into the sand, the ladder wouldn't be long enough. I climbed off the ladder and took a seat in the sand next to my pack. What was in the room that I could use to keep the ladder from sinking into the sand? All I could see was my pack, but I needed that. There were the rocks that dad used to mark the tunnels not to go into. The rocks . . . . Yes, that was it. I would place some rocks under the legs. Then I'd take what rocks were left and place them in front of the entrance to the right tunnel to take. I scrambled to gather the rocks and place them under the ladder. By the time I had enough rocks placed by the tunnel entrance, I had worked up quite a sweat. I had to rest and take a drink of water. As I tipped my head back, I thought I heard voices again. Quickly I crawled over to the tunnel entrance and put my head into it and listened.

I did hear voices and they were coming this way. I needed to move quickly and quietly. Tying a rope to my belt and then to my backpack and sack, I proceeded up the ladder one rung at a time until I reached the first handhold at the edge of the shaft. When I let go with my hands, I took hold of the cave walls and pulled myself up until my feet reached the first foothold. Now I was no longer on the ladder, but spread eagle on the shaft wall. I had forgotten my candle that was still burning in the sand, so I would have to climb up the shaft without any light. I groped for each hand and foothold until I reached the top. Feeling for each foothold and hand-hold came easier as I went along, and before I knew it, I was reaching out of the top of the shaft. Carefully, I pulled up my backpack and sack with my supplies in them without knocking over the ladder. Now with both packs up the shaft,

I needed to climb down the shaft and tie my rope onto the ladder so no one could follow me.

The climb down seemed easier because I knew where the foot and handholds were. I wondered how I would get my rope onto the ladder and still stay in the shaft. The voices of the people were still coming my way, so I had to move immediately. I placed my feet on the very edge of the shaft and bent over to reach for the top of the ladder closest to my right foot. With just my fingertips, I pulled the ladder toward me. It slipped from my fingers and bounced on the wall but didn't fall. That wasn't going to work. I would need to get lower and reach for the top rung some two feet below the edge of the hole. What I needed to do was place my back against one side of the shaft wall and my feet on the other side and not use any hand or footholds. Then with one leg I would stretch out and hook the top rung with my foot and pull it up to me so I could tie my rope onto it. If I should drop it, I would have to let it go and the people coming after me would hear it and know that I wasn't that far ahead of them. Then they would use the ladder to catch me.

As I shifted my feet and moved to place my back on the opposite side, I slipped and my hand shot out to grab anything I could to keep from falling down onto the ladder and the rocks that I had piled up below. After my heart started beating again, I worked my body into position to reach down and hook the top rung. I mustered all the strength that I had to reach down, hook it and pull it up. Then I tied my rope to it and let it down gently still having the top part of the ladder resting inside the shaft and the bottom resting on the pile of rocks. What was I going to do about my candle that was still burning? They would know that I hadn't been gone long if it was still burning. The sweat was running down my face, and I wiped it with my bloody bandages. All of a sudden an idea came to me. I would only have one chance to make it work. I unwrapped my right hand and formed a ball with my bandage. I took careful aim at the candle and let the bandage fly. It was a perfect shot. I was plunged into total darkness. I felt for the hand and footholds and worked my way into the spread eagle position again and proceeded up the shaft. I could hear the people even clearer so I had to make it to the top of the shaft and have the ladder out of the hole before the first person would poke their head into the room below with light and see the ladder going up. I grabbed the ladder hand over hand and pulled it up the shaft. I could feel it cut my right hand. It was bleeding again and blood ran down my finger. I couldn't stop! I had to get the ladder up!

As the bottom of the ladder cleared the top of the shaft I collapsed, falling over backwards with exhaustion. I lay there in the dark with every muscle in my body throbbing and filled with pain except my tongue. I said a prayer of thanks to God. Only a few minutes passed when hunger and the growling in my stomach became my main thought. I rolled over to the side of my backpack, untied the top flap and pulled out my food sack with the food I had saved out the past few weeks from some of the meals that mom fixed. I must be careful not to eat too much because I didn't know what I would have for a food source once I got to the city. I started with some dried apple slices. I placed a few on my lap and tied the bag shut. Then I took one slice of apple and placed it into my mouth. It tasted so good, and it also brought back memories of when mom let me help make my first batch of dried apple slices. She would say, "Carl, stop eating all the apples or there won't be any left to go into the drier." That night I lay in bed with the worst stomachache I had ever had in my short life of eight years. I finished my last piece of dried apple and reached for the bag that had the dried meat in it.

The sound of people was so clear I had to look to see if they were standing next to me. The voices were coming up the shaft. It was the group from the settlement coming to take me home. The light from their lanterns was so bright it shot up the shaft and filled my room with enough light I could see the size of the place where I would sleep for the night. Slowly I rolled to the edge of the shaft to look down and see who came looking for me. There was Brad, my best friend, and his dad just standing there looking but not saying anything. I could hear another voice off to the side. I knew that voice anywhere. It was Peter, the night guard. He was saying that it was entirely his fault, and this would never have happened if he had been watching better.

Then a voice from someone not yet in the room said, "Peter, stop that talk right now. If I told you once, I've told you a hundred times that Carl leaving was not your fault." That was the voice of my dad, and it sounded like he was struggling to enter the room. I could feel tears starting to well up in my eyes. "Carl is a skilled hunter, and he used those skills to get past you. If it was anyone's fault, you could say it was mine. I talked too much about missing my parents."

I listened to them all try to take the blame on themselves. I wanted to yell down the shaft that it was nobody's fault. I had thought of this day from the first time that I found out that I still had grandparents back in the city.

Brad broke the silence with a shout, "Hey, look at what I found over here! It is a bloody rag."

Brad's dad turned to my dad and said, "Now Mark, that doesn't mean anything bad has happened to Carl."

Brad was always blunt and blurted, "But Dad, look at how much blood is on this rag, and . . . ."

Then there was a muffled voice and I looked down the shaft to see Brad's dad's hand over Brad's mouth. Brad was looking up at his dad. At that moment I saw Brad's eyes get big. I wasn't sure if he saw me looking down or if he had just seen the shaft opening for the first time. Unable to say anything with his dad's hand clasped tightly over his mouth, Brad pointed up. I rolled away from the hole and lay as quiet as possible, trying to slow my breathing down so they wouldn't hear me.

Then Brad pulled his dad's hand away from his mouth and spoke, "Look Dad, is that the way we have to go next?"

"I don't know. I wouldn't think so. It would be impossible for Carl to reach up that high; he is too short."

I sat up and said to myself, "I'm not short . . . I'm just . . . not tall!"

"What if Carl had a ladder? Then he could reach up there!"

"Now Brad, where and how would Carl get a ladder in here? You saw how hard it was for all of us to fit into the tunnel. How would Carl get say an eight to ten foot ladder down the tunnel and into this room?"

Brad with a disappointed voice said, "I guess you're right, Dad."

"No, Brad, you're right," my dad answered. "Look over here. You can see in the sand the marking of a ladder."

"Mark, how could Carl have gotten a ladder in here?"

"From what I can tell, he must have brought in pieces and reassembled them in the room."

Brad's dad was skeptical of that idea. "Okay, say Carl got the material in here. What did he use to put it together with? Glue?"

There was silence. Come on, Dad. Tell them that I'm smarter than that. Dad, tell them! What was taking dad so long to say something?

Finally dad boomed out, "No, my boy, Carl, was using this."

Brad yelled, "Of course, that's why Carl was always willing to clean up the hide tanning area. He was collecting the leftover pieces of leather and cutting them into strips to tie together to make a ladder. Carl always was the smartest in the class."

"Yes he was!" I'm not sure who was beaming more, my dad or the lantern.

Brad's dad asked, "Where is the ladder now?"

Dad answered, "Well, seeing what he has done so far, I would assume that he brought it up the shaft with him so we couldn't follow him. I know that's what I would've done; and I do have to say that Carl is a chip off the old block, and I'm proud of him. Wherever he is now, I wish I could tell him how proud his mom and I are of him and how he has turned out to be a fine young man. It's time for us to head back to the settlement and do what Carl had scratched into the wall of the upper room."

I could hear them starting toward the tunnel to go back. No one was saying anything. I laid there in the dark thinking of the things that my dad had said about me and how proud he and mom were. The light up the shaft began to move. The last person must have picked up the lantern and headed to the tunnel opening. I rolled towards the shaft to look down hoping to see my dad's face one last time. Then, all of a sudden, the light in the shaft got brighter. I quickly rocked back from the opening; but before I cleared the edge, I looked into my dad's face that was streaked with tears and dirt.

"Carl, if you can hear me, I will pray for you every morning and every night. I'm proud of you. Be careful and come home soon. We miss you already."

"Pastor Mark, are you coming? We need the light in the tunnel."

"Yes, Brad. I'll be there in a few seconds. Carl, if you could look for my old friend Ernie, it would be good to know what has happened to him. He would be too old to make the trip back, but tell him hello from me. I'll miss you, Carl. Goodbye."

The light faded quickly from the room. I rolled to the edge and whispered, "I miss you all too."

Then I rolled away from the shaft and lay there in the dark feeling that I could cry at any time, but I was happy with the things that dad had said about me to the other men. I remembered I had eaten only a few dried apple slices and hadn't eaten the dried meat yet. There was a choice of venison, turkey or smoked fish. The smoked fish smelled real good after the hard, long day. I broke off a big hunk from one of the three fish that I brought and put it in my mouth. That and a carrot should keep my stomach happy for a while. Eating in the dark was not what I wanted to do, but I could not take a chance that the men from the settlement might double back and see the light and find out that I was only a few yards from them—listening.

I had climbed all night long, so sleep was the next thing in order for me to do. Unrolling my two blankets, I laid them out in the sand away from the shaft and placed the ladder in-between me and the shaft. It wouldn't be fun to fall down the shaft and land on that pile of rocks that I left at the bottom. The small sack that I brought with me would make a good pillow if it wasn't too hard. As I lay there, I thought back to the story that dad told about how slippery the next part of the tunnel was. I remember that he said it was very steep too. He also said that he hurt himself slamming into rocks. I would have to take my time and try not to rush it. There was plenty of food and water for a week to ten days if I cut back on how much or how often I ate. I took a small sip of water and called it a day. I would sleep as long as I needed to before venturing out on the next section of the tunnel. I lay back and pulled the blankets up around my neck to keep out the cool, damp air. It was not long till I felt my eyes getting heavy and I was drifting in and out of sleep.

My sleep was rudely interrupted when my head hit the ladder that I had laid in-between the shaft entrance and me. In spite of the hit on the head, I felt well rested. I reached for my backpack and found another candle and my flint and knife. I lit a candle feeling confident that the men were gone and not coming back. Breakfast was the first thing on my agenda for the day. I had a small handful of dried apples and some dried, wild berries. I would have a piece of venison that I could chew on along the way to keep my mouth from getting dry. That way I would be able to save on my water supply. I finished breakfast and was packed up and ready to go in just a few minutes. Next I worked all my supplies into my one backpack. It was a little heavy, but that would leave both hands free to help in the climb up the slippery section of the tunnel. I placed the candle into the specially-made candleholder that let me have the candle on the backside of my hand making it possible for me to grip the rocks while climbing. With the candleholder weighted to always keep the candle upright, I wouldn't have to worry about hot wax dripping and burning me while I climbed. I left the ladder here for my return trip. There was no need to drag that with me anymore.

As Great Grandpa Roy would say, "Well, what are we waiting for? Onward and upward!" He liked saying that when he would take Kayla and me hiking in the hills just outside the settlement. The three of us would sit and look out over this large valley that seemed to go on forever. We would watch the eagles float on the air currents, and at times they would get so close that it seemed that we could just reach out and touch their wings. The first time Great Grandpa Roy took Kayla and me up to see the eagles Kayla asked Great Grandpa Roy if Mr. Eagle would let us ride on his back, and then we could fly home because she was tired. We just laughed. Great Grandpa Roy was very strong and Kayla very light. He gave her a piggyback ride most of the way back to the settlement that day.

Well, I'm not getting anywhere just standing here. Onward and upward! It got steep soon into the climb, and the walls were wet, but the floor wasn't too slippery like dad had talked about. Maybe they weren't as slippery as he thought. Maybe he just tripped a lot. I chuckled to myself envisioning dad slipping and sliding down the tunnel. I made great time up that section, but I should rest once I get to that large rock sticking out just a few feet ahead of me. I was almost there but I saw something reflecting my candle back at me. I reached down and picked it up. My foot slipped and down I went sliding and bouncing off the walls of the tunnel. I wondered if I was ever going to stop. Stop I did with a suddenness that meant I hit a large rock jutting out from the wall. I felt the pain from the sudden stop, so I decided to rest there. I slid for a long distance. Very early in my climb I remember this rock jutting out. The object I had reached down to pick up was still in my hand. It was made of glass and metal. This must have been my dad's candle lantern that he lost. I guess dad was right after all that the floor of the tunnel was very slippery. What was I going to do to keep from slipping and sliding back to the starting point each time I fell? It's too bad that they didn't carve steps into the rock floor so you could just walk right to the top.

The ladder; I'd go back and get the ladder and use that as my steps. I wasn't that far from the beginning where I left it. I took my backpack off and left it propped up against the rock that stopped me so suddenly. I hurried back down the tunnel to the room that I had just come from earlier today. I only traveled about 30 yards and there was the room. I picked up the ladder. Now I remembered how heavy the ladder was; but if I was to get up the tunnel, I would need it. I put my right arm between the top two rungs of the ladder and began my trek back up the tunnel again. I met up with my backpack and pulled out two pieces of rope. One rope I tied to the top of the ladder and then to the bottom. The second piece I tied to that rope so it would slide up and down the rope freely, and the other end of the rope I tied to my waist. With the ropes tied to the ladder and to my waist I shouldn't have to worry about having it slip out of my hands and end up back at the bottom of the tunnel. With the one rope sliding up and down the other rope, I would be able to move up the ladder with both hands free to grab onto rocks. I slipped my backpack on and walked up the tunnel dragging the ladder, stopping every now and then to get it unhooked from a rock jutting out from the wall of the tunnel or pulling out a leg that was stuck in a crack. Getting close to where I had slipped the first time, I found a secure place to put my feet, took hold of the rope from around my waist, and pulled the ladder up to me and reached for one rung. I pushed the ladder up the tunnel ahead of me. Then I placed the bottom legs of the ladder in the crack in the wall where I had had my foot. Next I would slide the top of the ladder to the opposite side of the tunnel. I placed my hands on each side of the ladder and tested the positioning of it to make sure it was secure. Then I tried my full weight with backpack. It was a slow process, but I moved carefully and steadily up the ladder one rung at a time until I reached the top, always making sure the ladder was secure before I took the next step. I had made five lengths of the ladder and was at the top again, but I didn't see any rocks jutting out to place the ladder legs up against. The floor of the tunnel was very slippery. While I held my candle out in front of me, I looked for a way to secure the ladder. There was a great big rock sticking out on the other side of the tunnel. I knew it was too far out of reach for me. To try to step over to it by walking on the floor, I would surely slide uncontrollably into who knows how much pain and injury.

An idea came to me. If I could throw a rope around that rock sticking out, I could pull both the ladder and myself over to it. Then I could pull the ladder up and rest the legs there. I leaned out from the ladder to get as close to the rock as I could, because I didn't have a lot of room to throw the rope. My first few tries were close but didn't land good enough to stay on. My arm was getting tired from throwing the rope after I had dragged the ladder up after each climb. As I got ready to throw the rope, I felt the ground start to shake. I threw the rope and it landed. As I pulled it tight around the rock, the rock that the ladder was resting on broke loose because of the ground shaking. The ladder slid out from under me. I hung onto the rope that was around the rock because that was all I had. The top end of the ladder slid past my feet. There was a great jerk and the ladder came to an abrupt stop. That was when I remembered that the ladder was tied to my waist. The pain was intense from my waist to my shoulders. It was as if someone was trying to pull me apart because of the weight of the ladder. I took a deep breath and pulled myself up the rope to the rock dragging the ladder behind. I only had about another foot to go. I was stuck. The ladder was caught on something I couldn't see; I'd have to climb back down a little to see if I could set it free.

The ground shook again, and rocks and dirt began to hit me. I pulled on the rope as hard as I could. Either my pulling or the shaking freed the ladder, and I reached for the rock and covered my head to protect me from the falling rocks and dirt. After the ground stopped shaking, the dirt and rocks took a little time to stop falling. Then I pulled up the ladder and placed it against the other wall and kept climbing. I wanted to get out of the tunnel as soon as I could. I didn't want to stop, but my body was saying that it had had enough and I needed to make camp somehow. The floor of the tunnel was still too wet to sleep on. I would have to stretch out on top of the ladder. I would need to secure both top and bottom legs of the ladder to a few anchor points and tie my backpack to the ladder. After some work, I secured a place to rest. I would need to eat and drink something to keep my strength up for the next day's climb. I opened my backpack and could smell the fish. My mouth began to water. Another carrot was on the menu; and if that wasn't enough, maybe some of mom's hard candy she made last week. My candle was about to go out. The flame was flickering, and it would soon be dark in the tunnel again. Before I ate, I folded my hands, and I looked up and said, "Dear God, Thank you for helping me make it through the tight spot that I had today with the ground shaking and the slipping. I also pray that you would continue to be with me as I sleep. In Jesus' name, Amen."

My supper went down fast, and I dug out a piece of mom's hard candy and popped it into my mouth. It was so good to have something sweet after the salty, smoked fish. I grabbed another piece of leather strapping and tied myself to the ladder for the night. My bed was not the most comfortable bed to sleep on, but it was the only dry place to sleep. I lay there in the dark and tried to shut off the thoughts of the next day and what I may find as I continued to climb up to who knows what. The city may have changed so much that what dad and others had told me about it may not be of any use to me. Would I find Ernie to give me help, or was he gone? So many things to think about, but for now I needed to get some sleep or I wouldn't have the strength to do anything.

I drifted off to sleep and could almost see my family standing in the kitchen looking out over the settlement. Kayla and mom's eyes were red from crying, and dad had his arms around them. Dad would try to reassure them that I'd be fine and home soon. Only waking up for a short time to find a better sleeping position on the ladder, I fell back to sleep.

Next thing I knew, I was waking up to the ground shaking and groaning. I was also getting dirt in my eyes. It was not the best way to start the morning. I scrambled to get my things together and start my climb, hopefully for the last day. I would worry about eating later. Then maybe I'd have fresh air and daylight. The thought of fresh air and daylight gave me the drive to move up the tunnel. It wasn't long before I felt the steepness of the floor getting much less, and the floor was almost dry. Could I leave the ladder here and continue without it? I'd have to think on that while I got something to eat since I was rushed out of bed by the ground shaking. Come to think of it, the ground hadn't shaken since then. In the back of my mind I was always hoping that it wasn't an earthquake or a cave-in. I was afraid I would be crushed like a bug.

For this meal I would have some more dried fruit, and I'd soak some of my turkey meat in some water to soften it up. I didn't rush this meal because I felt that I didn't have far to go. There was a different smell in the air, and it wasn't my fish. I lit a candle and put it in the candleholder. Since the ground hadn't shaken for some time now, I decided that I wouldn't have to cover my head with both hands anymore. The candlelight should help me make better time. As the light filled the tunnel, I could see that the ceiling was higher; I would be able to walk almost standing up.

Once again I packed up my things and started to walk. Each step I took gave me a better idea of what dad was feeling when he journeyed to the settlement many years ago. There was a bend in the tunnel up ahead, and it wasn't feeling as cold and damp as before. Maybe this would be the end of the tunnel, and I would be at the base of the old mill. I slowed my pace as I rounded the bend to make sure there weren't any traps set by the state police. I didn't see anything but another bend to go around. And then, there it was; daylight peeking in around a small wooden door just as dad had said. I made it!

Suddenly there was a crash and a boom. The ground shook and dirt fell from the ceiling putting out my candle. The only light I had was from around the door. Then I heard voices of men not too far away. I froze there in place.

One man yelled, "How much of this old mill do we have to tear down?"

The other man yelled back, "The whole thing, but let's call it a day and we can finish the job tomorrow."

"That sounds good to me."

I heard the man walk away. He must have been very close to the door. I dropped to the floor and just sat there shaking with fear of having someone so close to me and not knowing if they were good or bad. For some time I listened to see if they were coming back. I could hear them making all kinds of noise cutting down trees. When they hit the ground, it would shake and dirt would fall from the ceiling into my eyes.

Finally it got quiet, so I went over to the small wooden door and peeked out the cracks on the sides to see what I could see. The big water wheel was still in place. There was no way of knowing what the outside world would hold for me until I climbed out and found a place to set up camp. I wouldn't be able to stay here with those men coming back tomorrow to finish the job. What did that mean? Would they take down the whole mill and find the tunnel? Would they destroy the only way I knew back to the settlement? Or would they stop soon enough and be satisfied with knocking the mill over and leaving it? I decided to rest for a time before I left the tunnel. A short nap would do me good.

Chapter 2

On the Edge

I swung open the wooden door and all my senses came alive after being in the tunnel for a long time. It was great to be able to breathe fresh air and not the damp, wet earth smell. The wildflowers were blooming and had a refreshing fragrance. The birds were all chirping their own songs. It was good to see other colors besides the black and brown of the tunnel walls.

Carefully I poked my head out the door to see if anyone was around to see me come out. All was clear. There was no way to get onto the water wheel. I would have to climb down the wall of the mill as far as I could and then drop to the ground below. I'd send my backpack down to the ground first using my rope. Looping the rope through the straps of the backpack, I lifted the pack out the door and gently slid it down the wall of the mill. As the backpack made its way down, it passed over a big metal ring coming out the side of the wall and that gave me a great idea. If I could get down to the ring by climbing on both the mill wall and the water wheel, I could then loop my rope through the ring and climb down the rope. When I got to the bottom, I could pull on the one end and retrieve my rope to use again. My backpack had made it safely to the ground below.

Suddenly I heard voices again. I shut the door partway so I could hear what was being said. It sounded like there were three, maybe four people, but they were talking too quietly. I couldn't hear what they were saying, or maybe they were too far away. Slowly I opened the door and poked my head out. I couldn't hear any more talking, so I climbed out the door and sat on the edge. I was ready to start my climb down the wall, but I had this strange feeling that someone was watching me. I looked around the side of the water wheel as much as I could, but there was no one to be seen. I heard a growling noise. Was that my stomach? There it was again; but this time it was a little bit louder.

I looked up, and there staring back at me was a set of eyes and the biggest set of teeth. It scared me, so I lost my footing on the wall and fell bouncing back and forth between the wheel and the wall until I hit the ground twisting my ankle. The pain in my ankle was great, but the pain I would feel if the state police caught me would be worse. I crawled over to my backpack and hugged the wall of the mill. The dog began to bark and growl more intensely. The dog's owner was coming. I could hear him yelling at the dog.

"King, get over here and be quiet. There's nothing out there, you silly dog." King wasn't quieting down any. Instead he picked up the intensity until King's owner must have given him a smack on the rump; then I heard a yelp. King's owner was not too happy with him because I heard him say, "I can't take you anywhere without you causing problems. Now get in the car."

Just then a few small rocks landed next to me, and my heart skipped a beat or two. Was the owner looking over? I hoped he couldn't see me. I didn't have time to look around so I didn't know where to run to get away. With my twisted ankle, how fast or how far could I run? Worse yet, what if they would let King come after me. Then I wouldn't only see his big teeth; I would feel him taking a bite out of me.

I'd have to stay put and hope for the best. I could feel my ankle swelling a little. If these people would hurry up and leave, I could take my shoe off and put my foot into the water to stop the swelling and help dull the pain. They must be leaving in a car. It would be interesting to see a car for my first time. Dad didn't draw the best pictures. His wheels were two different sizes, and that looked funny. The sound of the car was getting less. Now I could relax and unlace my shoe. I slipped my foot out and could see that it was turning color already.

I scooted over to the edge of the water and lowered my foot in. The water was cold, but it felt good. I lay back and rested while I could. My next item of business would be to find a place to set up a campsite where I wouldn't be seen by people. I'd start by walking the river on this side. For now all I needed to find was a temporary site. Tomorrow I could find a more permanent spot to set up camp. I pulled my foot out of the water and dried it off with my shirt. Then I put my shoe on and laced it up tight so I could walk to find a place to camp tonight. I wasn't looking forward to carrying my backpack with my ankle so sore, but I couldn't take the risk of someone finding it. Also, I didn't want to find a spot down river and then have to come back to get it.

I grabbed the straps, slung it onto my shoulders and headed down river. Looking at the sun, I guessed that I didn't have a lot of time before sunset to make camp. It would have to be a simple place. It didn't look like rain, so maybe just a lean-to with some pine boughs to help keep the dew off me would be good for tonight. I stepped out away from the mill for the first time and finally got to look at the mill that dad had talked about so much. The roof and one wall were gone. Those men that I heard earlier must have knocked it down with that thing there that had one big yellow arm with a scoop with teeth on the end. I would have to come back tomorrow to see how that worked, because that didn't look like anything in dad's pictures. It didn't have any wheels, so how did it move around?

As I made my way down the river, I saw up ahead an area with some pine trees and some low lying brush that would give me some cover to hide in for the night. The river wasn't very wide at this spot, and the water was running slow. The river water here didn't look too clean; not like back at the settlement where you could look down a long ways and could even see the fish swimming. I'm not even sure if there were any fish in the river here. I pushed my way past the first few rows of pine trees and came to a spot where someone had cut down a few. I'd make camp here for the night.

I slipped my backpack off and walked up to the front of a big pine tree with its branches reaching out so far that I could duck down a little and walk into the center of it. It was perfect. I wouldn't have to do any cutting. The tree would give me all the protection I needed for the night. As I ducked under the branches, I grabbed my backpack where I had dropped it earlier and carried it into my home for the night. It wasn't long after I sat down in my new home that I felt the pressure of my ankle swelling again. I needed to take care of that as soon as possible to keep it from getting any bigger.

While I walked to the river, I took my shirt off so I could get it wet and wrap it around my ankle for the night to help keep the swelling down. I found a calm, shallow pool in the river; and for the first time since I left the settlement, I saw my face. I was dirty from ear to ear, and I didn't smell too sweet either after being in the tunnel all that time. Maybe it was time for me to take a bath right here in this shallow little pool. At least I could get a couple layers of dirt off and soak my ankle at the same time. I slid into the water and swished my arms and legs back and forth. I could see big clouds of dirt coming out of my clothes changing the color of the water to a cloudy, light brown. I sat and rested as I watched the current take the dirt from my clothes and me and wash it down the river.

My teeth began chattering, so I should get out, get into some dry clothes and hang the wet ones up to dry. Wait until I tell mom that I took a bath and washed my own clothes all at the same time. And she didn't have to tell me to do it. No, maybe I shouldn't tell mom I did all this; she would want me to do that all the time. I think that is a secret I'd leave here in the river. I better quit dillydallying and get out of the water before I chatter my teeth out of my head. I could hear those cars on the road back at the mill again as if they were looking for something or somebody. Hopefully that somebody wasn't me. I tried to make sure I covered my tracks, because extra attention was not what I needed while I was here in the city. It would be hard enough to get around the city to look for grandma and grandpa without people looking to put me in jail.

I would have to have another cold meal because starting a fire would get too many people looking to see where the smoke was coming from.

As I ate, I started to think about mom and dad and, of course, Kayla. This would be about the same time that they would be sitting down to have supper. I wondered if they had been praying for me since I left the settlement. I know I had been thinking about and praying for them that they would get along without me until I got back with Grandma Ramona and Grandpa Russell. My thoughts were a blur. I had so many things to think about. Maybe I should just roll out my bed and listen to the activity of the woods and the creatures. That would clear my mind. It wasn't long until the trees became alive with chickadees darting from tree to tree and branch to branch for seeds. A chickadee landed where I had been eating supper. He must have found some of my crumbs that I had dropped. Two more chickadees flew in to clean up my campsite. Wow! Where did that blue jay come from? He chased off the other birds so he could have all the crumbs to himself. I lay back and listened to the wind blow through the pine trees, and every now and then I could hear a pine cone fall from the top of the tree and bounce off the branches until it hit the ground.

My eyes were getting heavy. It wouldn't be long till I'd be sleeping, so I better plan tomorrow's activities now. One thing I had to check on was to see how much of the mill they were going to destroy. Would it stop me from getting back into the tunnel to get back to the settlement? If they destroyed the tunnel entrance, I would be in big trouble. People back at the settlement had talked about someday looking for another way in and out of the settlement, but no one had ever looked into it. All I could say was that I hoped they left some of the tunnel intact so I could get home. I wouldn't want to have to be the person to blaze a new trail back home over the top of this mountain. The second thing I needed to do was find a more permanent campsite far enough away from people so I could have a fire to cook some food. A nice hot meal would taste good. I would also need to find a couple different ways to get to the campsite just in case there was a problem with the police; or if someone thought about following me, I might need to have a second place to hide. I would like to look at the Zabling farm; maybe there would be a place for me to hide out there if the police got too close. It would be nice if the old chicken coop was still there. Oh, I should look for the tunnel entrance at the farm while I'm there, because that could also be a place to hide.

I was yawning more and more. Maybe I should let myself go to sleep. Then I'd be rested and ready to start my search for Grandma and Grandpa Wilson. I had no sooner thought those words until I was sleeping.

Morning seemed to come fast and with a crash. I shot straight up out of my bed. I looked around and started to panic when I saw the tree around me. Then I remembered that I wasn't at home and that I had come to the city to search. Suddenly there was another big crash. It must be those men knocking down the mill. I grabbed my clothes and rushed to put them on. Then I raced out to the edge of the river. There was a voice inside my head that said slow down and look around. If they are knocking the mill down, then there will be people around to watch it come down, and they will see you running.

I froze in my tracks and crouched behind a group of bushes so I could look around. When I finished looking around, I saw that I had hidden myself in some bushes of what we called wild redcap berries, and some were ready to be eaten. I didn't see anyone as I looked up and down the riverbanks. I picked a few berries to have as a quick breakfast. Then I popped out of the bushes and hugged the tree line along the river as long as I could to give me as much protection as possible. All this time I could hear more crashing and metal grinding. I could see dust in the air, and it smelled like old rotted wood. It was like when we would knock down an old tree, and the tree would break apart as it would hit the ground. The dust would rise up, and it would have this same smell. The mill, or what was left of it, was coming into view.

I spotted a clump of trees I could hide in. It was a perfect spot to watch them knock down the mill. Also, I could see if anybody was coming down to the river's edge.

The machine with the big yellow arm took a swing at the mill and another wall came tumbling down. I couldn't believe the power that machine had. With each swing of that arm more and more of the mill came down until there was only one wall standing. As the arm of the machine rose up, the machine started to move. I couldn't tell how. There was too much debris in the way. I wanted to see how that thing moved, so I crept in closer.

Just then I heard a man yelling and pointing my way. I dropped to the ground and lay as flat as I could. I could hear somebody walking in the wooded area behind me. I was so afraid of being caught that I was having a hard time thinking about what to do. Do I run and take the chance that I could outrun whoever was in the woods behind me? What if there was a group of them? I surely couldn't outrun them all with my ankle still sore.

The sound of tree branches getting pushed back was getting closer. I couldn't tell how many there were walking in the woods. The man was still yelling for the man on the machine to look harder. He wanted to know if he could see it too. A flash of brown and white ran past me; then another and another. The man wanted the other man to see the white-tail deer running in the woods. I stopped hugging the ground and rolled over on my back to breathe a sigh of relief. When I rolled over and opened my eyes, there was a pair of eyes looking back at me. I couldn't move. I couldn't even take a breath. Fear was screaming out of every pore of my body; but I could not scream because I was too afraid.

My eyes were fixed on his eyes as he walked closer. I could see his teeth form what looked like a smile. He leaped into the air and landed on my chest; we were nose to nose. He licked my face again and again. I took a chance and grabbed hold of the dog's collar. I saw he had two tags. In between the licks in the face I saw that this dog was my old friend, King. I called him by name and he stopped licking my face just long enough for me to read the second tag that said: "Property of the state police. If found, please return."

"Well King, old friend, this is a better greeting than you gave me the last time our eyes met. Are you hungry, boy? I still have some berries that I picked this morning. They are a little crushed, but they're all yours if you would like."

I held out my hand with the five crushed berries. King licked the berries out of my hand in just a few seconds. Then he started to lick my face again.

A voice from not too far away yelled, "King, come on. We need to get back to work. Whatever you got over there, let it go. King, don't make me come over there and get you."

I whispered to King, "King, go! I'll see you later. Go now. I don't need your master to find me. But remember, I fed you the berries and my name is Carl."

"King, get over here!"

His master was getting madder by the minute, and it wouldn't be long before he found me. I gave King a push and motioned for him to go. He just looked at me and barked once. Then he took off to meet up with his master. I could hear his master give him praise.

"Good boy, King; but next time come when I call you the first time."

The smell of smoke was in the air. They must have finished knocking down the mill while I was getting licked to death by King. I rose up into a sitting position. Flames from the mill were growing higher with each passing minute. The whole thing was burning, and there was a small group of people standing in the distance watching. The wind was blowing the smoke my way, and it was very thick. It was causing my throat to burn, and it was getting hard to breathe or see anything. I saw all I needed to see though. They left the entrance to the tunnel in place. All I could hope for was that the intense heat from the fire didn't cause the ground to dry out and cave in. I would have to wait until the fire went out and the ground had cooled before I found out if it caved in. Right now I would go further into the woods and hope that the trees would block some of the smoke. I hadn't finished breakfast so I decided to head back to my camp.

When I got to my campsite, I found I could breathe a little easier and get a drink of water to help the burning in my throat. As I sat down on my bed, I grabbed for my food bag to get one of mom's bread rolls. I could chew on the roll while I packed up for the move to my next campsite a little closer to the city. Dad wanted me to search for his friend, Ernie, and see if I could find out what happened to him. He said that Ernie was old then. Ernie may not be around anymore, but I would look anyway. Somebody might know something about him. Besides, how many Ernie's are there in one town anyway? My packing was done, and I tried to spread out more pine needles and leaves over the area to cover up that I had been here.

I headed down river with my backpack on my shoulders. The flames from the mill were reaching high into the sky, and I could hear the crackling of the timbers as I walked along the river. The river was getting wider, and there was a bridge up ahead. The wooded area along this side of the river was getting thinner, so I must be getting closer to the city. I climbed up the riverbank and looked around to see if there was a place to make camp on this side of the river. If there wasn't a place, then I would have to cross that bridge when I came to it. Ha! I made a joke and there was no one to laugh at it but me.

I grabbed onto some tree roots and pulled my way up the side of the riverbank. I stayed low to the ground so that no one would see me. At first glance all I could see was a corn-field. Then I looked to my far left and there, half hidden by some trees, was a house. If I had my facts straight, that could be my dad's house; and that would make this cornfield the old Zabling farm. How could I be sure? I couldn't just walk up to the front door and knock. Then when they answered I would say, "Hello. My name is Carl Wilson. I'm your long lost son's boy."

Someone had come out the back door. I needed to get closer to see, so I would use the cornfield as my cover. Then I should be able to get close enough to see or hear something. Maybe, just maybe, I could find out if it was my grandparent's house. I hid my backpack behind a clump of fallen trees. Then I would be able to move faster and quieter through the corn. Again I looked to see if the person was still outside, and he or she was. Quickly I moved to the edge of the corn-field where I had a clear view into the backyard. It was a lady in the yard. I turned around and counted the number of rows of corn stalks so I would not get turned around and lost. I was ten rows in. Quietly I walked down the row keeping one eye on the house and the lady in the backyard. I got to a spot in the cornfield where I was directly in line with the back of the house. I could see that it was a large, two story house just like dad said his house was. There was a garage next to it plus a small shed beside it. This had to be the place, and that would make that lady hanging out the laundry my Grandma Ramona. I walked closer to the edge of the cornfield to get a better look. The excitement was building as I pushed past each row of corn. My stomach was doing flip-flops to see Grandma Ramona for the first time. I couldn't let her see me because I didn't know what she would do. She didn't know who I was, so she could call the police.

I'd stay three rows back and listen for a while to see if I could hear anything. The wind was rustling the leaves of the corn making it difficult to hear anything. I would have to take the chance and move closer because it sounded like she was saying something. I didn't see anyone else around, so whom would she be talking to? She wasn't talking to anyone; she was singing! Then she stopped. She was looking at me! What was she going to do now? She was waving to me. I waved back to her to let her know that I was friendly. She walked toward me very slowly and motioned for me to come closer, but I was afraid to and I shook my head no.

"Come closer; I won't hurt you. My name is Ramona Wilson. What is your name?"

Part of me wanted to burst out of the cornfield and run into her arms and say, "I'm Carl, your grandson." The other part of me was saying, "Get ready to run at the first sign of danger of getting caught." Grandma was getting too close, so I motioned for her to stop.

She spoke again, "I will not hurt you. Are you from around here? I didn't catch your name."

"My name is Carl. I'm not from around here."

She had the biggest smile just hearing me talk. "Are you lost?"

"No, I'm not lost. I'm looking for some friends of mine."

"What are their names? Maybe I know them. I have lived here in this town all my life."

"That's okay. I'll find them." I didn't want to give out too much information.

"You know, Carl, you could come a little closer." I was feeling comfortable so I stepped out of the cornfield and walked towards her. With each step I got closer, her eyes got bigger. "Come closer!" She motioned to me with her hand.

"I think this is close enough."

"Now that I can see you up close, Carl, I do have to say you look a lot like my son I had."

I could feel tears welling up in the corners of my eyes, but I couldn't let her see that. I wanted to tell her so badly that I knew her son. "What is your son's name? I would like to meet him."

She said nothing. Her head sank to one side and I could see tears running down her slightly wrinkled face. I didn't know what to do or what to say. Maybe I had said too much already. We just stood there in silence.

Then she spoke, "My son's name was Mark." My heart was screaming for joy. I had found my Grandma Ramona. She continued to speak, "He disappeared many years ago and we have not heard from him since then. I think of him often and wonder if he is okay and if he is happy."

"He thinks of you often too."

"What did you say, Carl?"

"I said I'm sure he thinks of you often, too." Oh boy, that was close.

"Would you like to come inside and get something to eat?"

"No, I'm sorry. I must go. I need to find my friends as soon as possible." I could hear a car coming down the road, and it was slowing down in front of the house. Grandma could see that the car was making me nervous. "I've got to go. It was nice meeting you Ramona Wilson."

"No, don't go. That is just my husband. He works for the state police. He would be able to help you find your friends."

"State police!"

I must have said it too loud because I scared her and she backed up and tripped over a tree root and fell to the ground. I ran to help her up. Just then grandpa got out of his car and started yelling at me.

"Hey you, leave her alone. Put your hands up in the air and don't move." Grandpa came running at me.

I finished helping grandma up and darted into the cornfield trying to count the corn stalks as I rushed past them. I stopped ten rows in and looked back to see if he was still coming after me. He was talking to grandma while she hung onto his arm. He wanted to catch me, but she wouldn't let go of his arm. Finally he quit fighting her, and they began to talk. Wanting to hear what they were saying, I quickly circled back to the edge of the cornfield a few yards away from them. I'm sure they thought I was long gone. Grandma was telling grandpa that I just popped up on the side of the cornfield.

"Russell, the boy looked so much like Mark; I didn't know what to do—cry or hug him." I could tell by grandma's voice that she was about to cry just telling grandpa what happened.

Grandpa answered, "Ramona, not every strange boy you see is Mark. I know how much you miss him. I miss him too. You can't just reach out and start talking to strange kids. They could hurt you."

Grandma said with a little fire in her words, "Carl was not hurting me."

"Ramona! I saw he had you down on the ground, and who knows what would have happened if I hadn't come home when I did."

"No, Carl is a nice boy." Hey, you tell him, Grandma. I'm a nice young man. "Besides, it was when I said you worked for the state police that frightened him. That in turn made me step back and trip on those tree roots that I have asked you to cut off for the past ten years. I most likely won't see Carl again the way you came running at him like he was some common criminal."

Boy, was Grandpa getting an earful. The only thing Grandpa could do was ask some questions hoping to stop Grandma from yelling at him because of the way he treated me.

"Does Carl have a last name? Did he say what he was doing out in the state's cornfield?"

"Yes, he does; but he didn't tell me."

"Why was he in the cornfield?"

"I didn't ask him that. I did ask if he was lost, and he said he was not lost but that he was looking for some friends of his. I told him that I could maybe help him find his friends for him. That seemed to make him nervous."

"Ramona, don't you find it a little strange that the boy wouldn't give you his last name, and he didn't want your help finding his friends? And when you said I worked for the state police he runs away into the cornfield? I find that very strange. I should report this and see if there are any bulletins out on this kid. What did he look like?"

"Russell Wilson, you will not be making any report to anybody. He is just a boy; let him be. Besides, I told you he looked just like Mark did at that age." Grandma started walking toward the cornfield.

"Ramona, where are you going?"

"I'm going to look for Mark; I mean Carl."

"The boy is probably long gone."

"I'm going anyway," Grandma answered with determination in her voice.

"Are you just going to stand there, Russell, like a bump on a log, or are you going to come here and help?"

Grandpa just shook his head and took Grandma's hand. They walked into the cornfield about ten yards away. Grandma called my name, "Carl! Carl!"

Then Grandpa started calling my name too. "Carl, it's okay. We won't hurt you. We would like to talk." They stopped and waited for me to call back to them. I could see my Grandma's face, and there were tears running down her cheeks.

Grandpa declared, "Here is what we'll do. I'll walk deeper into the cornfield and you walk along the edge of the field. That way we can cover more area."

Grandpa let go of Grandma's hand. Through Grandma's tears she told Grandpa, "Be careful and don't get lost out there. I don't want to be looking for two of you."

As they split up, Grandpa took off almost at a full run to get deeper into the cornfield, and Grandma was heading right for me. I should head back to my backpack and find a permanent campsite, but for some reason my feet weren't moving and grandma was getting closer. She was only two rows away. Her back was toward me looking deeper into the field.

Softly Grandma whispered, "Carl, come back, please."

I wanted to ease her pain and have her stop crying, so I spoke back to her, "I'll be back, and we'll have that talk."

Grandma spun around so fast that she almost fell down again. Our eyes met and I waved goodbye. I ran as fast as I could to the place where my backpack was.

All the time I could hear her calling my name, "Carl!" Then she yelled to Grandpa that she had found me.

When I reached the pile of fallen trees where I had hid my backpack, I rested a little while before heading out to find a place to spend the night. I couldn't see any place that would work for a shelter on this side of the river. With Grandma on the prowl looking for me, it would be best if I took a look on the other side of the river. I slipped my backpack on and wandered along the riverbank toward the bridge. From time to time I could hear my grandparents calling for me. I found myself walking half in a daze thinking about them and not watching where I was walking, tripping and stumbling over rocks and fallen trees. I stopped to clear my head. Then I walked to the edge of the riverbank to look at the other side to see if there were any places that I could call home. I saw nothing but fallen trees. The river at one time must have been very high and undercut the dirt out from under the trees along the river. The bridge was not too far now. I could see it from here. There were fewer trees and bushes to hide behind, so I would have to keep a sharp eye on the road to make sure there was no one coming. I hadn't heard my grandparents calling for a while. Either they gave up, or I was too far away to hear their voices.

It was amazing to see my grandparents for the first time. My dad looked just like his dad, and his mom looked just like he said she would, only with a few more wrinkles. Then again, it had been many years since dad left the city to find the settlement.

There was a car coming. I needed to find a place to hide. As I turned to run and find a place to hide, the ground under my feet started to break away. I reached for a small tree but missed. I tumbled down the riverbank, and the weight of the backpack made it impossible to stop. I tumbled to the river's edge where I had a soft landing. There was no time to stand around admiring the sites. There was no way of telling if the people in the car saw me or not, and I couldn't take that chance. I ran along the river's shoreline and spotted a place to hide until the car left the area. I scrambled up the dirt riverbank, reached for the dangling roots of an old elm tree and pulled myself and my backpack deep into its roots. This must be what it's like to be a baby chick under the cover of its mother's wings peering out between the feathers. The car slowed down. They must have seen me. I tried to see the car from my hiding place, but they hadn't driven far enough up the road. Just then the car stopped and I heard people getting out. I buried myself into the riverbank as far as I could. My heart was pounding with fear and sweat was running down my face and into my eyes. The salt from my sweat was making it hard to see anything, and my hands were covered in dirt from scrambling up the riverbank. I was blinking my eyes trying to get tears to form to wash the salt out. I could hear muffled voices what seemed to be right overhead.

"Carl!" It was Grandma. They were still looking for me.

"Ramona, come on. He's not here. You were just seeing things."

"No, I saw what I saw. He was standing right here by this tree!"

"I think you just wanted to see him again so bad that your mind was playing tricks with your eyes. Come along and we'll get back into the car and head on home."

For some reason I didn't think Grandma believed what Grandpa was saying. "Russell, I know I saw Carl right here!" Just then Grandma must have stomped her foot. The dirt that was clinging to the roots of the tree overhead came raining down on me.

Grandpa wasn't helping any by saying, "If the boy . . . ."

Grandma stomped her foot again. "Russell, the BOY has a name; it's Carl!"

"Okay! If Carl was here, where is he now? Did the ground all of a sudden open up and swallow him?"

Grandma was crying again, and through her tears I heard her say, "Carl, you come back to the house anytime, day or night. I'll leave the back door unlocked. I have cookies in the cookie jar just like I did when my son, Mark, was with us." Then she started crying harder, and the crying got muffled. Grandpa must be hugging her to help comfort her.

"Ramona, are you ready to go yet?" Grandpa questioned thoughtfully.

"No," Grandma replied softly. "I would like to stay a little longer. It's like I can feel him here."

They just stood there in silence. Every once in a while I would hear Grandma start to cry again. I couldn't stand hearing her cry. I was going to come out and tell them that I was here and who I am-just get it over with. I pushed my way past the tangled roots and clung to the largest root.

"Grandma, it's me, Carl. I'm your grandson!"

They didn't hear me because there was another car coming down the road making the loudest noise. It was a black car with flashing lights. It was the state police. Once again I buried myself deep into the riverbank. The only thing I could do was sit and listen for them to leave. I could hear the men rushing toward my grandparents. I hoped that I didn't cause them any trouble.

One of the men yelled out, "Alright you two, don't move and get on the ground now!" They sounded mean.

Grandpa barked at them, "What are they teaching you at the police academy nowadays? How can I do two things at once? You said don't move and get on the ground. So what is it, patrolman? Do I not move or do I get on the ground?"

I'm not sure what happened up there, but the policemen that came rushing at grandma and grandpa were sounding a little silly. "I'm sorry, Captain Wilson. I didn't know it was you and your wife down on the riverbank. We had a report on the radio that the kids had been on the move again. We will continue our search elsewhere."

"Patrolmen, aren't you forgetting something?"

"Sir, what's that?"

"A salute, Patrolmen, or don't they teach you that in the police academy anymore?"

"Sir, yes sir!"

I could hear them running back to their car. I also heard grandpa and grandma laughing. "Russell, you have too much fun with those rookies."

"Yes dear; you're right. But this time I had a purpose for doing what I did to the rookies."

"And what purpose was that, may I ask?"

"If this Carl is ever going to come back and see us again, we will need to keep the number of police patrols to as few as possible, or the next time we see Carl will be at the station behind bars."

"Thank you, dear. I have always said that you have a soft heart inside that gruff exterior."

"Well, don't tell anybody. I have a reputation to uphold. Let's go home."

When I heard them slam the doors of their car, I decided to head for the bridge. It felt a little strange to be walking down along the shoreline while my grandparents were up on the bank. They didn't even know how close they were to meeting their grandson.

Chapter 3

Bridge Closed

Wow, this bridge was bigger than I first thought. I'd have to wait here until Grandma and Grandpa drove away. Then I'd be able to cross the bridge to the other side to find me a new home for my time here. I had found my grandparents, but dad wanted me to look for his old friend Ernie. Then there were the kids that the patrolmen were looking for. They said the kids were on the move again. Here comes Grandpa's car. He must be turning around to head back home.

Oh no! It was that same loud noise I heard just before the police showed up. Could it be them again? It sounded like it was coming from the other side of the river. There it was, another black car with flashing lights. They must have seen me while I was walking. How silly that was for me to do. I should have been watching that side of the river.

With the blast of what sounded like thunder, I heard, "Hello, Captain Wilson."

Grandpa stopped the car, and I heard the car doors open. They were walking on the bridge right above me. "Well hello, Captain Novak. What brings you out this way?"

"Let me call into the station and have them turn off the bridge alarm system so we can get closer and don't have to yell so the whole world can hear us. Squad 117 to control, turn off bridge 12D. I will be meeting with Captain Wilson."

"That's a 10-4. Advise control when you are ready to activate the bridge again."

"10-4, will do."

"Control out."

"So, Ted, how are things on that side of the bridge?"

"Well, Russell, ever since we put the electric eye system in, we have had less of the dirty, little rotten kids from your city crossing over to our state."

"So, Ted, back to my first question. What brings you out this way?"

"Someone saw your patrol come up to the bridge with the sirens blasting and lights flashing. I thought I would come out and help back them up."

So that's what they call that loud noise, a siren. I remember dad talking about them, but he didn't say how loud they were.

"Ramona and I were just out for a ride. We haven't seen any signs of those kids."

"Hello, Ramona."

"Hello, Ted. How are Cathy and the kids?"

"They're all doing just fine. Russell, when are your people going to find the hiding spot of all those kids? You've had their parents locked up for how many years, and you haven't gotten anywhere. The parents aren't saying where the rest of their people have gone; when we catch one of the kids, they stop talking."

"We caught one of your kids and got him to talk. We told him that if he'd help us, we could help him get back together with his parents. He told us the most unbelievable tale."

"What did he say, Ted?"

"He went on about how they have tunnels all over the town. He said that . . . ."

"Squad 117, we need you back at the station. Please let us know when you are clear of the bridge so we can reactivate the alarm system."

"That's a 10-4. Russell, I've got to go."

"Okay, Ted, we'll see you another time."

As they walked away I heard grandma say, "You know, I never did like that Ted. He is so .... Well, you know what."

"Yes, Ramona, I know what you mean."

"Russell, do you believe the rumors that Mark, our son, might be the ringleader of those kids and that he has been in the city all these years and too afraid to come home?"

"No, not for a minute. I cling to the hope that he found the settlement before they found him."

"Russell, that is the first time in almost 20 years that you have talked about the settlement."

Yes, Ramona, it is. There hasn't been a day gone by that I haven't thought about my parents and Mark. I wonder if they are together. What I would give to see their faces again."

I wanted to tell Grandpa that he may just get his wish if I had anything to do with it. Grandpa and Grandma would have to give up all they had here to see them again.

"There goes Ted. Does he ever drive anyplace without his lights and siren going?"

I waited again to hear grandpa's car drive away. I had to think of a way to cross the bridge without setting the alarm system off. Out of the corner of my eye I saw a field mouse running along the beams of the bridge. He went back and forth picking up seeds that the birds had left behind. That's it! I would cross under the bridge using the crossbeams. It may take some time but it would be less painful than if the police caught me—unless I fell onto the rocks or into the river below. Maybe I should rethink that idea. Hey! If a mouse can do it, I can do it. I sat under the bridge and made plans on how I was going to cross the bridge. The beams were about 18 inches wide. I should be able to crawl on my hands and knees and be able to rest when I reached each of the two piers. I'd test my balance without my backpack on first, and then I would cross with my backpack on for real.

I crawled onto the cold steel and placed my hands and knees in a comfortable position. I'd crawl out to where the beams cross at the wide spot. Then I'd turn around, come back and get my backpack. Then it would be the real thing. I moved one hand and then the other along the beam trying not to look down at the rocks and river below. I would focus on the center of the beam and all would be fine. After only a few feet out onto the beam, the ground sharply dropped away, and the fear of falling was starting to increase. I had to do this because it was the only way across that I could see. I just had to focus on the center of the beam, and I would be at the center where the beam was wide and I would rest. Then I would head back. Slowly and steadily I crawled; before I knew it, I was in the center of the bridge. I didn't take time to rest and headed back. Once back where I started from, I rested and got some water. I cinched the straps on my backpack to keep it from shifting from side to side and throwing my balance off knocking me off the beam. One last check of the straps and I was ready to go across. I tried to stay steady and focus on the center of the beam. Oh my, I wasn't anticipating birds flying in at me. What seems to be their problem? Of course, the barn swallows had built their nests along the underside of the bridge. I was at the center of the first section. Do I continue diagonally or do I take the beam to the left? I decided to continue diagonally. That would be less turning and less chances to slip; because if I slipped here, there were no do-overs. I reached the first pier, and I rested before I did the next section of the bridge.

I grabbed onto the pier and peered over to the next section. I couldn't believe my eyes! There were no crossbeams in the next section like I had thought there would be.

I'd have to go back and find a different way across. All that work for nothing.

Wait a minute. If I can't cross on top or under the bridge, what about hanging on the side of the bridge? I'd climb out right here and see what it looked like. If there was no way across, I'd run as fast as I could. Even if the alarm went off, Captain Novak had gone back to his station. I would be long gone by the time he got here. When I got to the edge of the pier, I could see that there was a small walkway just three feet above my head that ran the length of the bridge. I just needed to find a way to get up there.

As I looked around for a way up to the walkway, I saw a small building through the trees that may be a place to make camp. Back to the problem at hand, how do I get up there? The large bolts sticking out would make a great place to put my hands and feet. But wait, I wouldn't be able to get by that beam with my backpack on. I'd have to get my rope out like I did in the tunnel and pull it up once I got on top of the walkway. I tied the rope to the frame of my backpack and the other end of the rope to me and started my climb. I reached for the first bolt and placed my foot on another. With each bolt I climbed higher and higher until I could touch the walkway with one foot and climb onto it. I took up the slack in the rope until I could feel the weight of the backpack. Then quickly and carefully I pulled it up to me. I coiled up the rope, placed it in my backpack and slung in onto my back. The walkway was more out in the open, so I would have to move fast and always be looking for those black cars with flashing lights. When I stood up, the top of my head was level with the top rail of the bridge. That would help hide me some from the right side, but my left side was wide open. I wanted to run, but there were no railings to keep me from falling. The walkway was about two feet, a little wider than the beams under the bridge; and there was no birds dive-bombing at me. This should be easy. All I had to do was put one foot in front of the other and I'd be on the other side in no time flat. No sooner had I had that thought and a gust of wind blew and I started to lose my balance. The weight of my backpack shifted and I felt myself starting to fall. I reached out and grabbed a steel cable and stopped myself from falling. Now if I could only get my heart started again, I could continue my walk across the bridge. All I needed to do was let go of the cable and keep walking, but for some reason I wasn't letting go of the cable.

"Carl," I said out loud, "just let go and trust God to get you across. He has gotten you this far. Why would he stop watching over you now? That's right."

Just then I felt a warm, gentle breeze blow across my face and fingers. They started to loosen from around the cable. I stood up straight and focused on the end of the bridge. As I walked, I began to sing a song that Kayla and I would sing when we were little. In no time I found myself at the end of the walkway.

There in front of me was a locked gate with an old sign that was hard to read because most of the lettering was gone. What I could read said: "Warning: You are now entering the state." (I was hoping to find out what state I was in. That part was missing.) Then it said: "Violators will be arrested." Well, I didn't come this far to turn around so I'd just climb over the gate. It wasn't that high so I grabbed a hold of the gate and pulled myself up.

Then the funniest thing happened. The door swung open. I climbed back down and shut the gate so everything would look normal for when the state police would come by. They wouldn't know that someone had crossed the bridge. I quickly looked to see if anybody was around.

I headed down to the little building that I saw when I was up on the bridge to see if it would work for a place for me to hide while I was here—until I found all my people and was ready to bring them home to the settlement. I stayed off the road and walked in the woods along the river until I came upon an old caboose with no wheels. Most of the windows had been broken, but the best thing was that it was off the road and it didn't look like anyone had been around it for some time. As I walked around the caboose, I remembered the stories about trains that mom would read to Kayla and me before we would go to sleep at night. I climbed up the stairs, pushed open the door and set my backpack down as I stepped inside. There was a table and a chair to sit on. To my surprise, there was also a bed. There was no mattress but I could sleep on the springs just fine. It sure would beat sleeping on the cold, wet ground. I sat on the edge of the bed and looked around. I said a short prayer of thanks to God for all that he had done for me today.

I would rest and then get some food in me. I couldn't remember when I ate last, but my stomach was growling so it must be time to eat. I decided to sit at my table and set out a small feast. I looked out the broken windows on the side of the caboose. I could see the city, and dad was right; it did look all gray and dreary. I had much to do while I was here in the city. I needed to find out if Ernie was alive after all these years. And what about the kids that the state police were all looking for? Why were their parents in prison, and what did they do wrong? It was like a big puzzle with so many pieces. Some of the pieces were missing, but I could do this. While I ate, I thought back on some of the things that had happened today. The best thing was to see my grandparents face to face for the first time in my life.

Someday soon they would find out who I really was and that I had come to take them home. I was getting tired even though the sun was still high in the sky. I decided to lie down and sleep for a while. I could feel the soreness in my muscles as I rolled out my bedroll on my new bed. Stretching out on the bed, I stared up at the ceiling of the caboose. There staring down at me was a sparrow.

I said to the sparrow, "I hope it's okay that I share your home. I didn't know that anyone was living in here. I will only be here for a short time, and then I will be off, back to my real home." The sparrow just cocked its head, and for just a moment it appeared the little sparrow winked at me as if to say okay.

I said, "Thank you," and drifted off to sleep.

I was awakened some time later. The sun was setting and my friend, the sparrow, had flown down to my table to clean up the crumbs that I had left from my feast earlier. Slowly I sat up and talked softly to my friend. "Good evening, my friend. I see you have come for supper. Please eat until you have had your fill. Consider it payment for letting me stay in your home. We will be eating light tonight as I'm still a little full from lunch. I'll be having only some dried fruit, a little fish and for you I will break off a small piece of bread."

I looked out the window toward the city and watched the sun set and the city lights come on. We would never light up our settlement like that. We were too afraid that the airplanes that flew over at night would see the settlement and the state police would come and take us away to prison. That's why we had a law in the settlement that there was only one light on in each home, and all lights were out as soon as total darkness settled in on the settlement. I looked at my little friend pecking at her piece of bread, and she chirped at me. I'm not sure what she was saying, but I would like to think that she was listening to me. My friend flew back up to her nest and settled in for the night.

I spoke to her, "If you don't mind, I'll sit up and look at the stars for a while until I get sleepy again."

There were not as many stars showing because of the city lights. Back at the settlement the sky would be full of stars; many nights the Milky Way was like a river of stars twinkling in the sky. I looked up to see if the sparrow was watching me, but I couldn't even see her head. She must be scrunched down in the nest hoping that I would be quiet so she could get some sleep. Maybe I should lie down and try to get some sleep even though I wasn't that tired. I would need to get up early to cross the bridge before full daylight came and the whole world would see me on the bridge walkway. One thing I would have to do in the morning was make sure that I was clean and had clean clothes on, so when I walked around in the city I wouldn't stand out. I would have to bring some food and water along with me because it would be a long day. I wouldn't be able to cross the bridge until dark. I was yawning, so I must be more tired than I thought. I would lay here and pray until I fell asleep. I had much to be thankful for and much that I needed God's help with when I got to the city. Where would I start to look for Ernie? And what about the kids? I couldn't stop thinking about those kids that everyone was talking about. Could I help them? Maybe they could help me find Ernie. So much to think about and do in a city I had never seen. There I go yawning again. I better get to praying before I fall asleep.

Tap, tap. Tap, tap. I opened my eyes slightly. It was too early to get up. "Mom, can I sleep a little bit longer?" Tap, tap. Tap, tap. My eyes sprung wide open and I sat up in bed quickly; so quickly that I frightened my friend, the sparrow. She flew out one of the broken windows. The sun was coming up, and I would have to move fast to get everything done so I could get into the city before too many people were up and moving about on the road into the city. While pulling out some clean clothes, my friend, the sparrow, flew back in.

"I would like to thank you for the early wake up. I'm sorry I frightened you when I sat up in bed so fast. For just a few seconds there I thought I was back home. When I opened my eyes to see where I was; well, it freaked me out just a little. It's kind of nice having someone to talk to even if you are a sparrow. I'm sure if the people back home would see me talking to you, they would think that I was a little crazy."

"Chirp, chirp."

"You didn't have to agree. I don't have time to sit down and have breakfast with you today. I'll have to eat on the run. I want to be on the other side of the river before full sun up. My knapsack is packed and I'm ready to go."

Cautiously I looked out the windows on all four sides of the caboose. I didn't see anyone. I'd put the rest of my things in the closet just in case someone would happen to look in here for curiosity, they wouldn't see it and take it or set a trap for me when I would come back later tonight. I closed the door on the back of the caboose, and could feel the excitement starting to build with each step down knowing that I could be that much closer to finding dad's friend Ernie and the other kids. First things first, though; I needed to find out if Ernie was still alive and if he was, where he was. Dad said that, for an old guy, he seemed to move mighty fast; because when the police would show up, Ernie would be gone. I asked dad once if he thought Ernie was an angel, and he said that Ernie was just a man with a mission to get people to the settlement if they were ready to give up what they had here in the city. It would be hard to find Ernie because dad said that he never did find out what his last name was or where he lived. The only thing for sure was that if you needed to talk to Ernie, you would just show up at the park and wait. Before you knew it, there would be Ernie sitting next to you on the park bench. So it was off to the park for me. Maybe I could talk to some of the older folks in the park. They would most likely know Ernie since he would be a little closer to them in age and would be less likely to tell the police that I was asking questions. The bridge was only another 50 feet away and all was still clear. I hadn't seen or heard any cars driving around on either side of the river, and that was good for me. I would run and get up next to the cement wall and look one more time before going up on the bridge walkway and passing through the gate. I ran to the bridge and could feel some pain in my ankle from my fall at the mill. I didn't think that it would be a problem unless I had to do a lot of running. I was just feet from the gate so I hugged up alongside the bridge. Now was the time to go. As fast as I started to go for the gate, I stopped and dropped to the ground and lay as flat and as still as I could. There were voices coming from the road leading up to the bridge. They must be walking because I didn't hear any cars. Then I saw them. It was three ladies walking fast. They were talking just as fast as they were walking. They weren't wearing black, so they must not be the police. I would have to wait until they passed by and got down the road a ways so they wouldn't see me as I crossed the bridge. As I listened for their voices to disappear, I prepared myself for the walk across on the narrow walkway. I didn't want to have what happened the first time happen this time. That was scary.

This morning there was no wind so that would help. I also had the smaller knapsack. It was time to move. Once I hit the gate and got on the walkway, I wouldn't stop until I got to the other side. Hopefully the gate on grandpa's side of the bridge was unlocked also. If not, I would have to climb the gate. Then I'd head for the cornfield to rest and decide whether or not to walk down the road or stay in the cornfield a few rows back using it as cover. Then I could keep the road in sight to guide me into the city. Once again I listened to see if I could hear the ladies talking; all was quiet. The small trees that were growing around the base of the bridge I used to pull my way up to the gate. I grabbed the gate with both hands and pulled it open. Then I raced through and closed it behind me. I looked straight ahead and moved quickly along the walkway. I didn't want to lose my concentration and my balance. The gate was only a few feet ahead of me. Oh no! There was a padlock, and it was very rusty. Climbing over it or climbing out and around the short little wall were my choices. To climb around would be faster, but there was a little more danger of falling. There was no time to stand here and think. A car was coming this way, so it would have to be the faster and more dangerous way. I grabbed onto the fence and pulled myself out over the rocks below. Because I could hear the car getting closer, I had to move fast. As I reached around the end of the fence I froze. At the end of the bridge was a black car just sitting there. They would see me if I moved. How long would they be there, and how long could I hang onto the fence? The muscles in my hands, arms and legs started to burn with pain as I waited for what seemed like forever for the car to leave. Inside my head I was yelling at the police to go; but it didn't do any good. Finally my legs began to shake uncontrollably. If they didn't move along soon, my muscles would give out, and I would have to climb onto the bridge. Then I'd be caught for sure. And dropping to the ground was not a possibility.

At that moment the siren howled and the lights on the police car started flashing. The engine roared as it backed up. The smoke was rolling off the tires. In a blink of an eye, the driver swung the car around and it was racing down the road toward the city. My muscles were screaming for relief as I grabbed the other side of the fence and made my way to the walkway. I couldn't stop to rest until I found some cover in the cornfield. There was a chance that the car could come back as fast as it left.

Hobbling across the road and into the cornfield, I collapsed a few rows in. I lay there in the dirt. Every muscle in my body throbbed with intense pain and needed to be rubbed to help the pain go away. Eventually I got into a sitting position that helped me keep an eye on the road to see how many people used it. Would this road lead into the city, or would I have to walk across the cornfield to get to the main road? Dad had talked about a road that went in front of his house and straight into the heart of the city. While watching and listening to nothing happening on the road, the pain in my body was now just a dull ache in my shoulders and legs.

Some of the cornstalks I used to help myself into a standing position. I found myself a little wobbly as I brushed off the dirt from my clothes. If someone passed me while on the road or in the city, I didn't want them to mistake me as one of the kids that the state police were looking for. It would be harder for me to move freely around town without having people possibly think that I belonged to that group of kids. Probably I was more like them than the people of the city. In order to find who I was looking for, I would need to play the part of a city dweller.

No one had used the road in some time. I would head out to the road so I could make better time. It felt good to be out of the cornfield. The green leaves made me itch when they dragged across my body. When I emerged from the cornfield, I made my way through a small ditch and up to the road. I walked towards town on the side of the road next to the corn; that would hide me the best if the police would come back down this road. My mind was going a mile a minute looking at and recording everything I saw to help me know where I was. That would help me when I had to travel in the dark or to find other hiding spots along the road in case I didn't have time to run up into the corn. There was a hole in the side of the road up ahead. That was so strange. Why would you put a hole in the side of your road?

As I left the road and walked down into the ditch, I stood in front of the hole. It all became clear to me then. The hole was to let the water from the spring that was in the bottom of the ditch drain into the river and not wash the road away. The hole was almost as high as I was. This would make a great place to hide. I could run in on one side of the road and come out on the other side next to the river. Curiosity was getting the best of me. I wanted to feel what it would be like to walk under the road, because we didn't have these back at the settlement.

There was a small trickle of water running through the tunnel; and when I entered, I had to straddle it. The tunnel was damp and cold. My footsteps echoed as I made my way to the other side. It reminded me of the tunnels that lead to the settlement. One nice thing was that this tunnel didn't get totally dark, and it was short. But it did have big frogs which was something to keep in mind when I started to run out of food.

The trickle of water had created a natural path to the river. There seemed to be a pile of junk next to the path. I couldn't make out what that stuff could be, but curiosity was getting the best of me again. I needed to find out what that stuff was. I needed to make it a quick trip and get back to my task at hand which was to get into the city and find Ernie. I started jogging toward the river but because of the water from the spring, the ground was slippery and I felt myself slipping and having to run faster to keep from falling. Suddenly I was out of control, and I hoped I could stop before I ended up in the river. I grabbed at a tree, but it slipped through my grasp. I was moving too fast and it spun me sideways. The tree slowed me down a little, so maybe I'd be able to grab onto the next tree. Using my arm as a hook instead of only using my hands to grab onto the tree, I found myself swinging in circles around a small poplar tree. I was happy that I stopped in time before hitting the river or falling down.

Now I could see the pile of stuff at the end of the path. I walked over to it slowly. According to the amount of dirt that had piled up around the stuff, it looked as if it had been there for many years. It looked as if it was deposited here by high water. There was an assortment of things tangled in amongst the driftwood and dirt. I picked through it quickly to see if there was anything that could be of use for me while I was here. There were mostly old worn out tires and bottles on the one side of the pile. I walked around the pile lifting up some weather-beaten boards. There I found a box partially buried. I found a stick and began to dig it out to see what was in it, if anything. Grabbing onto the handle I tried to remove it from the grasp of the dirt that had held it there for a long time. Finally with one more pull the box broke free, and I set it down on the ground and cleaned off the dirt to find the latch so I could open it up. The box was made out of plastic, and it rattled when I shook it. When I found the latch and opened it up, I was excited to find fishing tackle. That was something we needed badly at the settlement. We had gotten to the point where we had to fish with spears. As I set the box next to a tree, I thought to myself how nice it would be to find a fishing pole so I didn't have to use the long stick that dad found for me to use many years ago. When I pulled up more old boards from the pile, I found what I would say was a gold mine. There, in a long wooden box, was not just one fishing pole but three fishing poles. As I looked to the sky, I thanked God for leading me to these things. I rushed over to the tree where I had placed the box earlier and put the fishing poles down.

As I headed back to the pile to continue my search for more things, I once again looked up to the sky and said, "Would a boat be too much to ask for?"

I poked around in the pile until I thought I had found all the good stuff. There was no boat. I picked up my things and headed back up the hill to the hole in the side of the road. I would hide my things in there and pick them up when I came back tonight to take to the caboose to see if they worked.

As I approached the tunnel, I heard a car coming down the road; I hurried into the entrance before the people in the car could see me. The car drove on by, so I must have made it in time. Back out of the tunnel I went to pick up some leaves, dried grass and some sticks to cover my things so no one would happen to see them. Through the tunnel I ran hoping to make up some of the time I lost digging in the pile.

71

I had hoped to be into town by now, but finding the fishing tackle was great. I couldn't wait until I saw the look on the people's faces when I brought the fishing tackle back to them along with my grandparents. After I climbed up the bank, I looked up and down the road to see if anybody was coming. The coast was clear so I jogged down the road as if I jogged it my whole life.

It wasn't long before the cornfield came to an end. It was then that I could see the edge of the city not too far in the distance. The city got closer as I continued to jog. I looked for the steeple that my dad had talked about when he told me the story many times when I was younger. A large tree blocked the city skyline from my view, and that caused me to focus my eyes back on the road. That is when I saw there was a fork in the road. I stopped jogging and walked off the road and headed for the clump of trees. The trees would be a good cover and a welcome place to rest.

"Hello there! It sure is a nice day for a jog along the river, isn't it?"

There, standing next to a big old elm tree, was a man. His clothes helped him blend in with the color of the trees keeping me from seeing him standing there. My brain was scrambling to find the right words to say.

"Yes sir, it surely is a wonderful day for a jog."

He would have had to see me coming. Now that I had stopped jogging and walked off the road, he knew I was thinking of resting. That meant I would have to stop and talk with him. He wasn't that old of a gentleman, but there was gray hair sticking out from under his hat.

"My name is Christopher Kittleson. I'm a doctor at the city's hospital. Most of my friends call me Chris. What is your name?"

"My name is Carl Wilson."

"I don't think I've seen you jogging along this road before."

"Well, sir, I just moved here only a few days ago. I was heading into town for my first time to see what the city had to offer as far as parks and learning centers." The doctor had this funny look on his face like he was thinking a little too hard on my answer. "I must be going now. It sure was nice meeting you. Maybe we'll see each other again, and we can talk more."

I turned and ran back up to the road and then began to jog straight ahead when the doctor yelled, "Carl, stop!"

I was afraid to turn around but I knew I had to. "Yes, sir!" When I turned, I saw he was running up to me. Panic was setting in. Had he heard something strange in what I said to him?

"If you're heading into the city, you will need to take the road to the left. If you go straight, you will end up in the city dump. That, my friend, is not a place you want to be."

"Why is that, Doctor Kittleson?"

"The report I've read says that there is a band of renegade kids that live in the city dump."

Wanting to know more about the kids, I asked the doctor more questions. "Where do the kids come from, doctor?"

He didn't answer right away. He looked around as if to see if someone was watching or listening; I played along with the game and looked also. Then the doctor got closer and spoke softly to me, "The kids belong to prisoners of the state."

"Doctor Kittleson, why doesn't the state help them and put them in a home so they don't have to live in the city dump?"

"Carl, it's not that simple. You see, these kids' parents are Christians."

The doctor was really looking uncomfortable. To ease his mind, I gave him my best "I don't know what you're talking about" look.

"What is a Christian anyway?"

73

"Carl, if you don't know, I'll say that it would be good for you to stay away from the dump and stay away from those kids."

"Are these Christians bad people, doctor? Have you ever met one of these Christians face to face? What do they look like?"

The doctor waved his hands trying to keep me from asking anymore questions.

"Thank you for the directions to the city and for the helpful information on the dangers of the city dump. Have a good day."

I ran down the road going into the city hoping to make up more lost time. Besides, I was getting excited about seeing the city that my dad grew up in and to find his friend Ernie. At the intersection to the main road I decided to walk again so I would not draw any extra attention to myself. Up the road I could see the remains of a burned down house. From what my dad had said, the state police had burned the Zabling farmhouse to the ground. There was a sign at the end of the field I was curious to read. It read: "Warning! State property. Keep out." Well, I guess the farm belonged to the state and not the Zabling family anymore. I wondered whatever happened to the Zabling's kids. I didn't know of any at the settlement. Maybe they were in the city some-where. Turning to walk back up to the road, I saw my first car drive by. I was hoping that it wasn't the state police or my grandma and grandpa. Either one of them would ask too many questions. The car drove on kicking up dust into my eyes. I had to stop to rub the dirt out of my eyes because it was making it too hard to see where I was going. As I pulled my hands away from my eyes and my vision had not cleared yet, I was startled to see somebody standing at the edge of the road. I could feel myself starting to panic.

Then the person spoke, "What's wrong, Carl?"

It was the good doctor. "Hello again, Doctor Kittleson. There's nothing wrong. A car just drove by and kicked up some dirt in my eyes."

"Do you need me to take a look at it? After all, I am a doctor."

"No, thank you, I think I have gotten most of the dirt out now. By the way, weren't you running the other way last time I saw you?"

"Yes, I was until the hospital called me and said I needed to get back to the hospital as soon as I could. There was a lady coming in to have a baby, and it would be good if her doctor was there. I decided to run and catch up to you, and we could jog into town together."

"That would be great." Having the doctor jog with me would make it look as if I was his kid and maybe no one would stop and ask any questions.

"Carl, I saw you were reading the sign at the end of the cornfield."

"Yes, I was curious to see what it said. Why? Shouldn't I do that?"

"Well, let's say next time don't make it so obvious. The state gets a little funny when they see people walking on their land."

"Thanks for the tip. I'll keep that in mind next time. Say, Doctor Kittleson."

"Carl, why don't you just call me Chris, okay?"

"Sure! Now I forgot what I was going to ask you. Oh well, if it's important, I'll remember it sometime, and maybe I'll see you again and I could ask you then."

I had a hundred questions I wanted to ask Chris about the city before I got there; but if I did that, he might get suspicious and then start asking me questions that I wouldn't want to answer because it would put the settlement in danger of being found. That's why they didn't think that it was a good idea to come back to the city, because one could slip up and say the wrong thing. Then the state police would come down hard on the settlement and many would get hurt. Dad always said, "If the state police ever found the settlement, just start running and don't look back. Don't stop running because living out in the wilderness alone is better than living in the state prison. I can tell you firsthand, Carl, they do not like Christians. I don't know what they are afraid of."

"Carl, are you okay? Carl!"

"Yes, I'm fine."

"You looked deep in thought. What were you thinking about?"

"What was I thinking about? I was thinking about the wilderness and how you can run and run and never stop. I was wondering what it would be like to live alone in the wilderness."

"Carl, you are the most interesting young man I have talked to in a long time. I hope we will have more opportunities to talk."

"I would like that."

Our conversation was going to get interrupted. There was a black car speeding our way. It looked like a state police car. I couldn't run or they would suspect something.

"Hey Chris, I think they're coming after you. What did you do wrong now?"

Chris had no time to answer back before the car came to a screeching halt next to us. The police officer stuck his head out the window of the car and asked, "Are you Doctor Kittleson?"

Walking to the side of the police car Chris said, "Yes, I am Doctor Kittleson. What can I do for you officers?"

"The hospital sent us to come and get you. The baby is on its way, and it is not waiting. We need to get you to the hospital right away. You and your friend get in the car and we can be at the hospital in just a few minutes." We didn't have any choice. The back door swung open and the officer in the car said, "Move it! We don't have all day, Doctor!"

I thought it best that I too got in the car keeping up appearances that the doctor and I were old friends. Once they dropped us off at the hospital, I could go into town and look for Ernie starting at the park. I climbed into the back seat with Chris. The door to the car wasn't even closed and the officer started the car moving. Before I could blink my eyes, we were flying down the road heading into the city. We were going so fast that things on the side of the road were just a blur. I was starting to feel sick. I had to close my eyes or there would be a mess in the back seat. If this was what it was like to ride in a car, I would stick to walking.

Chris was getting a little worried about the way the policeman was driving. "Excuse me, Officers; do you really think it is necessary to drive so fast? It's not going to do anyone any good if we don't make it to the hospital in one piece."

"Don't worry, Doctor, you'll get there in one piece."

All of a sudden the car turned to the right sharply sending me up against the window of the car. The tires were squealing and Chris and I were being bounced around in the back seat, tossed from one side to the other as if we were a ball. I kept quiet during the ride. As quick as the ride started, the car came to an abrupt stop. There outside my window was one of the largest buildings that I had ever seen. It must be the hospital. It was so big. It had to be five stories high and had lots of windows. The biggest building at the settlement was the watchtower used to keep a lookout for the state police and bears.

"Here you go, Doctor, safe and sound."

"And in one piece I might add!" said the second officer.

As we exited the car, they began to laugh. Chris reached to shut the car door. The car's tires started to spin; then squealing and smoke started to roll off the tires. I jumped back, as did Chris, not knowing what those two crazy offi-cers were up to. The doors to the hospital flung open and out ran a lady dressed in a white uniform.

"Doctor Kittleson, your patient is in the delivery room as we speak. I will brief you on the way. Who is your young friend?"

"Oh yes, where are my manners? Lisa, this is my new friend, Carl. Carl, this is Nurse Lisa Glover. We met down by the river while I was out running. He is new to town."

I reached out to shake her hand and said, "Hello. It is very nice to meet you."

Nurse Glover looked at me strangely as we shook hands. I'm not sure what that look meant. Maybe it meant nothing at all.

"Well, Doctor, the baby isn't going to wait much longer!"

I reached out and grabbed a hold of Nurse Glover's arm before she went into the hospital. "Nurse Glover, could you tell me how to get to the city park, the one with all the statues?"

"Sure, you go straight down this street about eight blocks and then turn left. Go three more blocks and you'll be in the park."

"Thank you!"

"Carl, what are you going to do in the park?"

"I'm looking for a friend of my dad's."

Oooops! I couldn't believe I said that. I hope she lets that pass and doesn't ask any questions.

"What is your friend's name?"

What was I going to do now? I had to answer her. "His name is Ernie. You probably don't know him. He is very old." The look on Nurse Glover's face was as if she had heard that name before.

"Thank you again for the directions to the park. You'll have to hurry to catch up to the doctor so you can help with the delivery of the baby."

I turned to head for the park and Nurse Glover turned to go into the hospital. I was glad that she didn't ask any more questions. A sigh of relief slipped out of my mouth when I heard the door close behind Nurse Glover. I had only taken a few steps when the door opened again. I thought nothing of it because people were always coming and going at the hospital.

"Carl!" My heart skipped a beat. I spun around to see who had called my name, and there leaning out the door was Nurse Glover. So many things rushed through my head. What did she want? Had the doctor told her my last name, and she called the police because she remembered the story about what happened back when my dad took off to find the settlement? Did she know my grandma and grandpa? Maybe the strange look on her face meant that she knew something was not right with my story but she couldn't put her finger on it.

"I'm glad I caught you." I quickly looked around to see which way the police were coming from so I could run the other way. "Carl, you're a little jumpy. What is the matter?"

"Nothing, Nurse Glover! You just surprised me. I thought you had gone in to deliver the baby. I didn't expect to see you out here calling for me. What can I do for you?"

"I remember an elderly man that went by the name Ernie."

"Do you remember his last name?" I asked hoping to find out more information.

"No, I don't. One thing I do remember was that people said that he loved the park and always had a smile on his face. Some say that he was a little on the crazy side."

"What do you think? Do you think he was crazy, or was he just happy?"

"I don't really know. I've got to go now but, Carl, if you would like, I'll do some checking around and let you know what I have found?"

"That isn't necessary. I could stop by here tomorrow and talk to you then."

"That would be fine. I take a lunch about 12:30. Just come in and ask the ladies at the desk to call me when you get here, and we'll talk then. Maybe we can find your dad's friend."

"Thank you. That would be great. I'll see you at 12:30 tomorrow."

"Goodbye, Carl."

"Goodbye, Nurse Glover."

"Carl, why don't you just call me Lisa?"

"Okay, Lisa."

She waved goodbye and slipped back into the hospital, and I headed for the park to see what I could find out on my own about Ernie. The homes along the street came in all sizes. Some were small and some real big. They weren't like at the settlement where everybody's home was about the same size. Some of our homes were made of logs and some were made of sod. These homes were brick and wood planks, and they had different colors. At the settlement all the houses were brown. When the grass on the sod homes started to grow, they turned green. A few houses up ahead I could see a little elderly lady with gray hair sitting on her front porch. Her house seemed to be the most run down one that I had seen in the city. I kept my eye on her as I walked down the street. What would she do? A little dog lying in the long grass startled me when it began to bark and bark. I tried talking to the dog to get it to quiet down. "Hello, boy, how are you today?"

A voice from the porch yelled back, "My dog is not a boy. It is a girl, and her name is Simba Louise. Just let her smell you, and she will quit barking."

I held my hand out for Simba Louise to smell, and she did. Then she stopped barking. "That is a good watchdog you have there, Miss. The name is so different. I don't think I have ever heard of that name before."

"My great aunt and uncle had a dog named that, so I named my dog that. You're not from around here, are you?"

"No, I'm not. How did you know?"

"I have lived on this street for over 60 years, and I've been sitting on this old porch every day for the past 20 years. Do you have a name?"

"Carl is my name."

"So Carl, where are you going to?"

"I'm going to the park to look for a friend."

"You're not very quick with the dispensing of names, are you? Do you have something to hide?"

"No, my dad always says that when you're in the city, people don't need to know everything about everything."

"Your dad is mighty smart. You keep listening to him. I would like to talk more, but it's time for Simba's and my nap. Maybe you can come by this way again sometime and we can talk some more. And if you find your friend, he or she can come too. I have lots of cookies and juice."

"I'll try to do that. I don't even know your name."

"It's Mabel."

"Goodbye, Simba. Goodbye, Mabel."

"Carl, do you know how to get to the park?"

"Yes, I do. Thank you for asking."

Before turning the corner, I looked back at Mabel's house to help me remember where her house was so maybe I could stop there one more time before I left the city to go back home. As I looked ahead, I tried to see the park, but there were many large shade trees on both sides of the street making a canopy high above. I looked at the houses again as I walked down the sidewalk. There were so many different shapes.

Then I heard a car coming up from behind me. I wanted to look; but if it were the police, I didn't want to look guilty and have them stop me and ask questions. Why didn't they just hurry up and drive by so I wouldn't have to tie my stomach up in knots wondering who it was and if they were going to stop me and haul me off to jail. Suddenly there was a siren blast and squealing tires. A black car pulled up alongside me and a police officer poked his head out the window.

"Hey, boy, come here! Now!" I walked quickly to the edge of the street next to the police car. I recognized the officer as one of the two officers that gave Chris and me a ride to the hospital.

"Hey, boy, aren't you the kid we gave a ride to the hospital with Doctor Kittleson?"

"Yes, I am."

"So what are you doing down here?"

"I'm going to the park."

"Why aren't you in school?"

"I've just come to town and I haven't gotten enrolled in school yet. I probably will start next week, sir."

"Hey, kid, do you need a ride to the park?"

"No thank you, sir, I like to walk."

"Okay kid."

The lights on the car started to flash, the siren blasted away and smoke rolled off the tires as they turned the car around and went back up the street where they came from. I couldn't believe my ears when he asked me if I wanted a ride. I would like to have told them that if I rode with them, I may not make it to my next birthday. I could still hear the siren blasting away. They were just two little kids in big people's bodies. How did they ever get to be policemen? Walking back from the edge of the street to get on the sidewalk, I noticed that some people from the homes around me had come out to see what all the commotion was about. My eyes were focused on what looked like the main gate to the park. I tried not to make eye contact with any of the people, but out of the corner of my eye I saw a large man walking down his sidewalk from his house. He was going to intercept me. If I crossed the street, that would look too obvious that I was trying to avoid him.

I decided to start the conversation with a joyful greeting. "Good afternoon, sir."

"What's so good about it?"

"Well, the sun is out and the birds are singing."

"Cut the chatter! I'm a member of the 'Neighborhood Watch Dog' group. Who are you? What are you doing in the neighborhood? And why did the police stop you? Their siren woke me up from my nap."

"I'm sorry they woke you up from your nap, sir. They were some very nice friends of mine, and they thought that it would be funny to scare me with their siren. They didn't mean any harm. They just wanted to know if I wanted a ride to the park. I told them no, that I like to walk because the park wasn't that far away. Do you go to the park much, sir? It looks like a very nice park. I'm sure I will enjoy my time at the park. Maybe you and the Mrs. would like to join me for a walk in the park."

"Kid, do you ever stop to breathe, or do you just talk non-stop like an old lady?"

"Why sure I stop to breathe. I was trying to be friendly and answer your questions; and since you seemed like a nice man, I thought that it would only be kind if I would invite you and the Mrs. to enjoy a day at the park with me."

"Kid, me and the Mrs. aren't going to the park with you, so move along."

"Why? Was it something I said?"

"NO! It's because I'm afraid that you'll never stop talking; and if I wanted to hear non-stop chatter, I'd talk to my mother-in-law. So hit the road."

"I'm sorry that you feel that way. I'm also sorry it I have offended you and the Mrs. in any way. There is one thing I don't want to do. That's offend you or anyone else."

"Stop already! Just go! Get out of here! I think all your chatter has given me a headache."

"Goodbye, sir! Maybe when you are feeling better I could stop by again and we could talk."

"NO! Don't ever stop. Just walk on by."

"Well, if that's the way you want it, I suppose I could abide by your wishes. I was hoping we could be friends."

"Just go! Please!"

I walked away as fast as I could before he figured out that I didn't answer most of his questions. My plan to talk the guy's leg off worked. I'd have to remember that next time someone started to ask too many questions. I did feel bad that I gave him a headache.

Chapter 4

City Park

The park was in sight, and from what I could tell, it was a very large place. I knew dad said it was big, but I didn't think it would be this big. I passed under the steel arch with the words city park on it. The statues were what I was eager to see. Mostly I wanted to see the statue of the boy trying to fly. Dad had talked about that one the most. The park was so big I didn't know where to start looking; I found the nearest park bench and sat down to think. It felt good to sit down, because I had been walking for awhile and I was a little hungry. Maybe now would be a good time to eat something. That reminded me that I hadn't eaten breakfast. No wonder I was so hungry. I pulled out some food and thought about who I could trust to ask about Ernie when a shadow came across my feet and stopped. The way things were going, it was probably those two crazy police officers here to cause me more trouble. Maybe if I didn't look at them, they would go away. I continued to dig for some food in my knapsack. Good. It worked. The shadows were moving. No, they were getting closer.

"Excuse me. Is there anybody sitting next to you?"

When I looked up, I saw an elderly couple holding hands and looking very tired. "No, there's no one sitting there. I can move to another park bench and you two can have it all to yourselves."

"No! We don't want you to go. We were hoping that you would stay and talk awhile. It isn't very often that we find people to talk to. Everybody is always in too much of a hurry."

"Sure, I will stay and talk. Maybe you can help me out."

As the couple sat down on the bench, they said to me, "We would be glad to help if we can. Our minds are not as sharp as they were when we were your age. How can we be of help?"

"I'm new in town and I'm looking for a man that spends a lot of time here in the park."

"What is his name? Maybe we know him."

"I only know him as Ernie."

The couple looked at each other hoping that the other knew who Ernie was. I could tell that they wanted to help but nothing was coming to mind. "Could you tell us what he looks like? Maybe that would jog our memories."

"I have never seen the man myself. He is an old friend of my dad's that he knew back when he lived here in town and was just a kid himself. My dad said that he had white whiskers and white hair. Does that help?"

"As you can see, most of the people in the park have white hair, so that didn't narrow it down any."

"I don't know what else I can tell you about him that would help."

As I looked into the face of the old man, he began to smile. "I knew the man. He would come to the park almost every day to feed the birds. His favorite birds were the gold-finches and the chickadees. He would sit on that bench over there next to the statue of the governor."

I was excited to get a lead on Ernie. I had so many questions to ask, but before I could ask them his wife spoke, "No, no! Dear, that was Bernie, not Ernie. Besides, Bernie died two years ago while feeding the birds."

"That's right, dear. That was Bernie."

My heart sank when I heard that they had the wrong man. The three of us sat on the bench not knowing what to say to each other. To break the silence I said, "I should introduce myself to you. My name is Carl. What are your names?"

"We are the Abernathys; my first name is Aaron, and my wife's name is Marian. Carl, you said that you were new in town. Is there anything about the town that you would like to know about? You see, we have lived here all our lives."

"Oh yes, I have a lot of questions for you two."

"Fire away!" Aaron yelled enthusiastically.

Marian leaned over, put her hand on my arm and said, "Carl, you have just opened the floodgates. He will be talking until the cows come home."

"Don't listen to her, Carl. What is your first question?"

"When you said 'fire away,' that reminded me that I saw they burned down the old mill at the edge of town. Why did they do that?"

I don't know what I said, but tears began to well up in Aaron's eyes. "I'm sorry. Did I say something wrong?"

"No, Carl; it's okay," Marian replied. "Aaron worked there for many years, and many of his friends worked there, also. Then one day they shut it down and built a more modern mill."

"Why did they burn the old mill now if it has been closed for many years?"

"They are going to build a new state prison. Back in the olden days we didn't have that much crime that we needed to have so many prisons; but ever since the state cracked down on the black market, they don't seem to have enough room for all the people they arrest. Soon everybody will be in prison and there won't be anybody on the outside. When

I was young, if you did something wrong, they would make you pay a fine. They wouldn't put you in jail." Aaron was getting madder and madder as we talked.

Marian told Aaron, "I think it's time to talk about something else; people are starting to stare."

"I have another question for you folks. What time does the park close?"

"The park closes at 10:00 p.m., but the state police begin to sweep through the area about 9:30 p.m. Then they drive by every hour all night long, but you don't want to be out after dark."

"Why is that, Aaron?"

"Because of the kids," he said with fear in his voice.

Wanting to know more about these kids I asked, "What kids are they?"

"They are . . . ." Then both Aaron and Marian looked around to make sure no one was around to hear what they were about to say. "They are the kids that were forced out onto the street because their parents are in jail."

"Why are their parents in jail?"

"Their parents went to that old church just up the road from here. Most of them lost their jobs when the new governor took office, because he hates Christians. He says that it is their fault that the state is in the shape that it is. That doesn't make any sense to me, but then most of what the state does doesn't make any sense."

"There can't be that many kids out there, can there? Why would you be afraid of the Christian kids?"

"The state officials say that they are responsible for the break-ins at the government stores and people's homes."

"The state officials say this? Has anybody ever seen the kids doing the things that the state officials say that they are doing; or are the state officials just telling you these things to cover up their poor management of the state?"

"I heard that a group of these kids beat up a man and his wife over a bag of apples! Isn't that right, Marian?" Marian didn't answer Aaron.

"What's wrong, Marian?" I asked.

"You know, Aaron, when we were at that town meeting where the officials said those things, people asked who these people were that got beat up, and the state said that was classified information. For weeks we talked to others, and nobody knew of anybody that had gotten hurt by these kids."

"So, Marian, what you are telling me is that the state could be using these stories to keep people in line. And that most, if not all, of what they say is just made up."

"Yes, Carl, I guess you're right. They could be making it all up."

"Oh, a couple more things. You never told me how many kids were on the street. If their parents are in jail, where do the kids live?"

Marian spoke up before Aaron could say anything. "We really don't know for sure. The state officials say about 100, but we think there are maybe more. It is hard to tell. You never really see them, but you know that they have been around."

Aaron interjected excitedly, "I tried to set a trap for them." Marian began to laugh. "What is so funny, Marian?"

"Some trap!"

Aaron was looking a little mad and not saying anything. Marian was laughing so hard that she couldn't get the words out to tell me what kind of trap that Aaron had set.

Finally Aaron couldn't take it anymore and he blurted out, "It was a fine trap. It would have worked if I could have run a little faster. I had placed a few apples on the tree stump back by the alley, and I sat in the garage and waited for the kids to come out at night."

Marian jumped in on his telling of the story and said, "The reason he missed the kids was because he fell asleep.

The kids took the apples and he never saw them or the apples again."

Aaron's pride was a little bruised about now. I thought I would change the subject. I was sure Aaron wouldn't mind. He pulled back his shirt sleeve to look at his watch.

"Marian, we should be getting home."

"Would you like to have me walk with you a ways? I need to be going also."

"That would be very nice of you, Carl. Thank you."

Getting up I reached out my arm for Marian to take a hold of to help her up off the bench. She moaned a little. She must have gotten a little stiff sitting on the bench. I reached out my other arm for Aaron to take hold of, but he didn't take it. He struggled to get up and finally made it.

Aaron looked at me and spoke, "Carl, if you don't have to get old, don't. It's no fun."

"Carl, don't listen to him. He says silly things like that all the time. I don't know where he comes up with such things. It scares me sometimes."

Marian was still hanging onto my arm as we began walking down the sidewalk to leave the park. We were coming up to the statue that dad had talked about so many times. I didn't even have to read the words on the plaque. I knew immediately that this was the one because Dad had described it well and often.

Marian noticed that I was staring at the statue while we walked by. "Do you like that statue, Carl?"

"Yes, I do."

"Have you ever dreamed of being able to fly?"

"Sure, Marian, hasn't everyone at some time in their childhood dreamed that they could fly for some reason or another?"

"What are you looking at now, Carl?"

"What is that sticking out of his back pocket? Is that a stick?"

"Carl, surely you know what that is."

"No, Marian, I don't have a clue."

"Aaron, Carl doesn't know what is hanging out of the boy's pocket on the statue."

"It's a slingshot. You have never seen a slingshot before?"

"No, this is the first one I've seen. What is it for?"

"When I was a kid, every boy in town had a slingshot. Marian, do you think I still have a few of my old slingshots around that I could give one to Carl?"

Marian laughed and pulled my collar to bring my ear closer to hers. She whispered, "He doesn't throw anything away. Yes dear, I'm sure you can find one to give to Carl."

"Would you like one?" Aaron asked. "I'm not sure. You didn't say what they're used for."

"When we were kids, we would go hunting for rabbits; but mostly we would shoot tin cans off the fence. The people that lived around us didn't like it because it would be so noisy with the rocks hitting the tin cans and all."

Marian pulled on my collar again and said, "Come to our house and take a look at his collection. We'll set up a few cans back in the alley and the three of us will have some fun. After that I'll fix us something to eat. What do you say to that?"

What could I say? They had been so nice, and Marian was offering to feed me. I would be crazy to say no. "Of course, I'll come with you to your home."

I didn't think their smiles could have been any bigger when I said I would come with them to their home. They both seemed to have a little more spring in their step. If Marian didn't loosen her grip on my arm, I'd be black and blue. It took no time at all to get to the entrance where I entered earlier today.

Once outside the park Aaron spoke up, "We will go just a few blocks up this street here. We live next to an old boarded up building. I asked the state officials when they would tear it down and put something new it its place, but they said it was a reminder to 'those people' who was in control."

Aaron's jaw was starting to tense up as he talked. I wanted to ask him some questions, but my questions could wait until we got to their home. I wanted to see if the building that he was talking about was the old church that great grandma and grandpa went to and where my dad had spent so much time looking for clues to help him get to the settlement.

Aaron spoke again. He had calmed down and was smiling again. "Carl, this house here was where my best friend lived when I was growing up. We did everything together.

We would do all the stuff that boys did growing up like riding bike, camping and fishing."

I quickly jumped in there and said, "Don't forget about shooting tine cans with slingshots."

"Carl, you are looking forward to shooting the slingshot aren't you?"

"I do have to say that I am, and that is strange since it was only a few minutes ago that I saw one on that statue."

"Wait until we start shooting. You won't want to stop," said Marian.

"It is really that much fun?"

"My best friend, Dwayne, we called him the 'Z man', and I would shoot for hours until we couldn't pull our arm back to let the rocks fly. We even started a club called the A to Z Slingshot Shooting Club."

Aaron laughed, then stopped and stared at me. "Carl, do you get it? A to Z. My last name is Abernathy and my best friend's last name was Zabling."

I stopped walking and just stood there on the sidewalk. The only time I had heard that name was when dad told of the story about how Dwayne and Janice Zabling helped him get his journey started to the settlement with much sacrifice."

Marian pulled on my arm and asked me, "Carl, are you okay?"

I answered her quickly and started to walk again. "Yes, I'm fine."

She looked me in the eyes, and I could tell that she knew something wasn't right, but she didn't push it.

"Aaron, whatever happened to your friend Dwayne?"

"Dwayne met this farm girl, Janice, from a town down the road called Milltown. It doesn't exist anymore. Our town here was growing, and we swallowed it up. That old mill on the edge of town that you asked about earlier, that was part of Milltown. That girl started coming to our school; and the next thing after we graduated from high school, they got married and had a bunch of kids. They bought a hog farm."

"Do you see him anymore?"

Aaron got real quiet and just looked at the ground. I didn't know what to do, so I looked at Marian and mouthed the words, "What did I say wrong?"

Marian mouthed back to me, "You did nothing wrong."

Then I pointed to Aaron, shrugged my shoulders and mouthed, "What can I do?"

Marian had gotten closer to me and she whispered into my ear, "Give him a few minutes, and he will tell you the whole story. He needs that time to get past some of the things that hurt the most before he tells the story to anyone that asks."

Marian was right. She had no sooner finished whispering in my ear when Aaron's head rose up, and we could see that his eyes were red and there was a little tear in the corner of each eye. He reached for his handkerchief that was in his back pocket. He wrapped the handkerchief around his nose, took a big breath and blew. The sound that came out of that little man's nose was loud enough to wake the dead. It frightened me because I had never heard a person blow their nose like that with such volume. I must have made a funny face when Aaron blew his nose because Marian was laughing. Aaron looked at Marian and she imitated the face I had made. If that was the face I made, I could see why Marian was laughing so hard. Aaron had a smile on his face as he folded his hanky up and pushed it into his back pocket ready for the next time.

I asked Marian how much further before we got to their house. She pointed and said, "Do you see that blue and white house next to that boarded up building? That's our house."

"Wow, that's a nice house! What is that building next to you?"

"I'll let Aaron tell you about that building. It is part of his story."

We were right in front of the church that dad had told me about. It had gotten even more run down than what dad had said it looked like back when he was a kid. It must have been a wonderful building when it was new. I could see the windows that impressed dad so much when he first stepped foot in the church many years ago.

Marian must have let go of my arm and kept walking while I stood and stared at the church. She called to me, "Carl, are you coming?"

"Yes, I am." I ran to catch up to them as they stood in front of their house.

Marian had a smirk on her face. I wasn't quite sure why until she said, "You two boys head to the backyard and start looking for rocks. I'll get the slingshots."

Aaron questioned, "Marian, are you going to shoot also?"

"Well, that's a silly question. Who do you think is going to show you two boys the right way to shoot?"

Aaron gave me a poke in the ribs with his elbow and said, "She's right you know. She has always been able to outshoot me, even when we were kids."

We walked along the side of the house to get to the back-yard. I sneaked a glance at the side of the church whenever

Aaron wasn't looking, because I didn't want him to wonder why I had such a fascination with the church.

As we walked to the alley, Aaron said, "Carl, not every rock is a good rock."

"What do you mean? A rock is a rock, isn't it?"

"No, you want to find a rock that is as round as possible and not much bigger than the end of my thumb." Then Aaron bent down and picked up a rock. "Here you go, Carl. This is what I'm talking about. Now you got the idea. Start picking. We will need a lot of them if the three of us are going to be shooting."

I bent over and began to gather up as many rocks as I could find. My hands were getting full. As I reached for a nice round, black rock, I felt a sharp stinging pain in my butt. I stood up straight and grabbed my butt dropping all my rocks to the ground. The sting grew into a burning feeling. I turned to ask Aaron what had happened, but he was gone. Then I heard the two of them laughing.

Aaron yelled out, "I told you she was a good shot."

I could not believe what had just happened. Marian had just shot me in the butt. This sweet, little old lady shot me in the butt; and there was nothing I could do about it. She was up on the back porch laughing.

"Carl, pick up your rocks and come and get your second lesson on shooting."

"What do you mean, Marian, my second lesson? I haven't had my first."

Bending over to pick up my rocks that I dropped when I got shot in the butt, I quickly stood up and faced Aaron and Marian. "No need to explain about the first lesson. I know what that lesson was. Don't give you two such a tempting target."

"Carl, you are a fast learner. It took Aaron a long time to learn that lesson."

Marian was pulling back and taking aim again as I walked toward the porch. I dropped to the ground and lost my rocks again, but I didn't want another stinging reminder. A rock whizzed by and then there was a ting. A can fell to the ground. She was not aiming at me this time but at a row of tin cans that they had perched on a fence. I gathered up my rocks one more time and headed for the porch before they started shooting again. There on the table were five slingshots; some made with forked sticks and some made out of metal.

"Pick one," Marian said with a smile.

"I don't know which one to pick."

Aaron said, "Take the X-15. It shoots a long ways."

"Which one is that?"

He handed me the one that was made out of a forked stick, and there carved in the handle was X-15. "I made that one myself. It is my favorite one of them all."

Over the next few hours the three of us shot tin cans off the fence until we couldn't shoot anymore.

"Carl, you have become a great shot with the X-15."

"Thank you, Aaron, for the lessons and the opportunity to shoot with you folks. I had a lot of fun; it is something that I won't ever forget, especially lesson number one."

"Carl, we would like you to have the X-15 and this little slingshot also. I know it looks small, but it is good for when you don't have a lot of room to pull your arm back and shoot. It packs a whale of a sting though."

"Thank you. You really don't need to do that."

"But we want to."

"Now you two boys go wash your hands and get ready for supper. We will be eating in about 20 minutes. Aaron, that will give you enough time to answer Carl's question that he asked earlier today about what happened to Dwayne and Janice Zabling."

Marian walked into the house and closed the door behind her. Things felt a little awkward. Neither one of us knew what to say.

I spoke first, "You don't have to tell me if you don't want to."

"No, I want to tell the story. I'm just trying to figure out where to start my story."

"Well, I know that you two were the best of friends. Dwayne got married and had a lot of kids and lived on a hog farm."

"Alright, I'll take it from there. I started working at the old mill on the edge of town when I got out of school. I remember my first day there. I was late."

"That's not a good way to start a new job." Aaron gave me the same look that dad did when I would interrupt him when he was telling his stories. "Sorry! Go on. You were late and . . . ."

"I was late; and this cute, young lady in the office saw me running down the hall toward her office and figured I was a new employee. She started talking to what I found out later was the mill foreman. That gave me time to slip into the office and sit down next to two men starting the same day. The cute, young lady finished talking with the foreman, and she turned and gave me a wink. It surprised me. I looked at the other two guys, and they weren't even paying attention. All that week I tried to find any reason I could to go up to the office to thank her for distracting the foreman so I wouldn't be late for my first day. After my sixth time up front, the other secretary told me that I should give her my name and she'd tell her to find me. That way both of them could get some work done."

"Did she find you, and did you ask her out?"

Just then the door opened and Marian replied, "No, he didn't. He was too chicken. I had to ask him out to dinner. Carl, do you have a girlfriend?"

"No, but I'm looking. Maybe I'll find a good one like Aaron did."

"Carl, flattery like that will get you an extra big piece of pie. What I came out here to tell you, Aaron, is that when you two come in, I need you to go to the freezer in the back room and bring out the ice cream to go with our pie."

Before Marian went inside, she reminded us that we needed to wash our hands before we came to the table. After Marian left to go back inside, Aaron continued on with his story. "I had only been working at the mill for about three weeks when Dwayne came in and was getting some of his corn ground into feed for his hogs. That took awhile to grind up. It was a great time to get caught up on what had been happening with the two of us. That is when he invited Marian and me out to the farm the next weekend. They said they were going to have a little get-together with some of their friends. The weekend came, and Marian and I went out to the farm. When we pulled up, there had to be some 50 cars parked all over the yard and even into the woods. I looked at Marian and told her I was wondering what kind of party it was anyway. We didn't have to wonder very long."

"Why was that, Aaron?"

"The first person we ran into commented, 'Hello! It's another fine evening that the Lord has given us tonight. Let me introduce myself. My name is William Wilson, but everybody calls me Roy. That little lady next to the hay wagon is my wife Frieda. We just live down the road a piece. I would love to talk, but I need to get inside. The service is about to start. Maybe we could talk later. I think I've seen you at the mill. You work second shift, right?'"

"Right."

"I told Marian that it was a church service. I had heard talk that Dwayne had gotten mixed up with those Christian people from the church in town. I told her that we were going to get back in the car and head back to town. Dwayne wouldn't even know that we came out. That is when I heard my name called out. It was Dwayne and Janice, and they were waving their arms for us to hurry up and come to the barn. We sat through two hours of some guy talking about God and Jesus and a whole lot of other stuff. I leaned over and told Marian I was sorry that I got her into this. She told me to keep my voice down because she was trying to hear what the guy was saying."

"Are you and Marian Christians?"

"No, we're not; and don't you even think that."

"Why?"

"Why you ask? I'll tell you why. As the years rolled by, Dwayne and Janice asked us out to the farm and tried to talk to us about God. It got to the point that we started to make excuses why we couldn't make it out to the farm. We hadn't seen them for many years until the state took over the mill and everything changed. Dwayne was having a hard time paying the state's high prices to grind corn into feed. He came to me one night and asked if there was some way that I could take the corn in and get it ground up, because he heard that we mill workers could get it done cheaper. I did it a few times until I got called into the office one day. Three guys in black followed me in. They told me that if I planned on working at the mill one more day, I better stop grinding corn for Mr. Zabling."

"Why didn't they want you to grind corn for your friend?"

"I didn't ask why. I just said yes sir. Then the foreman told me to go back to work and not tell anyone what went on in the office. I told him yes sir. I heard a few days later that the state police raided Dwayne's farm and took control of it. They said that the Zablings now worked for the state. Word got around that the state was shutting down private businesses starting with the Christians first; and anybody that helped them would lose their jobs. I ran into Dwayne a few days after the state raided the farm. He looked bad; they beat him pretty good."

"What was the state looking for?"

"The state officials thought that somehow the Christians had found a place out in the wilderness where they could live and not be under control of the state."

"So is there such a place, and did Dwayne tell the police where it was?"

"Dwayne said that there was a place, and that if at anytime Marian and I would want to go there, he knew people that could get us there. He didn't tell the police about it though, and for that he took a beating."

"Aaron, where are the Zablings now?"

"A few years back, I'm not sure how many years, the police came to the farm again and beat both Dwayne and Janice. The state officials accused them of helping a young boy escape from the police."

"What did the boy do?"

"He broke into the state computer files and into the information center. Dwayne and Janice went to jail for ten years, but they never got out. Janice got sick and died, and it wasn't long after that Dwayne was gone too."

"Aaron, you said the Dwayne and Janice had a bunch of kids. Do they still live around here?"

"Just Kevin. He works at the hospital. I see him when we go to get our medicine. We just say hello and not much more than that."

"When did the state close down this church next to you?"

Aaron leaned back in his chair and tilted his head down so he could look over his glasses and questioned, "Who said that the state closed down this church?"

"I must have just assumed they did since you said that they were closing down private businesses and things." Where was Marian and her perfect timing to get me out of this mess? "Aaron, I think we should go and wash our hands before Marian tells us one more time."

"No, Carl, not yet. Why are you so fascinated with the church? I see you looking at it often. What is it about the church? You seemed to be somewhat sympathetic to the Christians when I was telling the story."

I heard the door behind me open and Marian announced, "Okay boys, it's time to eat. Now I don't want to have to tell you again to go wash your hands. Carl, I'll show you where the bathroom is and Aaron, you need to go get the ice cream."

"Marian, I was just about to ask Carl . . . ."

"You can ask Carl all the questions you want after you get the ice cream. And don't take too long. We don't want our food to get cold. Come, Carl, I'll show you the way to the bathroom."

I looked back at Aaron as Marian and I walked toward the bathroom. He had this look on his face that was saying, I know you have a secret, and I'm going to find out what it is.

"Carl, the bathroom is right here, and you can use the blue towel to dry your hands with."

"Thank you for everything. I've had a lot of fun today."

"It is we who should thank you. It has been a long time since we have had a young person in the house. You see, Aaron and I never had children. With the way the world is today, I'm glad we didn't have kids. You wash and we'll talk later."

She left the room and I turned on the water and washed the dirt from my hands from picking up all the rocks. I could smell the food. It was spaghetti and garlic bread, and Marian said I would be getting an extra big piece of pie.

"Carl." I dropped the bar of soap on the floor when Marian came back to the bathroom. "I'm sorry, Carl. I didn't mean to scare you like that, but I wanted to ask you a question before Aaron gets back with the ice cream."

"What question is that, Marian?"

"I was listening to you and Aaron talk as he told you the story of what happened to the Zabling's. I heard how Aaron was beginning to ask some hard questions about the church and how you feel about the Christians. That's why I came out when I did. You looked like you were trapped in a corner and there was no way out."

"Thank you again. He was asking a lot of questions."

"Carl, are you a Christian?"

Aaron yelled, "I've got the ice cream, and if you two can make a little room, I would like to wash my hands so we can sit down and eat."

When Marian asked if I was a Christian, I almost dropped the soap again. I was happy that Marian saved me from the questions that Aaron was asking, and now he saved me from having to answer Marian's question that I didn't think I was ready to answer yet. Marian left the room without getting her question answered, and I could see disappointment written all over her face. I wanted to trust her; but if she would tell Aaron, who knows what he would do with that information. I headed down the hallway and gave a tug on the back of Marian's dress. She turned and I could see a small tear in the corner of her eye.

I whispered to her, "I can't give you an answer to your question; but if you're as smart as I think you are, you may know the answer already." I gave her a smile, and she reached out and gave my hand a squeeze and smiled back.

"Come on you two; quit blocking the hallway and let's eat!"

We all walked down the hallway to the kitchen. "Carl, you will sit here," Marian said as she turned toward the oven.

"Okay."

"I'll get the garlic bread out of the oven, and we can get started."

I took both of my hands and pretended to rub my eyes and said a prayer of thanks for the food that God had provided through the Abernathy's hospitality. When I was done with my prayer, I looked up; Aaron was staring at me.

"Don't you just hate it when you've been outside all day and your eyes get dry? Rubbing them like this makes them feel better."

"I wasn't sure if by the time you got done rubbing your eyes that there would be any eyes left in your head for as long as you were rubbing them."

"Well, the trick is not to rub too hard but enough to get your eyes to water; and that makes them feel better."

"Here is the garlic bread. Now it is hot, so be careful not to burn yourself."

Supper was quiet and no one talked. All you could hear was the clanking of our silverware on the plates.

"Carl, are you ready for your apple pie with a scoop of ice cream on the side?"

"Yes. I saved enough room for pie and ice cream."

"Aaron, could you help me clear the dirty dishes off the table?"

"Sure, Marian, I can do that." As the two of them gathered up the dishes, they each took turns looking at me for some reason, and I couldn't figure it out.

"Do you need any help bringing them into the kitchen?"

"No, that is quite alright. You just sit there and take it easy."

When they reached the kitchen, I could barely hear them talking. It was killing me not to be able to hear what they were saying. I got up from the table, walked around over by the kitchen door and pretended to look at the pictures on the wall all the while trying to listen in on what they might be saying about me. All during the meal it looked like they wanted to ask me things, but they didn't. I needed to get a little closer because I still couldn't hear them. Maybe if I moved closer to the door I could hear something.

"Aaron, I've been looking at Carl today and I think he looks a lot like Roy Wilson's kid. What's his name?"

"I know who you're talking about. His name is Russell."

"That's it. Russell. Don't you think so?"

"Well, maybe a little."

"If you put the two together side by side, Carl could pass for his grandchild."

"Fat chance of the happening since their son, Mark, ran away some 15 or 20 years ago, and no one has ever seen him or found his body."

"Aaron, don't talk like that. Some day Mark Wilson will walk back into town . . . ."

"And the state police will be all over him like stink on manure."

"I'm going to ask Carl if he knows the Wilsons on the edge of town."

"No, Marian!"

"Yes, I'm going to ask and that is that. Now grab those two plates and give Carl the big piece."

I ran to the other side of the room and was looking out the front window as they came from the kitchen; they had no clue that I had heard what they were going to ask me. "Here it is, Carl. Just as I promised, I dished you up a big piece of apple pie with a scoop of ice cream."

"Wow! That is the biggest piece of pie I have ever seen. If it tastes as great as it looks, I may be back again tomorrow for more."

"Well, Carl, you will surely be welcomed. Carl, can I ask you something?"

"Sure, what is it?"

"Aaron and I . . . ."

"Leave me out of it, Marian."

"Okay; it's more me than Aaron. I was looking at you when we were out back, and I thought there just for a minute that you looked like a friend of ours named Russell Wilson." I gave them a blank stare and waited to see what they would say or do next. "Do you know the Wilsons? They live on the edge of town not too far from the old mill that the state burned down."

"I talked to a nice lady one day this week. I'm not sure what day that was. She <u>did</u> live down by the mill. I was walking along the river, and I heard her singing. Does she have a little gray in her hair? She's not tall, but at the same time she's not what you would call short either."

"That sounds like Ramona."

"Nice lady. We didn't talk much because a car pulled into the driveway, and we said goodbye."

"Was it a man driving the car?"

"Yes, it was."

"That would have been Russell, Ramona's husband. The one I think you look like."

"I'm sorry. I did not see what he looked like."

"That's okay."

There was an awkward silence as we were sitting around the table each of us picking away at our pie. They looked like they still had questions to ask me. I didn't want to answer too many questions because I didn't know enough about them to trust them yet. Both Marian and Aaron finished their pie and ice cream first and pushed their plates into the center of the table. I was still working on finishing mine. It worried me that that would give them time to ask more questions. Then Marian got up from the table and left the room. Aaron and I were left there sitting all alone.

I really began to sweat when Aaron remarked, "Carl, you never did say where you live and where you are staying."

Those two questions I had hoped to never hear while I was in the city. Now that I had been asked, what do I say? If I tell them where I'm from and why I'm here, the police would be here before I could put my fork down; but I couldn't lie to them either. Before Aaron had asked the two questions, I had just put a big bite of pie in my mouth. I motioned to him that my mouth was full, and as soon as I was done chewing, I would answer.

"Okay Carl, I can wait."

It took me a long time to chew the piece of pie in my mouth. I had to make it last as long as I could to give myself time to think of what to answer him. It had to be an answer that would not land me in jail and that I could feel comfortable telling them. The piece of pie was almost gone, and I didn't have answer. This must be the feeling that dad had when he was running from the state police. There was a tingling over my body. It seemed as if my hair was tingling, or maybe it was standing on end.

"To answer your question on where I live, I would have to say it is a small town not too far from here. I'm staying with a friend I met here. I'm not sure what he does for work but he flies around a lot."

"Carl, that didn't tell me much."

Then Marian came back with an armload of books. I jumped up from my chair to help her and to get out of answering Aaron. "Let me help you with those!"

"I thought that since we had talked about the Zablings and the Wilsons that you might like to see some pictures of them."

"That would be great!"

I could see Aaron was getting suspicious of me not answering his questions. "Aaron, are you going to look also?"

"No, I've seen them before. I was the one that took the pictures in the first place."

For the next hour we flipped through the books of pictures and I heard stories of the fun they had. We laughed at some of the pictures. Marian quit laughing all of a sudden and a strange look came over her face. She didn't say anything at first. She just stared at a picture in the book. Then her wrinkled, aged hand took the picture from its place in the book, held it up to my face and she stared not saying a word. Then a tear seeped out the corner of her eye. I gently took the picture from her hand and turned it around so I could look at it. I could see what she was staring at. It was a picture of my dad with his mom and dad standing on their steps in the back of the house. I looked so much like my dad. I wondered what questions were running through Marian's mind about now.

Not wanting to know, I said, "I would like to thank you for everything. The shooting lessons and the food were great. I hope that we can maybe do it again sometime soon. I need to be going and get back to my friend's place." They started to get up. "No need to see me to the door. You two just have a great evening together, and I'll see my way out." They both tried to say goodbye at the same time. Marian gave a little wave and a wink.

I waved back and replied, "Thank you so much."

As I hurried out the door and down the steps to the street, I heard the door of their house open up. When I looked back, I could see Marian and Aaron standing on the steps still waving to me. I waved again and didn't look back anymore. I had a long ways to go to get back to my caboose. I'd have to move fast to get to the bridge before it got too dark and made it more difficult to cross. The only way I knew to get back home was if I backtracked to the park and passed Mabel's house and hope that her dog didn't start barking. It didn't take me long to get to the park. I could see down the street where Mabel lived, and there was no one there. There wasn't much time before the sun would start to set, so I ran down the sidewalk nearing the house of the man that belonged to the neighborhood watch dog group. Oh no! The man was on his front steps. What was I going to do now? I started to laugh when I got an idea.

"Good evening, kind sir. We meet again. I hope that your headache went away." I waved, and he turned and grabbed the doorknob to the front door of his house. He was in such a hurry that the door hit him in the face.

Running up his front sidewalk I asked, "Sir, do you need any help?" He struggled even more to get the door to his house open and get inside before I started to talk his leg off.

I started running again and passed by Mabel's house; all was dark. I kept running until I could see the hospital. Then I had to decide whether to stay on the main road or head down to the river which would take me close to the city dump. The main road would be faster, but there was more of a chance that the police would stop me. Then I heard a car engine start and that made up my mind. I'd walk by the river. There was a sign that read city dump, so I turned off on that road because I figured that would get me to where I needed to go. The doctor said that the city dump was down the road from where we met. The car engine was getting louder, so I looked over my shoulder to see if it would drive by the road I had just turned down. It did, and I breathed a sigh of relief. Then I heard tires squealing, and I looked over on the road and saw red and blue lights flashing. I started to run looking for a place to hide, but the area was just an open field. The trees up ahead looked to be my only hope for hiding. All I needed to do was get there before the police got turned around. I heard their tires hit the gravel road surface, and I still had a ways to go before I reached the trees. I couldn't let them catch me; I just couldn't. I no sooner thought that when the car turned off the road and into the field. Then I saw what appeared to be silhouettes of two small people. The police car was chasing them down. I could hear them screaming. They sounded like just kids.

I stopped running to the woods and ran toward the kids being chased. The car stopped and the doors flew open. Two police officers grabbed the kids and began to hit them with their sticks. Their screams of fear and pain was hurting my ears. I wanted the police to stop hitting the kids with their sticks; I reached into my pocket and pulled out my X-15 and reached down and grabbed a handful of rocks from the gravel road. I put in as many rocks as I could and pulled back aiming at the police car. As the slingshot sent rocks flying toward the car, I could hear a rush of air pass by my ear. I dropped to the ground and looked up just in time to see the rocks hit their target. It was a direct hit on the police car breaking the flashing red light. The kids stopped screaming; now it was the police officers turn to be fearful of what was happening. I loaded up the X-15 again with another handful of rocks. There was another hit on the car. Marian would be proud of my shooting. I looked up and saw the two kids had escaped from the grasp of the police officers and were running for the trees, but the police officers were running after them. I loaded the X-15 with rocks, aimed at the police officers and let them fly. In seconds I heard one police officer cry out that he had been hit and dropped to the ground. The other police officer continued after the kids and was catching up to them. They were getting too far away, so I needed to reload fast and get another shot off before they were out of range. I only had one chance. I launched my last handful of rocks and waited. Then a scream of pain rang out and the officer fell to the ground.

He was rolling around on the ground yelling. "My knee. I twisted my knee!"

It was not my shot that took him down and twisted his knee. It was imperative that I made my escape to the trees while both police officers were down on the ground. I ran for the trees as fast as I could, not wanting them to get up and chase me and see who helped the kids get away.

One of the officers yelled, "Stop! Police!"

I kept running for the trees. A shot rang out and I felt something hit my shirt. I was too close to the trees to stop and see what hit my shirt and too afraid of getting caught. I kept running deep into the wooded area before I turned to see if the police were coming. When I looked back, I could see that the police car hadn't moved, so the police officers must not be able to move very well with their injuries. My arm was beginning to sting as if a bee had stung me. I could feel sweat running down my arm. As I made my way toward the river, I had time to look at my shirt. There was air coming in; I must have torn it when I dropped to the ground. With my right hand I reached around and grabbed my shirt. I felt a hole and my sleeve was wet. When I pulled my hand back, it was covered in blood. I stood there in the woods not knowing what to do. Was I going to need medical help, or was this something that I could take care of myself? If there was a bullet in my arm, was it going to have to come out so I didn't get an infection? One thing I did need to do was wash it out and try to stop the bleeding. If I ran to the river, that would only get my blood pumping harder, and then I would lose that much more blood.

Maybe it I used the little slingshot as a tourniquet to keep the bleeding down to a minimum, it would let me run to get out of the area in case the police officers called for backup. With the tourniquet in place, I jogged through the woods until I came to the road by the river. Cautiously I approached the edge of the woods looking to see if the police had anyone watching the road. Just ahead I could see a sign for the city dump and an arrow pointing to the left, but my home was to the right. With the way that my arm was, I would have to wait for another day to meet up with the kids from the dump.

I loosened the tourniquet on my arm hoping that I had stopped the bleeding. It took only a few seconds to see that the bleeding had not stopped. I was worried that I may lose too much blood before I could get it to stop. Before crossing the road and heading down to the river, I tightened the tourniquet again. Once at the river's edge, I took off the tourniquet and with my right hand ripped off the sleeve of my shirt. Just for a moment I wondered what mom would be madder about, me ripping my shirt or the bullet hole in my arm.

Dipping the sleeve into the water, I used it as a washrag and cleaned off the blood. Then I could see how big the wound was that I had received from the state police. I'm not sure if it was from the loss of blood or the sight of the hole in my arm, but feeling a little dizzy, I decided to sit down before I fell down. I rinsed out the blood from the sleeve and wrung out as much water as I could with my one hand. My other arm was hurting more, and it still hadn't stopped bleeding. Using my sleeve as a bandage, I wrapped my arm and place the tourniquet back on. What was I going to do tonight for a place to sleep? With my arm hurting and bleeding, I wouldn't be able to climb around the end gate of the bridge to get home.

As I sat on the riverbank thinking, I remembered that dad and the Zablings hid in the backyard shed at Grandma and Grandpa Wilson's house. If nothing changed since then, there should be some food supplies still there. In the morning I could eat, and then if my arm was better, I would meet up with Nurse Glover to find out about Ernie. No, that wouldn't work; my shirt was ripped and I had a hole in my arm. Someone at the hospital would notice that. I would have to get back home to the caboose to get another shirt and then head back into the hospital. There was no other way. I picked myself up off the ground and started walking along the river on the path staying off the road so that the police wouldn't see me as easily. The sun was almost set, and darkness was settling in. That was good because I would need the cover of darkness to slip into the shed.

I could hear a car coming down the road. It was the police. They were using a big spotlight to search the edge of the woods. They must be looking for me or the other kids. As the light approached, I ducked behind a big tree. The light went right on by, and so did the police. I hoped that was the last I would see of them tonight. I picked up my pace hoping to get to the shed that much faster. Then I could settle down for the night and take the tourniquet off hopefully for good. I passed the bridge and hurried down the road to reach the cornfield behind the house. The lights from the house could be seen through the corn stalks. As I weaved my way through the corn and came to the edge of the field, I could see someone walking past the window as if he or she were pacing. That could make it hard to get into the shed, but I had to take a chance because I needed a place to spend the night. I would have to time it just right with the person pacing. It was going to take about 15 seconds to get from the edge of the cornfield to the shed door. If the door was locked, I didn't want to think about that. The door would be unlocked, and I would slip in and make myself at home down under the floor.

Okay . . . now! Quickly I ran to the shed and grabbed the doorknob. It was opened. I slipped inside and closed the door behind me. There, safe at last, or was I? I could hear talking. Who was it? I pushed my face up to the wall and looked out a space between two boards. It was grandma and grandpa, and they were coming this way. Frantically I searched for the trap door in the floor but I wasn't finding it.

"Russell, I know I saw someone in the backyard over by the shed."

"Are you sure it wasn't a deer or something like that?"

"No, Russell. It had only two legs, not four."

"Ramona, there is no one out here. Let's go back in the house."

"I'm going to look in the shed." The door swung open.

"See Ramona, there is no one in the shed either. Come into the house and relax."

"How can I relax? You heard the police radio. Two officers not far from here shot and hit a larger child that had attacked them."

"And what! You think it's your friend out in the cornfield?"

"Yes, I do! If he's hurt, I want to help him."

"What do you think he is going to say? I just attacked two state police officers, and they shot me and I need help because I'm bleeding to death."

"No, I don't know what he would say. He may not even be able to say anything. He could be hurt lying out in the woods cold and alone."

"Oh Ramona, now what are you doing? Are you crying? You don't even know if he is hurt that bad."

"Hurt that bad. The police officers said they shot once and that they found blood leading into the woods and again down by the river. I would say that is hurt bad."

Just then grandma screamed. It sent shivers down my back. Grandpa Russell was surprised by the scream from grandma. "What is it, Ramona?"

"Look at my hand, Russell. I have blood on it."

Grandpa asked, "Did you cut yourself on something?"

"The only thing that I touched was the door to the shed."

"Well, that's it. You cut yourself on the handle to the shed. Let's go inside, get your hand cleaned up, put a bandage on it, and call it a night."

"Russell?"

"What is it now?"

"I don't see any cuts on my hand. It's not my blood."

"Alright, I'll call the police and they can send out the dogs to find this person."

"Russell, you will do no such thing! We'll go in the house now, and if this person needs our help, that is where we'll be."

"Ramona, what are you talking so loud for?"

"If he is out there needing our help, I want him to know we will help."

They talked as they walked back to the house but I couldn't hear what they were saying. As their voices drifted into the dark, I heard the porch door open and then close. I uncovered myself from the heavy tarp that was in the shed that I found just in the nick of time before grandma opened the shed door. I searched the floor until I found the handle to open the trap door. The tarp would help me to keep warm and protect me from the dampness of the dirt, so I decided to take it down the hole. Quickly I laid out the tarp and settled in. Then I took off the tourniquet. It looked as if it had stopped bleeding for now. I was looking forward to a good night's rest. The other half of the tarp I pulled up and covered myself.

"Thank you, God, for all that you have done for me today. I know some might think it crazy to thank you for getting shot, but I think you are going to use it somehow. Good night, God."

Chapter 5

Get the Lead Out

The sound of a car door slamming woke me up. It wasn't the most ideal way to greet the morning. That sound startled me so that I sat up too fast and hit my head on the floor of the shed. I struggled to get the tarp off me so I would be ready to run if I had been found out. All of my thrashing about to get the tarp off hurt my arm, and now I could feel a small trickle of blood running down it. Carefully I removed my makeshift bandage to take a look at it now that there was more light. The area around the entry wound was very red and swollen. I noticed that there was a lump about two inches to the left, and with my hand I reached up to feel what it was. I feared it was the bullet and that I would have to get it out or I would get an infection. That would slow me down to the point of having to go back to the settlement without Grandma and Grandpa Wilson. I couldn't let that happen. I came too far to go back empty-handed.

As my fingers felt around the lump, sharp bursts of pain would shoot up and down my arm; it was the bullet. If I could just work the bullet back over to the entry wound and push it out the hole, then I could wash out the wound and pray that I didn't get an infection. Firmly I braced my feet up against some boxes and pressed my back against the dirt wall. I could work the bullet only for a few seconds at a time before I got the feeling like I was going to pass out. The pain was intense as I maneuvered the bullet. For several minutes I worked at the bullet, but it seemed that the bullet just slid back and forth and didn't get any closer to the hole where it came in. The only thing I managed to do was get the blood flowing quite heavily. I put the bandage back on and wrapped it tight to help slow the bleeding.

Slowly I unplanted my feet off the boxes that I was using to brace myself and reached in the food packets that were left from when dad and the Zablings were down here many years ago. The great meal that I had at the Abernathys was gone from my belly, and now it was growling for more. Anything would do for now. The box I pulled out said spaghetti dinner. Spaghetti is what I would have for breakfast. Digging for the can opener that was in each packet, I found that there were some crackers, gum, toothpicks and toilet paper. There in the corner of the box was the can opener. It was hard grabbing onto the can with my hand because of the pain. I placed the can in the bend of my elbow and hugged it tight to my side and began to work the can opener around the top of the can until the lid fell to the ground. The smell of the spaghetti drifted up to my nose, and it smelled so good. Okay, maybe not as good as Marian's spaghetti that we had last night, but it was food. I opened up my crackers and placed a cold meatball on top of a cracker and popped the whole thing into my mouth all at once. I gathered up the garbage, put it in the little box that it came in and placed it in the pile where the other ones had been for years.

I took inventory on how much food was in the boxes just in case I needed to use them not knowing how long I would be in the city and how many would be coming back with me to the settlement. Would it be just grandma and grandpa, or would I be able to find Ernie? And would Ernie be in any shape to make the trip back with us? From what I had seen so far from my time in the city, I would not want to stay any longer that I had to. The state police don't greet their guests with open arms but with firearms, and that leaves a bad impression in a person's mind and holes in their body.

I reached to get something out of my knapsack. Oh no! I forgot it at the Abernathys. I knew exactly where it was. It was on the back porch. If there was time in the next few days, I would have to go back and get it. Hopefully it would be safe to return by then.

Alright, back to my original thought. There were 46 meal boxes. That should be plenty for the trip back home to the settlement, even if we have to go slower and take an extra day or two to get the older folks through the tunnel and out the other side to freedom.

Then I heard a car door slam, but the car never drove away. I had to see what was happening, so I carefully pushed open the trap door and rested it up against the wood that was piled in the shed. I found a crack between the boards and looked towards the house. I was right; the car was still there.

Suddenly the door to the back of the house flew open and grandpa came out and ran down the steps. He was halfway to the car when Grandma asked, "What? No kiss this morning?"

Grandpa dropped his stuff and ran back up the steps and kissed her while bending her backward and looking as if he was never going to stop kissing her. Then as fast as the kiss started, it was over and he straightened her up and ran down the steps toward the car.

He grabbed the car door, spun around and yelled, "I'll see you later!" Like my mom, grandma just stood there and waved goodbye.

Grandpa got into the car and drove off very fast. He must be late for something. Dizziness was beginning to overtake me, so I sat in an old chair in the shed before I fell down. I braced myself with one hand on the open trap door. Then things began to get blurry, the shed began to spin and I remember falling forward and things went dark.

When woke up, I found myself down under the shed and the door was closed. I had not been out long because the dust in the air had not settled yet. I could hear the shed door open. "Who is in here?" It was Grandma. She must have heard the trap door slam shut when I fainted. "I know someone is in here, so come out right now!" I could see her standing right above me. "I'll give you to the count of ten to come out. One, two, three." Grandma stopped counting. "I know you're hurt, and I can help. I won't hurt you or call the police. Come to the house, and I'll be there for you."

Right now I didn't know what was hurting more, my arm or my heart. I wanted to tell grandma that I was here and that I did need her help. My fear was what grandpa would do when he found out. Would he turn me in? He wanted to tell the chief of police I was here the first time I met them.

I watched grandma walk to the shed door to leave; but she stopped at the door and said, "You can trust me, and don't worry about my husband, Russell. I can handle him. He won't call the police either."

Then she walked out of the shed and the door closed behind her. Still a little dizzy, I lay there in the trap waiting for the dizziness to pass. I did need help with my arm so I would have to trust her. Sitting up slowly, I looked around and nothing was spinning. The dizziness was almost gone for now.

Once again I pushed open the trap door and crawled out of the hole. This time I closed the trap door quietly. I opened the shed door just enough to look up toward the house and then around the yard to see if the police had set a trap for me. All looked clear for now; I opened the door more and walked toward the house. There was fresh blood running down my arm mixing in with dried blood and dirt. As I walked through the backyard, I saw the fire pit that dad told me about where his mom and dad had burned many secrets years ago. I found myself at the steps leading up to the back porch door.

Then I heard tires squealing and engines roaring. Out of the corner of my eye, I saw flashing red and blue lights. It was the police. Grandma called the police on me! I turned to run for the cornfield. After only taking a few steps, I saw three police officers standing by the edge of the field cutting my way of escape off.

The back door of the house opened and I heard Grandma's plea, "Carl, don't go!"

I turned to her and answered, "You said I could trust you and that you wouldn't call the police."

Grandma saw the police by the cornfield. Then she saw the police cars streaming into her driveway and still more coming down the road.

"Carl, it was not me!"

I had no time to discuss whether she called the police or not. They were closing in on me fast. I ran inside the garage and headed to the back hoping the things that Great Grandpa Roy told me were true. Grandma was yelling at the police to stop. They yelled back at her to get in the house.

I heard one office say, "We are going to get this kid dead or alive. It doesn't matter to me one way or another."

Then the shooting began. I dropped to the floor and covered my head. Pieces of wood from where the bullets ripped through the side of the garage landed all around me. I crawled along the floor praying that the shooting would stop. No sooner had I prayed that to God and the shooting stopped. I could hear grandma screaming at the police. I heard grandpa's voice trying to calm her down.

Grandpa was mad and he yelled at the officers, "Who gave the order to shoot?" All was quiet but the crying of grandma. Grandpa barked out the question again to the police officers, "I said who gave the order to start shooting?"

An officer standing not far from where I was hiding said, "I did."

Grandpa yelled, "Who said that?"

"That would be me, Lieutenant Kyle Anderson."

"Well, Lieutenant Anderson, whatever did our suspect do that would warrant you to fill my garage full of bullet holes?"

"Sir, he started to run."

"He started to run. Is that all? Did he have a gun or knife?"

"No sir."

"We do not shoot suspects that aren't armed, or did you skip that chapter in the policeman's manual? Lieutenant Anderson, why don't you go in what is left of my garage and bring the suspect out and we will question him."

"Sir, don't you think it would be wise if I would take two other men in there with me to get him out?"

"Lieutenant Anderson, he is just a kid. For as many bullets as you put into my garage, there is a good chance that he wouldn't put up a fight. Now move out and bring the kid to me."

"Yes sir!"

Grandpa seemed to be stalling by asking the lieutenant so many questions before sending him in. I waited until I could see the lieutenant's face, and then I tossed a shovel at him.

"Captain Wilson, did you see that? The kid just threw a shovel at me and missed."

"That's too bad."

"What do you mean that's too bad? He could have hurt me or worse; he could have killed me."

"No, Lieutenant Anderson, you misunderstood me. It's too bad for the kid. Now we will have to put that in the report. We wouldn't want anything bad to happen to you. That would mean that I would have to fill our more paperwork. Now that we have that cleared up, go in and get that kid."

When the lieutenant came back into view, I took out my X-15 and found a clump of rock hard dirt next to some flowerpots. I waited for the lieutenant to get closer.

Grandpa yelled at the lieutenant, "What are you waiting for? Get the kid and get out here."

When the lieutenant turned around to answer Grandpa, I drew back and let the clump of dirt fly hitting the lieutenant square in the back of the head. He let out a scream like a little girl would. Then I took one of grandma's flowerpots and threw it through the window. In all the commotion I made my escape. Grandpa sent in the other officers to come and find me. To their surprise I was gone.

One officer came out and told Grandpa, "There was no one in the garage but the back window was broken out. The kid must have climbed out the window."

I heard grandpa talking to the officer as he walked into the garage to see for himself that I was gone. "Well, we are done here for now. Load up and head back to your areas of patrol. Take the lieutenant with you."

"Yes sir!"

Grandma ran into the garage and asked Grandpa, "Russell, where is Carl?"

"He's not here; he got away."

"How could that be, Russell?"

"The officer said he thought the boy climbed out the window that he broke."

"The window is too small and there is still too much glass in the frame. With that much glass he would have cut himself, and there is no trace of blood anywhere on the window frame or on the glass."

"Look at this, Ramona."

"What did you find?"

"You were looking for blood. There is blood here on this flowerpot. And look at this . . . a partial palm print and three fingers but no fingerprints."

"Russell, are you going to put that in the report that you found these prints?"

"What prints, Ramona?"

"These right here!"

"I'm not sure how old those prints are. They could be my prints from a few weeks ago or maybe a few months ago. I will have to just leave it out of the report since I'm not sure."

"Thank you, Russell. I see what you are doing."

"Ramona, why don't you go back into the house and take it easy. I'll be off work about 3 o'clock, and maybe we could grill something for supper tonight. How does that sound?"

"That sounds like a good idea. I'll see you a little after 3 o'clock."

Grandma and grandpa walked out of the garage so I reached down and opened up the second door to the tunnel that Great Grandpa Roy said he had put in the garage that lead into the basement of the house under the stairs. I was glad that Great Grandpa Roy and I had talked about the tunnels that he used to avoid the police back when they were looking for him and great grandma. I would have never thought about pushing the workbench to one side to find a trap door with a smaller door so that you could reach up and pull the workbench back into place. That way no one would know that you had gone down into the tunnel. Who would have thought that the tunnel was even there. Closing the second door to the tunnel plunged me back into darkness. Great Grandpa Roy said that it I placed my right hand on the wall and kept my left arm straight out in front of me and walked slowly for 50 paces, there I would find a small wooden door that would open up to the basement.

Slowly, as I walked, I could gee that Great Grandpa Roy had poured a lot of cement to make this tunnel so that it would not cave in. I should have counted my paces so that I would know about when to expect the tunnel to end and where the door entered into the basement.

"Ouch!" There was no need to count paces. I had found the end of the tunnel. Great Grandpa Roy said that there was a latch on the top and the bottom, but all I had to do was turn the handle in the middle of the door and it would open. Here was the handle. I gave it a twist and the door opened. First I listened to hear if anybody was in the basement; all was quiet. Then pushing the door open more, I stuck my head out to have a look around. It was strange to have my first look inside the house that dad grew up in, I thought as I stepped out of the tunnel into the basement. Dizziness was coming on again, so I sat in this big old chair to rest and to wait for it to pass. Grandma was walking around upstairs because with each step the floor would creak. I unwrapped my arm to look at the wound. It was bleeding and the skin around it was red like it was infected—just what I did not want to happen. I was going to have to trust grandma and ask for her help to get this taken care of before it got worse. Great Grandpa Roy said that there should be an old coal bin that was not used anymore. Inside of there was a way up to the storage space under the stairs on the first floor.

I stood up too fast and stumbled forward running into some boxes and making a loud crash. Quickly I rushed to the coal bin, shut the door behind me and waited to see if Grandma heard me. I was right; she did hear the crash.

The door at the top of the stairs opened up and Grandma yelled down, "Who's down there?" I could hear her take a few steps down the stairs and say, "I'm sure glad Russell isn't here. He would just say that I was getting old and that I was hearing things."

Grandma turned around and headed back upstairs and closed the basement door behind her. I groped around in the dark until I found a wood structure. This must be the steps that lead up into the storage area on the main level, but I didn't feel any steps. Great Grandpa Roy said that he designed it so that it could convert from steps when you needed to climb up or down; and if you needed to escape fast, all you had to do was pull a lever on the side and the steps converted into a slide. It must be in the slide mode from when Great Grandma Frieda and Great Grandpa Roy made their run for freedom many years ago. I found the lever as I ran my hand along the side. I heard the slide convert into steps when I pulled the lever toward me. There was just one problem; Grandma Ramona heard it upstairs too. She was running over to the basement door and would be yelling down the stairs right about now.

"Alright now! I know somebody is down there, so come out where I can see you."

I could hear her slowly inching her way down the stairs. Each time she took a step down towards the basement, I used the sound that she made to cover up and sound of my taking steps up to the storage room. My head was pressed up against the trap door. I had to be ready to open the door when and if Grandma Ramona made a loud noise to cover up the opening of the trap door. It didn't take long for her to help me. She ran into some old paint cans that were stacked up by the stairs, and now it sounded like they were all over the basement floor. I made my move and pushed open the door, crawled up into the storage room under the stairs and shut the door. Quickly I found the door leading out from the storage room under the stairs, and soon I was standing inside my dad's house. There would be only a short time before Grandma Ramona found out that there was no one in the basement and would be back upstairs. I had to find a place to hide until I knew that is was safe to talk to her and get her help to fix my arm. My dad's old bedroom would be a good place since they wouldn't think of looking in there for any reason. My dad had been gone for so long. If I remember right, dad's bedroom was at the top of the stairs and just a little to the left. Dad talked about his house a lot, and it was as if I had lived here myself.

Quietly I ran for the steps and made my way to my dad's bedroom. Once inside I found it necessary to rest because I was feeling faint again from the loss of blood. Just in case grandma would happen to look in the room I lay down next to the bed; that way she wouldn't see me unless she walked around the bed.

I heard a door open. I got up, ran to the door and opened it just a sliver. Grandma was bringing the clean laundry into the room next to me. As she walked into the room, I stepped out into the hallway and crept down the hall to see what she was doing. When I was a few steps from the doorway, the door flew open, and there was Grandma Ramona. She screamed, and I started to run for the steps. As I took hold of the railing, I started down the steps but then stopped myself. Why was I running? I needed her help, and she was my grandma. Just tell her who you are and get on with it. She was going to find out sooner or later who I was, so why not now? I turned around and came back up the steps. Grandma Ramona was still standing in the hallway when I got to the top of the steps.

"How did you get into my house?"

"How is not important right now. I need your help. I was shot by the police, and my arm is getting infected."

"I don't think I can help. I wasn't expecting it to be that bad. We will need to get you to the hospital so you can see a doctor and he can dig out the bullet. The bullet is still in your arm; that is why it is infected, right Carl?"

"Yes, I tried to work the bullet out, but it just keeps moving around and not moving out. As for going to the hospital, that I can't do."

"Why is that, Carl?"

"They would ask too many questions. Then they would call the police, and you would never see me again."

"How can you be sure that they would call the police?"

"Trust me; they would. All this standing is making me feel dizzy. Are you going to help me?" I could feel my legs turning to rubber and I knew that this time I was going to pass out. As I fell forward, I reached out my hand and said, "Please, Ramona, help me!" All went black before I hit the floor.

I don't know how long I was out, but coming to I could faintly hear grandma talking to me. I couldn't understand what she was saying because I was going in and out of consciousness and things were blurry. She was lightly slapping my face hoping to get me to come to. I struggled to regain consciousness just so I could tell her to stop slapping my face and that it wasn't helping.

Grandma got frightened when I took a couple of deep breaths to help get some oxygen to my brain. She must have thought I was dying because she cried out, "Carl, don't you die on me!"

I opened my eyes and stared up into her face. She had my head cradled in her lap. Tears began flowing down her cheeks when she saw that I had opened my eyes and that I had not died on her. "Carl, you are going to be alright. I will help you. I know a nurse that I can trust. She can come here to the house and get the bullet out and fix up your arm. She won't ask questions."

"Thank you!"

"I'm going to have to leave you for just a few minutes while I send a message to her. Will you be okay here?"

"Yes, I'll be fine. I'm feeling better." Grandma gently laid my head on the floor, stood up and walked to the stairs. I could see that her hands had blood on them. "Where did you get the blood on your hands?"

"It's from your head. When you passed out, your head hit the floor mighty hard and it split your forehead open. I got it to stop bleeding."

"Thank you again."

"That's okay. What else could I do? I could not have you bleeding all over my floor."

What she said took me by surprise, but it shouldn't have. Now I knew where dad got his humor from, Grandma Ramona.

"You just rest, and I'll be back up here and we'll talk."

I watched her descend down the stairs until she disappeared, and I could hear her moving around downstairs for what seemed like forever. I was feeling stronger, so I tried to sit up using the railing to pull myself up into a sitting position. That was I could see more what was happening. Besides, the floor was very hard. Grandma was coming to the stairs, and she had a tray with her.

"Carl, are you hungry? I've made you a sandwich and I've got some grapes. I hope you like grapes. And I know every boy loves cookies."

"Yes, I am very hungry, and what you have sounds great."

"Oh! There you are. I was starting to worry that you left because I didn't see you lying there on the floor where I had left you."

"I hope I didn't worry you too much. I was feeling stronger so I pulled myself up to see what was happening."

Grandma came over and sat next to me on the floor. "Carl, you eat; and if this is not enough food, I'll go get you more."

I grabbed the sandwich and took a big bite. As I chewed, the taste was unfamiliar and it must have shown on my face.

"What is wrong, Carl? Don't you like the sandwich?"

"The sandwich is good. It's just that I've never had this kind of sandwich before."

"You have never had a peanut butter and grape jelly sandwich before?"

"No, I have never had one before; but I like to very much."

"My son, Mark, always loved his peanut butter and jelly sandwiches. Carl, you may think I'm being a little silly, but sometimes when I look at you, I see my son Mark. I know that you're not, but you do look a lot like him."

"Do you think so?"

"Let me get the last picture we had taken of Mark, and you can see for yourself."

Grandma went into a room down the hall; it must be their bedroom. "Carl, I hope you don't mind. I found a few other pictures that you might find interesting. This picture here is my son, Mark, when he was 16; and this picture is a picture of Mark when he was just 1 year old."

"With Great Grandpa Roy."

"Carl, what did you say?" Oh no, I slipped up again. "Did you say Great Grandpa Roy?"

"Who is Great Grandpa Roy? This looks like a picture of a grandpa and baby boy."

"Oh, I thought you said Roy. My mistake." That was too close; I need to be more careful what I say. "Carl, as I was saying, this is a picture of Mark and his Grandpa Roy. And here is a picture of Mark, Grandpa Roy and Grandma Frieda."

"Who is this guy here in the picture?"

"Why, I never even noticed him before."

"Where was this picture taken, Ramona?"

"It was taken in the park in the city."

Suddenly I heard bells. "What's that?"

"Carl, it's the doorbell. It's the nurse friend of mine. I'll get her and bring her up here."

"No, I'll come downstairs. I'm feeling better now."

"Let me help you up; then I'll answer the door before she thinks that we aren't home and leaves."

Grandma grabbed hold of my good arm and helped me to my feet. I grabbed a hold of the railing and told her, "I'm okay; you can go and answer the door. I need the nurse's help. It feels like my arm is bleeding again."

"Take your time and don't hurry down the stairs. I don't want you to fall. You are banged up enough."

"Do you think the nurse can do something for this headache that I have?"

"Oops. There goes the doorbell again."

"Go ahead. I'll be fine."

Grandma scurried down the stairs while I watched from the top as she opened the door to let her nurse friend in. "Hello, Officer." What were the police doing here? I moved away from the railing and headed to my dad's room to hide. "What brings you out this way?"

"Your husband, Captain Wilson, said that I should stop in and see that you are okay after all the excitement that went on earlier in the day."

"Well, as you can see, I'm doing just fine."

"The captain wanted me to have a look around and to ask you if you had seen the boy."

"There is no need for you to look around, and I'll talk to my husband in just a few minutes and let him know that you have done a wonderful job making sure all is secure."

"Okay, Mrs. Wilson. You have a good day. If you need anything, don't hesitate to call."

"I won't. Goodbye, Officer."

My heart was beating so fast and hard; it was a great relief to hear the officer leave and the door close. I came out of the room and looked carefully over the railing. Grandma was looking up at me. "Its okay, Mark, the police are gone now."

"Ramona?"

"Yes, what is it?"

"You called me Mark."

"I'm sorry, Carl. It's just that I'm so used to having my son looking down at me from that very spot asking me questions."

Our conversation stopped when we heard a knock at the back door. Grandma motioned for me to hide. "I'll go see who it is, Carl."

I hurried to dad's room once again, but this time I stood in the doorway hoping to hear if it was the police. If it were the police, I would have enough time to get to the storage space under the stairs and escape.

"Carl, it's okay. It's my nurse friend. She has come to help. Come on down and meet her."

I headed for the stairs to meet the lady that was going to fix me up. For just a second things started to spin as I grabbed a hold of the railing and stood at the top of the stairs. I hung onto the railing even harder and closed my eyes hoping that it would stop the spinning. When I opened my eyes, the spinning had stopped. Grandma and her nurse friend were at the bottom of the stairs looking up at me.

Grandma said, "Lisa, this is my friend."

Lisa's eyes just about popped out of her head when she saw that I was the one in need of her help. "Hello, Nurse Glover."

Grandma was surprised that I knew Nurse Glover. "I see you two know each other already."

"Yes, Carl and I met at the hospital when the police brought Doctor Kittleson to the hospital to deliver a baby. Carl was with him."

"Carl, that sounds like a story I would like to hear on how you and Doctor Kittleson know each other."

Nurse Glover asked Grandma, "Where can we work on Carl? This could get a little messy."

"The best place would be on the kitchen floor. The sink isn't too far away."

"That will work just fine. Carl, if you are ready, let's go to the kitchen and we can get started."

The ladies went on ahead of me to the kitchen while I slowly walked down the stairs praying that I wouldn't have any more dizzy spells. As I entered the kitchen, Nurse Glover was opening her black bag and was setting out all kinds of first aid things. There were things that we back at the settlement would love to have. That could be something to think about trying to bring back when I got ready to go back to the settlement.

"Carl, if you would take off your shirt and let me look at what we have to work on." I took off the blood-soaked shirt and grandma took it from me and put it in the trash.

"Ramona, I'm going to need that shirt."

"No, Carl, you don't."

"What am I going to wear if I don't have that shirt?"

"My husband, Russell, has all kinds of shirts in his closet. You will fit into his shirts just fine."

"Carl, how do you want to do this? Would you like me to go slow, stopping to let you take a rest from the pain, or work as fast as I can and don't stop until the bullet is out?"

"I like the last one. Work as fast as you can and get that bullet out."

"Take this tongue depressor so you have something to bite on. We don't want you to crack a tooth from gritting your teeth because of the pain." I took her advice thinking that she would know about the pain if she had dug bullets out of people's arms before. I placed the tongue depressor between my teeth. "Carl, are you ready?" I nodded that I was ready.

Nurse Glover swabbed down my arm with some stuff that turned my skin an orangeish-brown. She then looked me in the eyes to say without words that this was going to hurt and hurt a lot. I nodded my head again to let her know that I knew it would hurt. I just wanted to do it and get it over with. Glancing towards Grandma, I was anxious to see how she was handling the whole ordeal. She looked a little worried, but most likely not as much as she could be worrying if she only knew who was lying on her kitchen floor getting worked on. Out of the corner of my eye I saw a flash of light. I turned in time to see the nurse plunge something that looked like a scissors into my arm. At that instant sharp pain ran up and down my arm with each twist of the instrument. Every muscle in my body tightened. The tongue depressor began to splinter under the tremendous pressure that my teeth were creating because of the pain. Grandma was beginning to shed tears, and the hand that she had on my head was no longer gently patting but holding me as still as she could so the nurse could continue to look for the bullet. The pain was incredible. There was frustration on Nurse Glover's face because she couldn't find the bullet. Her gloves were covered with my blood and you could see on her gown where blood had splattered on her. She stopped digging and pulled the instrument out of my arm.

"I can't find the bullet. I'm sorry."

I spit the depressor out of my mouth and said firmly, "Don't stop! Keep trying!"

"Carl, if I go in again, I could do more damage to your arm."

"If you don't get the bullet out, my arm will get infected, and then I could lose my whole arm. I'll take the chance on possible damage to the arm over the thought of losing the whole arm later. Go in and get that bullet! Before you do, though, I'll need another tongue depressor. Maybe two this time."

Now with two new sticks in my mouth, I braced myself for another rush of pain. The three of us looked into each other's eyes, and without saying a word she started the search for the bullet. The pain this time was not as intense as the first time. My mind must be blocking out most of the pain. It had been a few minutes and Nurse Glover said calmly, "I found it."

Grandma said, "Thank you, God."

For just as few seconds the three of us looked at each other and said nothing. Nurse Glover gave a few twists of the instrument, and out came the bullet and a sigh of relief. Once again I spit out the depressors that were tightly clinched in my teeth.

"Thank you so much." Grandma was crying. "Why are you crying? It's all over."

"These are tears of joy, Carl."

"Carl."

"Yes, Nurse Glover."

"You will need to rest for several days in order to give your arm time to heal. There are no stitches to hold the wound closed. You could start bleeding if you do too much."

"I can't wait. I have so much to do."

"Whatever it is can wait."

"You don't understand."

Grandma then put her hand over my mouth and said, "He will get the rest he needs." I tried to speak but grandma had her hand clamped down on my mouth so hard I'd probably have bruises. Grandma and Nurse Glover got up off the floor and pulled out chairs to sit at the kitchen table.

I rolled over to one side and started to get up. They both said at the same time, "And where do you think you are going, mister?"

"I thought I would get up and sit at the table with you ladies."

"Well, you thought wrong," Grandma said. "You just lie there on the floor and rest. We will tell you when it is time for you to get up."

The two ladies talked and talked for how long I'm not sure. I fell asleep, and when I awoke I was in the kitchen alone. I struggled to sit up. The chair at the kitchen table helped me get to my feet. I headed for my escape route.

"You're going to need a new shirt, Carl." It was Grandma but where was she? I was spinning around to see where she was. "Carl, look up!" There, at the top of the stairs, was Grandma with two shirts in her hands. "Do you like the blue shirt or the green one? Ah, who cares; take them both. Russell will never miss them."

"Where did the nurse go?"

"She had to go back to the hospital. They sent a message here telling her to come back. There was another lady coming in to deliver a baby. She left enough bandages and things to keep it clean for the next two weeks. She said that she would try to stop by and check on your arm in a few days."

"That was nice of her to leave the bandages."

"Oh, Carl, she also told me to tell you that she may have found your friend Ernie."

"Ernie! Where is he? I would like to see him."

"She thought that is what you might say. I'm supposed to tell you that you will not be able to see him."

"Is Ernie dead?"

"No, Ernie is not dead. He is . . . ."

"He is what?"

"He is in the mental ward at the hospital. She said that is if this is the same Ernie that you are looking for." My heart sank about as low as it could get, and my face must have showed it. "Carl, maybe next week when you are feeling stronger I could try to get us in to maybe see if this is your friend. I know that there is an observation station where you can look in at the patients, but they can't see you. That way you could see if that is your friend. What do you think of that, Carl?"

"That would be great if I knew what Ernie looked like."

"That is strange. You don't know what your friend looks like?"

"Well, Ernie is really my dad's friend, and he wanted me to look him up when I was in town. I have a slight picture in my mind from what my dad has told me of him over the years; but I'm sure Ernie has aged a little since my dad met him about 20 years ago, give or take a year or two."

"Carl, if you would like to go up to Mark's room and lie down and rest for a while before Russell comes home for supper, I'll call you when he gets here."

"That sounds like a good idea. I think I'll do that."

I made my way upstairs to dad's old room and walked in. I wondered what the folks back home were doing about now. If dad only knew that I was in his old bedroom about to take a nap on his bed. Sitting on the edge of the bed, I took off my shoes and lay back on the pillow. What was I going to do when Grandpa Russell came home? I knew what would be the first thing out of grandma's mouth. "Russell, you'll never guess who dropped in for a visit today. It was that young man, Carl."

Grandpa could do one of two things: He could get his gun and arrest me, or he could help me hide from the police. Who knew which one it would be until that time comes. Depending on his reaction, I would need to take action and find a way to escape; or I would sit down and tell them who I was and what I was doing here. I was tired, but I couldn't take the chance of falling asleep when it was so close to the time when grandpa would come home. Lying here is nice, but I know me, and if I lie here too long, I would be sleeping in no time flat. I better get up and find something to do. Just then I looked over at my dad's desk. That must be the computer thing that dad was always talking about. I pulled out the chair and took a seat to look at this thing. I pushed a few of the buttons that had letters and numbers but nothing happened. There was a box with an orange light on. I touched the box and could feel it was vibrating. Curiosity was getting the best of me. I had to push the lighted button. The light was no longer orange but green now, and a picture appeared in that black picture frame in front of me. Now what do I do? Maybe I should shut it off with the same button that turned it on. Oops! I hit some of the other buttons and now the picture was changing. I reached over and pushed the green button, and the picture frame went black again.

A car was coming down the road. That must be grandpa and hopefully not the police. I looked out the window to see grandma meet grandpa in the driveway. Grandma must have told him that I was in the house. Grandpa drove forward out of my sight leaving grandma standing in the driveway. This did not look good for me. I better get downstairs and head for my escape route and hide there until I found out what was going to happen. I rushed to the stairs and descended them as fast as I could. Once at the bottom of the stairs, I could hear grandma yelling for grandpa to stop and listen to what she had to say. When I looked out the back door towards the garage, I looked straight into the face of my grandpa.

"Hey you, stop right there!"

That was my answer as to which way my grandpa was going to take to the news that I was in his house; it wasn't the one that I was hoping for. Hurriedly I turned and ran for my escape route. I flung open the trap door, dropped down in and shut the door over me. Now I would sit and listen. The back door opened.

"Alright Carl, come out with your hands in the air. I don't want to hurt you, but I do have to do my duty and bring you in for questioning."

"I don't think so, Grandpa," I whispered to myself. "I've heard from my dad how the police question kids, and I'm not going to give you the chance of questioning me if at all possible."

"Russell Wilson!" Oops, Grandma to the rescue. "What did I say about you pulling that gun out? Carl is just a child. Those animals that you call policemen have already shot him once, but thanks to a nurse friend of mine, he is going to be alright. Now put that gun away and maybe Carl will come out and talk with us, and we can get to know him. Then maybe you won't be so quick to pull your gun. Carl, Carl. It's okay. Russell has put his gun away, and we just want to talk."

"He's got to be in the house. I saw his face as I was walking up the sidewalk in the back yard. Ramona, why don't you check the front door just in case he went out that way."

"Good idea." I could hear the two of them running around the house looking for me and calling my name. "Russell, the front door is still locked, so he has got to still be in the house. I'm going to look upstairs in Mark's room. He was lying down taking a nap. Maybe he went back up there."

I could hear the footsteps of grandma going up the stairs, and she was still calling my name. The floor was creaking above me, so I figured grandpa must be near the storage room. Then I heard the door to the storage room open. Grandpa was inside the storage room. If he knew about the trap door in the floor, I'd be caught for sure, and no amount of yelling on grandma's part would stop grandpa from bringing me to the police.

"Russell, what are you doing?"

"Ah, Ramona, don't sneak up on me like that."

"What are you doing in the storage room?"

"The last time I saw Carl he was standing right around here, and then poof, he was gone."

"So what are you trying to tell me, Russell? That the floor opened up and swallowed Carl?"

"No, don't be silly. Of course the floor didn't swallow him up."

You know Grandma and Grandpa, the floor did open up and swallow me, and as soon as you two get out of the storage room I'm going to finish my escape. No, I can't leave because all the extra bandages are still on the kitchen table, and I'm going to need them. I'd have to wait until they were both far enough away so I could get to the kitchen and back in here without them seeing me enter the storage room.

"Russell, let's go into the living room. I need to talk to you about what happened here today. When I first saw Carl, he was all bloody."

Grandma and grandpa's voices faded as they walked into the living room. This could be the best time to get my bandages. If I didn't go now, grandma would start fixing supper, and then I would have to wait all night until they went to bed. Then I would have to walk back to my camp in the dark. The thought of walking across the bridge in the dark was not my idea of fun. The bridge gate was locked, and with only one good arm, I would not be able to climb the fence. What was I going to do? First things first. I needed my bandages, and then I could get out of the house. If nothing else, I may have to spend the night under the shed in the hole.

Slowly I opened the trap door again and listened. I could hear them talking in the other room. Carefully I turned to knob on the storage room door so as not to make a sound that would cause them to start searching for me. I pushed the door open and slipped out into the hall listening to make sure they were still discussing the day's events and not going to come out and surprise me. Quietly I walked to the kitchen. There on the table was a brown paper bag with my bandages. As I reached for the bag, I had this feeling that someone else was in the room. Quickly I turned and there was Grandma. She started turning to call Grandpa, "Russ . . . !"

I reached out and touched her arm and said, "I need to go."

Grandpa yelled from the other room, "Ramona, did you call me?"

138

"No Russell, I'll be in there in a minute."

"Thank you for all that you have done. I will never forget it."

"Carl, you need to rest."

"That is what I'm going to do."

"Carl, you can rest here in this house."

"As nice an offer as that is, I need to go for my safety and yours, because I am wanted by the police, and I don't want to get you folks in trouble."

"Carl, will we see you again?"

"Oh yes! You can count on that."

That brought a smile to Grandma's face. "Russell is sitting in his chair and he can see both doors from there. What can I do to help you get out of the house?"

"Don't worry. What I need you to do is to just go back into the living room and act as if nothing has changed. In less than five minutes I'll be gone."

"When will I see you again?"

"If all goes well, you should be able to see me in three days."

"And if things don't go well?"

"We don't want to think about that. Now go in and talk to Russell, and I'll see you in a few days."

Grandma had tears in the corner of her eyes. "Ramona, why are you crying?"

"I don't know. It's like I'm saying goodbye to my son or grandson."

"You need to wipe those tears out of your eyes before you get into the living room and Russell asks what the tears are for."

"No, Russell won't ask. I've been crying about our son, Mark, for so many years, Russell doesn't even see the tears."

"Give me ten minutes before you allow Russell to get up out of the living room."

Grandma left the kitchen and then came back, "Carl, you know that if I did have a grandson, I'd want him to be just like you."

"Ramona, remember I'm wanted by the police."

"That's okay. So was my son, and I still love him."

With that grandma spun around and went back into the living room. What she said took me by surprise. I was a chip off the old block; both dad and I are wanted men. I grabbed my bag of bandages and hurried to the storage room, slipped inside through the trap door and down the stairs. As I opened the coal bin door, I listened hoping not to hear any footsteps. Where were those old paint cans that grandma knocked over while she was looking for me? I had to make sure I didn't run into them as I crossed the basement. There were so many paint cans I had to take a different path to get to the tunnel door. Passing by grandpa's workbench reminded me that I had to find something that would help me get the lock off the gate on the bridge catwalk or I wasn't going to get to my camp. I needed something that would cut the padlock off because I didn't think I could break it by hitting it with a hammer. From the looks of the workbench, I could see where my dad got his messiness from. All the tools were in one big pile in the middle. Grandpa had so many saws I may have to take two or three to make sure I'd get one that worked on the lock. Just then the floorboards creaked. I froze in place.

"Russell, where are you going?"

"I was just going to get a glass of water, Ramona."

"I'll get it for you. You just sit down and relax."

Good job, Grandma! I needed to select my saws, get into the tunnel and head for home. In less than five minutes I would be gone just as I told Grandma. Quickly I moved through the tunnel and up into the garage.

As I left the garage, I carefully scanned the area to make sure there were no police sitting there waiting for me. All was clear. I jogged into the cornfield and then towards the bridge. The bridge was just ahead; I was make good time. It would be nice to have time to rest at my camp and not always have to be on guard as to what I do or say. That was one perk about having a sparrow for a roommate. She didn't say much, and she didn't borrow my clothes.

Hurriedly I cut through the lock on the gate at the bridge. It was much easier than I thought it would be. I whipped open the gate and passed on through. Carefully I placed the lock back on so when the police would drive by, it would look locked. I moved along the catwalk like I had been doing it for years. When I reached the other side, I ran for home.

Chapter 6

Quiet Time

Through the trees I could see my little caboose. It was a lovely sight for these eyes. Even for as weather-beaten as it was, it was home. The next few days I would just rest like the nurse said I should, and that would give me time to plan how I was going to find the kids in the city dump. When grabbing the handrail to help myself up the few stairs on the caboose, I looked down and noticed that I was wearing Grandpa Russell's shirt. It looked nice. It was too bad I had to leave in such a hurry that I left the other shirt that grandma said I could have back at the house. Maybe when I got back it would still be there.

I surprised my roommate, Mrs. Sparrow, when I opened the door to the caboose. She flew out the broken window and didn't even say so much as hello, or where have you been or the least you could have done was call when you're going to be gone so long. Oh boy, do I need time to rest. I was starting to ramble on just like my dad about the silliest things.

Just then the sparrow flew back in and she landed on the headboard of my bed. "Hello, Mrs. Sparrow. I did not mean to surprise you when I came in a few minutes ago. It's nice to be back home. Are you a little hungry? I know I am. You would not believe what has happened to me since I left. I talked with my grandma and grandpa; okay grandma and I talked. Grandpa was always yelling at me and pointing his gun at me. I wonder what he would think if someone would do that to him? Oh, and speaking of guns, I got shot. Look! A nurse friend of grandma's had to dig the bullet out."

"Chirp, chirp!"

"No, I didn't cry! Grandma cried, and I think that if she only knew that I was her grandson, she would have cried a river of tears and she would have hunted down the policeman that shot me and would have yelled at him a lot."

"Chirp, chirp."

"I know; stop talking and break out the food."

Grabbing my sack with the food in it, I set out some dried meat, dried fruit and some bread for us to share. I pinched off a piece of the bread and set it out on the table for my room-mate. She began to peck at it.

Next I bowed my head and said a prayer: "Dear God, Thank you for bringing me home to rest. Thank you for the people that have come into my life to help me, feed me, clothe me, hide me and help heal me by getting the bullet out of my arm. I hope that the next few days will be a time of quiet and a time to plan. Help me with those plans, God, for I am unsure as to how to go about finding the kids. Thank you for this food I'm about to eat. In Jesus' name I pray, Amen!"

I gathered up some food and put it on a makeshift plate so I could stretch out on my bed and relax, something I had not been able to do for quite some time. This quiet time to rest up and heal was needed before I found the kids.

After finishing my food I put my plate on the table, and as usual my roommate cleaned up any crumbs I may have left. Since tiredness was overtaking me, I decided to turn in early, get some sleep and start planning in the morning. I unrolled my blanket, covered up, and that's the last thing I remember.

The morning brought sounds of kids laughing. Maybe it was my mind playing tricks on me because I had not fully woke up. I rolled over onto my back and stared at the ceiling. Again I heard the laughter of the kids, but this time it was closer. I threw off my blanket and scrambled to find my shoes and put them on so I could get outside and talk to the kids. As I was tying the laces, I heard a thump on the side of the caboose. And then another one. The kid's laughter was right outside the caboose. Then came a series of thumps along with the laughter of the kids. As quickly as the thumping started, it stopped and the laughter was fading away. I jumped to my feet to look out the door at the end of the caboose; two boys were running away with sticks in their hands. They had run their sticks along the side of the caboose just like I did on Mr. Brown's fence back at the settlement.

I followed them keeping my distance so as not to spook them. Hopefully they would not lead me on a wild goose chase but would lead me to their camp. My hope was that they were the kids from the city dump. One thing that worried me about the kids was that they were not heading to the bridge that I use but were heading in the opposite direction from the bridge. They were heading in the direction of the dump though. Across the river I could see the road that I traveled on when I met Doctor Kittleson. That was when he told me about the fork in the road. One way would lead me to the city, and the other road he told me I should not go on because it went to the dump. He said to stay out of there.

The two boys hadn't noticed me following them. They were playing like they didn't have a care in the world. Following them for what seemed like several minutes at their slow, carefree pace was making me wonder how much longer I would have to follow them before they got to their camp. For some time now I had been smelling the city dump in the air, and now through the brief openings in the trees I could see the city dump. I wondered how the kids were going to cross the river. Surely they weren't going to swim the river because the current was too swift and the water was too deep to walk across.

In my excitement of seeing the dump I had not noticed that the kids had stopped to play, and now they had noticed that I was following them. They started to run along the road. Since the boys had noticed me, I came up out of the woods and ran on the road to catch them so I could talk with them. I was making up some of the distance on the boys by running on the road. It was then that we all heard the police sirens.

We stopped for a second and looked at each other; then we ran into the woods down along the river. The boys weren't so carefree anymore; they were running for their lives just as I was. As I ran along the riverbank, I was looking for a place to hide. Up ahead was an old railroad bridge that looked half dismantled spanning the river and leading into the city dump. There was nothing to give me cover and the police sirens were on the road just above me. The two boys were on the bridge climbing along and through the crossbeams. I heard a loud crack. I was afraid that they were shooting at me again. I was too far from the railroad bridge that the boys used to escape. I would have to jump into the river and swim to the other side. I saw flashes of white bouncing off the tree trunk and heard a loud crack. Not giving it a second thought, I jumped into the river and started to swim for the other side.

As I picked myself up off the floor of the caboose, I realized that I had dreaming. It was storming outside and the rain was coming in the broken windows. I hurried to the end of the caboose to look out the door to make sure that there were no kids outside. It was dark, and the rain was coming down very hard. I looked to see if Mrs. Sparrow was in the caboose; there she was, looking down at me all nice and dry. I grabbed anything I could find to cover up the broken windows to keep the rain from coming in and flooding my house. After placing the last board across the side window, I took a seat at the table to rest. I must have hit my arm while I was dreaming because it was a little sore; but with it being dark out, I couldn't take a look at it until it got lighter. There was nothing I could do now but to go back to sleep, wait until morning and hope that the rain would stop.

Lying down on my bed, I covered up with my blanket and watched the lightning through what windows had not been covered up. I hadn't seen lightning that bright for such a long time. It was good to see the awesome power of God. It hit me while I was lying there waiting for God to flex his muscle and send more lightning that the dream I had was maybe God telling me how to meet up with the kids from the city dump and that there was another way to cross the river. I would have to explore the possibility that my dream was God helping me just as I had asked Him. I watched the lightning and listened to the thunder and rain until I drifted back to sleep.

Morning came and Mrs. Sparrow began to chirp what seemed like in my ear. The rain had stopped. Sunlight was shining in the window that I had been watching the lightning through earlier in the night. I got up and uncovered some of the windows to let more sunlight in and make a way for Mrs. Sparrow to fly in and out. After all, it was her house first; I was just a guest.

The next item of business was breakfast. My food sack was getting quite light, and I'd have to start looking for other means of food. I would have to make a trip back to the side of the road where I hid those fishing poles and tackle box. Then I could fish very early in the morning or late in the evening when there would be fewer people out to see me. While I placed my breakfast on the table, I noticed that my arm had bled a little, and it was coming through the bandage. After breakfast I'd need to change the bandage and look to see how it was doing. I took less food out for breakfast than I had other mornings thinking that I should save some food not knowing how long I would be here with still so much yet to do.

I put the food sack away, reached for the brown paper bag with the clean bandages and took a seat at the table. Carefully removing the bandage, I could see that much of the redness had started to go away and now it was black and blue from all the digging that Nurse Glover did to get the bullet out. I dug in the brown paper bag and set out all the different things that the nurse had packed in there: tape, gauze pads and first aid antibiotic ointment to help prevent infection in minor cuts, scrapes and burns. It didn't say anything about big holes in your body left by bullets, but if it stopped infection, I was going to use it. After reading the rest of the directions, I applied it as it said to and wrapped up my arm. Then I placed the stuff back in the bag and hid it with the rest of my things.

As I looked out the window, I was trying to decide what I should do next. Do I cross over and get my fishing poles and tackle, or do I explore the possibility that I would find that railroad bridge down river. The best thing would be to explore the possibility of a better way across the river where I would not be so visible to the police and the world. It sounded like the police had the whole town worried about the kids that live in the city dump and that they were like a band of thieves looking for the next poor victim to walk into their trap. It was pretty smart of the police to make the kids look like the bad guys. That way if anything went wrong with what the police or the government was doing, they could always blame the kids for it. That is kind of what I did when I was much younger so that I wouldn't get into trouble with mom and dad. I would say that Kayla did it. It wouldn't be long, of course, and mom and dad figured out what I was doing. Why hadn't the people of this city figured out what the police and the government were doing?

If I headed out now, I wouldn't need to pack a lunch. I shouldn't be gone that long. My X-15 slingshot was coming with me just in case I ran into trouble or if I saw some food running around. The air outside was very humid. That could mean that there may be more storms tonight. Closing the door to the caboose, I went in the direction that the boys in my dream too me—towards the dump. I walked on the road as long as I could to make good time and not work so hard that my arm would start bleeding again.

After walking for what seemed like 10 to 15 minutes, I could see what looked like a road that turned to the left toward the river. As I got closer, I could see that it was an old railroad bed with all the rails removed, and excitement began to build inside me. When I turned left I could see the railroad bridge plainly. Carefully I looked around to see if there were any signs or alarms; there was nothing but one chain stretched across between two large posts. Cautiously I walked out onto the bridge; it didn't take long for me to see why the two boys in my dream didn't cross the bridge on top but worked their way across using the crossbeams. Someone had removed a section of the bridge on top so that no one could walk or drive across the bridge to escape or to enter from one side to the other. While on the bridge I could see into the city dump. There was a smell that was drifting my way from the dump, and sometimes it almost took my breath away. If the stories were true about these kids, how could they live in that dump?

I looked for a way to the area where I saw the two boys in my dream walk across the bridge. There were some unusual wear marks on two of the beams that were about two feet apart. As I looked down between the beams, I could see that someone had nailed boards to the beams that were vertical to make a ladder. I worked my way into position. After taking a quick look around, I started down the ladder. The ladder took me down about ten feet under the bridge. The people that put the ladder in had made a catwalk right down the middle of the bridge with a railing on one side. The river was passing below me about 15 feet. I grabbed a hold of the railing and began to walk across the bridge when I looked down at my hands. There were spots of black, sticky stuff on them. I raised my hands to my nose and took a sniff to see if they smelled like what I was smelling now that I was in the bridge's framework. Pew!! My hands did smell like the bridge. It must be what they use to preserve the bridge's wood from rotting away. I noticed that there was no build up of dust or dirt on the boards, so that told me that this catwalk was used often. If I were on this end of town, I would cross over on this bridge because it was much easier than the other bridge. If I were at grandma and grandpa's house, I would use the other bridge.

Just two more sections of bridge left and I would be on the other side. There should maybe be another ladder to take me up to the topside of the bridge just like it did on the other side. Speaking of a ladder, there it was. I peeked around to make sure there was no one waiting for me to pop my head up from under the bridge. Hurriedly I climbed up the ladder. Once on top of the bridge, I looked for a place to hide while I checked out the dump to see if there was any movement of people. There on the right side of the road was a little shack.

As I was running to the shack, I saw something out of the corner of my eye. I wasn't sure what it was. It could have been just an animal. When I reached the shack, I ran around to find the side with the door and slipped inside. The shack had four windows, one on each side, and a table and chair. One wall had some shelves that at one time maybe held books and things. The shack must have been used to collect payment to dump trash. I pulled the chair up to the window and made myself comfortable so I could watch to see if there was anybody living in the dump. I would wait awhile to see if there was any movement down in the dump; and if I didn't see anything now, I would come back tonight and hopefully see something when it got toward sunset. If there was no movement, then I would walk down into the dump and make a final search. Then if there was nothing or nobody to be found, I would forget about the kids and concentrate on finding Ernie. From time to time I checked out each window to make sure no one was sneaking up on me. That kept me from falling asleep sitting there waiting for something to happen inside the dump. I'm not sure how long it had been, but I thought I had given them enough time to make a move. I would have to come back tonight just a little before sunset and check out the dump then. Another look out the windows of the shack before stepping out turned up nothing. I would take the road back to the area where I hid the fishing poles and tackle box. Then I'd decide which bridge was closer to the caboose and take that bridge home. There should be enough time to fish for my food for supper and get it cooked before dark so that the light from the fire wouldn't attract unwanted guests.

Down the road I walked watching goldfinches fly from tree to tree trying to stay ahead of me as I walked. Eventually they flew deeper into the woods. My walk was very peaceful. The only sounds I heard were the many birds and the sound of the river flowing by.

The place where I hid the fishing stuff should be along here someplace. Then I saw the hole in the side of the road that would lead me down to the pile of things that got trapped in what looked like a flood. I hurried down into the ditch towards the hole when I heard a car coming. I dashed back up the ditch and across the road into the cornfield and pushed my way back deep enough not to be seen but close enough to see who was in the car. It was not just one car but three cars; all of them were black and one had the red and blue lights on top. It was the state policemen, and they must be looking for somebody because they weren't driving very fast. I stepped back a few rows to make sure that they didn't see me.

They were stopping! The car doors flung open and men dressed in black poured out like black ants when you tip over an old, rotten tree stump. One of the policemen had a dog, and he was going crazy on the end of the leash. One man began barking out orders to line up along the road next to the cars. The dog calmed down when the man patted him on the head. I stepped forward a few rows to hear what the man in charge was saying to the other men.

"Men, today we are going to make a sweep of this area looking for several things. You know what they are. We talked about them in the squad room before we left, but I want to emphasize my personal goal and that is to find the boy that was seen over at Captain Wilson's home. He attacked the captain's wife; and worse yet, he escaped our grasp when we had him supposedly cornered in the captain's garage. We know he is hurt and bleeding. A couple of our officers put a bullet in him before he got away the first time. I want this boy found! Do not let this boy outsmart us again. Do I make myself perfectly clear?"

With a mighty roar the men answered altogether, "Sir, yes sir!"

"Move out!" the man in charge yelled.

Four men crossed the road heading for the cornfield where I was standing. I needed to push deeper still into the cornfield and hope the men only searched a few rows deep. As I began to move back into the cornfield, I heard the man in charge yell for the men to stop.

"You four men stop and come over here to search this section. Let the canine and his handler search the corn-field. They will be able to search the field faster and more completely."

The four of them turned and were walking right towards where I hid my great find of fishing stuff. If I was lucky, the police wouldn't find where I hid the fishing stuff; and once they cleared the area, I could go and get it and head on home. Before I could worry about finding my stuff though, I had to figure out how I was going to hide from this dog and the policeman attached to him.

With each step they took crossing the street, I slowly backed up into the corn. The dog was getting a little crazy on the end of the leash, and the policeman was having a hard time keeping him under control. Should I run? Where would I run? There were police everywhere. If I walked in large circles through the cornfield crossing over my own tracks, maybe, just maybe, the dog would get confused. After running in several circles, I stopped to rest and listen to where the dog and the policeman were. Had they entered the cornfield yet I wondered. I heard nothing from the dog, but I could hear the other policemen yelling back and forth. I decided to run two more circles and then sit and wait for the police to leave.

Just as I turned to run another circle, there standing behind me was the very dog and policeman I thought I outfoxed by running in circles. Our eyes were locked on each other for what seemed like forever. When I glanced down at the dog, his eyes were locked on me too.

I thought about running, but the dog started to growl and the policeman said, "Don't even think about running. King will take you down before you even get past one row of corn." The policeman smiled and showed me King's leash. The end was no longer clipped to King's collar.

"What is your name, boy?"

"Carl."

"Now, Carl, when I asked you for your name, I expected to hear your full name. So I will ask you again and give you one more try. Let's see if you can get it right this time."

I didn't even let him ask again. "My name is Carl Russell Wilson."

153

The look on the policeman's face changed in an instant from mean to surprised and then back to mean again. I wonder what that was all about. Did he forget that he was supposed to keep the mean look on his face when questioning people?

"Carl, what are you doing in the cornfield?"

"I saw all the police cars coming, and I didn't want to be in the way of whatever you were doing, so I thought that walking in the cornfield would be a good way to get out of your way."

"Oh really."

"Yes, sir."

"Carl, let me ask you another question. What are you doing down by the river?"

"I'm looking for a good place to go fishing."

"Carl, there is one thing wrong with your story."

"It's not a story. I'm hoping to go fishing in a few days, and I thought it would be a good idea to look for some good places along the riverbank to fish from."

"Did you find any good fishing spots?"

"I like the one by the bridge. The water looks deep, and hopefully there will be some fish in there. Do you know of any good fishing spots along the river, Officer?"

"I don't fish this river. Enough about fishing. You said that your last name was Wilson."

"Yes, sir, I did."

"Are you related to Captain Wilson who lives just on the other said of this cornfield?" I just stood there not knowing what to say. Running away was not an option with King off his leash. My body temperature was rising and the sweat began to form on my forehead. "Did you hear what I asked you, Carl? Are you related to Captain Wilson? A simple yes or no answer is all I need, and sometime today would be nice."

"I . . . ."

"I . . . what, Carl? I . . . does not answer the question. I need a yes or no answer."

I was scrambling to come up with an answer when the radio on his belt started to blast. "Control to K-9 unit 1."

"K-9 unit 1, Officer Shawn Murphy here."

"What do you have to report on your search of the cornfield?"

The strangest thing happened right there before my eyes. Office Murphy closed his eyes and said, "Control, I see no one or no signs of anyone being in the cornfield at this time; do you copy?"

"That's 10-4. A big negative on your search."

"K-9 unit 1 to Control, I will continue my search and will meet up with my unit at the corner of the cornfield at Old Mill Road and River Drive. Advise my unit of that. My ETA is about 30 minutes, give or take a few minutes."

"That's 10-4; will advise your unit."

Officer Murphy opened his eyes and looked at me and said, "So, Carl, now that you have had more time to think about your answer, I would like to hear it now."

"Yes, Russell Wilson is my grandpa; but he doesn't know."

"Captain Wilson is your grandpa. That would mean that his son, Mark, is your father."

"Am I going to jail now?"

"No, Carl, you're not going to jail."

"I'm not?"

"You sound disappointed."

"No, no! It's not that. I just thought that once you found out what my name was and that my father was Mark Wilson and that his dad is Russell Wilson that I would be going to jail. I'm not disappointed. I'm happy and confused all at the same time. Can I ask why not?"

"Your father was two years ahead of me in school. He did not know me, but I knew him. My grandpa talked about

Mark Wilson and about the times that he would come over to the farm when he was little and play with the pigs. My grandpa was Dwayne Zabling."

"Your last name is Murphy!"

"My mother's maiden name was Natalie Zabling and she married my dad, Patrick Murphy."

"I was talking with some people, and they said there was only one Zabling relative living in this town and his name is . . . ."

"Kevin Zabling. He works at the hospital. Kevin is my uncle. The rest of my family moved away shortly after grandpa and grandma were arrested."

"Why did they move away?'

"My mother said that grandpa told her that would be the safest thing for us to do. At least until they could get out of jail; but as you may know, Dwayne and Janice were in jail for ten years until grandma got sick and died and grandpa was not too far behind her."

"So your family moved back here?"

"No, they are still up in the northeastern part of the state. Only I moved back hoping to do some good. I wanted to pick up where Grandma and Grandpa Zabling left off. I try to help steer people looking for freedom one way and the police the other."

"What do we do now?" I asked.

"I'm not sure. I've never had anybody from the settlement come back before. What is it that you came back to the city for?"

"There are some missing pieces in my life. One is Grandma and Grandpa Wilson. Two is a man called Ernie that helped my dad escape along with the help of the Zablings. The third is to see if there are any others ready to give up their life here for a life of freedom to worship and not be oppressed by the government."

"That is a big list, Carl. How do you plan on doing all that?"

"With my grandparents help."

"Carl, you said they don't even know that you are here, much less that you exist; they think that their son may be dead."

"I've talked with my grandma, and she very much thinks that her son, Mark, is alive and will someplace. She just doesn't know where."

"Okay, I'll give you the first missing piece of getting your grandparents back with you; but the second missing piece, as you call it, of getting Ernie out will take an act of God."

"You know of Ernie!"

"Yes, Ernie and I were working to get some people ready to make the trip to the settlement when the police raided the park. Ernie punched me in the face just as the police closed in on us. He grabbed me by my jacket and pulled me close to his face and said, 'Don't say anything, Shawn. My time is up.' Then he told me to pray that God would send me a helper to continue the work."

"And where is your helper, Shawn? When will I meet this person?"

"Carl, as strange as this may seem, I think you have met this person already."

"I have? Who is it?"

"Carl, it is you. You are my helper."

"Wait a minute here. Things are moving a little too fast for my liking. I have no way of telling if your story is true and if you are who you say you are. Maybe you just have a lot of information on me and my family and friends and you are luring me into a trap."

"Carl, if I was luring you into a trap, the trap would have snapped shut on you the second I saw you; but it didn't, did it?"

"Well, that is not to say that you may want to use me to get more people in your trap before you snap it shut."

"I'll tell you what, Carl. You think about it and let me know if you want my help. I already know that I want your help."

Shawn turned and was clipping the leash back on King and was getting ready to leave for the other end of the corn-field to meet up with his unit. "Shawn, wait! I'll meet you tonight at the shack by the railroad bridge just outside the city dump, and I'll let you know what I think then. I was going there to try to meet up with the kids to see what I can do to get them back to the settlement."

"Yes, that's right. That is your other goal that you have now that you are in the city. What time?"

"Shawn, I don't have a watch. It will have to be after sunset."

"After sunset it is. I'm looking forward to working with you, Carl. May God bless you."

"Before you go, how long has it been since Ernie got arrested?"

"Six months ago."

"How did he end up in the mental ward at the hospital?"

"Uncle Kevin told him that it would be much easier to take care of him if he was at the hospital than in jail. Ernie did a little acting for about a week until the guards at the jail could not stand his singing and laughing and shouting until all hours of the night."

"Is Uncle Kevin on our side?"

"That depends on what side you are on, Carl."

With that he turned and started walking through the corn. I had not heard any shouting from the other policemen for quite some time. Hopefully they had moved on and I could pick up my fishing things and head home until tonight. I hoped I knew what direction to go to get to the river. It would be bad to walk out where the rest of the police unit was meeting.

"Carl, you go that way." I spun around to see who was talking to me. It was Shawn. My heart was racing a mile a minute. "I came back because I thought you might not remember which way to the river."

"Thanks! I was wondering a little." He gave me that look of I think you were wondering a lot on which way to go. "Okay, I was wondering a lot."

"It's okay, Carl. I was going the wrong way too. When I ended up in the Wilson's backyard, I knew I was going the wrong way. When I saw you still standing there in the same spot as I left you, I figured that you needed some help. Be careful out there!"

"I'll see you tonight."

We parted ways. As I walked through the cornfield, I had some time to think about all that Shawn said. He knew a lot about me and still did not report me to the police. Walking through the last few rows of corn, I could see the road ahead. My pace slowed as I surveyed the situation on the road and where the police were now. No one was on the road from what I could see. Hurriedly I crossed the road and moved into the ditch and over to the tunnel at the side of the road. A quick look into the tunnel revealed no one was there either, so I ran through the tunnel and stopped just before coming out on the other side. Slowly poking my head out to see if there were any police on the riverbank, I uncovered my fishing stuff and gathered them into my arm and headed for the bridge. My pace must have been a little too fast, because I could see that I had got my blood pumping too hard and the wound on my arm was bleeding a little. I had to slow down even though I didn't want to until I got to the caboose.

The bridge gate was just ahead. I picked up the pace again and then stopped dead in my tracks. It was the police again, and they were getting out of their car. I pushed myself into a clump of birch trees to hide until they left. This was one way to slow me down so I wouldn't break open the wound on my arm. I wondered what they were looking for. They had searched this area already. No! Don't go up to the gate! Please don't go up to the gate. They were going up to the gate! Now they would see that the lock had been cut. Please don't have another lock in your car, or I will have to walk back to the other bridge. This way would be so much shorter. Good, it looked like they were leaving; they must not have a lock. I was sure they would be back soon, though, with a new lock. When they left, I would have to move quickly and get across the bridge. Then I would have to remember that next time I plan to use this bridge, I'd have to use grandpa's saw again and cut the new lock off. The only bad thing about that was that then they would know that somebody was crossing the bridge, and that would not make the government on either side happy. I let them get out of sight before I plucked myself out of the clump of trees. To cross the bridge with the fishing poles and tackle could be a little tricky; I'd have to divide the things so I'd be balanced.

At the gate I took careful notice of how the lock was positioned so I could put it back in the same position not letting the police know that the bridge was used some time soon after they left and before they got back with a new lock. I slipped the lock off, pushed the gate open, moved my fishing stuff onto the catwalk and closed the gate. Squeezing my hand between the gate and the post, I placed the lock back just the way that the police had left it. The fishing poles I put in my right hand, and the tackle box I put in my left, checking to see how the balance was; it felt good.

Quickly I moved across the catwalk looking forward to the other side and hoping that the police would not come back before I got home to the caboose. Out of the corner of my eye I could see flashing lights on the side that I was crossing over to. I needed to make it to the other side before the police could see that I was on the bridge. The policemen that found the lock cut must have called the policemen on the other side.

I had only ten feet of catwalk left. The police were so close, and there was no place to hide on the bridge. As the police car approached, I wasn't watching where I was walking. My foot missed the catwalk and I began to fall; but with both hands full of fishing poles and tackle box, I couldn't grab on to anything. I was so close to the other side I didn't know what I was going to land on. Would I land in the water or the rocks along the shore? As the earth rushed towards me, I passed a pine tree. I let go of the fishing stuff and tried grabbing for a branch, knowing that if I couldn't stop myself or slow my fall, I could be hurt very badly and wouldn't be able to run away. Then I'd be caught on this side of the river in this state. That wouldn't be good because Grandpa and Grandma Wilson wouldn't be able to help me.

As I grabbed for a branch it would slip out of my hands, and then I would reach for the next branch and the same thing would happen. I could see that it was impossible to stop myself. My only hope was that I would be able to slow down so the impact would not be too great. In just seconds I found my answer. The pine tree that was on the very edge of the riverbank that I was desperately grabbing at had guided me away from the rocky shoreline, and with a small thud I stopped, but my fishing poles and tackle box followed me down. The corner of the tackle box hit me in the arm. I was so happy it wasn't the arm with the bullet wound.

The police car was at the bridge, and I had no place to run and hide. They were getting out of the police car and one man was barking out orders to search the area and leave no stone unturned. Grabbing the fishing poles and tackle box, I lifted up the lower branches of the pine tree and curled up around the trunk praying that the branches that slowed my fall would now hide me from the police until they left. I tried to slow my breathing so they wouldn't hear me. I peered out between the branches and saw the policemen searching the area, and my heart stopped.

Too frightened to move, I could only pray that the policeman standing only inches from me wouldn't look down to see me curled up around the tree trunk. I said a quick prayer: "Dear God, have the policeman's eyes be blinded so that he sees nothing when he looks into this tree." I could feel the branches move over my head and the pine needles falling on me. My shoulder was only inches from the policeman's boot.

The man barking out orders yelled from the side of the bridge to the policeman standing next to me, "What have you found?"

"Sir!" The policeman was so surprised when the officer barked at him that he turned quickly and that is when he kicked me in the back. I was sure to be caught now. I prepared myself to surrender to them when the policeman said to the officer, "I have found nothing down here. My search is finished, Sir!"

"I'm calling off the search. Report back up here, and we will go back to the station and debrief. It looks like we were sent on a wild goose chase again. Every time the policemen on the other side see or hear something, they call us and we scramble to go look. Sometimes I think they are on the other side of the river watching us run around and they're over there laughing at us. When will our top people get a clue?"

"Yes, sir. I agree."

"Just remember that we never had this conversation, or we will both be in jail. Do I make myself clear?"

"Sir, yes sir. We never talked."

"Good. Now get up here!"

I listened to the policeman make his way up the side of the riverbank to the bridge deck. Now I could breathe a little easier. I could not hear very well what the other policemen of the search team were saying because they were too far away, but I was not about to get closer to hear. When the policeman kicked me in the back, that was too close for me.

The police cars drove away slowly. I would wait a little longer here under this tree to make sure that no one stayed behind. I sat up between two branches to see what damage I had done to myself when I fell off the catwalk. There was no pain anywhere, and as I rubbed my hand along my arms and legs, I found no blood. To my surprise the bullet wound was looking good.

What was that noise? Quickly I lay back down and quieted my breathing to listen. As I lay on my back looking up through the tree branches, I could see part of the catwalk and bridge. There was someone walking on the bridge. I only caught glimpses of maybe an arm or leg but not the face. I was sure of one thing: this person was looking for me, and they were with the police because of the uniform.

"Control to Alpha 1."

"Alpha 1 here."

"Captain Novak, will you be coming into the station anytime soon? We are waiting to debrief."

"Control, I'm getting into the squad car now and my ETA will be about ten minutes."

I watched Captain Novak run to his car. I thought the voice that was barking out orders sounded familiar, but I couldn't figure out why or where I would have heard this person's voice. Now I knew. This was the same captain that grandpa talked to on the bridge a few days ago. I'm so glad that he didn't find me, because from what I remember, he did not sound like a nice person even on a good day. The police car's engine started, and the tires slung gravel up against the bridge. It rained down on me, but the wide, full branches protected me from the rocks. It's like a hen gathering her chicks under her wings to protect them. The tree gathered me in to protect me from all kinds of danger. I waited a little while longer before crawling out from under my hiding spot and looked around to make sure there were no eyes on the other side of the river watching. There was no movement for as far as I could see. I would need to get out of the area before the police came back with the lock for the bridge gate. I wouldn't want them to see me walking along the riverbank and have them call Captain Novak to pick me up and throw me in jail. Gathering my things, I walked up the path to the road that would take me to the caboose. It was peaceful out here in the woods when the police weren't around; it almost reminded me of home. My mind wandered back to the settlement thinking of what I would be doing now if I were home. Most likely I would be picking on Kayla and getting in trouble with mom because of it. I miss Kayla, mom and dad, but I didn't like the idea of never meeting my grandparents on dad's side of the family. When I bring back Grandma, Grandpa, Ernie and possibly the kids from the dump, I'd have all the pieces to the puzzle of my life with me.

When I saw the caboose, I came back to the real world and took hold of the railing to climb the steps. I went inside and sat down at the table. I looked around to see if my roommate, Mrs. Sparrow, was around, but she was out looking for seeds and bugs to eat, I suppose. I was hoping to do some fishing, but with the police all stirred up, I would have to wait until tomorrow.

Maybe I should take a nap so I would be fresh for when I met up with Shawn at the dump tonight. Still I didn't know what to think about him and his willingness to help me. I would have to think of some things that only a close Zabling family member would know. I'd give him a test, and that would let me know whether to trust him or not. Thoughts of the many stories dad told me of the things he did on the Zabling farm when he was young went through my head as I lay down to rest. I wish dad were here now; he would know what to do.

Chapter 7

Questions & Answers

The pecking of my roommate on the table where she had a seed trapped between the table and her foot awakened me. "Good evening, Mrs. Sparrow. I hope your day went better than mine did." She didn't even look up. She kept pecking away at the seed. "When you're done with supper, I have a few crumbs for you."

I dug into my food sack and found some smoked meat and some dried fruit. The amount of food I had left told me I would have to cut back to only two meals a day unless I could find another food source. I could ask Shawn where I could get more food. That was if he passed the test on Zabling family history. I still needed to come up with five or six questions that only a close family member would know the answer to.

As I sat at the table chewing on a piece of smoked venison, I came up with a few questions; a thought came to me to put in a trick question that had nothing to do with the Zabling family. I'd have to remember not to let him turn the tables and start asking me questions. I wouldn't want to give out any information that would lead the police to the settlement. I'd ask the questions slowly and show no reaction to his answer one way or another as to whether his answer was right or wrong. One question that I would have to ask him was who was Big Bertha? For the trick question, who was Big Bertha named after? With my head in my hands I stared out the window, trying to think up more questions to ask Shawn. Mrs. Sparrow flew up onto my shoulder, and I slowly and carefully turned my head. There we were beak to beak, or should I say beak to nose. We said nothing for the first few seconds. Then I asked Mrs. Sparrow, "Is there something you want?"

"Chirp, chirp."

"I truly wish I could speak sparrow so I knew what you wanted; but until I do learn to speak sparrow, I will just pretend that I know what you are saying and give you a piece of dried fruit and say that is what you asked for."

I set a small piece of dried apple from my handful of fruit on the table; it wasn't long until Mrs. Sparrow flew down from my shoulder and picked up the piece of apple and flew up to her nest. Mrs. Sparrow looked so contented in her nest. Maybe I did understand sparrow . . . ; I don't think so!"

The sun had almost set. I had to get going to meet up with Shawn at the shack. I'd use the glow from the sunset to find my way to the shack; and with the sky clear, I'd be able to use the moonlight from the half moon to find my way home.

"Chirp, chirp, chirp."

"Yes, Mrs. Sparrow, I'll be careful. The way that you are fussing, one would think that you were my mother. Oh, don't wait up. I don't know how long this will take."

I grabbed my jacket and headed for the door. As I grabbed the handle, I could feel the butterflies in my stomach from the excitement and the fear at the same time. Once I got out the door, I moved quickly to the road. The meeting with Shawn could be the answer I was looking for or a trap that the police had set for me. For some reason the railroad bridge seemed closer this time than the first time I was at the bridge. It must be the excitement of the meeting, and hoping that he was going to be able to help me get my people home.

Once I got along the side of the bridge, I crouched down and scanned the horizon for any signs of the police or Shawn. I wanted to be there before him to make sure that this was not a trap set up by the police to catch both the kids and me. When I looked to the right and then to the left, the only movement was two deer down by the river on the side of the dump. Hopefully Shawn wouldn't come in his uniform; because if the kids saw that uniform or his dog, they would never come out of hiding, and I wouldn't be able to help them if I couldn't find them.

I ran up to the spot where the ladder was and dropped down the ladder making sure each time I moved my foot that it was firmly on the step, because I didn't want to make a misstep because of the darkness. When I reached the bottom of the ladder, I stood on the catwalk under the bridge. Without hesitation I started walking across the catwalk, but about ten feet out from the start I heard a faint sound coming closer to me. Each time I moved from section to section I stopped, checking to see where the sound was at. The middle section was the longest and the most open to anybody watching. The sound kept getting closer but I couldn't see where it was coming from. Sometimes the sound seemed like it was coming up the river, and then it sounded like it was on land. I decided to hurry across the next section and rest behind some post until whatever was making that noise passed by or turned around and went back the other way.

The sound suddenly got quite loud and a white light flashed across part of the bridge in front of me. I turned and hid myself in the crossbeams of the bridge positioning myself so I could see who was on the river with the big light. Underneath me a police boat with a spotlight checking the shoreline and the bridge went by. Maybe this was not a good night to meet up with Shawn if the police were out looking for me and the kids. Maybe it was too dangerous to be out.

What were they doing now? Why were they turning around when they had not even gotten to the bridge? What was wrong with me? I should want them to leave, but it seemed odd that they would stop before searching the area around the bridge. As soon as they rounded the bend in the river, I scurried for the other side. So much for getting to the shack earlier than Shawn. I thought for a second to stop and rest, but I pushed on and got to the ladder. With one hand I grabbed the ladder and pulled myself towards it.

The sun was setting fast, so I poked my head out when I got to the top of the bridge and hoped that there was no one out there waiting for me. It wouldn't be good if Shawn saw me come up out of the bridge like this. Even if he were a good guy, I won't tell him where I'm staying just in case the police turn on him and make him talk; he wouldn't be able to tell them what he didn't know.

As I reached the shack I carefully looked in the windows to see if there was anybody in there, but it looked empty. When I got inside the shack and closed the door behind me, I looked out the windows to see if Shawn was anywhere near. The setting sun had turned the white clouds pink and purple. No one was lurking in the shadows outside. I'd hide in the storage closet and listen to see if Shawn would say anything that would give me a clue on whether to trust him or not.

I found a chair and placed it up against the wall facing the bridge because I didn't expect him to come from that side of the bridge. As I panned back and forth looking out the windows straining to see something of Shawn, doubt began to creep into my head. Maybe Shawn wasn't coming! What if the police had figured him out and had him in a room and were interrogating him right now to find out where I was. He could lead them right to me.

"Stop it!" Ooops, that came out kind of loud. Shawn would show up . . . alone! He could be coming any minute now because I told him not until after sunset; the sun had only really set just a little while ago, so I'd give him some time. It wasn't like I had someplace to be tonight other than the dump, and that wasn't going anywhere.

I had been sitting in the dark for so long I was starting to get sleepy even with the nap I took this afternoon. I'd like to get up and walk around, but I wanted the element of surprise, and I'd lose that if Shawn saw my silhouette walking around in the shack. When I looked out the left window, I thought I saw something moving. Even squinting didn't help because I couldn't tell if it was a deer or a person.

I would get into the storage closet and wait a while until I thought it was safe to come out; or if it was Shawn, I could surprise him. Staying low, I opened up the closet doors and moved a broom and shovel over and then closed the doors leaving them open slightly so I could see and hear what was going on outside the closet. I settled into place not knowing how long it would be. To my surprise, I heard the door to the shack open and heard footsteps come in. I held my breath waiting to hear if it was Shawn or someone else. The person always kept his back towards me, so it was hard to tell if it was Shawn, even when I placed my eye close to the door. The person would have to speak before I would come out and confront him.

While pulling back from the door my foot kicked the shovel and the handle slid along the back of the closet. I grabbed it and stopped it from hitting the broom and making more noise. I looked out the crack in the door to see if the person had heard the noise, but he didn't move; his back was still facing me. When was the person going to say something so I could tell if he were the good guy or the bad guy? Time seemed like it stood still as I waited.

"I know Carl said he didn't have a watch, but it is way past sunset."

It was Shawn so I could relax a little. He was starting to talk, so maybe he would say something that would help me decide whether or not to trust him.

"I'll give Carl one hour. Then I'll have to go, and I'll have to figure out how to meet up at another time."

Then all went silent. If he wasn't going to talk, I may as well come out and start the questioning. Placing a hand on each of the doors, I quietly opened the doors and stepped out. Shawn didn't hear me come out, so I moved towards him from the back, reached out with a stick that I found in the closet, tapped him on the shoulder and said, "Good evening, Shawn."

He shot up out of the chair that he was sitting in just as if he had sat on a porcupine and yelled as loud as if he had also. "AH!" Shawn shot across the shack trying to get away from whatever had just scared the living daylights out of him. "Carl, is that you?"

"Yes, Shawn. Who did you think it was? The boogey man?"

"No, of course not! You could have said something to warn me that you were here. That was you that made the noise a little while ago, wasn't it?"

"Yes it was. I kicked a shovel."

"Well, the way that you scared me, you're lucky that you're not using the shovel to bury me. You about gave me a heart attack."

"Sorry!"

"No you're not. You think it was funny, don't you?"

"I do have to say it was funny to see you shoot up out of that chair."

"So you decided that you could trust me."

"No, I came here to find out if I could trust you by asking some questions that only a true Zabling would know."

"Okay, fair enough. Let's have the first question."

"Who is Big Bertha?"

"What kind of question is that?"

"Having problems with the questions already and that was the easiest one. They only get harder."

"The question is so easy I'm surprised you even asked it. Big Bertha was Dwayne's prize pig. It died after it crashed through a fence and fell into an empty manure pit. Next question."

"Who was Big Bertha named after?"

Shawn just shook his head and asked, "Are you sure the questions are going to get harder? Big Bertha was not named after anybody. Dwayne didn't like doing that because it could hurt someone's feelings. Next question, Carl."

"That's all the questions I have. I couldn't think of any more. I thought I would have stumped you with those two questions. You answered them correctly, so there is no need to ask you anymore about the Zablings. I do have some other questions about the kids in the dump. Who are they, and why does the state not help them?"

"Who they are is easy. They belong to the parents that have been arrested over the years because the parents have tried to start an underground church. Why doesn't the state help the kids? I think that may have many answers. The state would have to have a heart to even care about these kids, much less want to help them."

"I was talking with someone in town and he said that the kids are dangerous; is that true?"

"I'm not sure, Carl, on that question. I have not yet been able to make contact with the kids. I know that they live somewhere in the city dump, but I don't know where, and the state doesn't know where either. Otherwise they would be in jail too."

"What I'd like to do tonight is to walk through the dump and let them see us together. We can talk amongst ourselves loud enough for them to hear us say that we want to help them and that they need to let us know when and where they would like to get together and talk about how we can help them."

"Carl, do you think that is really going to work?"

"Well, whatever you have been trying has not worked so far. What can this hurt?"

"Okay, Carl, you got me there. Lead on; I'm right behind you."

"Shawn, why don't you lead since I have never been in the city dump before? I wouldn't know where to begin to look for the kids."

"Okay. Follow me, Carl."

We left the shack and headed toward a broken down gate that was hanging by one hinge. We squeezed through an opening and walked to the biggest building in the dump.

"Shawn, what is in that building?"

"That is the old garbage incinerator. It broke down about five years ago, and the city doesn't have the means to fix it."

"What do they do with their garbage?"

"They burn it in big piles on the other side of town. Some days the smoke and smell is so bad that a lot of the older people get sick. They burn once a week, and when the workers go in to light the fire, the police have to go out there with them just to shoot the rats that run out from under all that garbage. The rats would overrun the town if the police weren't there to shoot them."

"Why doesn't the city find the means to fix the incinerator?"

"It's not that simple, Carl. The part that they need is made in another state, that right now our state is fighting with them about how it is going to fix the lock and dams on the big river. So it may never get fixed."

"Is the building locked, Shawn?"

"No, the door is stuck. I'd stand back if I were you."

"Why?"

"Remember the rats that I told you about where they burn? They have them here also."

I moved off to the side so when the door would come open, the rats would run one way and I could run the other, if I needed to. Shawn grabbed the door handle with both hands, and I could hear him count to himself, "One, two and three." Then he pulled back with everything he could muster up. First there was a whoosh sound like when Great Grandma Frieda would open up some of her pickled beets; then came the high pitched squeaking of the rats running out the door. It looked like black water spilling out the door and flowing everywhere. Once the rats stopped coming out the door, we stepped inside; then the smell hit us. It was so bad it took our breath away. It was very hard to breathe.

"Hey, Shawn, do you think the kids live in here with the smell this bad?"

"No, but if we get through here and get into the offices, it may not be as bad."

"Let's get out of here then as fast as we can."

We could barely see our way through the garage. If it wasn't for the few streetlights in the dump, it would have been pitch black in the building and we would not see anything. I still tripped on all kinds of stuff that had been pushed into piles along the walls waiting to be incinerated. There were old chairs, rugs, beds and a basket with a broken handle. If the handle wasn't broken, I'd take that back to mom. She liked baskets to put vegetables in. I reached down to pick up the basket to take a closer look at it, and a rat ran across it. That made up my mind that I wouldn't take it home to mom.

"Carl, are you coming?"

"Where are you?"

"Up here! Take the stairs over there to the right of that big pile of old furniture." I ran to get caught up to him. "What were you looking at, Carl? This is all garbage. Broken, used up junk."

"There was this basket and . . . never mind."

"The offices are through this door. We should look in every room to see if there has been anybody in here in the past year or so." We searched the rooms one by one and found no traces of the kids.

"Shawn, is there any other building that the kids could live in?"

"There are two buildings out back. We could go out the back door and look there to find traces of the kids. If they aren't there, then I don't know where the kids are."

We didn't say anything to each other as we walked across the dump to the next building. The next building to search was a large garage; the door was wide open. We walked in and looked around. There were big trucks that were parked all in a row. I climbed up on the side of the first truck in the row and looked into the window and saw nothing unusual, so I went to the next truck and then to the next. When I climbed up on the last truck, I grabbed onto the door handle like I did all the others to help myself up, but this time the door was already open. It swung open wide and I lost my balance and fell to the floor; thankfully I landed on my feet and didn't get hurt. I jumped back up on the truck and crawled inside and sat in the driver's seat to look at the things on the other part of the seat. There were old papers and cups on the seat and on the floor also. There, sticking out from under a pile of papers, was an apple core. It wasn't bone dry but slightly crusty like it had been in the truck for a day or two.

"Shawn, I think I've found something that might be of interest."

I could hear Shawn running from the other side of the garage. "Where are you, Carl?"

"I'm in the last truck."

Within seconds Shawn was standing in front of the truck, and I motioned for him to climb up with me. When he opened the passenger side door, an avalanche of junk poured down on him. "Is this what you wanted to show me? Old papers and used coffee cups?"

"No, look at what's on the seat. An apple core that is not all dried up. To me it looks like it has been here a day or two at the most. What do you think?"

"That is great that you found that apple. That could prove that the kids have been here lately unless one of the city workers has used this truck in the last few days."

"I don't think so."

"What makes you think that?"

"Look at the tire back here. It's flat."

"Well, maybe it went flat, and then they parked it here yesterday."

"Again I don't think so, because there is too much dust and spider webs with a lot of dust clinging from the truck to the tire. I don't think that much dust can collect on a tire in just two days. I only clean my room once a week and I don't have this much dust."

"I can't argue with that deductive reasoning."

"Should we look for footprints? Maybe we can follow them to where they live."

"No, it wouldn't do any good, Carl. It's too dark. We would not be able to see anything."

"I guess you're right. I don't know what I was thinking."

"That's okay. You just got excited when you found the apple, and you were hopeful to find the kids. There is nothing wrong with that. I want to find the kids too."

"Do we want to look in the other building to see if there are any clues in there?"

"I would like to, but I have to go and get some sleep. I have to work tomorrow."

175

"I'm going to stay and look in the other building. I'll let you know what I find."

"Carl, how will I find you? Where are you staying?"

"Don't worry; I'll find you."

"Carl, I sense that you don't trust me yet."

"Oh, I trust you. It's that just in case you get caught by some other police and they make you talk, you would not be able to tell them where I am because you don't know."

"That is an excellent thought, Carl. I'm sure glad that you're on my side. I wouldn't want to match wits with you."

I stuck out my hand to shake hands with Shawn. He looked at me for just a second not knowing what I was going to do, and then he noticed I wanted to shake hands; then he put his hand out.

"Thank you, Shawn, for meeting with me tonight. I think our partnership will work out well and we will be able to help a lot of people to find the freedom they're looking for. Shawn, maybe before you leave, we should pray and thank God for all that we found out today and that He will keep us safe."

"Sure, that would be a great idea. 'Dear God, thank you for bringing Carl into my path that now we can do a great work. I pray that you will keep a watchful eye on us as we work to find freedom for all that want it. Amen!'"

"I'll try to meet up with you again, Shawn, in two or three days to let you know what I have found."

"How will I know when or where to meet with you?"

"You know the park in the center of the city with all the statues, right?"

"Yes."

"Each day look by the statue of the boy that looks like he is trying to fly. I will leave a simple note as to when and where to meet."

"Until we meet again take care, Carl."

"Same to you!"

"No, they just don't think that it's right what the government is doing to us children just because of what they think that our parents have done. I have asked some of these people if they would take some of the children into their homes, and there was no hesitation for them to answer no."

"Amber, is it because if they are found helping the children, they would lose everything and could end up in jail themselves?"

"That's exactly the reason."

A small girl was walking toward our table carrying two plates, one had muffins and the other had fresh fruit. "Carl, would you pray for the food?"

"Yes, I will." I felt a small hand take my hand. I looked down into the smiling face of a little boy with his eyes closed tightly. I leaned over to Amber and remarked, "Isn't he cute with his eyes shut tight so we can pray?"

"Yes, Carl, he is cute, but his eyes are shut like that because he is blind. His name is . . . ."

"Hi. My name is Karl too. I spell my name with a K. How do you spell your name?"

I turned to face Karl and replied, "I spell my name with the letter C."

"Have you come to help us?"

"Yes, I have."

Amber interrupted, "Karl, we need to have this Carl pray so we can eat."

"Okay. Carl, will you stop over by my bed and talk to me later?"

"I will, Karl." He was so happy he squeezed my hand really hard and the smile on his face went from ear to ear.

"Quiet children. Carl is going to pray. Go ahead, Carl."

"Dear Heavenly Father, we come to you today with thankful hearts for all that you have done for us by providing this food. Watch over us all in whatever we do today, and keep us safe. In Jesus' name, Amen."

The children at our table watched me the whole time that I ate. It was like having 20 mothers make sure that I ate all that was on my plate. Amber turned to me and questioned, "Are you done eating?"

"Yes."

"We need to talk about a few things before you go. There is a room where we can talk and the children won't interrupt us. Follow me!"

"Carl, where are you going? You said that you would come and talk with me," Karl said with his head hung down.

"Karl, I'm not leaving. I just need to talk with Amber, and then I'll be back and we can talk."

A smile returned to Karl's face as he said, "Amber, don't talk too long. I need to talk with Carl too."

It was the first time I had seen Amber smile. She should do that more often. She bent down and rubbed Karl's head and answered back, "As soon as we are done talking, I'll send him over to talk with you." That was good enough for Karl, and he made his way over to his bed to wait for me to come back and talk.

"We need to go this way, Carl."

"Lead on."

We walked out the end of the dining car and then into the next car. It was crushed and damaged more than the other cars that I had seen. There were no chairs or tables on the car. It had been stripped bare.

"I'm sorry that there is nothing to sit on, but we needed all the things in this room to have enough chairs for all the children to sit down and eat together as a family."

"That's fine. At the settlement we do not have that much furniture anyway. I usually have to sit on the floor when grandma and grandpa come over or . . . ."

"Wait a minute! You said that your grandparents live here in the city, but now you say that they are in the settlement. So what is it? Are they here or there?"

190

"My dad's parents live in the city but my mom's parents live in the settlement. My mom was born in the settlement. She has never been to the city, and as she says, 'I never will either!'"

"Sorry, I didn't mean to jump down your throat, Carl, but I do need to be careful."

"You said that we needed to talk about some things. What questions do you have for me?"

"When do you plan on leaving for the settlement?"

"As soon as we can get things ready. The sooner we are out of here, the better, and once you see the settlement you will agree."

"When do you plan to talk to your grandparents here in the city to let them know who you are and what you hope to do?"

"That is a good question, and I don't have an answer for that. I had thought that when I go back to get my things from the caboose, I could stop by their house and see if they are home and talk to them then. If you think that is a good idea, then I could do it today. What do you think?"

"I think that is a good idea. The sooner we know what they want to do, the easier it will be to make plans to include them or to avoid them."

"Then I will talk to them today; and if I can't get a hold of them, do you want me to come back here, or should I wait until I have an answer?"

"Wait until you can talk to your grandparents before coming back here."

"How will I let you know that I have an answer?"

"Do you remember the gate that you had to squeeze past to get into the dump?"

"Yes, what about it?"

"The metal cap on the post comes off. Put a piece of paper in there to let me know that you are ready to come home."

"What do I use for paper? And I have nothing to write with."

"You don't have to write anything. Just find a piece of paper somewhere in the dump and put it in the cap. If you write anything, it could be found by the police, and we don't need that. Not when we are getting closer to finding freedom from this way of life."

"Is that it for questions?"

"No, what are you going to do about this Ernie person?"

"From what I have found out, Ernie is in the mental ward at the hospital. He's a friend of my dad's. The Zablings, along with Ernie, helped my dad escape. The Zabling's son works at the hospital. I'm hoping he will help. I'm also hoping that the nurse friend of my grandma will help. I'm not sure, but there is a Doctor Kittleson that may be of help also."

"You know Doctor Kittleson?"

"We met on the road down by the river one day. Why? Is he a bad guy too?"

"No, he is the doctor that I take the children to see when they get sick. This Ernie is not dangerous, is he?"

"No, I don't think so. Shawn told me that Kevin Zabling told Ernie to act crazy so he would be moved into the mental ward. That way he would get a little better treatment than in jail. My dad said that Ernie was old back when he was young, so he may be too old to make the trip. We will have to find that out and decide on what is best for the group."

"That is all the questions that I have."

"I have a question for you, Amber. What are we going to do with Officer Murphy?"

"When were you supposed to meet up with him again?"

"I told him that it would be about two or three days and that I would place a note by a statue in the park when I had something to talk with him about."

"No problem. We have a few days to think about how we can use him, but we can't wait too long or he'll get jumpy and will be hard to control."

I would also be halfway up the ladder for when it was time to go.

As I climbed up into my resting place, I kept one eye on the road and one eye on the river. Now I could see the car, and it was the state police. Just above me I heard somebody walking on the bridge. I froze with fear and hoped that they didn't climb down the ladder, because I would be right there for them to see; I would have no place to hide. My only way of escape would be to jump into the river and hope I could get to the riverbank and run. That would be a very slim chance to get away. The footsteps were getting closer; the pace was slow and steady. The car stopped and I heard car doors slamming shut. Next I could hear footsteps from the city dump side of the bridge. The person walking was right overhead because I could see them walking by as I looked between the beams. They must be walking out to the edge of the bridge where they had removed part of the bridge so no one could cross. The person on my side of the bridge had gone as far as he could go. The police from the other side were still walking, and it sounded like there were maybe two of them.

They began to talk. "Good day, officers."

"Good day." As I listened to them exchange greetings, I could sense that they did not totally trust each other even though they were all policemen for their states.

"What brings you out this way?"

"Nothing special. Just out on routine patrol. How about you? What brings you out to the bridge?"

"Someone said they thought they saw somebody hanging out around the old caboose down the road. I looked around and went inside to see if somebody had set up home in there, but there was nothing except for this sparrow. It started to dive bomb at my head. I figured if the bird wouldn't let me in there, then nobody would be crazy enough to live in there with that bird."

"You are most likely right about that. Your people should just burn that caboose and be done with it."

"The captain is working on getting the county commissioner to let us burn it sometime today or tomorrow."

"We need to continue our patrol. Maybe we can stop by when we see the smoke from the caboose."

"You'll have to do that. I'm sure it will burn real nice as old as it is."

"Have a good day."

"I'm going to try."

I heard the three police depart and head back to their sides of the bridge. This time I heard both cars start their engines and drive away. The one police car must have driven up at the same time that I was hearing the police car on the other side drive up thinking that it was just one car.

It was a good thing I was moving to grandma's house for a few days and then in with the kids knowing the information I just heard. Getting up from my hiding place I stretched to reach the ladder. Just a couple of rungs of the ladder and my head popped out the tope of the bridge, and I was looking around to see if the police on both sides of the river were indeed gone. All was clear, so I popped up from between the bridge deck and to the tree line. I looked over my shoulder wondering where that policeman's car went. Taking a chance that the police on this side of the bridge was long gone, I headed for the road. I could get to the caboose and get my things cleared out of there and get back over the bridge and to the shed at grandma's house. I was glad that I hid my backpack out of sight. When I heard that the policeman went inside the caboose to look around, he would have surely found my stuff. Then they would have been watching for me to come home, and I would have been in jail for sure.

As I approached the caboose, I looked to see if anyone was around. I placed my ear to the side of the caboose to hear if anyone was inside waiting for me, but I heard nothing. I grabbed the railing and pulled myself up the stairs and opened the door. The bed, table and chair had all been tipped over. I wasted no time getting my things together. As I strapped my backpack on, Mrs. Sparrow flew in and landed on my shoulder.

"Chirp, chirp!"

"Yes, Mrs. Sparrow, I'm leaving, and this time I will not be coming back. Thank you so much for sharing your house with me. If you are ever flying over the settlement, stop in and say hello. I'm not sure how I would know that it was you and not one of your relatives. Oh, by the way, the police are coming back sometime soon, and they are planning to burn the caboose down, so you may want to move your house to some tree nearby."

Just then she flew out the window. I better leave before the police come again. One last look around to make sure I didn't leave anything that would tip the police off that I was here in their state. It looked like I had gotten everything, and now I needed to move to one of my bridges, but which one? There were two black cars coming down the road towards me when I opened the door at the end of the caboose facing grandma's house. Like I was saying, I'll be taking the bridge over by the dump since the police had come so soon to burn the caboose. Quickly shutting the door I ran for the other end of the caboose and out the other door. I made sure that I closed the door, because that is the way the policeman had left it the last time that he was here. I ran through the trees as fast as I could to the riverbank grabbing small trees to try to slow me down so I would not lose control and end up in the river making a big splash and letting the police know that I was here. No one was yelling at me, so I must have gotten away without anyone seeing me. I walked along the path on the riverbank towards the bridge to the dump.

All at once there was a boom and the ground shook. Things began to hit the trees around me and were landing in the river. I lay down on the ground and covered my head. Just when I thought that it was all over, a large piece of wood landed next to me. I reached out and grabbed the wood; it read Northland Railroad Co. The police decided not to burn down the caboose but to blow it up into little pieces. I could hear them laughing; the sound of their voices carried well along the river. As fast as the police came, they drove away. I got up off the ground and headed to the bridge. With my backpack on, it was a tight squeeze, but I made it. This would be the last time I crossed this bridge, I hoped. I walked across the catwalk and to the other ladder in what seemed like record time. I scurried up the ladder and onto the road to grandma's house keeping both my eyes and ears open to see or hear if someone was coming and to give myself enough time to run into the cornfield.

When I walked by the bridge, this crazy idea came across me that I should throw something onto it and set the alarms off. That would get the police all worked up thinking that someone was crossing the bridge and it would pull any away that might be watching grandma and grandpa's house so that I could get into the shed without them seeing me. They would be too busy looking to see who set the alarm off. As I stood on the edge of the cornfield, I looked down and saw some of last year's corn cobs and that gave me an idea. If I put a cob in the slingshot and aimed high enough to get the cob to land on the bridge and then shot as many cobs as I could, then I could make it appear as if someone was running to their side.

I gathered as many old cobs as I could and placed them in a pile in front of me and prepared myself for rapid firing of the cobs. I started with the smaller cobs hoping that they would fly far enough to reach the other side and saved the bigger cobs. The first cob I launched hit the crossbeams and bounced into the water. The next cob I grabbed hit directly on the far end of the bridge. Now that I had my range figured out, I would start the rapid firing. After ten or so cobs, I ran out of the cobs that I had piled up. I picked up my stuff and pushed into the cornfield to wait and see if there was a response to the corncob bombardment.

As I walked back into the corn I could hear some sirens on the other side of the river racing towards the bridge. Then I heard sirens on this side of the bridge, and they sounded like they were coming from the area of grandma and grandpa's house. I would wait until the police converged on the bridge and then I would make a dash to the shed and set up a short stay camp until I could return to Amber and the kids. The police reached the bridge at the same time. The doors of the squad cars flew open and the men poured out like they were black ants. That was the signal for me to head to the shed.

Pushing my way through the corn to the back edge of Grandma Wilson's backyard, I stopped just short of stepping into the backyard. I needed to make sure the police didn't leave a man behind to watch the house. Nobody was lurking about, and I didn't see any light on in the house either. As I ran to the shed, I could hear that the sirens were on the move again. They must have given up on looking for the mystery person. I grabbed the door handle, opened it, slipped inside and quickly opened the trap door. The backpack I took off and dropped down the hole. Then I sent down the rest of the things that I had picked up along the way. I wasn't going to leave these nice fishing poles behind. Never did get a chance to use them in the river here, but when I get home, I will be the envy of all the guys.

Into the hole I crawled to set up an area where I could take a little nap and rest up and think about what I would say to my grandparents to persuade them to help me and get them to come back to the settlement. My biggest fear was that grandpa wouldn't believe what I had to say and grandma would. I didn't want to have one come with me and the other stay, but I couldn't force them or I'd be as bad as the state government that they live under now. I closed the trap door and settled into the cozy little spot next to the food. That reminded me; I should eat something now. I wouldn't even look; I'd just pick one out and eat it cold, of course. My hand found a small box when I reached into the big box. When I brought it up and put it close to my face to try to read what it said with what little light that was coming in through the floor, it looked like I'd be eating breakfast. I had selected scrambled eggs and ham.

After eating, my stomach was satisfied. I dug in my backpack, pulled out my blanket and settled in for a short nap hoping that I would be able to sleep with all the thoughts swirling in my head about what to say to my grandparents. I'd have to close my eyes and maybe, just maybe, my mind would slow down enough to let me sleep.

Chapter 8

Facing the Truth

I was awakened by a loud engine. It was not the way I was
hoping to wake up since I was having such a nice dream
of me and the guys back at the settlement fishing on the river.
I was right; I was the envy of them all. My stringer was full
of fish, enough to eat some fresh fish that night for supper
and still have a few fish to put into the smokehouse to save
up for winter when food got a little thin.

Here comes that noisy engine again. I opened up the trap
door and crawled up into the shed and found a crack between
the boards to look out and see what was going on outside.
It was grandpa, and it looked like the machine that he was
using was cutting off the top of the grass. That must me that
lawn mower thing that dad always talked about that he hated
to do every week only to do it again the next week. I'm glad
we don't have to do that at the settlement. We have all trees
covering us and that way the grass doesn't grow much. Here
he comes again. If grandpa had to cut the grass in front of
the house, I could either slip into the house through the back
door or I could use the tunnel from the garage to the house.
I'd have to wait and see what he does. Grandpa went back
and forth across the lawn. I could see why dad hated cutting
the grass. Grandpa was going up to the front of the house.

Oops, the engine stopped. No, don't stop now. You are just getting to where I can make a run for the house. He was coming this way. No, he was going to the garage. He must have run out of gas. Yup, he picked up some gas and was going back to the lawn mower. Now Grandpa, don't bring the can back; just leave it there, and then I can make my move to the house. Good, grandpa listened to me this time and put the gas can down and started the engine up again. There he goes to the front of the house. I thought it would be best if I went through the tunnel to get into the house just in case grandpa came back. It was a shorter run to the garage than to the back door of the house. I made sure I closed the trap door so grandpa wouldn't accidentally find it open if he would go to the shed for some reason. I listened to the sound of the engine to make sure that grandpa was in the far corner of their lot. That way he couldn't see me run into the garage.

Grandpa went a little further, and I pushed open the door to the shed and raced to the garage with only some clean bandages in hand. I ducked into the garage and went straight to the workbench and pulled it out far enough to open the trap door to the tunnel. As I was pushing the workbench back into place, I noticed something that I had not seen the last time I was this way. Grandpa had a shotgun hidden under part of the workbench. I wonder why he had it there. I finished pushing the workbench back into place and made my way through the tunnel and into the basement.

Grandpa was still cutting the grass, and that was good because I wanted to talk with grandma before he came in. She could help me keep him from calling the police or arresting me himself and hauling me off to jail. I thought I'd use the coal bin stairs up to the storage room and pop out there. Hopefully grandma was home. If she wasn't, I would have to go back to the shed and try another time or maybe another day.

206

I could hear someone walking across the floor above me when I walked through the basement. The kitchen could be above me, and that would be great because grandma wouldn't see me come out of the storage room. I hurried into the coal bin and up the stairs and pushed open the trap door. Excitement about what could happen when they found out that I was their grandson and that their son, Mark, was still alive was overtaking me. I needed to slow down. Pressing my ear to the storage room door, I listened to find out where grandma was. My heart almost skipped a beat when she walked by the door on her way to the living room. Now what do I do? She was supposed to stay in the kitchen so I could come out and not be seen, and I can't do that if she is walking about the house. There she went back into the kitchen. Now I could make my move to get out of here and get ready to enter the kitchen. I popped the door open a little and then all the way. I stepped out into the hallway carrying my bandages with me. She was sitting at the table rolling cookie dough in her hands and placing them on a baking sheet.

"Hello, Ramona," I said softly.

Grandma's head popped up, and her eyes got as big as the mixing bowl on the table. "Hello, Carl. How is your arm doing?"

"Well, I need my bandage changed. I brought the bandages with me; could you help me change it?"

"Sure, I would be happy to do that for you. I need to wash my hands because I don't want to get your bandages all greasy." As she walked over to the kitchen sink she asked, "Would you like a cookie and something to drink?"

"Yes, that would be nice. Thank you!"

"Go ahead, Carl. Sit down at the table, and we can talk while you eat your cookies and drink your milk. Is milk okay?"

"Yes, milk would be great."

"So, Carl, last time you were here you came in bleeding. I'm glad to see you in better shape this time. Now let me look at this wound of yours. Does it still hurt a lot?"

"No, it hardly hurts at all. I've changed the bandage once, but it didn't look as good as what you and Nurse Glover did that first day." Grandma carefully unwrapped my arm as I enjoyed the cookies that she put on a plate in front of me along with a glass of cold milk.

"Carl, your arm is looking pretty good. I don't see any infection, and it looks like you have rested enough that you did not bust open the wound since Nurse Glover didn't put any stitches in to hold it together."

"Ramona, do you remember the first time we met at the edge of the cornfield in the backyard?"

"Yes, I do. You were shy and would not come out of the cornfield very far."

"Do you remember that you said I looked a lot like your son, Mark?"

"Yes, and I still think you look like him even though Russell says that I think every young man I see looks like Mark. What are you getting at? Don't beat around the bush. Just say what you need to say, Carl."

"I have met your son, Mark, and he is alive."

"Carl, it is not very nice to say something like that if it is not true."

"It is true."

Grandma fired back at me, "How do you know this?"

"I know this to be true because Mark Wilson is my dad and you are my grandma." Grandma sat back in her chair and said nothing. Her eyes began to well up with tears. "I have been wanting to tell you that I'm your grandson from the first time we met."

"How can I be sure this is not a trick?"

"Grandma, I can tell you things that only Mark would know, and I could only know it because I heard it from him."

"What kind of things could you tell me?"

"Roy and Frieda Wilson ran from the state police and missed Mark's birthday. Your mother and father are in two urns in the living room. The key to the attic is behind the picture in the hallway upstairs. And I have saved the best for last. Your favorite saying is: 'There is a place for everything, and everything in its place.'"

The tears came gushing out and grandma grabbed me and put a bear hug on me that only a grandma could. She released the bear hug on me only to grab my face with both hands and pull it close to hers and said, "My boy is alive, and I have a grandson."

With grandma's hand clamped on my face so tightly, I tried to say, "Grandma, you not only have a grandson but you also have a granddaughter."

She asked through her tears, "Where is Mark? Where is my granddaughter?"

"That I cannot tell you."

"Why not? Why did you come here? To tell me that my son is alive and that I'm a grandmother, but you won't tell me where they are?"

"It is for the safety of all. Like my dad for many years, I wondered who my grandparents were. What did they look like? I haven't come just to get my questions answered but to bring you back with me."

"When do we leave?"

"As soon as we convince Grandpa Russell that I'm his grandson and not some dirty kid from the street."

"You'll have a hard time convincing me that you're my grandson."

I had not noticed that the engine had stopped and grandpa had walked into the kitchen without either grandma or me noticing him. After what he said, I didn't know if I should run now or take the chance and try to convince him that I was his grandson. Grandpa must have sensed that making a run for the door was crossing my mind.

"You won't get far, Carl, if you run. The police will be here in a flash. All I have to do is call on my radio."

"Do you mean this radio, Grandpa?" The look on grandpa's face that I had outfoxed him was priceless. A smile came across his face and he started to run for the back door. I said, "Grandpa, you wouldn't be going to get your shotgun that you stash under your workbench out in the garage, would you, because I have moved it someplace else."

Grandpa slammed his hands on the cupboard door so hard you could hear the dishes rattle. "You think that you're pretty smart don't you, Carl?"

"No, Grandpa, I don't."

"Don't call me Grandpa! I'm not your grandpa!"

"Russell, he knows things that only Mark would know."

"Like what, Ramona? That your favorite saying is 'There is a place for everything, and everything in its place?' I heard him say that, but that doesn't prove anything. All mothers say that to their kids, and the kids say that to their kids."

"Well then, Grandpa, I mean Mr. Wilson, should I tell you the time that you and Ramona took things from the attic and burned them in the pit in the backyard so Mark wouldn't know of your past? Do you still have the wooden box that your father made that held the letter asking you to come to the settlement? The letter with the first clue that read: 'Start in the center of the city park. Find the statue of the child with its hands reaching towards heaven. Place your chin on the top of the child's head. Look between the child's hands and you will see the place to find clue number 2. It will ring a bell.'"

Grandpa leaned up against the counter in the kitchen not knowing what to say. Grandma and Grandpa turned and looked at each other as if they had never read the letter.

I questioned them, "Surely you have read the letter that was in the wooden box."

"We started to read the letter, but when we saw it was from Roy and Frieda, we placed it in the wooden box and locked it up in the attic along with other things of theirs. The state was still very actively searching for them, and the police were coming to the house almost every other day looking for things."

"What things were they looking for?"

"We asked them that same question. They never told us, and sometimes they would escort us out of our house, search for hours and then tell us nothing."

"My dad told me that when you were at the capital city meeting with the governor, that is when he pursued more heavily his search for the clues to find his grandparent's location. He had a few run-ins with the police, but there was not enough evidence to hold him. While he was in jail, the police came to the house and hid listening devices around. They even hid one in the bathroom upstairs."

Grandma leaned over to grandpa and whispered something in his ear. He just frowned and shook his head no. Grandma looked disgusted at grandpa; I just continued my story. "The Zablings came one day and helped dad escape from the police that had come to take him away. The Zablings paid for it with beatings, and from what I have found out since coming back to the city, they both died in jail. Have I convinced you enough that I am who I say I am?"

Grandma smiled and replied, "Yes, I believe you, Carl."

Grandpa sat there at the table and looked at me. Then he reached for his back pocket and pulled out an old worn billfold. He opened it up and flipped through some pictures until he stopped and pulled one out. He held it out across the table towards me as if he was comparing what was on the picture to me. Not saying anything, he got up and walked around the table. He reached out his hand and gave me the picture that he had in his billfold. It had yellowed over the years, and the edges were very worn. There was a fold going

211

through the middle of the face of the person in the picture, but I could tell that it was my dad. I looked up into the eyes of my grandpa. I did not say anything; I did not have to, and neither did Grandpa.

Grandpa's tears ran down his face at the same time that his arms wrapped around me, "I believe you too, Carl." Grandma came from the other side of the table and joined in the hugging.

Our reunion was interrupted with pounding on the front door. We separated and grandpa went to answer the door. Grandma whispered to me, "Carl, you will need to hide. It is the police. It may be nothing, and they just might want to talk to your grandpa, but we cannot take a chance."

"I'll hide in the basement."

"Carl, where are you going?"

"I'm heading for the basement, why?"

"The basement is not that way. It is over here and down these stairs."

"Okay, Grandma; I'll follow you."

I walked towards the basement door but stopped in my tracks. There was a dark figure showing on the window shade. I grabbed grandma by the arm and motioned for her to say nothing. Then I pointed to the window, and she saw the dark figure move. It pounded on the back door so hard that the door shook on its hinges. I pulled grandma away from the door and walked her out into the hall and opened up the door to the storage room.

I began to walk into the storage room when Grandma pulled on my arm and whispered into my ear, "Carl, if I was a policeman, this would be the first place that I would look if I was looking for someone that was hiding."

"I know, but would they look in here?" I lifted up the trap door and dropped down inside. As I looked up, I could see that grandma had no idea that there was a trap door in the storage room. "I'll come back later after things have

cooled down and when the police have gone. I'll be okay!
Go let the police in the back door before they think that you
have something to hide. Let Grandpa know that I'm in a safe
place and that it is okay to let the police in. Keep them from
looking out the windows to the backyard."

"Why the backyard?"

"I don't have time to tell you why. You will have to trust
me on this."

"I love you, Carl." It was the first time I had heard those
words from my grandparents.

"I love you too, Grandma." I waved goodbye and shut the
trap door. I slid down into the basement and moved across
the floor quickly.

Grandpa was talking to the police officer upstairs. "Good
evening, Shawn. What brings you out this way?" I couldn't
figure out why grandpa was talking so loud. Was he nervous,
or was he hoping that I was listening? The air duct by the
furnace carried their voices well, so I stood and listened
for awhile. "Is this a social call, or are you here on police
business?"

"Police business, Captain Wilson."

Hoping to let Grandpa know that there was a policeman
at the back door also, I heard Grandma say, "Look, Russell.
It's Kyle, Steve's boy."

That didn't make Kyle happy. He snapped back at
Grandma, "I'm an officer of the state, and you will address
me as such."

I could feel the hair on the back of my neck stand on end
when Kyle snapped at grandma. If my dad were here, Kyle,
you would not be talking to Grandma or anybody else that
way. There was a loud thump as if something or somebody
hit the door to the basement. Kyle better not have hit my
grandma.

That was when I heard Grandma yelling at Officer Kyle,
"You listen here you little snot nose kid. I, too, am an officer

of the state, and I just so happen to be a captain; so if you don't want to be walking the streets of the warehouse district until you are old and gray, you better watch what you're saying and to whom you are saying it to. Are we clear on that, Officer Anderson?"

"Yes, M'am!"

"Now state your business!"

"We have come to ask you if you have had any contact or sightings of the boy that we, the state, have been looking for the past few days."

"If we had seen this boy that you are talking about, don't you think that we would have called it in and asked for backup to cordon off the area and bring him in for questioning?"

"Yes, Captain Wilson."

"And did we make the call?"

"No, Captain Wilson."

Then I heard Grandpa and Officer Shawn walk into the kitchen where Grandma and Kyle were. I moved to the bottom of the stairs so I could hear better.

"Ramona, look who was at the front door. Officer Shawn Murphy. Well, I see you have a friend back here also. My, we are so lucky to have two of the states finest here at our house at the same time. Ramona, you'll never guess what Officer Shawn was just asking me."

"Where is the mystery boy, and have we had any more sightings. Officer Shawn, I'll tell you the same thing that I told Officer Anderson; and that is if and when we see the mystery boy, you'd be the first person we'd call. By the way, has anybody found out anything about this boy?"

"No, we have not. He is smarter than most kids. He leaves no clues, fingerprints or anything that can help us find out who he is. The police across the river blew up that old caboose. They looked to see if he had been in there, but they found nothing."

"Well Officers, it has been nice talking, but Mr. Wilson and I would like to get back to a quiet evening alone. We'll call you if anything changes."

Oh how I would have liked to be a mouse in the corner to watch grandma put Kyle in his place. Dad would have wanted to be there beside me to watch Kyle being put in his place. It was then I heard the back door open and then close. I'd wait a while before I went up just in case the police would come back to surprise us. I walked back across the basement, found a big chair and sat down in it. It was so old that the springs were weak, and it seemed as if the chair was swallowing me up.

I could hear my grandparents walking around upstairs. I'm sure they think that I left the house. I closed my eyes to get a little rest. Tap, tap, tap. My eyes popped open and I looked around but didn't see anything. Tap, tap, tap. There it was again. Then out of the corner of my eye I could see a body crouched in front of the basement window. The person was trying to clean off the dirt hoping to see into the basement. I needed to let grandma and grandpa know that the police were still in the area. If I could get over to the stairs going up to the storage room, I could let them know that way. The person had stopped wiping the window and was no longer looking in. Now was the time to run to the secret stairs. Getting out of the chair was harder than I thought; I had sunk into it so deep. I flipped the lever by the stairs to go from a slide to stairs, and I made my way up the stairs into the storage room. I opened the door and talked softly so if the police were by a door or window, they would not hear me call out for my grandparents.

"Grandma!"

"Carl, is that you? I thought you escaped and were long gone."

"There are still police outside your house. I saw one looking in the basement window."

215

"It was a good thing you stayed in the house."

"Russell, Carl said there are still some police outside looking in windows."

"Where are they now, Carl?"

"I'm not sure. They couldn't get the window clean enough to see in. They might be looking for another window to look into."

"Russell, the best window to look into would be the window in the study. Why don't I go in there and look around? If they are there, I will sit down and give them something to watch while you sneak outside and scare them. Tell them to get moving."

"I'm going to hide down the basement and wait for the all clear sign before I come up."

I closed the storage room door and made my way to the basement when Grandpa opened the door and said, "Carl, you can't get to the basement that way. You need to use the basement stairs in the kitchen."

I opened the trap door and dropped down in. Grandpa's eyes popped wide open. I flipped the lever to make it a slide just for fun and knew that would make grandpa's eyes pop open again. As the stairs changed into a slide, not only did grandpa's eyes become as big as saucers but his jaw dropped to the floor.

"I'll tell you later about this, but for now we need to get rid of the police. Then I can tell you all the cool stuff that your dad made."

I turned and slid to the basement. I had forgotten to close the trap door, so I whispered up to Grandpa, "Grandpa Russell, could you close the trap door for me?"

"Sure!"

"Thank you! I'll see you in a little bit."

I must have fallen asleep in my big, old, overstuffed chair waiting for the all clear. Grandma and Grandpa had come down the basement and woke me up.

"How long have I been sleeping?"

"Not long."

"Are they gone?"

"Yes, Carl, they are gone."

"I better make my way out to my hiding spot and get ready to go to bed for the night. I'll see you in the morning."

"No, Carl, you will be sleeping up in your dad's room. There is no need for you to sleep outside when we have an empty bed upstairs."

"Thank you. I'm sure it will be a lot softer than the spot in the dirt that I had picked out."

We all headed for the stairs. No one said a word until Grandma broke the silence. "Carl, your grandpa and I were talking a little while ago, and we were saying that we were sure glad you came back to the city. We wouldn't have ever met you and wouldn't have ever known that our son is alive and well." Grandma turned and gave me a hug. Then we continued up the stairs in silence all the way to dad's bedroom.

"There should be something that you can use to sleep in of your dad's in one of the drawers."

"Thank you!" I walked into the room and sat at the end of the bed looking back at grandma and grandpa, each leaning on the doorpost. "My dad talked about you a lot to Kayla and me. He always said that if there would ever be a time when we would get to meet you, that we would think that you were the best grandparents in the world. He is right; you are the best. My dad misses you a lot. Sometimes when he comes in from outside his face is wet and his eyes are red. When I was little I would ask him if he was crying. I think he wanted to say no so I would think that he was big and strong, but he would take a deep breath and say yes. He would say that he was missing his mom and dad. Now I know a little of what he has been going through. I'm missing my mom, dad and even my little sister, Kayla. I'm looking forward to going home soon."

"Carl, you get some sleep, and we will talk in the morning."

"Good night, Grandma. Good night, Grandpa."

They both replied at the same time, "Good night, Carl."

It sounded good to hear that. They turned and grandpa went downstairs while grandma went down the hall to another room. Grandma said that there would be something that I could use to sleep in, so I looked in the drawers and found some pajamas.

Suddenly I heard water sloshing, so I ran to the hallway and looked around. It sounded like it was down the hall. Slowly I walked toward the sound; but before I got to the door at the end of the hall, it opened and Grandma walked out and said, "Carl, I'm running you some bath water. I thought that you would like to get cleaned up before you went to bed." I must have had a funny look on my face because Grandma said, "You do know what a bath is, don't you?"

"Yes, I do, but we don't have one in our house at the settlement. There is a men's bathhouse and a women's bath-house. We heat water over a fire and then pour it into a big bathtub. When I was a little boy, they would put three or four of us kids in the tub at the same time to save on heating up the water. We did more splashing than washing, but we always seemed to come out clean."

"Well, Carl, things are a little different here. The tub is not that big and we have plenty of hot water without starting a fire."

I walked into the bathroom and I could not believe my eyes. There was a white bathtub; Grandma had set out a washcloth and towel for me. I placed my hand in the water. It was very warm but not too hot like when we would first pour the water just taken off the fire.

"Carl, take as long as you like; and when you are done, just pull the plug and drain the water out."

"Grandma, won't the floor get all wet?"

"Carl, there is a pipe that the water will drain into and go down to the basement and then outside."

"Oh!"

Grandma just smiled and closed the door behind her. I remember when dad told me the story that the state police had planted a listening device in the upstairs bathroom up in the light. I looked up at the light and saw nothing. Still I wasn't sure.

I called out to grandma, "Grandma!"

"Yes, Carl, what is it?"

"My dad told me that before he left to come to the settlement, the state police had come into the house and planted listening devices around the house, and one was in this bathroom. Did you . . . ?"

"Find them all?" Grandma finished my sentence for me. "Yes, Carl, we found many listening devices."

"My dad said that they even put a tracking device on his bicycle. He said it was in the handlebars."

"We will look tomorrow; and if there is, we will take care of it."

"Grandma, do you think it would be possible for me to learn how to ride my dad's bicycle?"

"Certainly. Now you get cleaned up and ready for bed. Then I'll be in to tuck you in."

"Dad was right."

"What do you mean, Carl?"

"Dad said that you would still try to tuck him into bed even when he was 16. To tell you the truth, Grandma, I think he liked that you did that; and I'll be waiting for you to do that for me."

Grandma's eyes were getting a little watery, but she said nothing. She just smiled and headed back into their bedroom.

I closed the bathroom door and got ready to get into the water. The warm water felt good, and it would be good to wash my wound. Leaning back in the tub, I stretched out my legs and placed them at the end of the tub to keep myself from sliding under the water. I closed my eyes for what I thought was only a few seconds when suddenly I was awakened by a knock at the bathroom door. "Carl, are you okay in there?"

"Yes, Grandma. I must have fallen asleep. I'll be out in just a few minutes!"

"No hurry. I just wanted to make sure that you were okay and had not drowned. I just got a grandson. I don't want to lose you now."

I unfolded the washcloth, rubbed the soap on and scrubbed off the dirt and grime from my body. While I was drying off, I made sure I didn't get too close to the window just in case the police had someone posted across the street to watch the house for anything unusual. I reached into the water and pulled the drain plug to let the water out. Just as fast as grandma put the water in the tub, it went down the drain.

"Carl," Grandma yelled through the door, "I laid out some clean clothes that you can wear for tomorrow. They were your father's. I don't think he would mind you wearing them. I don't think he would fit them anymore."

"Grandma, you are so right. Dad is much bigger than any picture that I have seen of him as a kid. He has a lot of muscles and is just as tall as grandpa," I yelled back to her.

I put on the robe that grandma had left in the bathroom, opened up the bathroom door and stepped out into the hall and headed to my room for the night. There were the clothes set out on the chair next to the bed: socks, underwear, pants and shirt. It was like Christmas without the snow. I slipped into the pajamas I had picked out and pulled back the blankets to slide in-between the sheets. It had only been a few seconds when grandma appeared in the doorway just like my mom did when I was young. It must be a motherly thing to know when it is time to tuck kids into bed. They must not lose it when they become grandmas.

"Carl, are you ready for me to tuck you in for the first time?"

"Yes I am!"

Grandma had a huge smile on her face as she walked toward me. Suddenly we heard grandpa running up the stairs. I shot up in bed waiting to hear what he had to say that would cause him to run up the stairs. He reached the doorway to my room; grandma and I both looked at him waiting for him to speak and tell us something bad like the police were coming, but he said nothing. Finally Grandma could not wait any longer and asked, "What is it, Russell?"

Grandpa didn't know what she was talking about judging by the look on his face. "What is what? I just came up so I could help tuck Carl in. I don't want to miss all the fun."

"The way that you ran up the stairs, Russell, we thought that the police were on their way."

Then both of them tucked me in bed. Between the two of them, the covers were so tight around me I didn't think I could move. Grandma leaned over to kiss me on the forehead and I felt tears land on my face. Looking up into her tear-filled eyes I said, "Mark misses you too, Grandma."

I had hoped that what I said to her would make her happy, but she cried even harder putting her hands over her face as she ran from the room. Grandpa could see that I was afraid that I had said something wrong and he quickly assured me, "Carl, it's okay. Just go to sleep; we can talk in the morning."

"Good night, Grandpa. Say good night to Grandma for me."

"I will, Carl." Grandpa patted me on the shoulder and headed for the door; but after only taking a few steps, he turned to me and said, "Before you even say it, I'm going to say that your grandma is okay and you did nothing wrong."

"How did you know what I was thinking, Grandpa?"

"We grandpas just know these things." Then he winked and turned, walked out the door and hit the light switch. The room went black. I hoped that I would be as smart as my dad and grandparents when I got that old.

As I lay in the dark, I replayed parts of today's events over again in my head, cherishing the moments when grandma and grandpa realized who I was. I could feel my eyes getting heavy and my thoughts were getting all jumbled up; they weren't making much sense anymore. I should let myself go to sleep and get ready to plan my next move.

Chapter 9

Plan "A"

A gentle rapping on the door to my room made me open my eyes in time to see a hand reach around the edge of the door. Next came a slightly gray head of hair, and then came eyes that sparkled in the morning light. "Good morning, Carl," Grandma said cheerily. The door pushed open wide, and there was grandpa standing next to grandma.

"Well, son, are you going to get up, or are you going to lie in bed all day and rot?"

Seeing that grandpa had a half smile on his face when he was saying it, I decided that I would have a little fun back at him. "You know, Grandpa, that is an excellent idea. I think I'll lie here and rot until . . . say lunch. No, make that a late lunch, around 2 o'clock. Yes, I think that will do quite nicely. Thank you."

I pulled the blankets up around my neck and closed one eye. The look on their faces was priceless. I could not hold in the laughter; it burst forth. Then grandma and grandpa joined in with me. They rushed into the room and plopped down at the end of the bed. Grandma had a ton of questions.

"Carl, how did you sleep? Was the bed okay? It wasn't too hard or soft, was it?"

Grandpa jumped in to save me. "Ramona, give the boy a chance to answer."

"Grandma, I slept fine, and the bed was great."

"Carl, what would you like to have for breakfast?"

"Don't make anything special for me. I'll eat whatever you make."

"Do you like pancakes?"

"Yes I do."

"Well, then that's what we are going to have."

I really hated to say what I had to say but it had to be said sooner or later. "Grandma and grandpa, we need to talk about how we are going to get Ernie out of the hospital and how we are going to get all those kids back to the settlement, and soon. The longer I'm here, the greater the danger for all of us."

"You're right, Carl. We can talk after breakfast. Your grandma and I have been thinking about it. Get dressed, and when you are ready, come on down."

"Grandpa, have you seen any signs of the police yet today?"

"No, I haven't seen any police yet."

"Good. I'll be down in a few minutes."

They left the room. I slid out from under the covers and changed into the clothes that grandma had set out for me last night. I walked over to the side of the window still careful just in case the police had the house under surveillance. As I looked down the road towards where the old mill once stood, my thoughts were on what might be going on at the settlement. I could only hope that I was not putting mom, dad and Kayla through too much worry since I had been gone so long. I missed them so much. I could feel tears welling up in my eyes. The longer I stared at the hills and trees, the more I missed my family. Tears were running down my face as I stood there in silence in front of the window picturing the faces of my family.

It must have taken too long for me to come down for breakfast. Once again there was a gentle rap on the door. Quickly I wiped the tears from my eyes and tried to dry my face. I turned and looked into my grandpa's face. I didn't fool him. He knew there were tears on my sleeves.

"Your grandma said that I should come up and see what was taking you so long to get down to the table."

"Grandpa, I miss my family so much, and I have only been gone for a few days. How could you and grandma go so long without seeing your son?"

"It wasn't that we didn't want to see Mark. We didn't know what had happened to him. As you know, we were in the capital city working with the governor. When we came home, we found out that the police had chased, beaten and imprisoned Mark, but he still escaped. They didn't know where he went, and they were not telling us anything. Like I had told you earlier, they came to the house often to search and ask questions thinking that we still had contact with Mark; but as you know, we didn't. We tried to seek help from anybody that might have helped him. I had talked with my informants on the street, and they knew nothing. It was like the earth had opened up and swallowed him never to be seen again. For many years we would make his favorite cake on his birthday, but after about five or six years, we stopped. There were many times I found your grandma crying at night while she was either cooking one of Mark's favorite meals or when she was putting the dishes she had just washed away. I found her holding his baby cup; the one he first learned how to drink from."

"Grandpa, didn't you ever cry because you missed your son?"

"Oh yes! I cried rivers of tears while I was out working in the garage. When I would feel a tear coming, I would tell your grandma that I had something to do in the garage.

225

I would head out there and have a good cry. Your grandma never knew."

"That is where you're wrong, Russell." Grandma had come into the room, and we didn't even hear her. Grandpa spun around with his mouth wide open. "Russell, you were not hiding anything from me; because when you came in from the garage, the tears that you had cried left watermarks on your shirt. I was just being sensitive by not saying anything. Let's go down and eat before the pancakes get cold."

The three of us all nodded our heads saying nothing and headed out of the room. We didn't say anything for what seemed like an eternity. We walked down the stairs and into the kitchen. Grandpa and I took a seat at the table across from each other; grandma brought the pancakes and set them on the table and then took a seat herself. We just sat there looking at each other not saying anything or even eating.

We all spoke at once. "I'm sorry!" We all said the same thing at the same time, and then again we all spoke at the same time. "What did you say? I'm sorry!" We did it again, talking at the same time and not being able to hear or understand what each other had said. We could do nothing else but laugh.

Once we stopped laughing I spoke first saying, "I'm sorry for thinking that you didn't care about your son."

Grandpa spoke, "That's okay. I should have tried harder to find him."

Grandma started to cry. Through her tears she said, "I'm sorry I stopped you, Russell, from looking more; but I was afraid of what we might find. It was easier to think that he was alive and happy someplace."

Once again we spoke in unison, "Can you forgive me?"

Grandpa just shook his head and said, "Let me say a prayer before we eat. 'Dear Heavenly Father, thank you for all that you have given each of us sitting around this table. Bless the food, and bless all that are here at the table. Help us plan our exodus from here into freedom. Give us wisdom. In Jesus' holy name we pray, Amen!'"

I opened my eyes in time to see a smile of grandpa's face. I could tell it had been a long time since he had prayed openly. As grandma wiped away tears she spoke, "It is so good to hear prayer in this house again. It has been gone too long."

I was so happy that I blurted out, "Amen to that!"

Grandpa took hold of the plate of pancakes and handed them to me. I plunged my fork deep into the stack of pancakes and placed four of them on my plate. Then I handed the plate to grandma. She just smiled at me. She copied me and put four pancakes on her plate also. We laughed and talked all through breakfast and then some.

As I helped grandma clear the table of dishes I said, "We should talk about the next stop to get ready to head to the settlement."

My grandparents looked at each other and then at me. Grandma spoke softly, "Yes, Carl, you are right. These dishes can wait until later; we need to get a plan in place."

Grandpa said, "We need to get the children gathered together in one place close to the starting point."

"Wait a minute, Grandpa. Aren't you forgetting that we still have to see if we can get Ernie out of the hospital?"

"Carl, I don't think that is a good idea. Ernie is very old, and he would only slow us down. We could all get caught."

"I would like to at least meet him and see what kind of physical condition he is in. If he is too old to make the trip, I will then make the decision to go without him."

Grandpa chuckled and said, "Carl, it sounded like for a minute there you were in charge of this operation."

"You are right, Grandpa. I am in charge."

"But, Carl, you are just a boy."

"You are right again, Grandpa, and I'm the one and only person here that knows the way to the settlement, and it will stay that way for security reasons."

"Why?"

"If someone would get caught and forced to talk, the police would then know where the settlement was, and they wouldn't have a chance."

"Carl, you think that if the police caught you that they wouldn't make you talk?"

"No, Grandpa, I would give up my life to make sure that the secret location of the settlement would stay with me. I don't mean to be harsh, but this is the way it has to be."

Grandpa was silent for a few seconds with his head slightly bowed looking at the table. As his head rose up he said, "Okay, Carl, you're the boss of this operation. What do you have in mind?"

"First we need to get in to see Ernie and make the decision whether he will come with us or stay here. Second we need to gather supplies and backpacks to carry as much back to the settlement as we can without slowing us down."

"Carl, why do you need more supplies if the settlement has been going strong for so many years?"

"Grandpa, we will bring about 50 to 70 more people into the settlement, and some of our equipment is worn out. One thing we need is seeds to plant more food for the increase of the people."

"Carl, you are wise beyond your years. I wouldn't have thought of that."

Grandma turned and looked grandpa in the face and said, "And that is why Carl is in charge."

"Okay you two; I get it. Now Carl, where are these children at now?"

"I don't know yet. I will meet up with them later tomorrow hopefully, and we will have a planning time like we are having now."

"Wait a minute. You don't know where these kids are, but yet somehow you are going to have a meeting with them. How can that be?"

"Well, Grandpa, it is like this. The leader of their group is also very careful not to let out their location. If the police would find them, they would all end up in jail. I was blind-folded and taken to their place where their leader, Amber, and I talked."

Grandpa was getting a little uncomfortable. I could tell by the way he squirmed in his chair. "The leader of the kids is a girl!"

"Watch it, Russell. Remember I'm a girl too!" Grandma said with a look that, well, let's say it was not a good look.

"I have the kids looking for some supplies also. They have some people that have been helping them for many years that they hope will be able to gather together the things that we will need to make the trip. Grandma, are there any people at the hospital that we can trust to help us get in to see Ernie?"

"Yes, there is that nurse that took the bullet out of your arm."

"Good! Is there any others?"

"I don't know."

"What about Kevin Zabling? Can we trust him?"

"I think so."

"Grandma, what I'll need you to do is to talk to Kevin Zabling and see if he is willing to help us get Ernie out if need be."

"Carl, what do you want me to do?"

"Don't worry, Grandpa. I have a big job for you. I need you to get into the police records and erase as much informa-tion that the police might have on anybody that is suspected of helping us. If they have spies around town, we need to know who they are and what their location is so we can stay clear of them as much as possible. Also, find out what patrols will be out for each day for the next week so we can pick the best day to leave when they have their least amount of me on duty."

"Is that all?"

"No, but that will give you enough to do for now. Later we may need you to put inn some false information to send the police off in the wrong direction by chasing some of the police's own informants thinking that they may be double agents and may be working for us. Grandpa, do you think you have a police uniform my size? It would be easier for me to move around in the daytime with you and grandma if I looked like I was a young police officer."

"Carl, if they would catch you in the police uniform, they would put you in jail for impersonating a police officer."

"Grandpa, I don't think it will really matter if I'm in or out of a police uniform. If they catch me, I will be in jail no matter what."

"He's right, Russell," Grandma interjected. "Carl, I'll look in some of the closets. There may be a uniform or two that your grandpa thought that he might fit into if he ever started to work out and lose some weight."

"If I could get that for today, that would be great, Grandma. Thanks!"

Grandpa had a worried look on his face as he asked, "Carl, why do you need it today?"

"Because you and I are going into town and make a few stops so I can set up a meeting with Amber."

"What kind of stops are you talking about?"

"Well, I need to stop at the Abernathys. I left my backpack at their house one night when I was having dinner with them."

"You know Aaron and Marian Abernathy?"

"Yes, I met them in the park one day and we talked. The next thing I knew I was shooting rocks in their backyard. Then Marian said that I would be welcome to stay for dinner, and I'm not one to turn down food when it is home cooked and free. We can ask them a few questions to find out whose side they are on, the states or ours. If they are on our side, we

230

can ask them if they would like to help or would they like to come with us when we head to the settlement."

"Carl, what if they are on the state's side? What do we do with them then?"

"We'll use them to feed bad information to the police."

"Carl, how do you plan to get them to say what side they are on?"

"I don't know. I don't have a plan. We'll have to make it up as we go. Besides, you're a long-time policeman; I'm sure you'll think of something."

Grandma asked, "Carl, you said that you need supplies. What kind of supplies are you talking about? We could buy them."

"No, that would draw too much attention to you because of the things that you would be buying and the amount. We will need to gather them together by other means. You will be able to buy some of them, but you may have to ask some other people to get them for you, and you will have to buy something they need and trade them for the supplies. That way the supplies will be spread out over a number of people, and the police would not be able to put all the pieces together in time to stop us. I'll make a list later tonight when grandpa and I come back from our little trip into town to tie up loose ends with the Abernathys and make arrangements to meet up with Amber."

"You two men continue talking. I'm going to get that uniform ready for you to go into town. Carl, you are going to wait until after lunch, aren't you?"

"Yes, I'll wait. I would not want to miss lunch."

Grandpa and I talked a couple more hours to come up with a plan. We also came up with a back-up plan if there was a problem and the police would outmaneuver us. These entire plans would have to work with what happened when I met up with Amber in the next few days. Grandpa and I had finished up the last few items, and grandma came back into the kitchen holding something behind her back and a big smile on her face. Grandpa and I looked at each other and then looked back at grandma. Grandma spoke before we could even ask what she had behind her back.

"Well, I think I have outdone myself this time. It had to be taken in, but I think it looks very nice. What do you think, men?"

Grandma brought her hand around to the front; there, on a hanger, was the sharpest black state police uniform complete with a badge, nametag and a stripe on the sleeves. I could not believe my eyes; the uniform was fantastic.

"Grandma, you are right. You have outdone yourself. What do have in your other hand?"

Grandma swung her other hand to the front. She was holding a policeman's hat. She handed it to me. As I reached out my hand to take hold of it, my eye caught the shine on the jet black bill. It was so shiny that I could see myself in it.

Grandpa said, "Carl, the important thing is to make sure that when you wear it, you don't leave fingerprints on the bill. If a high ranking officer would see fingerprints or smears, they may call you to the side and reprimand you and start asking questions. We know that would not be a good thing."

"Well, Grandpa, if you can't get any fingerprints on the bill, how do you put it on?"

"Let mw show you how. First you place a hand on each side of the hat and place it on your head like so. Then you take your handkerchief from your pocket and use it to cover your fingers while you gently tug on the bill pulling it down until the brim of the hat rests just slightly above your eyebrows like this."

"I can't wait to try it on."

"I will need to know if it fits, Carl, so you go to your room and try it on. Then come back down and let me see if there is anything that needs to be fixed."

232

I took the hanger from grandma's hand and headed for my room. I had gotten partway down the hall and it hit me. Here I am with a policeman's uniform in my hand running to try it on, but it was only a few days ago men in this same uniform were shooting at me. I guess I was most excited about what the uniform would allow me to do, and that was getting my people home to the settlement. How sharp I would look init was second. I walked up the stairs to my room and put it on. I looked into the full-length mirror, and I thought it fit well. Reaching for the hat that I had carefully place on the bed so as not to make any smears on the bill, I placed it on my head. For a moment I thought about what to use to pull the bill of the hat down since I did not have a handkerchief. There on the chest of drawers was a pair of socks. I put my hand inside the sock and reached up to pull the hat down to the proper place on my head. As I looked in the mirror once more, I saw a policeman for the state. Shivers went down my spine even though I knew that it was me looking back. With the bill of the hat pulled down so far, I could barely see my eyes. Maybe that was why they wore their hat so low so people they were questioning couldn't read their eyes. I turned to head back downstairs to show grandma and grandpa how it looked in the uniform. Just then I walked past a picture of my dad when he was a boy. I wondered what dad would think if he could see me now all dressed in black.

They must have heard me coming down the stairs because they came out of the kitchen and met me at the foot of the stairs. They said nothing. Grandma just made swirling motions with her hand telling me to turn around so she could see the uniform from all sides. Still nothing was said.

There was a knock at the door. I stared at the dark shape moving back and forth in front of the window of the door, but the curtains kept the person from looking in. I turned to run upstairs. Grandpa ran up the stairs after me and grabbed my arm to pull me back down the few steps that I had gone up.

As I stood next to him he said, "Carl, this is a test to see if you can pass as a state policeman or not. I'll do all the talking and you just stand there and try not to shake so much."

Grandpa was right. I was shaking so much that the badge on my chest was flopping up and down. I took a deep breath and then exhaled. I gave grandpa a nod to open the door. As the door swung open, there standing at the door was another police officer. The officer popped a salute to grandpa, and grandpa returned the salute back to the officer. The officer fixed his eyes on me.

"State your purpose, Officer!" Grandpa said with a stern voice.

The officer snapped to attention and said, "Sir, the officer of the day requested that I check with you to see if you had seen any sign of the mysterious boy since his last showing."

"You tell the officer of the day that there has not been any activity of any kind." The officer was staring at me again and not listening to what grandpa was saying and grandpa knew it. "Officer, do you understand?"

"Yes sir!"

"Good. Repeat what I said."

The officer fumbled and mumbled and finally spoke, "Sorry sir. I can't repeat what you said."

"Sorry. You sure are a sorry excuse for an officer." That is when Grandpa turned to me and said, "Tell the officer what I said."

I snapped to attention and said with a loud crisp voice, "Sir, yes sir! You tell the officer of the day that there has not been any activity of any kind."

"That is correct; very well done. Stand at ease."

"Thank you, sir."

Grandpa took two steps forward and was only inches from the officer's face. He whispered to the officer, "Do you know what to tell the officer of the day now?"

"Yes sir, I do."

"Good. Now get out of my house."

"Yes sir!" The officer spun on his heels and headed out the door.

Grandpa yelled, "Officer, where are you going?"

"Sir, to report to the officer of the day."

"Did you forget something?"

The officer looked around and fumbled with his hands not having a clue what grandpa was wanting. I felt sorry for him so I made a gesture to give a salute. Then it was as if the lights had been turned on. The officer came to attention, gave a salute and waited for a return salute. Then he ran out the door. Grandpa shut the door and looked at me with the same look he had given the other officer. Then slowly a smile began to grow on grandpa's face. It turned into laughter. We all laughed together.

Grandpa reached out his hand and said, "Very nice job, Officer Wilson. You have passed your first test, but there will be more, and they will get harder as we encounter more seasoned police officers."

"I was so afraid that the other police officer would be able to tell that I was not one of them, but I did as you said and tried not to shake too much and didn't say anything. I was glad I had listened to what you had told the other officer so that I could repeat it. I think that comes from my mom asking me to repeat what she had told me to do if she thought I was not listening to her. I did not like the consequences if I got it wrong."

"Carl, you have a wise mother. I'm looking forward to meeting her soon."

Grandma said, "Okay, boys, let's go into the kitchen and have lunch so you can go out this afternoon and play cops and robbers in the city."

Us boys, as Grandma called us, just shrugged our shoulders and followed her into the kitchen.

Grandpa asked, "What are we having for lunch anyway?"

"Leftovers. I need to clean out the refrigerator of as much food as possible before we leave. I don't want anything to go to waste."

Grandpa opened the refrigerator and started pulling out bowls, jars and platters of food. I didn't think he'd stop putting out the food.

"Russell, there are only three of us here to eat lunch, not thirty-three."

When grandpa pulled his head out of the refrigerator and looked at us, he had a piece of cold chicken in his mouth. As silly as he looked, he tried talking to us with the chicken in his mouth; both of his hands were full of other food. Grandma buried her face in her hands and shook her head. She walked over to the cupboard and got out some dishes to use for lunch.

With a mouthful of chicken grandpa said, "What? There is more chicken in here for you two. Carl, do you want any?"

"Sure, that looks good, but I'll take mine on a plate." Out of the corner of my eye I saw grandma give me that look to see if I was going to eat my chicken like a caveman or with a plate. A smile came across her face as I asked for a plate to put my food on.

"Russell, maybe you can learn some manners from Carl."

Grandpa reached over and gave me a slight push on the shoulder; at the same time he said, "Show off."

We loaded our plates as if it were our last meal. In between bites we filled grandma in on some of our plans that we had worked out earlier while she was working on my uniform.

It had been quiet for some time because everyone had their mouths full of food. Grandma asked, "Carl what is this Amber like?"

"What do you mean, what is she like? She's a girl that leads a band of kids as if she was their mother."

"Is Amber pretty? Is she smart?"

"Well, I would say that Amber is pretty . . . smart."

236

"Carl, that is not what I was asking."

"Grandma, I'm not dating her. I'm just trying to save her and the kids that she is mothering from living a life without food, clothing and a family setting."

"So what you're trying to say is that you didn't notice if she was pretty."

"Okay! I noticed she is pretty. Grandpa, I think it is time for us to go into town, don't you think?"

"No, I would wait a little longer. That way your grandma can ask you more questions about your girlfriend."

"She's not my girlfriend!"

"No, seriously Carl, I think we should wait about a half hour before 3 o'clock when there is a shift change. There will be about an hour to an hour and a half that there will not be many, if any, police out on the road, and we could move easily about town."

"Grandpa, what time is it now?"

"It is only 1:30."

Grandma got a smile on her face, and I got a worried look on my face. Grandpa said, "Carl, why don't we go up to the attic and see what we have up there that we would be able to use for our trip to the settlement."

"Yes! That is an excellent idea!"

I took off for the stairs, but before I left the kitchen, I said, "Thank you, Grandma, for the lunch."

"You're welcome, Carl."

Quickly I headed for the stairs because it looked like grandma was about to ask me another question. I grabbed a hold of the end post of the hand railing, swung around and started up the stairs taking two steps at a time like my dad said that he did. Halfway up the stairs I slowed down and started to take only one step at a time. Grandma's questions about Amber rang in my head, "Is Amber pretty? Is she smart?" I thought back to when I first saw her in some good light; Amber was actually kind of cute.

I must not have been paying attention to how I was climbing the stairs that I did not get my foot up high enough and tripped on the top step crashing to the floor and making a loud noise. It must have sounded terrible because both grandma and grandpa came running. I jumped to my feet; that would be my two left feet for as graceful as I maneuvered up the stairs. I yelled out to let them know that I was okay but nothing came out. Apparently I had knocked the wind out of myself and it was very hard to talk. I put on my best face to say that I was okay. I clung onto the hand railing at the top of the stairs and waved to them as they looked up the staircase at me. They didn't know what to say, so they just looked at me funny and waved back. Grandma went back to the kitchen and grandpa started to climb the stairs. He just shook his head.

I squeaked out a few words, "What are you shaking your head about, Grandpa?"

"You tripped up the stairs because you were thinking about that girl, Amber, weren't you?" I just shook my head yes. "I thought so. That was the same way I was when I would think about your grandma back in high school a long time ago."

Grandpa put his arm around me as we made our way to the attic door. Grandpa grabbed the doorknob and gave it a twist; the door opened up to my surprise.

"Grandpa, don't you lock the attic door anymore?"

"No, Carl. After your dad left, there was no reason to lock the door. Come on up and take a look around at this old stuff and see if there is anything that you can use."

As I climbed the stairs, I remembered back when dad told the story about the time when he first got up into the attic and saw all the stuff up there that he had never known was up there. I, too, was getting excited about when I might find.

"Grandpa."

"What is it, Carl?"

238

"My dad told me the story of when he was up in the attic, and he told me about a uniform."

Even before I could finish my thought grandpa said, "Is this the uniform that you are talking about?"

"Yes, that is what dad described. Can I try it on like my dad did when he was up here?"

"Mark, I mean your dad, tried it on, did he?"

"Yes, he did. He talked about how it would be great to someday meet the man that wore this uniform."

"Carl, I wish you could have met my father, which would be your great grandfather."

"But I have met Great Grandpa Roy and Great Grandma Frieda."

As I told grandpa that I had met his mom and dad, he got the strangest look on his face; then he began to wobble a little. Then he sort of half sat down and half fell down onto a pile of junk. I got scared and didn't know what to do. Was he having a heart attack?

I yelled as loud as I could, "Grandma! Come up to the attic! Hurry! Grandpa is sick or something!"

Grandpa grabbed my arm and pulled me toward him and said, "Carl, I'm okay. You just surprised me when you said that you had met my father and mother."

I could hear grandma running up the attic stairs. I turned to her and said, "He is okay. I'm sorry I scared you, but I did not know what to do. Grandpa wobbled and sat down so strangely. I did the only thing that I could think of to do, and that was to call for you."

"Russell, are you really all right?"

"Yes, Ramona, I'm fine. Carl said that he met Roy and Frieda before they died."

"Carl, is that true?"

"No!"

Grandpa quickly turned his head to look at me and replied, "Carl, you just said that you had met them, and now you say no, you didn't?"

"No, I did meet them."

"Carl, make up your mind. Either you did meet Roy and Frieda or you didn't. What is it now?"

"Okay. Yes, I did meet Great Grandpa Roy and Great Grandma Frieda, but not before they died."

"Carl Wilson, what kind of story are you telling us?"

"Listen to me. I'm not telling you a story. The reason I said I did not meet Great Grandpa Roy and Great Grandma Frieda Wilson before they died is because they are not dead. They are very much alive."

I'm not sure what happened; but the next thing that I saw was grandpa lying on the attic floor yelling, "They're alive; they're alive!"

Grandma had her hands clamped onto the sides of my face so hard I was sure there would be permanent handprints. While grandma still had a hold of me, grandpa came up from behind me and gave me a bear hug and said, "Carl, do you have any more surprises that you would like to tell us?"

I paused and give them that look like I had to think about it for a minute. Then I took a big, deep breath and opened my mouth as if to tell them another secret. "No, that's it!"

Grandma clamped onto my face again and said, "You little rascal. I thought you had something to tell us."

Grandpa released his bear hug that he had on me and said, "We need to get back to work on finding things that we will be able to use for the t rip. Carl, why don't you start over there in that corner and work your way over to here. I'll be by this side of the stairs, and I'll meet up with you back by the window."

Grandma looked at me and then at grandpa; and with her hands on her hips, she coughed as if to say, "What is my assignment?"

240

Grandpa figured it out quickly and said as if he had not forgotten her, "Ramona, we'll need you to take the center of the attic and organize what things we do find. Now does everybody know what their assignments are?"

We both said that we did. We went to work looking for things. A lot of it was old stuff that would be of no use at the settlement. I lifted up a worn out suitcase and pulled it toward me. It was heavy. Before I it got it to me, the handle broke and the suitcase crashed to the floor. The locks popped open and all that was in there spilled out onto the floor of the attic. There on the floor were 50 to maybe 100 little books.

"Grandpa, what are these little books?"

"They are what some people would call gospel tracks. My mother and father would hand them out to people on the streets and in the city parks until the state started cracking down on Christians. The state said that the little books caused people to fight the good that the state was trying to do."

"Russell, I thought we had found all that they had in the house and had burned them out back shortly after they left for the settlement."

I watched grandpa's eyes look over the books and in a half-dazed voice he said, "I guess we missed a few."

Grandpa then reached down and picked up a handful and began to page through them one at a time. With each turn of the page a smile on his face began to grow and grow. Then his head began to bob slightly, and that smile he had turned into a smirk.

"Russell, you know how I worry when you start to smirk, and you start that head bobbing. What are you thinking of doing?"

"Well, I was just thinking. Why should these books sit up in the attic turning yellow when they could be out on the street and into the hands of the people that need to hear the good new of Jesus Christ? Carl, put them in the pile of something we can use."

"Grandpa, we don't need them at the settlement."

"No, Carl, they are not for the settlement. They are for the city. I hope to hand them out before we leave. The state police will think the people from the settlement have come back and they will be looking for them to be moving back in. They will not be looking for us to be moving out."

"Grandpa, I'm confused. How will that help us?"

"We will spread the gospel tracks on the opposite end of the city from where we will be leaving from. The state police will think that is the area where they will be settling in."

"Grandpa, what section of the city would you hand them out in?"

"That is easy. It would be on the west side of the city."

"Grandpa, I never told you what direction that we would be leaving."

"Carl, it is not that hard to figure out what direction we are going."

"What makes you think you know what way we are going?"

"Carl, this is what I have seen since we met you. One, you have stayed on this side of the city. Two, you are always looking to the east when you look out the window. Three, if you would go west, you would head for the capital city and there is nothing good there. Trust me. I know. I've been there."

"Okay, you're right. We are going east, but I'm not going to tell you anymore."

"Alright boys, let's get back to the task at hand, to find useful things to bring with us."

We split up and went to our areas that grandpa had assigned to us. I remembered dad saying that there was some camping equipment back over by the window that he had to crawl out of when he got locked in the attic. I pushed my way past the piles of boxes and stacks of bags with old clothes until I came to the box of camping equipment that dad had talked about. There, right on top of the pile, was the shovel. I set if off to one side and continued to dig. There was large, heavy metal cooking kettles, candles, water bottles, and so much other stuff that I stopped digging and piled it back into the box and hauled it out to the center of the attic floor. It was placed next to the things that my grandparents had found. My eyes lit up when I saw that someone had found a large amount of thick rope. It took only a second for me to think of the many uses for that rope, and that was just to help us get through the tunnels.

"Hey! Who found the rope?"

Grandma spoke up and said, "I found it, Carl, next to that old suitcase that you found with the gospel tracks in it."

Grandma, that was the best thing that you could have found. Rope is like gold to us back to the settlement."

I heard grandpa struggling with something behind a pile of stuff. Crash, bang and then grandpa fell over backwards. Grandma and I tried to rush to help him, but there was so much junk up in the attic that we could not get to him; and when we did get near him, grandpa sprang to his feet and hollered, "I got it!" There in his hand was a backpack just like the one I was using. I was just as excited as grandpa.

"Grandpa, that is a great find also. That will be able to haul a lot of equipment. What time is it now, Grandpa?"

"It is 2:35. We should get going if we hope to get every-thing we had planned done before supper."

"You two go ahead. I'm going to stay up in the attic a while longer to finish searching. Then I'll bring it down to the living room and we can sort through it and weed out some of the stuff that we don't really need."

"Grandma, that sounds like a great plan. We'll see you in about what, Grandpa? Two, maybe three hours?"

"Yes, that would be a good guess."

Grandpa and I made our way to the stairs. I was watching grandma out of the corner of my eye, and I could tell that she wanted to say something. I stopped at the top of the stairs; grandpa kept on going down the stairs.

I spun around and said to grandma, "Go ahead, Grandma, you can say it. You don't need to, but I think it will make you feel better."

"Okay, Mister Smarty Pants, what am I thinking?"

"You want to say, 'You two boys be careful out there. Oh, and Carl, make sure Russell doesn't drive too fast.'"

"Carl, how did you know that you grandfather drives too fast?"

"I didn't. But if he drives anything like the two policemen that drove Doctor Kittleson and me to the hospital, he drives too fast."

"Thank you, Carl."

"Thank you for what?"

"Thank you for letting me say what I wanted to say. I do feel better. You are very wise for your age."

"I'm not so wise. It is just that you are a lot like my Grandma Rachel. She would say the same thing to me even if I was only going down to the river to fish."

I must have been taking too long because grandpa yelled up from the bottom of the stairs by the living room, "Carl, are you coming? We don't have all day. Our window of opportunity is small the way it is, and for each minute that you dillydally, that window gets smaller."

I turned and yelled back down the stairs, "I'm coming, Grandpa." Looking back at grandma, I knelt down and gave her a big hug and then whispered in her ear, "I'll be careful, and I'll make sure that we both come home safe and sound."

As I was standing up grandma grabbed a hold of my right ear, "Carl, I want you to really be careful. I just got myself a grandson, and I don't want to lose you now."

"I'll be back."

"Okay now, go, before your grandpa starts yelling again, and I start crying."

I tried to leave, but I couldn't. "Grandma, I need you to let go of my ear now."

"Oh! I'm sorry!"

Grandpa met me in the hallway. "What was taking you so long?"

"Grandma wanted to say . . . ."

"Stop. You don't need to say anymore. I know what she said. Be careful!"

"She also said that I should make sure that you don't drive too fast."

"She did not!"

"Yes she did!"

"She did not say that. You just made that up."

"Yes, Russell, you do drive too fast."

The voice from above, Grandma's, froze both of us in our tracks for just a few seconds. Then we ran down the stairs and made a mad dash to the car not looking back, afraid grandma was going to lecture us.

Once in the car grandpa turned to me and said, "I bet you your dessert tonight that your grandma will be looking out the attic window to make sure that I'm driving slow."

"I'm not crazy enough to make a bet like that." Grandpa and I laughed as he started the car, drove out of the driveway and headed into town.

"Grandpa, I'll need you to stop by the city dump. I need to leave a note for someone."

"Carl, you will not be able to call me grandpa anymore when we are out in public. When you are in uniform, you will have to call me Captain Wilson. If we are in street clothes, you will have to call me Mr. Wilson or Russell, since many people in the city know that our son disappeared many years ago; and there would be no way that we should have anyone around that would be calling me grandpa."

"Yes Sir, Captain Wilson."

"If we have any slip-ups, we could all end up in jail, and no one will be going home. Now Carl, where abouts do you need me to stop so you can leave your note?"

"Pull up to the fence by the main gate. This won't take long."

"Do you need any paper or something to write with?"

"No, I prepared the note earlier, and it is all ready to go."

Grandpa stopped the car and I got out and walked over to the gate and lifted up the cap to place my note in the end cap. As I lifted it up, a piece of paper fell out of the cap and floated to the ground. I looked around and then looked at grandpa to see what his reaction was to the paper note floating to the ground. Grandpa had no reaction; maybe he did not see the paper fall. I gracefully reached down and picked up the note. The note read: "Hurry! Meet tonight here at dusk."

I read the note twice more, and then I put the paper in my mouth, chewed it into small pieces and spit them out. I didn't know what to do about the note. Amber had said to me not to write anything on my paper when I left the note. I would have to be very careful when I came back tonight just in case it was a trap, but I would have to come because the note sounded so urgent. I walked back to the car and got in.

Grandpa looked at me and asked, "Well, Carl, what did the note say that hit the ground, and why didn't you leave your note?"

"The note said to hurry and that we should meet tonight."

"What about your note? Don't you have to leave it here?"

"No, it doesn't matter now. We need to get to the Abernathys and talk with them to find out if they will help us."

"Carl, you look like you're a little puzzled. What is wrong?"

"Amber left a note for me."

"What is wrong with that?"

246

"That was not the plan. I was to leave a piece of paper in the end cap of the gatepost to let her know that I had an answer and that we should meet."

"Carl, I do have to say that I'm a little puzzled myself. You wrote a note but you did not leave it behind, but you are worried because Amber left you a note. Can you explain?"

"Grandpa, here is the paper I was going to leave for Amber."

"The paper is blank!"

"That's right. Amber did not want me to write anything on my note in case the police would happen to see me leave it there, and they would then know when and where to set up a trap."

"Carl, I see now why you are a little puzzled. Do you think the note is from Amber or from the state police?"

"That is a good question; one I will not have the answer for until I meet tonight."

"Carl, hearing what you have told me, I don't think it is a good idea to meet tonight. It sounds too much like a trap the police would set up."

"How would the police know to put the note in the end cap?"

"Maybe the police saw Amber put her note in and then they came and switched it out with their note to set up a trap to catch you."

"Grandpa, you have a point there. But I'm still going to come here and see who shows up."

"Okay, Carl, do what you think is best, but I'm coming with."

"No, I must go alone because if it is Amber, she would not show herself. Then she would think I had set a trap for her. No, I must go alone."

The car got very quiet during the ride to see the Abernathys. Grandpa pulled the car up to the curb and shut off the engine. I reached out my hand and placed in on grandpa's arm.

"Grandpa, are you mad at me?"

"No, Carl, I'm not mad at you. I'm just worried that you may get caught."

"Grandpa, it will be all right. I'll meet with Amber, and I'll be home either tonight or in the morning, but I will be careful."

"Okay, Carl. I believe you and enough said. What do you say we go talk with our friends, Aaron and Marian."

"Yes sir, Captain Wilson."

"Oh, Carl, I like that! It sounded like you are a real police officer."

"Well, let's see what they have to say, Captain Wilson."

"Carl, you will have to let me do the talking since I am the captain."

"Yes sir."

We had not yet reached the front steps to the house and the front door opened. Grandpa and I both slowed our pace to see what was about to take place. Aaron came out the door and asked, "What can I do for you, Officers?"

"Aaron, it's me, Russell Wilson."

"Good afternoon, Russell. I did not recognize you with the sun in my eyes. What brings you out our way?"

"I was wondering if we could go inside. I have a few questions for you and Marian."

"Sure, come on in. I'll have Marian put a pot of coffee on."

"That won't be necessary. We won't take up much of your time."

"You will be here long enough to eat a piece of Marian's pie, won't you?"

I leaned over and whispered in grandpa's ear, "Take the pie. It is the best."

"Well, Russell, from the way it looks, your partner here is a pie eater."

"Aaron, you have talked us into it. Bring on the pie."

I was surprised that Aaron had not recognized me, but maybe the sun was still in his eyes. As I passed through the door, I looked down and away from Aaron. I would wait until grandpa said it was okay to reveal myself to the Abernathys; because as far as Aaron knew, I was just another police officer.

"Russell, come in and take a seat over there on the couch. Let's talk, and you can ask your questions. Marian, we have guests. It's Russell Wilson and another officer."

Marian came into the living room. I looked her in the eyes and her face lit up. "Carl, we meet again," said Marian.

"It is nice to see you again, too, Marian."

"Good afternoon, Russell. I see you are in your uniform. I would suppose this is a business call."

"I do have a few questions that I would like to ask you and Aaron about some things that have taken place in the past few days."

Aaron was nervous. He was wringing his hands and his right foot was moving non-stop. Marian on the other hand was calm and had leaned back in her chair.

"Ask your questions, Russell. We are all friends, and we have nothing to hide from you and the state. Aaron, quit wringing your hands. It makes you look like you're guilty of something. Go ahead, Russell. What is your first question?"

"A few days ago this officer met with you in the park, and you invited him into your home. He said that you had talked about the Zablings and about the activities that happened on the farm over a large period of time. Is that true?"

Aaron spoke in a very nervous voice and asked grandpa, "Why does the state care about what we said about something that happened so many years ago? Don't they have anything better to do?"

"Hush up, Aaron! I'll answer that question, Russell. Yes, we did talk about our good friends, the Zablings. As I remember, your mother and father were very good friends to

249

the Zablings also, and they were your neighbors. Surely the state is not forbidding us to talk about old friends."

"No, Marian, the state has not gone that far."

Aaron leaned forward in his chair and blurted out, "Yet!"

Marian rolled up the dish towel in her hand and threw it into the face of Aaron. "Aaron, would you please be quiet? Continue Russell."

"This officer said that you made mention of the Christians and that the state had imprisoned the parents. You felt that the state had forced the kids to live on the street. Is that true?"

"Well, Russell, if Carl here said that is what we talked about; well then, it must be true. I don't think that a fine young man like Carl would lie about a thing like that, with him being a Christian himself."

"Marian, now I may be a friend; but I am also an officer of the state."

Grandpa was about to say more but Marian cut him off, "Yes, Russell, I know that. Have you noticed how much Carl looks like someone we know?" Marian didn't even give grandpa time to take a breath before she jumped in again and said, "Your son, Mark, was about this age when he came up missing. If one would put a picture of Mark next to Carl's face, I would think that there would be a lot of similarities. You know, I think it would be very interesting if I would call my old friend at the state and they could do a blood test and check his DNA. There were some simple questions that Carl could not or would not answer when we were talking with him."

Now grandpa was starting to wring his hands. I didn't know what to do to help him get out of this jam. I don't think he had expected to have the questioning turn on him.

"Well, I think we have enough answers to our questions. I think we should be getting back to the station," Grandpa said as we both stood up.

"Sit down, Russell. And that goes for you too, Carl. I think that would be Carl Wilson, isn't that right?"

"Yes, Marian, you are right. Grandpa, I think we will have to trust them. Marian, when did you put it all together?"

"When I held the picture up to your face the first time that you were here. Then when I saw you and your grandfather in the same room, I knew."

"Do you know what we are here for?"

"Now that I have no idea except that you must need our help."

"You're right. We need your help."

"What is that you need help with?"

"I'm planning to take as many people as I can back to the settlement that the Zablings had talked about."

"So this settlement does exist."

"Yes, it does."

"Aaron and I would like to help in any way we can. If we were younger, we would go with you, but our health is not very good. Russell, you tell us what you want us to do, and we will do it."

"It is not for me to say, Marian. Carl is in charge of the operation."

"What? How can that be? He is just a boy."

"He may be a young man, but he is the only one that knows the way to the settlement. He thinks that if he is the only one that knows the way, the police cannot force us to tell and put the settlement in danger."

"Thank you, Grandpa. With that out of the way, here is how you can help. I will give you a list of things that you can look for that we can take back to the settlement. Also, we may need to use your house as a place that if anything would go wrong, some of our people would be able to make it here and be safe until new plans can be made to get them out of the city. Is that a possibility?"

Aaron spoke up, "Yes, we would be happy to do this. It would be like taking the place of Dwayne and Janice and the work that they did so many years ago."

"Aaron," Carl said hesitantly, "the young boy that Dwayne and Janice took a beating for the last time was my dad."

A stunned look came across Aaron's face. Then he spoke, "The sacrifice that Dwayne and Janice gave has made it possible to have you come back and bring more people to freedom." Marian grabbed Aaron's arm and pulled him close. Aaron looked into her eyes and without a word said between them Aaron said, "We . . . will do what needs to be done."

"Thank you, Aaron and Marian. We do have a few problems. One is that there is a K-9 officer named Shawn Murphy that knows I'm here from the settlement, so we can assume that the state knows also."

"Shawn Murphy is related to the Zablings. How can that be a problem?" asked Aaron.

"He is playing both sides. He says one thing to me, and then turns around and tells the state what we are doing."

"That can't be true!" Aaron and Marian exclaimed in unison.

"I'm sorry to say, but it is true. I heard it myself on a police radio that the kids have."

Grandpa said, "So that is how the kids always seem to be one step ahead of us."

"The leader of the kids said that we could possibly use Shawn to our advantage somehow."

"Carl, who is this leader of the kids?" asked Aaron. Grandpa started to laugh before I could answer. "Russell, what is so funny?"

"Oh, you'll see."

"No!" Aaron shouted. "Don't tell me it's another kid."

"Even better, Aaron. The leader of the kids is Amber."

"Russell, what is going on here? Has everyone gone mad? You can't have two kids run an operation like this and expect to win against the state."

I stood up and looked Aaron in the eyes and proudly stated, "It was a kid that outfoxed the state many years ago to make it to the settlement, and to this day they still wonder where he is. And we will do it again."

"I believe you will, Carl."

"Thank you, Marian. I'm glad someone believes in me."

Marian stood up and said, "Why don't I get us all some pie and eat while we finish talking about how we can help you."

We talked for the next half hour about the plans that we had made while we were at grandma and grandpa's house. Aaron and Marian agreed that the plan should work.

As the four of us finished up our pie, Aaron said, "I'm still wondering whether or not Ernie will be able to make the trip."

"Grandpa and I will be going to the hospital now after we leave here and try to get in to talk with Ernie and let him know what we are planning. Then we can see if he would like to go back with us or if we think that he would be able to make the trip without jeopardizing the operation."

"Leave a message at grandma and grandpa's saying the apple pie is done and you can pick it up tonight. Then I'll come by at night and load the supplies up in the dark so that your neighbors won't be able to see what is happening."

Aaron had this look on his face as if to say, don't you think that the message is a little silly? Grandpa saw it too. "Aaron, you're probably thinking we are a little silly with the coded message, but we're not. The state police had our computer bugged. It has been that way ever since Mark left, and there is nothing we can do about it. If we tried to take it out, the state would be over to our house so fast, and we would be in jail. We should be able to use the computer bugging to our advantage."

"Again, Grandpa and I would like to thank you for being on our side and helping with 'Operation Exodus'. Marian, I need to get my knapsack that I left the first time I was here."

"I put it in the other room for safekeeping. Come with me and get it."

I followed Marian down the hall to the back room. Once we got into the room, I saw that she had my knapsack hanging on the closet doorknob. I grabbed the knapsack and made my way to the door. Then I stopped.

"What's wrong, Carl?"

"You asked me once if I was a Christian, and I told you that I thought you knew. I need to ask you. Are you and Aaron Christians?"

"Aaron and I are Christians."

"But Aaron gave me the impression he was not a Christian."

"That was an act. We were not sure if you were the police or not. It wasn't until we met you that we could see that there was so much more we could do than to keep it to ourselves. I had a dream last night that Aaron and I were at the police station being questioned about the street kids, about the amount of time we spend in the park, and what did we know about a Carl Wilson. I did not know what to think of that dream; but now, after today, the dream makes a lot more sense."

I walked over to Marian and gave her a hug and whispered, "We will be praying for you that God will use you more and more each day not just to help us get out of the city, but that you will be bold enough to tell others about the truth of the gospel of Jesus Christ. Grandpa and I found some gospel tracks up in their attic. I'd like to give them to you and Aaron to hand out."

Unclenching from our hug Marian said, "For a young man, you are very wise. Aaron and I will need every one of your prayers, even when you get back to the settlement."

"You can count on that. I will never forget you. My butt is still al little sore from when you shot me with that rock from your slingshot."

"Yes, that was a good shot."

"We better get back to the others before they wonder what we are doing."

"Yes."

"Well, Grandpa, are you ready to go to the hospital and see if we can find Ernie?"

"Yes I am, Officer Wilson."

"I will have to remember to call you Captain Wilson while we are at the hospital, or we could blow our cover."

"Captain Wilson, I was talking with Marian, and I think it would be good to give them the little books we found in the attic. They can distribute them for us. They would be able to talk with the people that will want to receive Christ."

Grandpa looked a little disappointed; I think he wanted to give them out. I could tell by the way he asked Marian, "Is that true, Marian? You want to hand out the gospel tracks? The state police will put a lot of pressure on you, and it could mean jail."

Aaron moved next to Marian and took her hand into his. "Yes, Russell, we are ready to stand for what we believe in and not sit here and do nothing. We need to share it with our friends, our city and if we can, to the governor himself."

"All right, Aaron. I'll take that as a yes, you want the books. When I come to get the supplies you have gathered for us, I'll bring the books."

Marian grabbed Aaron's arm and gave it a squeeze. She looked at him and smiled saying, "We can do this. We <u>will</u> do this."

Aaron and Marian walked us out to the car and watched us drive away. We had only driven a few blocks when grandpa said, "That did not go quite as well as I had hoped, but all in all, things turned out very nicely. If the hospital visit goes well and we can convince Ernie that we are the good guys even though we are in state uniform, we will have a good start on 'Operation Exodus.'"

"Carl, we are coming up to the front of the hospital. I'll park over here next to the side exit for a fast get away if we run into trouble. Don't head for the main entrance; run for the car."

"Why? The main entrance would be the easiest way out."

"The reason why is that if they have a security problem at the hospital, they flip a switch and all the main doors lock first. Then the smaller side doors lock after that. It takes about five to ten minutes to lock down the hospital so you will have to move fast to the side entrance."

"What if I don't make it out in time?"

"You will only be able to hide for a while until they bring in the dogs. Then they will find you, and I will have to figure out how to get you out of jail."

"I tell you what. Let's not have any problems, and we'll all be much happier."

"Amen to that, Carl. Amen!"

Grandpa parked next to the door that said Same Day Surgery. It should help seeing that the door is red. If I got separated from grandpa, all I'd have to do is ask which way to Same Day Surgery, and they would point the way.

Grandpa turned the key and the engine shut off. That is when my stomach started to feel funny; I must be nervous. I was not this nervous when we stopped to see Aaron and Marian.

"Are you ready, Carl? You look scared."

"No Grandpa, I'm not scared; I'm just a little nervous. I don't want to say or do the wrong thing."

"Carl, being a little nervous is good. It will keep you on your toes; you will be just fine. Just let me to the talking, take off that nervous look and put on your mean look. Remember, you are playing the part of a police officer of the state."

"Yes Sir!"

"Let's go find Ernie!"

"Wait Grandpa!"

"Wait for what?"

"Do we know what Ernie looks like?"

"I'll just ask someone at the front desk."

"Can you do that?"

"Of course! I am a captain in the State Police Force."

"No need to wait any longer. Let's go find Ernie."

As we walked up the sidewalk toward the front door, I looked over at grandpa. He walked with authority radiating from him, and for just a moment, I had no fear.

"Good afternoon, Captain Wilson."

I stopped and looked at Grandpa, and then toward the voice that greeted him. It was another police officer. I looked to see if he was an officer that I would have to salute.

Grandpa helped me out by saying, "Good afternoon, Sergeant." We stopped walking and grandpa asked the sergeant a question. "Sergeant, do they still have that nut case locked up in the mental ward?"

"Which one, sir?"

"Oh, I'm not sure. I think that they call him Bernie or Ernie or something like that."

"Sir, there is an Ernie in cell 14 at the end of the ward."

"Thank you, Sergeant."

"Sir, can I ask you why you're looking for him?"

"Training for this rookie. They need to see what kind of nut cases they will have to deal with once they join the force."

"That is an excellent idea, Captain Wilson. I wish I would have had that training when I was a rookie."

Grandpa received a salute from the sergeant and he returned a salute back and said, "Carry on, Sergeant."

"Yes sir!"

We turned toward the front door again and the sergeant walked to a waiting squad car. "That was a great job on getting the information that we needed to find Ernie fast. We should be in and out in no time."

"Hold on there, Carl. Just because we know the cell number that Ernie is in does not get us inn to see him. We have to have a good reason to get into the ward first."

"Well, can't you use the same reason that you told the sergeant? That it is for training for a rookie?"

"We can give it a try, but I was hoping to avoid that by maybe finding someone there on the ward that I knew that would let us in without recording that we entered the ward. That way they wouldn't have any record of us even being here at the hospital."

"What about the sergeant? He knows that we were here and that we asked about Ernie."

"Yes, that is true. He knows, but without proof, he would not dare say anything for fear that I would get him posted on the worst job for what would seem like life."

"Could you really do that?"

"No, but this is what we officers tell them every day starting from their first day as a rookie. It helps keep them in line."

We were standing in front of the door to the hospital, but I couldn't see any doorknobs or handle to get in. Grandpa kept walking toward the door; it slid open without him even touching it. We walked quickly through the doors. I turned in time to see the door slide shut behind us. I so wanted to ask grandpa how he did that, but there was no time, and there were people running every which way. I needed to be close by grandpa so I didn't get lost in the sea of people that was swirling around us.

"Carl, follow me."

"Yes sir."

We headed down a corridor next to a small café. I saw a lady getting food. She held out her hand palm side down; the hand behind the counter passed a purple light over her hand and then she said thank you. The lady took her food and sat down at the table.

"Carl! What are you looking at?"

"That lady just got some food, the man passed a purple light over the back of her hand, and then she took the food. What just went on there?"

"Didn't your dad tell you that is how we pay for things in the city?"

"Yes. He said something about a tattoo, but I didn't see anything on her hand."

"They don't use the tattoo method anymore. Too many people were forging the tattoos, and it would goof up the system. Now they implant a microchip that can't be forged. The purple light reads the chip's code and whatever you're wanting is paid for if you have the credit with the state. How do they pay for things at the settlement?"

"We don't pay for anything."

"What? You don't have to pay for anything? We will have to talk about this later. There is a friend of mine at the desk we need to report to. Ben, my old friend, how are you doing?"

"Russell, it's been a long time since I've seen you. Who is the rookie?"

"Ben, you are just not going to believe this but his name is Carl . . . Get this now. It's Carl Wilson."

"No, you're pulling my leg. Well, now that you mention it, he does look like you, but only a whole lot better looking! Captain Wilson and I go way back to the good old days in high school. What can I do for you, Russell?"

"We would like to get in off the record to do a little training for the rookie."

"No problem, Russell. You know the routine. Ring the bell when you're ready to leave or if there is any trouble. Is there any person you're looking to see?"

"No, no one special. I just want the rookie to see what he will be in for when he gets done with his orientation for the state police."

"Remember, ring the bell to leave."

"Oh, Ben, I was going to ask you. Does Kevin Zabling still work this ward?"

"Yes he does, but he doesn't work for another two days. He just finished his week yesterday."

"I'll have to give him a call. It has been a long time since I've seen him too."

There was a loud buzz and then grandpa grabbed the handle to the heavy door and pulled it open. I was not ready for what I heard. There was screaming, yelling and crying from the people walking around this large open room. There were men dressed in white sitting behind a table reading newspapers. They dropped their papers for just a moment to see who entered the room, and then they went back to reading. All the windows had bars across them, and the chairs were chained to the walls. At a table in the center of the room were four men sitting and a fifth man was standing. It looked as if they were playing a game. I walked over to the table slowly to see what they were playing. One of the men sitting down looked at me with short, quick glances and the yelled at me, "Hey! You quit looking at my cards!"

"Sir, I'm not looking at your cards."

"Yes, you are. You're telling Perry what I have. Go away!"

I could see that my presence was upsetting him, so I turned to walk back over by grandpa. As I did, I ran into a man. I said I was sorry, but he said nothing back to me. I stepped to the right to walk around him, but he stepped in front of me. Then I stepped to the left and he once again followed my

same movements. This time I started to the right, then darted
to the left and I got around him. When I got over by grandpa,
I looked back at the man; he was walking toward me.

"Grandpa, this guy I ran into is coming over here, and he
is freaking me out. What do I do?"

"Show no fear. Look him in the eyes and tell him he
needs to go sit down over there by the window. We are trying
to talk here."

"Grandpa, do you see the size of this guy?"

"So what is the problem, Carl?"

"Okay. Here I go. Hey buddy, you need to go sit down
over by the window. The captain and I are talking."

The guy turned, walked away, and took a seat over by the
window just as I told him. He curled up in the chair and sat
there watching us. Each time I looked over at him, he would
wave to me as a little kid would wave. He was as gentle as
he was big.

Grandpa said, "Carl, we need to go down this hall to cell
14. It's down at the end of the hall. I talked to the men at the
table, and they said Ernie stays in his room most of the time.
I'm going to go in first and talk to him."

"I thought I would get a chance to talk with him."

"You will get your chance, but first I need to talk with
him. What I need you to do is see where those stairs go. Go as
far as you can go, but don't open any doors. If you come to a
door, stop, look at the door, and see if there are any wires that
would tell us if it is alarmed. Then come back up here and
wait outside the door until I tell you to come in. Got it?"

"Yes sir!"

"I'll see you in a little bit."

Grandpa entered Ernie's room. I watched through the
window hoping to see his face, but his back was toward me.
I glanced around to see if anybody was watching. The men
in white had their heads buried in their papers, and the men
playing cards were still playing. I could see now why they

were in this ward; they had no cards in their hands or on the table. It was all in their mind. My eye caught "the big guy" sneaking a peek at me from around a post. He waved at me and, of course, I waved back.

Standing at the tope of the stairs I listened. There was dead silence. I walked down the first length of stairs talking my time so as not to be surprised by someone other than Ben that would not like me snooping around. All was clear so I headed down the next length of stairs. There was a hallway with not much lighting. Just then a door partway down the hall flew open and a basket on wheels rolled out into the hallway. Then the door slammed shut. Quickly I moved with my back pressed tightly along the side of the wall that the door opened on so that if the door would open up again, whoever was in the room would not be able to see me. I came closer to the door and could hear muffled talking and some banging, but I couldn't tell what they were saying or what the banging was. Just a few feet from the door I had to make a decision to run past the door and move on down the hall or turn back. Grandpa wanted me to see what I could find down the stairs. I needed to move past the door. Now I could not hear much banging and the talking was faint, but I could tell there were still people in that room. I would run past the door. I pushed off the wall and crossed in front of the door when it flew open and another basket on wheels rolled out the door and into my leg.

I found myself looking directly into the faces of two men who were working in the laundry room of the hospital. When they saw me in the state uniform, it struck them with fear. I grabbed the basket, pushed it back into the room that it came from, and began to yell at the two men asking them all kinds of questions and not giving them time to answer before I shouted out the next question. The men were shaking so much I started to feel bad that I was so hard on them.

"You, what's your name?"

"Bruce, sir."

"Where does that door there lead to?"

Bruce was shaking so much he could hardly talk. "Sir, that leads to the outside courtyard."

"Can you get to the parking lot from there?"

"No sir. The courtyard is all fenced in with razor wire on top."

"Let's take a walk outside, men."

"Sir, we need to get our work done."

"Bruce, if I remember right, I didn't give you a choice. So move it!"

"Yes sir!"

Once outside I could see the courtyard was about 30 square feet with a ten-foot high fence with the razor wire on top just like Bruce had said. One thing I noticed was a manhole cover in the center of the court.

"Bruce, come here. Those windows up there, where do they go to?"

"Those windows go to the doctor's lounge. Why do you ask?"

The question caught me off guard for just a few seconds, and then I answered Bruce, "I'm the one that asks the questions, not you."

"Yes sir."

"Now just get back in the building."

While the men ran back to the door, I took one more quick look around hoping to find a way out of the hospital besides the front door. The only thing was if the tunnel under the manhole cover would link up with the tunnels that my dad talked about; then that could be of some help, if Ernie was able to move well enough. When I walked back in, I saw a bag of dirty laundry come crashing through two doors on the far wall. There were two sets of doors.

"Bruce, where does that door lead to?"

"That is the dirty linens shoot. Each floor has a room where they drop the soiled linens down the shoot to us here."

"How do you get the clean linens back up to them?"

"That is easy. We push the carts over to the "cart only" elevator and send it up to the floor we want it to go to. Then we walk up the stairs, pull it off the elevator and push the cart to the linen closet on each floor."

"Have you ever taken a ride in this elevator?"

"No sir!"

Just then I saw his co-worker look at Bruce and give him a funny look. "Bruce, you would not be lying to me, are you? Because if you are and I find out . . . . Well, let's just say it would not be a fun time for you."

Bruce began to stammer, "Well, let me think now. Now that I think about it, I may have at one time ridden up the elevator a while back. Yes, now that I think about it more, I did."

"How much weight will it carry?"

"Our boss said that it would hold 400 pounds and not much more."

"Show me how it works."

Bruce raced over to the controls and showed me the buttons to push. "Well Gentlemen, you have been a great help. I expect you to keep our conversation a secret. Our time together never happened, did it?"

"What conversation, sir?"

Bruce was only too willing to please me. I didn't trust him. I headed for the hallway, but as I reached for the door, I stopped, turned quickly and said, "If you men would ever like to join the state police, we are always looking for a few good men like you."

I rushed out the door and made my way to the stairs to meet up with grandpa and to see what he had found out about Ernie. When I reached the main lobby of the hospital, I did not see grandpa anywhere around, so I walked up the hallway to look for him. It was sad to see so many people in this condition. This strange feeling came over me that someone was watching me. I turned around, and there was "the big guy" just three feet behind me.

"What is your name?" I asked.

"I'm called Bear."

"Why do they call you that?"

"That's the name my parents gave me. It's a nice name. Don't you think, Mr. Policeman?"

"Yes I do. It is a very nice name."

"Are you going to go into Ernie's room too? That's where the other policeman went."

"Yes I am, Bear. Does Ernie have a lot of people visit him?"

"No, not for a long time."

"Thank you, Bear. You have been a big help. Say, Bear, would you like to help some more?"

"You just ask, and I will do anything."

"Well, Bear, there is nothing you can do now." Bear looked so sad when I told him there was nothing for him to do. "Bear, if there is anything for you to do, you'll be the first I will look up to have help me."

"Yes, sir, I'll be waiting."

Bear stuck his hand out for me to shake. The size of his hand was huge. As I reached out to shake his hand, my hand was swallowed up inside of his. Bear smiled that we shook hands. I could feel the strength that he possessed, and I was very glad Bear was my friend.

"Goodbye, Mr. Policeman."

"Bear, you can call me Carl. That's what friends do."

"Okay! Goodbye, Carl."

As I approached the door to Ernie's cell, I could hear grandpa talking to Ernie. "Ernie, in just a little while, you will meet a young man that came to my home with an amazing story. At first I did not want to believe, but later on I thought, how could I not."

"Russell, who is this young man that you would come here to talk to me about him?"

Ernie's voice was strong and clear for as old as I imagined him. Grandpa was about to tell Ernie who I was when I walked in and introduced myself. "If I may, Sir. I would like to tell Ernie who I am."

Ernie spoke before I could tell him who I was. "Mark Wilson, is that you?"

"No, sir, my name is . . . ."

"You sure look like a kid I knew a long time ago. His name was Mark Wilson."

"Yes sir. I know Mark Wilson very well. He is my dad, and he said that when I got to the city, I should look you up and say hello from him."

"Mark made it to the settlement and he still remembers me."

"Ernie, my dad talks about you often and how you helped him."

"How is Mark doing there in the settlement?"

"My dad is a pastor at the church, and he helps in the school."

"Mark was a smart kid. I knew he could find the settlement; but for him to become a pastor, now that is amazing. Did Mark send you to come and get me?"

"Ernie, I'm sorry to say, no. This was my decision to come back to the city and find my grandparents. It was when my father was unaware that I was listening when he spoke into the darkness of the tunnel maybe hoping that the sound would carry to my ears. His wish was to see you again."

"Carl, as I was telling Russell, I'm too old to make the trip. I would just slow you down. It would be like you trying to bring back a bunch of kids. You would have to be insane to try something like that."

"Well, Ernie, call me crazy, because that is what I'm going to do. I have about 50-70 kids ranging from age 5 to 16 that will be making the trip along with my grandparents and you."

"Russell, he can't be serious. Stop him from this crazy plan."

"I would like to, but I'm not the one in charge of 'Operation Exodus.'"

"Who is in charge?"

When Ernie looked at me; I just smiled and said, "The person in charge. That would be me! Now that we have that all straightened out, I'll get a message to you as to what day we will be leaving. Have your things and self ready in two days, because we could leave at any time from then on."

"What would the staff think if I had my things packed as if I was going someplace?"

"Tell them you're taking a trip to a far away land flowing with milk and honey. They would just think you're crazy, but then they think that already. We know that is not true."

"Carl, I'll be ready."

"Ernie, I have one question. What can you tell me about a fellow inmate called Bear?"

"Bear has been in here for a long time. Most of the staff can't remember when he got here, and some are not sure why he was put in here. Some say he hurt a man during a fight over a loaf of bread that he had found in the trash out behind the store. The story goes that he was bringing it home to his three children."

"Can he be trusted?"

"That is a tough question to answer, but I would think so."

"We may need him if there happens to be any problems. Ernie, whatever happened to Bear's kids?"

"No one really knows. Some say they died out in the forest. Others say they're still out there waiting for their father to come home to them."

"That is very interesting. I think it is time to head home and see what grandma has cooking for us for supper."

"Carl, that is a great idea," Grandpa answered.

"Carl, I have one more question."

"What is that, Ernie?"

"How will you get a message in here?"

"Trust me. I'll get it in here, and you'll know it is from me." I reached out my hand to shake Ernie's. "Ernie, it has been a pleasure to meet you. Now I have a face to go with all the stories that my dad has told me for all these years."

Grandpa patted Ernie on the back as we walked to the doorway of his room. Ernie watched as Grandpa and I walked to the desk area to get let out. The buzzer sounded and Grandpa grabbed the door handle. We exited and quickly headed down the hall to the main door. As we approached the main door, I could see out of the corner of my eye that someone was walking along side us trying to cut us off from exiting the hospital.

I could not see who it was, so I whispered to grandpa what I was seeing. He quickly glanced over and then said, "Carl, it's okay. It is Doctor Kittleson, my doctor. Hello, Doctor Kittleson. Are you needing to talk to me?"

"Yes, I would like to talk to you, but I see you are working." The look on the doctor's face when he realized that I was the boy on the road a few days back was priceless. "Carl!"

"Yes sir."

"You are Carl, the one I met on the road while I was out running down by the river?"

"Yes sir, I am that Carl."

"I'm just a little surprised to see you in . . . ."

"In the uniform of the state police."

"Yes!"

"Captain Wilson, I think it would be a good idea to move this conversation into my private office so we don't have any extra ears listening in on what we have to say."

"That is a very good idea. Yes, by all means; let's go to your office."

The three of us moved swiftly to the office and shut the door. Grandpa asked the doctor if the office was clean of listening devices by writing a message on a notepad on the doctor's desk.

"Yes, we are safe to talk. What are you doing here in the hospital today? Our appointment isn't for another two weeks."

When I heard that, I looked at grandpa to see if I could figure out what was wrong with him that he would need to see the doctor. "Carl, I'm okay. Don't worry."

Now the doctor was looking at both Grandpa and I wondering why grandpa was sharing personal information with a rookie. "Doctor Kittleson, I can see by your face that you're a little confused with the conversation I'm having with my rookie. Well, let me clear things up for you since you're a man that can be trusted. Carl here is not really a rookie. He is my grandson."

"No Russell, that can't be. That would mean that your son would have had to get a wife and have a child. And you yourself once said that the odds of Mark being alive was very small."

"Well, Doctor, believe it. My son it alive and has not only a son but a daughter as well."

"Where has he been living all this time? Have you talked with him?"

"No. Not yet."

"Why not?"

"Doctor Kittleson, it is not that easy."

Just then you could see that the light had come on in the good doctor's brain. "Russell, are you trying to tell me that the stories of the secret settlement are true?"

"Yes I am."

"Carl, did you come from that settlement?"

I looked at Grandpa for some kind of help not knowing if I should answer the question. "It is okay, Carl. You can tell him."

"Yes, Doctor Kittleson, I'm from the settlement."

"Are you going back?"

"Yes we are," answered Grandpa.

The doctor didn't say anything. He pulled out his chair from behind his desk, sat down and stared at the mountain of paperwork. His head shot up and he entreated grandpa, "Russell, take me with you. I can be of great help to the people out in the wilderness. I have been studying up on the subject of medicine back when this country was first settled. Please take me with you."

"It is not up to me, Doctor Kittleson."

"Then who? Let me talk to the one in charge. I'll plead my case in front of him."

Grandpa said to the doctor, "You just did."

"Russell, you are confusing me. You just got done saying that you were not in charge; and the only other person in the room is Carl, your grandson." There was silence in the room. I looked over at Grandpa. He looked at me and just raised his eyebrows. The doctor then blurted out, "Carl! Carl is in charge?"

"SHHH! Yes, I'm in charge, Doctor Kittleson. The settlement can use a doctor."

"Thank you! Could you use a great nurse?"

"Who is this nurse?"

"Nurse Glover."

"Can she be trusted?"

"She would work on many of the Christians before they were locked up. From time to time she would see kids out by the dump and would work on them. She told me that a few days ago she worked on a young man to pull a bullet out of his arm."

I rolled up my sleeve and showed him the damage the bullet did.

"It was you!"

"Yes, it was me."

"Can I take a look at it?" I moved around to the other side of the desk. "Hmmm. It looks very good for not making a trip into the hospital. I told you that Nurse Glover was a great nurse."

"Would she go with us?"

"Yes, she has no family."

"Doctor Kittleson, you know that once you leave here and enter the settlement that you can no longer return to the city."

"Yes, I know. That is the way that it will have to be."

"Is Nurse Glover working today?"

"Yes she is."

"Would it be possible to talk with her now? You see, we will be leaving in less than a week, and as short as two days from now. We will need her answer."

"I'll page her to my office, and you can ask her yourself."

While the doctor paged for Nurse Glover to come to his office, I leaned over and whispered, "It will be good to have more help from adults for when we make the trip back to the settlement. It is not an easy trip, and some of the kids will need some help."

The door opened behind us. Nurse Glover walked in and said, "Yes, Doctor. What is it that I can do for you? Oh, I'm sorry. I didn't know that you had someone in the office with you."

"It is all right, Nurse Glover. These men would like to ask you a few questions."

"Yes, anything for the state police."

You could hear the fear in her voice as she answered. "Is that true, Nurse Glover?" I questioned. I had not turned around so she did not know who asked the question.

"Yes sir."

"Is it true that you helped a young man that had a bullet in his arm?"

She said nothing. I stood up, turned around and said, "Thank you for doing that."

The look of relief on Nurse Glover's face said it all. Then she came over and gave me a tap along side the head. "Don't ever do that again. You about gave me a heart attack. Now you said that you had a few questions for me. What are they?"

"What do you know about a place called by some as the settlement?" asked grandpa.

"Some say there is one."

"No, Nurse Glover. I don't want to know what others think. I want to know what you know or think about the settlement."

"I believe there is a place. Where it is, I don't know. I wish I did know where it was; because if I did, I would be gone in a heartbeat leaving this nasty old city behind and never ever coming back."

"Nurse Glover, what would you say if I told you that I know a person that has been to the settlement and has come here to bring back some people."

"Tell me who that person is. I need to talk to that person."

"What would you say to the person in charge?"

The doctor began to snicker. Nurse Glover turned to look at him to see what he thought was so funny. The light must have come on in Nurse Glover's mind. There was another tap up along the side of my head.

I spun around and said, "What was that for?"

"You know very well what that is for. You are the person in charge, as silly as that sounds. But right now I don't care who is in charge; I want to go to the settlement. So Carl, will you take me with you?"

"Yes. Welcome to the team."

"When do we leave?"

"You will need to be ready any time from two days from now to as long as a week depending on how long it will take to get the rest of the people ready. There are some things that you both will need to bring with you, but only the necessities. One being as many medical supplies as you can get your hands on. Our time is getting short, and we need to get going."

We said our goodbyes and left the doctor's office. We took a side entrance to get to the parking lot so we wouldn't run into any people that would wonder why we were at the hospital and start to ask questions or, worse yet, inquire about our activities to police headquarters. We had just left the building when grandpa pushed me into the bushes along the side of the building. I fell to the ground next to a large bush. Grandpa stepped over me and crouched down.

I said, "Hey, what did you do . . . ?"

Grandpa's big hand clamped over my mouth and with his other hand pressed a finger up to his lips to tell me not to say anything. I nodded my head and he removed his hand from my mouth. Then he placed it on top of my head and pivoted my head to show me that there were three police cars pulling up to the front of the hospital. We couldn't do anything until they left. Grandpa whispered in my ear that this could be coincidental that the police were here, or someone called us into the police. We would have to check that out before we made our next appearance at the hospital so we knew who to watch out for next time.

I leaned over and asked grandpa, "Are you okay?"

"Yes, I'll be fine. These old knees of mine don't like being crouched like this, so I hope that the police move on soon. I still have to go into work tonight, and I was hoping to get some supper before I dropped you off at the dump. I need to take care of the things in the state computers that we had talked about."

The side door opened up. The same door that grandpa and I came out of. I parted some of the branches of the bush to see who was coming down the sidewalk. I was not happy to see that it was Shawn Murphy and King, his dog. We would be caught for sure once King caught our scent. I turned to grandpa and spoke without saying anything hoping that he would be able to read my lips and that Shawn Murphy and his dog were about to find us. Grandpa read my lips just fine, and his eyes grew large. All he could do was shake his head. King started to bark and pull Shawn in our direction, but Shawn pulled him back next to him. King darted off the sidewalk toward the bushes that we were hiding in. King had now peaked the interest of Shawn as to what he was alerted about.

"What is it, King? Did you find yourself a rabbit?"

King barked and barked as he drew nearer to our hiding place. When I looked through the bushes, King was getting so close it was like he was looking into my eyes and was determined to find me. Just then Shawn's police radio blasted out to call off the search for the lady stealing food from the kitchen.

"Come on, King. Let's go back to the car."

Shawn pulled on the leash to get King turned around and headed back to the car. King's nose was only a few feet from the bushes. King let loose with a couple more barks so loud that it made my ears ring.

"That's right, King. You tell that rabbit that it is his lucky day, because you have to go back to work or you would give him a run for his money."

Little did Shawn know that we were the rabbits and that it would have been his lucky day to catch both grandpa and me at the same time. King kept looking back at the bushes and would bark a little token bark to let us know that he almost had us. The three police cars drove out of the driveway and headed back into the city the opposite direction that we would be going.

Grandpa tapped me on the shoulder and said, "Carl, I'm going to need a little help getting up. My knee has been bent this way too long."

Grandpa placed one hand on my shoulder and the other on my knee to push himself up. I could see that there was a lot of pain in just getting up. He rubbed his knew a little and looked at me seeing that I was concerned for him.

"I'll be okay, Carl. Just don't say anything to your Grandma, or I'll never hear the end of it. A while back the doctors said that I should have my knee worked on, but I put it off. Now I think I should have let them work on it. Let's get to the car and get home before something else happens."

I stood up and grandpa and I looked around to make sure that it was safe to come out of the bushes. "Grandpa, it looks clear to me. What do you think?"

"You're right, Carl. I don't see anybody. Let's go now."

We walked out of the bushes as if there was nothing wrong and made our way to the car in the parking lot. Safely in the car, we both looked at each other and breathed a sigh of relief.

"Carl, I hope we don't have too many run-ins with the police like that before we leave. That was a little too close for comfort."

"I remember my dad saying how the police treated him each time they got a hold of him. Then he would say, 'Carl, be glad that you are here in the settlement and you will never have to feel the heavy hand of the police or a swift kick to the body.' Wait until I tell him that I may have missed the hand and the boot, but the bullet was not much fun."

"Carl, I sure can tell you are my grandson just by some of the things that you say. It is so much like Mark. I have to keep reminding myself to call you Carl and not Mark."

"Let's head for home. We both still have a very long night ahead of us."

"I hope your Grandma has something good cooking."

The trip home was fast. We said nothing to each other. We put all our attention on looking for the police. As we pulled into the driveway, we could see that Grandma was standing in the window.

"Grandpa, what is Grandma doing in the window with her hands?"

"She is giving a signal that there are police waiting in the house and that I should pull the car all the way into the garage and come in alone. You better duck down until we get into the garage."

"Then what? Should I take the tunnel into the basement?"

"NO! Wait until I come and get you; but if by chance the police would come looking in the garage, go into the tunnel but do not come into the house until I come and get you."

"How did you know that grandma was saying all that?"

"When your dad left, the police came often, and I would come into the house talking about things that we didn't want the police to know. There sitting in my living room would be the police, and I would have to somehow explain what I was saying. We came up with some simple signals to let each other know the status of the house."

Grandpa turned into the driveway. From the floor of the car I watched him wave to grandma with the back of his hand. "Grandpa, why are you waving like that?"

Grandpa looked straight ahead and talked with his teeth clinched tightly together, but I could understand what he was saying. "Carl, I can't look at you just in case there are police with binoculars watching. If I would look down at you, then they would know that there was someone else in the car with me. The reason I waved backward to your grandma is because that was a sign that I did receive the message and we are ready. Be prepared to be out in the garage for a while."

"Grandpa, I need to get back into town to meet up with Amber to get things ready so we can leave."

"Carl, right now neither one of us can do anything until the police back off. I'm thinking that they will back off when I go to work in a few hours." I felt us pull into the garage and grandpa pushed a button to the garage door so it would close by itself. "Carl, don't move. There is a policeman by the back window of the garage. I'll go out and talk to him and draw him away from the window. You better make your way into the tunnel and stay there. We will try to get you in the house as soon as possible. What I need you to do is to be ready to slightly open the door on your side of the car, but don't get out until I draw the policeman away. Then slip out and don't shut the door. It will make too much noise." I nodded my head. "On the count of three. One, two, three. Very good, Carl. Now, give me two minutes to draw the policeman away from the garage so he doesn't hear you moving around as the work your way into the tunnel."

Grandpa slammed his car door and the car shook back and forth. He started talking to the policeman even before he got out of the garage. I heard the service door on the side of the garage slam. I couldn't hear well enough to understand what they were talking about. I raised my head slightly and looked over the seat toward grandpa. Grandpa had worked it so that the policeman's back was facing the garage and I could see grandpa's face. He must have seen me looking because he started to rub his eye and the hand he rubbed it with had his pinky finger sticking out. For just a second I thought about what an odd way it was to rub his eye. Then it hit me. It was grandpa's signal for me to move to the tunnel now. I opened the door and slid out of the car as if I was a snake crawling on the floor to stay out of sight. I made my way into the tunnel and closed the trap door behind me.

Grandpa's voice became quite loud and clear. They were in the garage.

"Captain Wilson, thank you for cooperating with us."

"It is my duty to help find those scummy kids. They say that the kids have been on the move a lot more this week. What does the state think is happening?"

"The state is not sure, but they have us searching all the outer edges of town to see if we can find anything."

"If you need to look in the house, we would be happy to have you look."

"I don't think that will be necessary with you being a captain in the state police. A kid would have to be out of his mind to hide in your house."

"You have a point there, Officer. Are you done here? I need to get in and eat, because I still have to go to work tonight."

"Yes Sir. I'm all done here."

I heard them both leave so I moved my way to the end of the tunnel. Then when it was time to enter the house, I'd be there ready to move. It seemed like forever as I sat in the dark waiting for them to say it was clear and that is was all right to come out. Finally I heard grandma's voice calling me.

"Carl, it is all right to come out. Supper is ready."

I opened the tunnel door and made my way out. There was grandma waiting for me. "Are you hungry, Carl?"

"Hungry! It's like I haven't eaten in days."

"Let's go up, and you tell me all that happened."

"Grandma, how come grandpa didn't come down and get me?"

"It seems that his knee has blown up like a balloon. I have him sitting in his chair with ice on it since he still has to go to work yet tonight. We will need to get it so he can walk."

"What is for supper, Grandma?"

"Well, we had some chicken in the freezer, and I fried that up. We have white rice, salad and some blueberry muffins."

"My dad always did say that you were a great cook, and now I can say for sure it is true. You are the best."

I closed up the tunnel and followed grandma upstairs to the kitchen table. There was grandpa with a huge bag of ice on his knee sitting at the table waiting for us to come up from the basement.

Grandma said, "I will pray for our food. 'Dear Lord, Thank you for this food that we have before us tonight. Bless it to our bodies, and heal the old broken bodies that are around this table. Thank you, Lord, for bringing my men home to me, and watch over them as they go out into the night. Bring them home again. Amen!"

I opened my eyes and Grandma was wiping tears from her eyes. Grandpa was comforting her by rubbing her back. Through her tears Grandma said, "I want you two men to be very careful when you are out tonight. Most certainly you, Carl."

"I will."

"Because you know that the police are out looking for you and the kids that you will be meeting with later tonight."

"Yes, I know. I figured that the police would be stepping up the pressure to find me. The longer I'm here and the more that we prepare to leave, we become more visible by the things that happen in town."

Nothing more was said as we filled our plates with the food that Grandma had prepared for supper and began to eat. There would be times when Grandpa and I would think of something that happened while we were in town that we thought Grandma would want to know about. Grandma was most curious about our time at the Abernathy's house and wondering how well they received the news that I was from the settlement. Grandma was most pleased to hear that Aaron took the news well and that they were willing to help.

"There are four muffins left, men. Go ahead and eat them up. I don't want to save them."

Grandpa reached for two muffins and put them on his plate. I said, "I'll take mine with me and let the kids share."

Grandpa took the muffins from his plate and said, "Give them my muffins too."

Grandma said, "I'll get you a plastic bag to put them in. Why don't I put some cookies in another bag."

"They would like that very much. I don't think they get many sweets."

"Carl, I will be leaving for work in about a half hour. You will need to be ready and in the garage to get in the car for your ride to your meeting with Amber and the kids."

"I'll find my own way home and will enter in the house from the garage tunnel. If there is trouble and the police are in the house, have the shade open if it is at night; and if it is in the daylight, have the shade pulled down on the kitchen door. I will stay away until they are gone."

"That sounds like a good plan, Carl," Grandma and Grandpa both agreed.

"Carl, before you go to the basement, remember to stop in here and pick up the food for the kids."

"Yes, Grandma, I'll try to remember. May I be excused to go upstairs and get ready for my trip into town? I surely can't meet up with the kids wearing this police uniform. They would go crazy."

"Yes, Carl, you may be excused."

As I walked past Grandma, she reached out her hand and grabbed my arm and pulled me close to her and said, "Be very careful."

"I know, Grandma. I will be careful."

I started to walk away, but she pulled me back and hugged me without saying anything. When she released me from her hug, she said, "And don't be gone all night. You know I will not get any sleep until I know that you are up in that bed safe and sound."

"I'll try to be back as soon as I can, but I can't promise you that I will. I just don't know how soon I will meet up with the kids and what things we will have to get worked out to get them ready to leave."

The look on grandma's face said it all. She did not want to hear what I said, but that is the way it had to be. I rounded the corner into the hallway heading for the steps and met up with Grandpa.

"Carl, you handled that situation with your Grandma very well. She will still worry about you, but she knows that you are a very smart young man and that you will make it back; just not as fast as she would like you back."

"Grandpa, what time will your shift end?"

"Not until 6 am if all goes well and I get all the things I'll need to get done plus my police duties. My work on the computer will not take that long, but to find the time to get into the file when no one is monitoring them is a small window of opportunity. It has to be when they take their coffee breaks. I'll tell them they both can go at the same time and that I will monitor any computer activities that the state would want to know about."

"Would you be able to come to my rescue if the police happened to get too close to catching me?

There was a long pause, a very long pause before grandpa spoke, "No, I would not be able to. That would blow my cover and everything would be lost. We would all end up in jail. Carl, you are on your own tonight."

We walked up the stairs together and then separated at the top of the stairs. We went to our rooms to get ready for our missions.

Chapter 10

Men's Night Out

G randpa yelled from his room, "Carl, I'm leaving in three minutes. You need to be in the garage by then."

"No need to yell, Grandpa. I'm on my way downstairs now. I just need to stop by the kitchen and pick up the food for the kids from Grandma."

Grandpa quieted his voice and said, "I'll be right behind you."

With my knapsack strapped to my back, I swung my leg over the stairs railing and slid to the bottom of the stairs. I would miss doing that when we went back to the settlement. I slowly approached the kitchen because I could hear someone talking in the kitchen. I left Grandpa upstairs, so it should only be Grandma in the kitchen unless that police came back while we were upstairs. I hugged the wall and moved as close to the doorway as I could to listen to what was being said and to find out who was in the kitchen with Grandma. I strained my ears to hear. I could only hear one voice and that was Grandma's. I peeked around the corner and there was Grandma on her knees. She was praying for us. Mom always said that some of the strangest prayers came from grandmas on their knees praying for their family. I cleared my throat in the hallway and waited a few seconds before I entered the kitchen. It gave Grandma enough time to get up off her knees.

"I have your food ready, Carl."

"Thank you for doing that, Grandma. I know the kids will love getting fresh food. Most of what they eat is old food that people have thrown out."

"Maybe I should give you more."

"No, this is enough. If I take anymore, it will slow me down, and I think tonight is a night that I'll have to be able to move quickly. I've got to go. I need to be in the garage soon so grandpa can give me a ride to the dump."

"Carl . . . ."

"I know, Grandma. I'll be careful, and I will be back as soon as I can, but I've got to go now. I love you, Grandma."

"I love you too, Carl."

I opened the basement door and ran down the steps as fast as I could so I wouldn't hear Grandma crying. I moved through the tunnel like a rat in the sewer. Crouching next to the passenger side of the car I waited for Grandpa. I heard the door open, and Grandpa was talking to someone, but it was not Grandma's voice I heard. It was that pesky policeman that was by earlier.

"Excuse me, Captain Wilson; do you think I could catch a ride into the station? It seems that the other officer thought it would be funny to take off without me. I sure do get tired of these rookie pranks."

Grandpa didn't know what to say, because he knew I was in the garage already. I moved to the front of the car and motioned to grandpa that I would go down into the tunnel, and that I would walk to the dump. He motioned back okay.

"Why sure. I can give you a ride into the station. I remember the pranks that were played on me my rookie year."

Grandpa took one more look to make sure I was safely in the tunnel. I peered out a crack in the floor and watched the police officer take my seat in the car. I would have to come up with another way to the dump. I heard the car start, and that was my cue to move back through the tunnel and into the house.

I ran up the basement stairs and called for Grandma, "Grandma, I'm still here!"

She came running down the hallway and met me in the kitchen. "Carl," she said, "I thought you were caught when I saw that police officer enter the garage with your Grandpa."

"Grandpa stalled him long enough for me to get back into the tunnel. There was nothing that Grandpa could do. He was stuck. He had to give him a ride into the station. I have to figure out a way to get to the dump."

We sat at the table with blank looks on our faces until Grandma got a smile on her face. "What is it, Grandma? Do you have an idea?"

"Yes I do. You can take Mark's bicycle and ride down the road by the river."

"That is a great idea, but I don't know how to ride a bicycle."

"We have only a small amount of time to teach you before the next shift of police will come by to set up their surveillance. Let's go get your dad's bike."

"Grandma, will I learn how to ride well enough in such a short time?"

"Carl, you'll get better the longer you ride it, and it will be a lot faster than walking to the dump."

"You have a point there, Grandma."

Grandma and I flew out the back door towards the garage. Once inside I looked around, but I could not see my dad's bike.

"Grandma, where is the bike?"

"Calm down, Carl. Knowing Russell like I do, he has most likely buried it with his junk. We just have to look around starting with the biggest piles."

285

I lifted up a pile of lumber and there it was. "Grandma, I found it!"

Frantically I started to dig it out from the pile of lumber Grandpa had thrown on it. As I wheeled the bike out into the center of the garage, I could see that my dad had taken very good care of it. It looked almost new.

I looked at Grandma and said, "Now what do I do?"

As Grandma told me about having to balance, steer and pedal, I thought maybe I could run down to the dump. "Well, Carl, I'll show you how it is done, and then it will be your turn."

Grandma pushed off and pedaled. Away she went out the garage and down the driveway. She turned around at the street and came back to the garage. "Okay, Carl, your turn."

I took a hold of the handlebars, swung my leg over and sat down on the seat. "Now Carl, put your one foot on this pedal. Now push and pedal while I hold onto the back of the seat and run alongside to help you get started."

I pushed off with my one foot and struggled to get it on the pedal. I should have been watching where I was going instead of watching my feet, because I ran into the garbage can inside the garage and tipped it over. Grandma laughed and helped me up.

"Carl, it's just like a horse. If the horse bucks you off, you get back on. So get on and give it another try. This time, watch where you're going. You will be riding in no time flat."

After a few more times of trying and falling over, I finally got the hang of it. I rode down to the street and back without falling or running into anything. As I rode into the garage I told Grandma, "I think I got it. I can ride a bike."

Just then I remembered dad had said the police had put a tracking device in the handlebar. I grabbed the plastic grip and pulled it off. A small black thing hit the garage floor and broke open. Grandma reached down, picked it up and looked at it.

"I don't think we will have to worry about this device tracking anybody. It is broken. I'll just throw it in the garbage where it belongs."

"Grandma, I better get my things and make my way to the dump to meet up with the kids. I'll see you later tonight or tomorrow morning."

"You'll need to ride through the backyard and head down along the cornfield until you get to the river road. Ride as fast as you can until you get to the dump. You can hide the bicycle there and pick it up later."

"Pray that I don't crash."

"You'll do just fine, Carl."

I pushed off with my one foot and began to pedal my way out across the backyard. I caught only a glimpse of Grandma's face in the kitchen window as I made my way to the cornfield. Riding the bicycle on the grass was very hard and bumpy and I almost tipped over when I drove over some big tree roots. When I reached the cornfield, I found the ground to be a little smoother. Grandma was right again; the longer I rode the bicycle, the better I was doing. No sooner did I say that in my head when I tipped over because I hit a rock. Down I went, knocking the wind out of me. I lay there on the edge of the cornfield gasping for air. There were car headlights coming my way. It was the state police with their searchlights checking the edge of the cornfield. I needed to lay as flat as possible and hope that they didn't see me or the bicycle. The air had only partly returned to my lungs, so I was in no shape to make a run for it. Since the police were not stopping, I could continue to lie here and catch my breath. They would be back shortly to make a second pass to search the cornfield.

They drove slowly along the rest of the cornfield and then turned around. Here they come again right on time. I'd give them a few minutes to get ahead of me, and then I would ride to the dump behind them. That way I could keep an eye on them, and they wouldn't be able to surprise me. I stood up, brushed off the dirt, reached for the handlebars and looked at the bicycle to see if I broke anything. Everything looked good to me. The police had a big enough head start that I should be able to ride to the dump to meet up with Amber.

I walked the bicycle to the road and threw my leg over. With the surface of the road being loose gravel I would have to take it easy. I pushed off and pedaled slowly at first to get a feel of riding on gravel. It would be easy to fall down; and after the last fall, I didn't want to do that too many times. I was making great time as I realized that I was picking up speed as I went. I could see the taillights of the police car ahead of me. I slowed down until they had driven past the dump. The moon was about full; that was good as far as for me seeing Amber so we could meet; but with the police out, they would be able to see me also.

The main gate to the dump was up ahead. I would check the end cap of the post to see if there were any other notes left by Amber. I sure hope that it was her that left the first note for me to meet her here tonight. One thing was for sure; if it were the police that left the note, I would know about it in a flash because they would swarm the area, and that would be it for me. I leaned the bicycle up against the fence and reached for the end cap. I lifted it off and looked inside. There was no note, and there were no police. I would hide the bicycle and find a place that I could watch as much of the dump as possible to see if anybody approached the dump area. That would give me as much time as possible to get away if there was danger of getting caught. If I stationed myself in one of those upper offices, I should be high enough to see most of the dump and the roads coming and going.

I opened the door. The smell of the garbage had not gotten any better since the last time that I was here. There were no rats tonight. I pushed the bicycle through the door and laid it in the pile of junk next to the door. When the bicycle handlebar hit a bag of stuff, some tin cans came rolling out and made some clanging noise. That gave me an idea. I gathered up as many cans as I could and placed them next to all the doors that anybody would enter this building. It would be an alarm to let me know if someone had slipped passed me while I was not looking. Hopefully it wouldn't be a long wait before my meeting, so I found a chair and settled in. I would have to make sure that I stayed awake, or I could miss out on the meeting, and that would set our leaving back. I was ready to go back home. All this sneaking around was tiring.

I would sit for awhile and then my butt would get sore and I would have to walk around. That was good to help keep me awake. I came back to my chair after a short walk to the back room to look out those windows to see if there was anybody coming up from the back of the dump. There was nothing. As I stood next to the window, I saw car lights coming down the road. I backed away from the window just in time as the police searchlight on the side of their car streaked across the window. The police needed to just drive on by. If they stopped, it could spook Amber away or worse; she could think that I had set her up to get caught. I found myself telling the car to drive on by and don't stop. Please don't stop.

"You're stopping," I said out loud to myself. "I told you to drive on by. But did you listen? No! You had to stop. Now that you stopped, look around real quick and move along on down the road. Don't come in the dump whatever you to. You're coming into the dump. Don't you ever listen? Oh, this is not good. The policeman has a dog. The best thing I could hope for is that it is Shawn and his dog, King; but that most likely will not be because nothing has gone my way yet tonight. I better stop talking out loud or the dog will hear me."

289

There were many buildings so hopefully he and the dog would not come into this one. I should go and stand next to the stairs to see if the police officer comes in. That way I can make a dash out the back door if it was not Shawn and King. The police officer's silhouette was on the front door. I moved back down the hallway a few steps. The cans crashed and I could hear the dog barking wildly. I wanted to run, but I needed to find out if it was Shawn. The police officer was not coming in. What was he waiting for? Come in so I can see your face from what light is coming in from the moon. The dog came into the building and there was no police officer attached to him.

Then I heard the officer say loudly, "Search, Rex, search. Find them!"

I ran to get my knapsack. The dog was barking close behind. I entered the room and grabbed the knapsack. The doge had stopped barking. Maybe the officer had called him back and I wouldn't have to leave. I stepped out into the hallway to hear if they had gone. All was quiet, but for some reason I had this feeling that it was not a good sign. I decided to slip out the back door and maybe make my way to another building and wait there. As I turned to head for the back door, there was the dog staring me right in the eye. His nose was twitching. When he flashed his white teeth, there was a soft growl. My heart was racing. I could feel the sweat running down my face because of the fear. Slowly I slid my knapsack off my shoulder. If the dog would attack, I could use the knapsack to protect myself. My hand ran into the muffins and cookies that grandma had given me to give to the kids. I'd see if I could distract the dog with the food long enough to make my way out the back door.

"Hi there, dog." The dog growled louder. "I'm not sure if I liked your answer."

I reached into the knapsack and pulled out one of the blueberry muffins. I broke off a small piece and tossed it in front of the dog. He didn't even attempt to catch it; his eyes never moved off of me. This time I took a bigger piece—about half of the muffin—and tossed it so it almost hit him in the nose. His head shot down to the floor, searched quickly for the food and then snapped back up; his eyes were glued back on me as if nothing had ever happened. I wondered if I could make my way to the room and shut the door fast enough so the dog would be out in the hallway and I would try to crawl out a window and get away. I would need to bait him with more food. I reached into my knapsack again and grabbed another muffin. When I pulled my hand out, a second muffin hit the floor and rolled into the room where I was hoping to go. The dog darted after the rolling muffin. I seized the chance, grabbed the doorknob and pulled the door shut trapping the dog in the room.

As I ran down the hallway to the back door that lead out, I could hear the officer calling his dog. "Rex, come! Rex, where did you go now?"

I wasn't going to stick around to wait for him to find his dog. When he did let the dog out, Rex would be looking for more food. I pushed open the back door and hurried down the stairs. There at the bottom of the stairs were Amber and Sticks. They motioned for me to follow them. We ran from building to building until we came to the back fence of the dump.

"Now what do we do? The fence is too high and it has razor wire on top."

"Nothing to worry about, Carl."

Sticks took his large stick and pushed it under the fence to lift it up. Amber slid under and motioned for me to follow her. Once on the other side of the fence, Sticks handed me his stick. I then lifted the fence up from my side. In a matter of seconds he was standing next to me. We ran through the woods along a dimly moonlit path. Sirens started to sound. The officer must have found his dog shut in the room and assumed someone had trapped him in there.

"What did you do in there that's gotten the police in a frenzy?"

"Well, it must have been that I trapped the officer's dog in a room while I made my escape."

"That would do it. The police have for years thought that us kids lived in the dump; this will seal that idea in their heads. Come on. We have a lot to talk about."

"Do you need to blindfold me or something?"

"No, Carl. It would be too hard for you to run with a blindfold. And besides, if you were any kind of threat to us and the kids, we would have known by now."

The three of us ran through the woods dodging low branches, rocks and tree roots until we came to a clearing. I couldn't believe my eyes. There in front of me was a pile of railroad cars scattered around and lying on top of each other.

"What a mess!"

"That mess as you call it, Carl, is our home."

"I didn't mean anything by that. It's just that there are so many railroad cars lying on top of each other."

"I know, Carl. It looks like a mess, but it has been our home for many years."

"I'm sorry, Amber, that I called your home a mess."

"It's okay, Carl. Just don't say it in front of the kids. This is for some the only home that they can ever remember, and it would hurt them deeply."

"I'll never say it again."

"Come on! The kids have been so excited to see you ever since we said that you would be coming back tonight with us. There is one little guy that has been asking about you all day long. It has about driven my crazy."

"Would that be Karl with a 'K'?"

"You guessed it."

"My Grandma gave me some food to give to the kids. Do you want to wait until morning to give it to them, or should we give it to them tonight?"

"How much food is it, and what did you bring?"

"I brought a lot of cookies, and I had four muffins, but I fed the dog some."

"We'll give them the cookies. That way with cookies in their mouths, they won't ask so many questions. That will give us some time to get things worked out to make our leaving as smooth as possible."

We slid down a dirt embankment and came to the first railcar. Amber looked at me and asked, "Are you ready?"

"As ready as I'll ever be."

Sticks pushed open the door, and with his stick held back to first wave of kids. The kids kept coming and coming. I didn't know if there would ever be an end to the kids.

"Amber, are there more kids than the last time when I was here?"

"Yes, Carl. We found four more kids on the street when we were out gathering food."

"Where are they coming from?"

"These kids came from the other side of the river."

"You mean they're not even from this state? That could mean that there may be more kids on the other side of the river that could use your help."

"Now Carl, don't get any grand idea of searching the countryside for more lost kids. It will be a big enough task to get all these kids to the settlement. I'm sorry to say that they will have to have their own Carl in their state come and rescue them." Sticks was standing next to his sister shaking his head in agreement with her.

"I know you're right, Amber, but I feel bad for them."

"Maybe next time you come back to the city you can work that side of the river and find all the forgotten kids."

"I don't think there will be a next time. Once is enough for me, and besides, my mom most likely will ground me for about 50 years before she will let me out of the house after this adventure."

"Carl, give Sticks your food for the kids. The sooner they eat their cookies, the sooner they can go to sleep and we can start planning our exodus from the city."

"Here, Sticks. Make sure you tell Karl I say hello, and if possible, I'll try to stop by before I leave; but if not, it won't be long and we will be together for a long time."

Amber told Sticks, "When you are done dividing the food, make sure the group leaders get their kids in bed. We have another big day ahead of us."

"Okay, Amber."

"Sticks, Carl and I will need you in the meeting room to help us plan."

"It shouldn't take me long to distribute the food, and I'll be there."

Amber and I walked down the hall and into the meeting room. It was the same room they used to spy on me when I first came here."

"Carl, fill me in on what has happened since we last talked."

"There have been so many things that have happened. All our adults are lined up and will be ready to move out in as short as two days. I told them I didn't want to still be here in a week. The longer we are here, the better the possibilities of the state finding us."

"I agree; the sooner the better. But what did you mean, 'all our adults'? How many adults are you talking about?"

"Let's see. There is my Grandma and Grandpa, Ernie, Doctor Kittleson and Nurse Glover. The Abernathys will be working with us but will not be going with us. They will not know a lot of what we are doing until after we leave for the launch spot. That is in case the police would find out that they are helping, they would not be able to tell the police anything because they don't know anything."

"That is a smart idea, Carl."

"Oh, I forgot. We may pick up a Kevin Zabling. I'm not sure if we have that worked out yet, but most people think he will come with us."

The door to the room opened and in came Karl. Right behind him Sticks. Sticks lead Karl to my side, and Karl hugged me. "You're back, Carl. You're back!"

"Yes, Karl. I'm back, but I will be leaving again."

"No, Carl, you must stay here with us."

Karl was crying in my arms. I looked to Amber and Sticks for some help, but they just leaned back in their chairs and smiled.

"Thanks guys for the help." I grabbed Karl, sat him next to me and said, "Karl, I need you to listen to me. You need to stop crying so you can hear what I have to say, okay?"

Karl nodded his head and wiped the tears from his eyes. I could see that his nose had started to run. I turned to ask Amber if she had a hanky or a rag. But before I could get the words out, Karl had taken care of the problem with one wipe of his sleeve.

"Carl, I've stopped crying. What is it that you need to say?"

"Karl, I need to leave. Now Karl, don't start crying again. I need you to listen to all of what I have to say. I need to leave but I will be back. I have some work to do with some other people that will be helping us get to a safe place where you and the other kids can play outside in the sunlight and not worry about the police coming and putting you in jail."

"Will there be other kids there to play with?"

"Yes, Karl, there will be many kids to play with and to make new friends with. What I need you to do is to be strong and to listen to what we tell you to do. Can you do that for me?"

"I sure can!"

295

"That is great. What I'm going to need you to do is to run off to bed and let Amber, Sticks and me work on some plans to get us out of here."

Karl hugged me again and hugged Amber also. He gave Sticks a high five and then made his way out of the room. I looked over at Amber. There was a smile on her face again. "What is that smile for?"

"You'll make a great dad someday."

"Well, I learned from the best, and if I can be even half the dad he is, I'll do just fine. And don't think I haven't seen your mothering skills. You have done a great job keeping these kids fed and clothed for all these years."

"Oh! Please stop!" pleaded Sticks.

"What? It's true. Your sister would make a good mother."

"Let's get to the planning before my teeth rot out from all the sweetness being said in this room."

"Carl told me that all the adults are ready to go in as short as two days and not longer than a week. Carl, are these adults getting supplies also?"

"Yes, I have given them a list of important items; just as I did with your list."

"Are you still in charge, or is one of the adults in charge?"

"I will be in charge and they are okay with that. I will want you to be a leader and lead your kids; I'll work with the adults."

"What about me, Carl?"

"Sticks, you will be the link between the two groups. I will be counting on you to help me communicate between the two groups once we leave the city. Any questions so far?"

Amber spoke, "Some of the kids have been asking what will happen to them once they leave here and go to their new home. Will they have a place to stay?"

"My plan is to have the families there at the settlement become adopted parents to your kids. No one will be left along anymore."

Amber got up from her chair and walked away from the table. I started to get up to see what was the matter, but Sticks grabbed my arm and motioned for me to sit down and let her be. We sat it silence for what seemed like forever. I could hear Amber crying, but every time I would twitch in my seat because I wanted to comfort her, Sticks would give me that look. Soon Amber wiped her eyes and came back to the table.

"Sorry about that. It just hit me that I'll not be their mother anymore once we get to the settlement. That is hard for me, but I will have to get used to it."

"Amber, I think the kids will think of you as their mother until the day they turn old and gray. Their kids will call you Grandma."

"Thank you, Carl. I'll remember that."

"How are you coming along with the list of things I asked you to try to find?"

"We have had great success finding most of what you have asked for. Most of it has been given by our friends that help us from time to time. They worry that the state might find out that they have been helping us and hurt them. There is talk that the state has a list of people that help us. There are those that help us and help the state also. We are never fully trusting of anyone because of that."

"Do not tell anybody what I'm about to tell you. I told my Grandpa to break into the state computers and see if they have any files of sympathizers and those people passing as sympathizers but betray us when our backs are turned. On the tope of the list is most likely Shawn Murphy. My Grandpa will wipe out those files and put in bogus information to get the state to start mistrusting their own people. Hopefully they will turn on themselves and forget about us."

"Can your grandpa really do that?"

"I think he can, and I'll know for sure when he gets home later in the morning. We will talk about what he found and what he did. We hope to have a day and time that will be best for us to leave the city. As soon as we know that information, we will get it to you."

"How Carl?"

"Our friend, Shawn Murphy, will tell you."

"Are you crazy? I'm not going to meet with him. You just said he is a bad person pretending to be good."

"You're right. He is rotten to the core, but I will tell him a day and time and all you . . . ."

"You're going to tell the state police the day and time when we are leaving the city? Do you think they are going to let us go?"

"Amber, if you would let me finish, I'll tell you how this will work."

"Okay. Tell us." She folded her arms and leaned back in her chair.

"I will tell Shawn the wrong day and time. He will radio headquarters, and all you have to do is listen."

"But how will that help us know . . . ?"

"Amber, I'm not finished yet. You will need to be at the dump two days earlier and two hours earlier. Someone will get you to the safe area, and we will leave from there."

"What if we miss the transmission?"

"Don't. Have someone on the radio at all times."

We sat around and talked over some of the small details of the plan until Amber yawned. That made me think that I still needed to go back to the dump and pick up my bicycle and ride home before I could go to bed.

"Let's call it a night, guys. We have talked about everything I can think of, and of every possible situation."

"We need to get some sleep. The kids will be getting up in a few hours. We will be listening to hear from our friend, Shawn."

"Until we meet again on the day of our exodus, be safe."

I stood up and shook Sticks' hand, and then reached my hand out to Amber. She stood up, gave me a hug and said, "Thank you for all that you are doing for the kids." I didn't know what to say, so I just stood there looking at her. "Carl, are you okay? You better get going. You have a long way to go before you get home."

"Yeah, you're right. Say goodbye to the kids and let them know that it will not be long."

I grabbed my knapsack and hurried out the train car into the early dawn air and took off running down the path to the dump. The run to the dump went fast, probably because I was thinking about Amber and the kids. As I approached the back fence to the dump, I remembered that I needed to have a stick to lift the bottom of the fence up so I could slide under it to get back into the dump. When I was looking around in the woods for a stick that would work, I kept one eye on the dump and the road to make sure no one was around. Over by an old rotted stump was a log about as big around as my arm and almost as long as I was tall with a stub of a branch sticking out about a foot. This was the stick I was looking for. I would be able to use the stub of the branch to get leverage to lift the fence. Then I could use logs on the one end to hold it up while I crawled under the fence. I'd need to kick the logs out from under the fence afterwards so the police didn't see that people had been crawling under the fence, and then find the path that lead back to the train.

Running the log under the fence went easy. Now I needed to find enough other logs to hold the fence up. I scrounged around and found some logs and big rocks and placed them on the one end of my log and the fence lifted up and stayed. My knapsack I threw under the fence and then I got onto my belly and wiggled my way under. I kicked the log with my foot and made the counterweight of logs and rocks fall of the other end. The fence fell back down to the ground. The log was still under the fence and that looked unnatural so I grasped the bottom of the fence and lifted it to kick the log away.

I picked up my knapsack and began to walk toward the building that I hid my bicycle in. When I looked back over my shoulder at the fence, I noticed that the area where we had crawled in and out looked disturbed like a lot of people had been going in and out. I ran back and stood there thinking of what I would do to cover that up. There, next to the fence, was a black garbage bag. When I ripped into the bag, I found that it was not garbage as I had thought; but it was a bag of leaves and grass. This would look even better than garbage. I spread it around as if I was feeding the chickens we have at the settlement. The ground looked good where I hid the marks.

With knapsack in hand, I made a dash to the first building and looked to see if it was clear to run in where I had left the bicycle. I walked to the corner of the building and checked the road in front of the dump to see that nobody was driving down the road. All was clear; now was a good time to get the bicycle and head for home. I slipped into the building, pulled the bicycle out of my hiding spot and walked it to the main gate of the dump. I swung my leg over and pushed off pedaling for home. Grandma hopefully did not stay up all night waiting for me to come, because it looked like it would be sunrise in about an hour. Grandpa and I would have to get some sleep before we talked about what we got worked out while we were in town all night.

I could see headlights up ahead, but they weren't on this side of the river. It looked like they were near the bridge. I'd have to ride by at a nice speed not showing any fear and not looking at them in case they talked with the state police on this side of the river asking them what I was doing out so early in the morning. It seemed as if they were looking for something or maybe somebody. I pedaled by the front of the bridge and sneaked a peek out of the corner of my eye so they couldn't tell that I was interested in what they were doing. This was not good; they had stopped whatever they were doing, and now they were watching me. The two of them were pointing. Now one of them was running across the bridge. I wanted to pedal faster, but that would give them the idea that I was guilty of something. I kept at the same speed and kept looking ahead. I pedaled until I thought that I was out of sight. Then I looked over my shoulder and could see a car was driving parallel with me on the other side of the river.

I wouldn't be able to take the easy, fast way home by the cornfield into the backyard or they would know where I lived and call the police since they were so interested in me. I turned and headed up to the road in front of grandma and grandpa's house. I'd have to take a chance that there wouldn't be any police out on the main road. I made the turn and picked up the pace pedaling. I heard the car on the other side of the river slam on the brakes, but I couldn't look back.

The road thankfully curved some so the car wouldn't have a line of sight to see which way I was turning. I coasted up to the intersection and stopped, looking both ways to see that there were no cars on the road. I pushed off again and pedaled hard and fast to get into the driveway at home. I slammed on the brakes and stopped next to the garage struggling to get the bicycle in through the service door. I didn't want to open the big garage door because it would make too much noise and it might scare grandma if she was sleeping. I wheeled the bicycle to the far back corner out of the way for when grandpa came home, rested it along the wall and headed for the house.

There was a crash and a bang. The garage door was opening so I dove under the workbench to get to the trap door leading to the tunnel. I didn't know who this was coming in. It could be grandpa, or it could be the police. They could be inside the house. I forgot to look to see if there was a signal saying if the house was safe. Thankfully the door opened slowly because it gave me time to get into the tunnel and the trap door shut. Once inside I tried to slow my breathing down so I could hear who was up in the garage. There was a car driving in so it must be Grandpa. I'd head to the basement and wait down there until I heard if it was safe to come up.

As I entered the basement, I listened to hear if anybody was moving about the house and who it might be. Slowly I tiptoed up the stairs and sat next to the door. It wasn't the best place to be if the police would hear me and open the door. I would be caught instantly, but I could hear the best from here. Not hearing anything, I pressed my ear to the door hoping to hear something if they might be talking in another room.

Oh! Now I could hear footsteps coming down the hall. The footsteps sounded heavy—too heavy to be Grandma—so maybe it was Grandpa home from work. I'd just crack the door a little and see. I looked through the crack and could see only the back of a black police uniform. That must be Grandpa; I could see Grandma talking to him. It must be okay to come out; I pushed the door open more. I saw Grandma's eyes get as big as dinner plates. The person in black turned around, and it was not grandpa. It was another police officer. I shut the door quickly but quietly and tiptoed back down the steps with my heart pounding so hard I thought it might jump out of my chest. I flew to the tunnel. Just as I reached the tunnel, I heard the heavy footsteps coming down the stairs to the basement.

The man yelled as he came down the stairs, "Who is down here? You may as well tell me because I will find you. There is no way out."

"Who are you looking for, Kyle Anderson?"

"You know who I'm looking for. You're hiding the dirty little street kids. I'm going to find them; and you, Mrs.

302

Wilson, will be sitting in jail the rest of your life. You kids come out where I can see you. Do you hear me?"

"Yes, I hear you."

That was not Grandma's voice; it was Grandpa's. So that was Grandpa opening up the garage door and driving in. Kyle Anderson was in big trouble now.

"Kyle Anderson, get up out of my basement now!"

"I'm looking for those dirty street kids that you and your wife are hiding from the state."

"Are you out of your mind, Anderson? Get up out of the basement now before I come down there and drag you out by your little, scrawny neck. Do you hear me?"

"Yes sir!"

Kyle slammed his hand on the wall just inches from the door to the tunnel. I jumped back because it scared me. He must have noticed that the wall sounded funny because he started hitting all around on the wall looking for something, but I don't think he knew what. I grabbed the door handles on the tunnel door to keep him from coming in.

"Kyle Anderson, my basement is not that big that you should be standing here in front of me now!"

"But sir, I heard something when I hit the wall."

"Why are you hitting my walls? Don't make me come down and get you; you will not like it."

Kyle stopped hitting the wall. I could hear him run across the basement and up the stairs. I could tell when he reached the bottom of the stairs. Grandpa was yelling at him all the way up to the top, and he didn't stop then. I stayed in the tunnel until the yelling stopped and I heard the front door slam shut. Then there was silence in the house. I opened up the tunnel door and listened. The basement door opened up, and I heard laughter.

"Carl, it is okay to come up now. Kyle is gone; and after that chewing out that Grandpa gave him, I don't think he will be back for a long time." I crawled out from the tunnel.

When I got to the bottom of the stairs, there was Grandma's face with a big smile. "Carl, what took you so long to get home? And when you did get home, you didn't look for the signal in the window."

"The state police like to park their cars down the road and walk up to surprise people."

"Well, he certainly surprised me. I thought my heart was going to jump out of my chest when I saw his face as he turned around to see what made your eyes get so big."

"Well, he is gone now. Get up here and I'll fix us three something to eat."

When we entered the kitchen, Grandpa was sitting at the table still laughing but not as hard. "So Carl, how did things go for you? Did you run into any dogs?"

"Yes, there was one dog that was looking to meet me."

Grandma's eyes were getting big again. "Carl, what dog?"

"Rex was his name."

"Oh no! He has got to be the meanest dog on the police force. How did you get away?"

"I fed him one of your muffins and . . . ."

Grandpa jumped in and said, "The dog died."

"No he didn't, Grandpa."

"Russell Wilson, I thought you liked my muffins."

"Ramona, I'm just kidding. Go on, Carl. Tell us what happened."

"Like I said, I fed him a muffin when it fell out of my knapsack and rolled across the floor into a room. When the dog went for the muffin, I reached for the door handle and closed the door behind him."

"Where was the handler?"

"He was too lazy to walk into the building until he heard his dog barking, and that gave me time to run out the back door."

"Carl, you should have heard the commotion that it caused for the police on the night shift. They were looking for all kinds of people."

"Why? There was only me, and the police officer never saw me."

"Well, that's not the story that Rex's handler was telling."

"What did he say?"

"It went into the report that there were about 10, maybe as many as 15 kids running around in the buildings at the dump."

"He's lying. I ran into Amber and her brother when I ran out the back door. Then we hurried straight for the back fence."

"I knew he was lying, but I thought I would let it go. If they were busy chasing phantom kids, then they wouldn't be chasing my grandkid. You said that you met up with Amber and her brother. How did that meeting go?"

"That went well. They will be ready as soon as we tell them when the day and time is."

"And how do you plan on telling them? The dump is going to be hot for a day or two."

"I thought I would let Shawn Murphy tell them."

"Carl, did you hit your head on something? Shawn is on the list of people that the police use to help find the kids. He's the worst one to tell. He'll have those kids in jail so fast."

"That is what I'm counting on."

"How do you figure?"

"His quest for power and promotion will drive him to help us. Once we decide the day and time, I will meet him just like I had told him I would before I had found out that he was working for the wrong side. I'll tell him a day and time. And remember, Grandpa, the kids have a police radio that they listen to all the time."

"Oh yeah, I forgot."

"Shawn will be so excited to hear the date and time that he will quickly radio in what he found out to show off to the other officers. All the kids have to do is be there at the dump two days earlier and two hours sooner than what I tell him."

"Russell, I have to say that is such a crazy plan it might work, because we know how power hungry Shawn is."

"Just to make sure it happens, I'll try to work that shift with him, and if he has not radioed in anything by a set time, I'll question him and get him all excited until he makes the call with my encouragement."

"Grandpa, that is a great backup plan; because if Shawn would think about grabbing me, you could swoop in and save me. We would have to take Shawn with us and let him go after we leave the city. Did you have time to get your computer work done with all that commotion?"

"Oh yes! There were all kinds of lists. There were lists of the good people that are suspected of helping the kids. There were lists of the bad people that pretend to be good and then tell the state what the kids are doing. There was even a list of people that are suspected of being possible Christians. Yes, Ramona, our names were on that list along with Nurse Glover and Ernie, but not anymore. I deleted them and added a few new names to the bad people's list. I set up a program so when we decide what day we are taking off to the settlement, it will scramble the police communications computer and alarm systems all across town. I can set it all into motion from home."

"Russell, won't they trace it back to us?"

"Ramona, by the time they get things unscrambled, we will be long gone and safe at the settlement. What do you think of that, Carl?"

"That will work. Now for the big question. When will we be ready to go?"

"I think we adults will be ready in three days," Grandpa answered.

"Carl, do you think the kids could be ready in three days?" Grandma asked.

"Yes, I think so. That's it then. We leave in three days. When would be the best time to take off, Grandpa?"

"I would think about three in the morning. Most of the police have had their break, and they pretty much are settled in for the night in one spot."

"Then it is settled. We leave in three days at 3 o'clock in the morning. I will set up a meeting with Shawn and tell him the good news, and he will tell the kids to get ready."

"Carl, what else do we have to do to get ready on our part?" Grandpa asked.

"We still have to find out if Kevin Zabling is going to come with us. I think, Grandma, you were going to take care of that."

"I'll go into town when you two head off to bed to get some sleep since you were out on the town all night long. I'll stop at his house first; if he is not there, I'll stop at the hospital."

"Grandpa, do you think we need to let Ernie know when we are coming, or do you think that he will be ready anytime we show up?"

"I think that he will be ready. It's not like he has anything there of value. The state took it all away from him to try to break him down to tell where the settlement was. They burned his house and burned his Bible in front of his eyes."

"It must have been hard to see that burn."

"On the contrary, Ernie laughed as they tore out each page and threw it on the fire."

"Grandpa, why did he laugh? Is Ernie really crazy?"

"No, Carl. Ernie is not. In fact, what Ernie did as they burned each page was he would ask the police what book of the Bible they were burning. They would tell him thinking it would break his spirit and tell them what they wanted to know. Ernie would not break. He quoted Bible verse from the book of the Bible that they were about to burn. The police thought he was just making up things to make them mad, so before they would throw it in the fire, they would look up the chapter and verse and read it out loud. Of course Ernie had memorized much of the Bible, so in a very shrewd way he was telling the police about Jesus while they thought that they were persecuting him. It's a perfect example of what man intended to be bad and God turned it around and made an opportunity for Ernie to be a witness and tell of God's power."

"Grandpa, did any of the police that day become Christians?"

"I'm not sure. There were two officers that the state was watching for the longest time thinking that they had converted, but they could not prove it. It wasn't for the lack of trying to prove it on the state's part. The two men retired as soon as the state said it was time."

"Are the men still in town? Maybe they would like to come to the settlement."

"A crazy thing happened. A few years ago the state lost track of the two men and their entire families. It was like the earth swallowed them up, and no one has found them or any traces of their families."

"I don't remember any new people coming to the settlement back then. Maybe there are other settlements out there that we don't know about."

"I don't know, Carl, but I think it is time to go to bed and get some rest. I have to go to work again tonight. I'll keep watch to make sure the police are not getting wise to any plans. Carl, when are you going to meet up with Shawn?"

"I told him that I would leave a note in the park and that we would talk. I said I would let him know what he could do to help. Later this afternoon I will go to the park and drop the note off and get back home as soon as possible."

"Just be careful, Carl. The police watch the parks often, especially the park in the center of town. Which park are you going to?"

"The one in the center of town."

Grandpa asked, "Is there any way that you could change the place where you leave your note?"

"No, that is the only place that we talked about."

"I got it! Carl, you write the note and I'll drop it off at the park. Where in the park are you supposed to drop the note?"

"It will be by the statue of the boy that could fly."

"That is the statue where the police caught your dad climbing many years ago."

"I know. I'll write you a note. All you have to do is set it by the base of the statue. He is to look each day to see if I have been there."

"I can do that. He is working my shift tonight, so I can send him into the park to make a few rounds. Then he will have opportunity to find the note."

"That would be great. That would save on a trip into town and one less times for the police to have a chance to catch me. Well, with that all worked out, there is nothing left to do but say good night. It seems silly to go to bed when it is light out, but I'm very tired. I know I'll sleep well. Good night, Grandma and Grandpa."

As I walked by each of them, I gave them a good night hug and headed upstairs to my room. When I grabbed the hand railing, I could feel the sleepiness come over me in waves. At the top of the stairs I wobbled to my room and collapsed on the edge of the bed. I kicked off my shoes and pushed them under the chair next to the desk. Then I lay down and closed my eyes for just a few seconds, I thought.

"Carl, why don't you finish getting ready for bed and crawl under the covers?"

Opening one eye I saw that it was Grandma. I had fallen asleep and was still in my clothes. I tried to talk, but I was still half asleep, so it came out in a mumble, "Okay. I'll do that right now."

I finished getting undressed as grandma suggested and then crawled under the covers. Once again I closed my eyes.

"Carl, it's time for supper!" It was Grandma's voice, so I struggled to wake from the deep sleep that I was in. My mind was saying, "Open your eyes and sit up", but my body was saying, "No. I want to sleep more."

Grandma did not hear me say anything, so she came into the room and said again, "Carl, it is time for supper."

Hearing her voice once again broke the hold that my body had over my mind. My eyes popped open, and I sat up as if I had been shot out of a cannon. I sat up so fast that it frightened Grandma.

"Oh! Carl, are you okay? I didn't mean to frighten you."

"You didn't frighten me, Grandma. Have you ever slept so hard that when you wanted to wake up, your body fought with itself?"

"Yes, Carl. I know what you mean. It is a frightening experience."

"You can say that again. I hope I don't ever do that again. Grandpa hasn't left yet, has he?"

"No. He is downstairs waiting to eat. He said that you still had to write the note that he would leave for Shawn at the park."

"I have to think of a place for us to meet that will not be too out in the open, but someplace where I can see if trouble is approaching from many directions."

"Why don't you meet in front of the information center? You could hide in the deep doorway in the front of the building until Shawn shows up. You can watch the street and not be seen," Grandma suggested.

"That is an excellent idea, but I'm not sure where the information building is."

"It is only a few blocks from the park in the center of town. I'll show you on a map that we have downstairs. You'll have no problem finding it. Hurry and get dressed and come down; we will eat supper."

"I'll hurry."

I put on the darkest colored clothes that I had so I would be able to move around at night while I waited for Shawn. I hurried down the stairs, entered the kitchen and asked, "Grandma, where can I get some paper and a pen? I need to write that note so Grandpa can drop it off on his way to work."

"Carl, when and where have you planned to set up your meeting with Shawn?" Grandpa questioned.

"Grandma thought I should meet Shawn at the information center in the front so I can hide in the dark doorway. I will tell him to meet me there at 10 o'clock tonight."

"That is a great place because you will be up high, but the time will have to be later because he won't get done with his security checks on the other end of town until almost midnight. I would set it up for 1 o'clock."

"But Grandpa, if I make it 1 o'clock, won't he think that it is funny that I set the time so he could get his checks completed? I think I'll say midnight. He will have to hurry to meet me. That way the pressure is on him."

"You do have a point there, Carl. Midnight it is."

"Here is the paper and pen, Carl."

"Thank you, Grandma."

Quickly I wrote out a short note saying, "Meet at information center midnight tonight."

"So Carl, what did you write?" Grandpa asked.

"I'll let you read it. I kept it short."

I gave the paper to him, and he read it and said, "I like it; short and to the point."

"I think I will have to leave here about 11 o'clock in order to get there in time. I'll use my dad's bicycle to get into town and back."

"I made a lot of spaghetti and meatballs, so eat up."

It wasn't long until it was time for Grandpa to go to work. Grandma and I went into the living room. She showed me the map of the town. She point out where the information center was and a few ways to get there. I memorized the routes while Grandma did some work on the computer.

"Grandma, did you ever get to talk with Kevin Zabling?"

"Yes, I did. You slept so long, and then we hurried to eat that I forgot to tell you what happened. Your grandpa and I talked about it before you got up. I found Kevin at home and told him the whole story. He is excited to meet you and will be ready at the drop of a hat. He plans to have a bag packed with him at all times whether at work or at home. I gave him a few items to pick up to bring to the settlement, mostly medical supplies."

"That is good news. Will you be going into town before we take off? If you do, try to let Kevin know what day he will need to be ready. If he is working at that time, we can use his help in getting Ernie out of the hospital. If not, have him meet at your house and park his car deep into the cornfield so the police don't see a gathering of cars."

For the next few hours Grandma and I talked and laughed about the silly things that my dad did when he was my age and younger. The clock on the wall chimed 11 o'clock. I jumped up off the floor and told Grandma, "It is time for me to go. Grandma, could you look to see if it is clear to leave? I'm going to leave from the garage by way of the tunnel, and I'll come in the same way, but this time I'll look for the signal that it is all clear before I come upstairs."

Grandma went to the front window to see if it was all clear, and I made my way to the basement tunnel. Standing at the window in the garage I looked for grandma to say that it was okay to leave the garage for town. There was the signal.

I pushed the bicycle out the door, drove down the driveway and out onto the main road so I could make good time and be in position before midnight. When I got to the side roads, I looked for lights. In surprising speed I was in the center of town and heading for the information center. Grandma said that I should stay off the streets near the park, because that was where the police patrol the most. If I remembered right, I should be only two blocks from the place. And there it was — the information center. Dad parked his bicycle in the front, but I didn't think that would be a good idea this time. I would have to find something on the side or in the back it I had to. Hopping off the bicycle, I walked it around to the side of the building and pushed it between some bushes. I felt good about my hiding place and walked to my hiding place at the front door. A quick peak around the side of the building revealed no one moving. I jogged up the stone stairs and slipped into the pitch black alcove of the information center. All I had to do was wait for Shawn to show up and give him the information that I needed him to pass on to the kids. Then the plan for our exodus would be in motion.

I rode the bicycle so hard that I was breathing heavy. Someone might hear me if they were to walk by, so I needed to try to quiet my breathing. I placed my hands over my mouth to help quiet my breathing some, but it still was too loud. I held my breath and fear shot through my body; I could still hear breathing.

Someone grabbed me by the shoulder and arm when I tried to dart from my hiding place. As I fought to get away, another set of hands grabbed my other arm, and I was thrown into the stone pillar knocking the wind out of my lungs. There was a pop when my face hit the pillar and blood was running down my face. I had broken my nose, and my lungs were gasping for air. The people that had a hold of me had not said anything, and there was no light to see who had captured me. I felt my legs getting weak from the lack of oxygen, and I started to sink to the ground. Just then a large hand grabbed me by the throat and lifted me to me feet.

A voice in the dark whispered in my ear, "Where do you think you are going, boy?"

With his hand around my throat and squeezing tighter as each second passed, I could not say anything. "What is your name, boy?" Still unable to catch my breath with his hand around my throat, I could not answer his question.

A voice from the other side of me said, "Let go of his throat, and maybe he would be able to answer you; if you don't kill him first." Finally, a voice of reason.

I slumped to the ground, but my capturers did not let go of my arms. One capturer was twisting my arm as I could twist the clothes to wring out the water when I was young and helped my mom with the wash. I was in great pain, but I couldn't let my capturers know, so I had to hold it in. It must have disappointed him because he stopped twisting my arm.

The voice of reason spoke, "What do we do with the boy now?"

"I say we drag him out into the streetlight and see what we have caught."

I could feel their grasps getting tighter on my arms. With their other hand they grabbed under my armpits and walked forward toward the stairs. I wasn't sure what was wrong. Why couldn't I feel the ground under me? Had they hurt me so bad that I had lost feeling in my feet and legs? As the three of us broke from the darkness, I looked to the right and then to my left to see that my capturers were indeed the state police. I had been caught. My heart sank. So many people's hopes of getting out of the city were now lost. Pain was shooting through my body with each step down the stairs, but I needed to maintain my silence. When we reached the sidewalk they dropped me. I crumbled to the ground too weak and dazed to run. I laid there until I felt a hand grab a handful of hair and wrench my head back.

"Let's see what we have here. Why, it is a dirty little kid. I think we have caught us one of those kids from the dump."

He then pushed my head forward with such force I ended up sprawled out on the sidewalk. Then I received a boot to my already sore ribs again and again. I looked up to find the voice of reason standing there not knowing whether to stop him or to join in on trying to break my ribs. I looked him in the eye and mouthed, "Please stop." Then I saw a boot and all went black. I'm not sure how long I was out cold; but when I awoke, the voice of Shawn was yelling at the two men that were trying to kill me.

"How dumb are you men anyway? Did you not hear the order given not to hurt any of the kids that you may encounter because we needed them to help the state track down the rest of the group?"

"He resisted us, and when he ran away, he fell down the steps."

"How dumb do you think I am? No one looks like that from falling down a few stairs."

"That is what happened, Sarg! So what are we going to do with this little dirtball?"

"We aren't going to do anything with him."

"What do you mean? We caught him, and we are going to bring him in. They can interrogate him and beat the answers out of him."

"I would like to inform you two that he is not one of those kids from the dump but that he is my informant. He has been working with me to infiltrate their group. He was about to tell me some good news if you haven't killed him."

I had not moved a muscle in fear that I would get more of a beating. To my surprise, Shawn had put his neck out by saying I was working with him and that I was about to tell him something.

"Carl, are you alright?"

Shawn reached down and helped me sit up, leaning me against the streetlight post. I struggled to get enough air in my lungs to answer Shawn.

"Answer the Sergeant, boy!"

Then I felt a swift blow to the side of my head that knocked me to the ground. Shawn pulled his gun and pointed it not at me but at the officer that kicked me in the side of the head.

"If you so much as even look at that boy the wrong way, I'll . . . ."

He didn't finish his sentence and put his gun away slowly. The man that kicked me chuckled. Then I heard a smack and a thud. There, lying next to me with blood running from his nose was the officer that had beaten me the most. Shawn must have punched him in the face and knocked him out. I looked up at the other officer. The look on his face was as if nothing happened.

Shawn said, "Help me get him to his feet." The officer reached for his partner and began to help him. "Not him! The kid!"

He quickly dropped his partner back onto the sidewalk and carefully helped me to my feet with the help of Shawn. They walked me to the steps of the information center."

"Carl, you left a note saying to meet you here. What is happening?"

I looked at Shawn and motioned with my head to the other officer sitting next to me. "I don't think I want him to hear what I have to say."

"Okay, Carl, this fine officer needs to check the doors to the back of the information center to see if they are locked, don't you?"

"We have already checked the doors and they are secure."

"Well, check them again, now! And take your partner with you."

"Yes Sir!" His partner was beginning to come to as he was being helped to the back of the building.

"They're gone now, Carl. How did you let these two catch you anyway?"

"I was going to hide up in the dark area by the main door, and there they were hiding in the dark. They must have known that I was coming."

"No, Carl. Knowing these two, it was just dumb luck on their part. And I would like to emphasize the dumb part."

"Shawn, first of all I wanted to let you know that I found the kids. Things are going well and the kids and I are going to leave Saturday at 5am from the north side of the school. Meet us there. You can bring King with if you would like. Bring only what you can carry on your back. You will not see or hear from me or any of the kids until you meet with us on Saturday. We are going to stay in hiding until that time. Do you have any questions?"

"No questions. It sounds like you got things worked out. I'll wait until I see you on Saturday. Oh, I do have one question now."

"What question is that?"

"If the state would happen to find out about you leaving, then what?"

"We had thought of that. We would go back into hiding and leave three days later at the same time and place, but I don't see that happening."

"Well, you never can tell where the police might show up just out of dumb luck like tonight."

"I see what you mean, Shawn."

"Do you need a ride home?"

"No, Shawn, I got here by myself, and I'll get home. Just make sure those two are nowhere near me. Send them to the park looking for somebody that is not really there. That would give me enough time to get away without them following me. Oh, and that goes for you too; or you'll never see me again. Am I clear?"

"Very clear, Carl."

"I'll see you Saturday."

When I went to get the bicycle, I had to walk past the two officers coming from the back of the building. I didn't even look at them as I walked by.

Shawn yelled at them, "Hey you two! What you need to do is go to the park. They say there is some crazed lady running around with a knife. Control wants you to find her and bring her in."

Pulling the bicycle from the bushes where I hid it, I turned down the alley and back to Grandma and Grandpa's house as fast as I could. I looked over my shoulder to make sure no one was following me. When I pulled up to the house, I saw that I had the all clear sign. I put the bicycle back in the garage and hurried through the tunnel into the basement. When I entered the kitchen, there was Grandma waiting up for me.

"Carl, what happened to you? Never mind. We'll talk later. Come here quickly. It's Shawn on the radio to control."

"K-9 unit to control."

"Go ahead K-9."

"I have received information on the movement of the dump kids. They will be leaving the city for the wilderness settlement on Saturday at 5am. They will be leaving from the north side of the school. Do you copy?"

"That is a 10-4. We copy. Great work! We will pass this on to the state."

"Control, I would like to request that I be allowed to be a part of the raid."

"10-4. We will advise if that is a go for you, K-9. Control out."

"Well, Carl, it seems as if everything is set to go."

"Grandma, I can't wait. I'm looking forward to going home."

"Let's go up to the bathroom and get you cleaned up. Then you can tell me what happened to you. I'm sure the police had something to do with your condition. I'll have to throw those clothes away. I'll never get the blood out."

"Sorry about that, Grandma."

"The important thing is that you made it home. With a few days to rest up before we leave, you will have time to heal from tonight's encounter with the police."

"One good thing about having to stay put; I'll have almost no chance of meeting up with the police unless they come knocking. I just don't know what I'm going to do for the next few days."

"Carl, don't you worry. I will find things for you to do."

"Oh Grandma, now you sound like my mom."

"Carl, it's not all bad. There is also your dad's computer upstairs that you can play on."

"I don't know anything about those things. Dad talked to us kids about it, but we couldn't picture it and how it would work."

"Carl, we have a few days to waste. I'll help you learn. There are some fun games on your dad's computer. For right now we need to get you cleaned up and in bed. It is getting late."

"I think I'm going to be black and blue for some time. The police worked me over pretty good before Shawn got them to stop—before they killed me. The officers wanted to take me to the station to get questioned, but Shawn made up some story that I was his informant and that it was okay to let me go."

"Carl, Shawn didn't do that for you. He did it for himself. He is hoping to catch not just one fish, but he is hoping to catch us all."

"I know, Grandma. It is kind of funny when you think about it. Shawn thinks that he is using me to get the kids, but we are using him to set the police up to miss our leaving by two days. Oh Grandma, what if the police get the dogs out and they track us to the settlement?"

"That is a good question, Carl. We will have to ask your grandpa when he gets home in the morning what we can do to cover our trail."

In the bathroom I scrubbed my face and hands to get the dried blood off. When I looked in the mirror, I didn't look so rough with the blood gone. I could see a bruise starting to form from when the officer kicked me in the side of the head.

"I'm ready to go to bed, Grandma. I'll see you and Grandpa in the morning. I hope this waiting to leave isn't as bad as I think it is going to be."

"Carl, you will survive the wait. I'll see to it that you keep busy and have some fun."

"Good night, Grandma."

"Good night, Carl."

Grandma was right. The next few days she taught me how to use the computer and play games on it. We had fun, and I got pretty good at getting around in the files and programs on the computer. The days went quickly.

Chapter 11

The Wait is Over

"Carl, wake up! This is the day you have been waiting for." It was Grandma's voice saying some of the sweetest words in my ear. This was the day we would start our journey back home.

"Good morning, Grandma! Is Grandpa up yet?"

"Yes, Carl, I have been up for hours," Grandpa answered as Grandma left the room.

"Good morning, Grandpa!"

"Carl, we have a lot of things left to do before we leave tonight."

"I know, Grandpa. I hope that everybody is ready to do their job so we don't run into any trouble."

Grandma poked her head into my room again and said, "When you two are ready, breakfast is on the table. You can finish talking downstairs."

"She's right, Carl. Let's go eat. We can talk later."

Grandpa and I both rushed for the door of my room as if we were two brothers racing to get downstairs to the kitchen table first. I wouldn't tell him, but I'd let him win this time. My ribs still hurt a little from a few nights ago.

"Come on, Carl. Are you going to let this old man beat you?"

That did it. So much for letting him win. Racing down the hall towards the kitchen, I made a move to the right and then quickly to the left. I began to shoot past Grandpa when he reached out his arm to block me from getting around him. The pain was so intense when I ran into his arm that I dropped to the floor of the hall and slid along until I came to rest in front of Grandma's feet.

"Russell Wilson, what did you do?"

"It's okay, Grandma. We were just playing around."

"Russell, don't just stand there. Help the poor boy to his feet; and while you are down there, say that you're sorry."

"Carl, I'm really sorry I hit you in the ribs."

"That's okay, Grandpa. I'll live."

Grandma went into the kitchen leaving Grandpa and me out in the hall staring at each other. We both bolted for the kitchen at the same time when we realized that the race was not over, because no one had entered the kitchen. We reached the doorway at the same time hitting our shoulders on the edge of the door so hard that it knocked us to the floor. We made such a large thud when we hit the door; we scared Grandma so much that she dropped her toast into her coffee cup.

"Would you two kids quit horsing around and get in here before you hurt each other anymore."

Grandpa whispered to me, "I won! See? My foot is in the kitchen."

"Alright. You won this time, but wait until next time."

At the table we ate and talked about the different jobs that we all had to do today. Grandma needed to drive to the dump late tonight and pick up as many of the small kids that she could fit in her car and brings them to the house. The rest of the older kids would have to walk along the river road in small groups. Grandpa would drop me off at the hospital to get Ernie. Kevin would stop and pick up Doctor Kittleson and Nurse Glover, and he would hide his car in the corn-field in the backyard. The plan was simple. Get the people to the house, move to the tunnel entrance, and get everyone inside before dawn's early light could give us away. If the plan went as smooth as we planned it, we would all be on the other side standing in freedom before the state would even know that we were gone; and they wouldn't have a clue where we were.

"Carl, are you okay?" Grandma asked.

"I'm fine. I was just running the plan through in my head to make sure that we have everything covered. Once we start, there is no turning back unless the jeopardy of the location of the settlement is at risk; then I will have to go to plan 'B'."

"Carl, you never told us about plan 'B'."

"I know. I don't have a plan 'B'-only plan 'A'."

"No! Carl's plan will work if everybody does their jobs. The plan is simple, so it should work. There is some room to make a few changes as we go if we need to; right, Carl?"

"That's right. But change the plan as little as possible."

Suddenly there was a loud boom and the house shook. "What was that?"

"That's the state starting to work on the new prison. At work they said that they needed to blast some rock away to get the footings in for the one side of the wall that would surround the prison," Grandpa answered.

"Carl, you look worried," said Grandma. "Is that a problem?"

"I hope not."

"Carl, that was not a very reassuring answer."

"I know."

"Carl, why would the state blasting at the old mill be of concern to us? Unless . . . ."

Grandma stopped in mid-sentence and covered her mouth with her hand, and her eyes opened wide with fear of what might be my answer. I didn't want to tell them which way we were going to go, but I think they were going to need to know.

"All right. I'll tell you now since we are so close to leaving. Some of the time we will be underground, and if their blasting has disturbed our route, I don't know of another way home."

There was a silence at the table, and no one was even looking at each other. We must be afraid of what questions we would ask each other.

Grandpa broke the silence. "It will work, and we will make it! I'm going to see my son no matter what it takes!"

"Amen to that," Grandma agreed.

"Okay then. There is nothing to worry about."

Just then there was another blast at the prison. For the next eight hours there were several more blasts shaking the house and making Grandma's dishes rattle in the cupboard. Grandma was in the kitchen fixing what she called the last supper.

"Carl, Russell," yelled Grandma.

Grandpa and I were upstairs playing computer games. We looked at each other and said, "It must be the police. Let's go see what is happening."

We ran out of my room to the top of the stairs. We stopped dead in our tracks when we saw grandma at the bottom of the stairs. "They stopped blasting!"

"Grandma, don't scare us like that. We thought the police were at the door."

"I'm sorry. I didn't mean to scare you boys. It is time to eat. Shut the computer off and wash your hands."

"Carl, I'll shut the computer off. You go wash your hands first."

Ding dong! Grandpa and I froze and looked down at grandma. "It's okay. I told Kevin to pick up the other two and come for supper. It would look a lot more normal having them come to the house for supper than at 3:00 in the morning."

"Grandpa, she has a point there."

"I'm going to get the door. I told them to come in the back."

I heard cornstalks crashing. That must be Kevin parking his car in the corn out back. As I washed my hands upstairs in the bathroom, I could hear talking downstairs. I recognized Doctor Kittleson's and Nurse Glover's voices. Little twinges of excitement came over me as I dried my hands. When I got to the top of the stairs I could hear another voice. That must be Kevin Zabling. This would be the first time meeting him. Sliding down the hand railing for what could be the last time, I got my first look at Kevin coming down the hall. I swung my leg over and stood on the last step.

"Hello. My name is Kevin Zabling. I hear you are the young man that I need to thank for asking me along on your trip."

"Yes, I am. My name is Carl Wilson, and I should be thanking you for what the Zabling family gave up so that my dad could find freedom at the settlement."

"Carl, could you tell me where the bathroom is? I need to wash my hands. I fell in the cornfield as I made my way out after parking my car. The state is not going to be very happy when they find it in their cornfield."

"Why is that, Kevin?"

"I'm still making payments on it."

"Come, boys. The rest of us are hungry."

"You better hurry and wash your hands. Grandpa doesn't like to eat cold food." I passed Kevin to make my way to the kitchen.

"Carl."

"What?"

"You didn't tell me where the bathroom was."

"Oh. Sorry. Go to the top of the stairs and take a left. It is at the end of the hall. You can't miss it."

"Thanks. Tell your Grandma to start without me."

"I don't think so. Grandma is going to want us all there for prayer."

"I'll hurry then."

As Kevin ran upstairs, I ran down the hall and turned into the kitchen to see smiling faces looking at me. "Kevin will be here as soon as he can. He needed to wash his hands. He fell in the cornfield."

Nurse Glover said, "Good evening, Carl. It is nice to see you again. How is your arm?"

"Good evening to you, Nurse Glover. My arm has healed quite well. Thank you for asking."

Grandma said, "Carl, you will sit next to Miss Glover, and Kevin will sit next to you."

"Did someone say my name?" Kevin had finished washing his hands and entered the kitchen.

I spoke up and said to Kevin, "Grandma said that you are to sit next to me."

"Sounds good to me."

"Who would like to say a prayer before we eat?"

Both Grandpa and Doctor Kittleson spoke up at the same time, "I will!"

Grandpa said, "Doctor Kittleson, why don't you say the prayer since you are our guest tonight."

Doctor Kittleson began to pray. I should have listened to his prayer, but I felt I needed to pray by myself. I tuned out the doctor's voice and words in my mind and began thanking God for all the people that were sitting around the table, and for all the supplies we had found to bring to the settlement. I tuned out so much I didn't hear when the doctor had stopped praying. There was so much more I had to thank God for. I ended my prayer by saying, "God, I'll talk to you in a little bit and finish what I started. These fine people are ready to eat. Amen."

Grandpa said loudly, "Let's eat!"

Grandma had found all the odds and ends around the kitchen to make a meal big enough for 12 people and not just for the 6 of us. As the food was being passed, I felt something stirring in me.

"I would like to thank you all for helping me while I have been here in your city. In a little while I will be able to return the favor by leading you to my city, showing you your new home, and helping you get settled. Thank you!"

Nurse Glover reached out her hand and placed it on my arm. I looked into her face; tears were running down her cheeks and a smile at the same time. With a shaky voice she said, "I'm sure I speak for all of us around the table and say thank you for asking us to join you." The others around the table agreed.

"I must tell you. I did not pick you to come with me. I came only for Grandma, Grandpa and Ernie. God picked the rest of you to come with me back to the settlement. God has seen your hearts and knows you are good, caring people; you all will be an asset and make good contributions to the settlement."

My little speech had stopped them in their tracks. They stopped passing the food and listened. Nurse Glover was crying even more, and Grandma had joined her in crying tears of joy.

Grandpa, on the other hand, said, "Carl, are you going to pass the potatoes or hold them all night?"

I passed the bowl of potatoes to Grandpa at the same time Grandma reached over and tapped him in the back of the head. The look on Grandpa's face was probably the same look I had when my dad would tap me in the back of my head. He must have learned that little move from Grandma. We ate and talked for awhile until Grandma suggested that we all take a little nap before we started our trip.

I spoke first. "I think that is a great idea. This trip will be no walk in the park, and we will need all the rest we can get. We will have to set the alarm clock to get us up by 1am."

To my surprise Grandma said, "Just leave the dishes. We won't be needing them anymore." We all left the kitchen and found places to take our naps.

I heard the alarm go off in Grandma and Grandpa's room. I threw back the covers, grabbed my clothes, got dressed and rushed out to the hall. Grandpa met me at the top of the stairs.

"Carl, are you ready? You and I should leave as soon as possible to give us some extra time. We will need to stay on schedule. Do you have your escape route planned and your back-up plan also?"

"Yes, I do. I hope not to have to use my back-up plan. That will take more time for us to get to the pick-up point."

"Everything will go fine, Carl."

"Grandpa, before I fell asleep for our nap, I thought of something."

"What is that, Carl?"

"When Grandma drives down to get the little kids, what if Kevin and the doctor would ride with her and walk with the kids to help them move along and get here safely without attracting any police?"

"The guys are in the den. We can talk to them and Ramona about the change in plans."

"Nurse Glover will stay here and continue to get things lined up so we can leave as soon as all arrive at the house."

I heard the clanking of dishes. Poking my head into the kitchen, I found Grandma was picking up the dirty dishes from the table.

"You just couldn't leave them, could you?"

"Carl! Don't sneak up on me like that; and no, I couldn't. Sooner or later someone will buy the house from the state, and I don't want them to think I was a bad housewife."

"Grandpa and I will be taking off shortly to the city to get Ernie. Remember, when you go to get the little kids, the two people that you will need to talk to are Amber and her brother, Stan. Explain to them who you are and that you, Kevin and the doc have come to help them."

"Wait a minute. I didn't know that Kevin and the doctor were coming with me!"

"I know. They don't know either. It is something I thought about before the nap. They will walk with the older kids to make sure they get here safely and without any police following them."

"I still just get the little ones, right?"

"Right. As many as you can fit in the car, but only make the one trip. We don't want any extra attention drawn to us by making a number of trips."

Grandpa poked his head in the kitchen. "Carl, are you ready?"

"Yes, I'll meet you out in the car."

"Don't be long."

No sooner had Grandpa left the kitchen doorway then Kevin and Doc appeared. "I hear we have a job to do tonight," said Kevin.

"Yes. You two will help get the kids back here as fast as you can. You will need to find dark clothing, black if you have it. It will help you hide if you need to. I have to go now. Grandma will fill you in on how the operation will go. Remember Grandma, only you go out and meet with the kids. If you all go, the kids might think you are police. You two stay out in the car outside the dump while grandma goes in to meet with the leaders of the kids. If all goes well, we hope to see you at the house by about 2:45."

"Carl, you be careful."

"I will."

I left the kitchen and ran out the back door to the car. After sliding into the passenger seat, I ducked down below the window and looked up to give him the go ahead nod, and he nodded back. His face was dimly lit from the lights on the dashboard. There was no way of telling what Grandpa was thinking. He just stared out the window as he drove.

My rescue plan I played in my head over and over again until Grandpa said, "We are about one block away from the hospital. I'll drop you off at the side door. Wait in the bushes until I come to open the door."

The car came to a stop. I reached up and grabbed the door handle to let myself out. Then I ran to the bushes and pushed my way as deep into them as I could. I heard the car drive away.

Grandpa parked in front and went inside. Now all I could do was wait. The side door opened. I rose up and turned to climb out of the bushes. I heard two voices. Both were women, so I dropped to the ground and waited for them to pass. They stopped right in front of me. Inside I was screaming for them to go away. Oh no! They were going to stop and smoke. With precision timing they both lit their cigarettes. Oh, this is just great. The smoke was drifting down toward me. I don't know what it was about that smoke from those cigarettes, but it was like two hands around my throat. I pulled my shirttails out and brought them up to my face trying to breathe through them, but it wasn't helping. I coughed into my shirt to muffle it, and the ladies stopped talking and looked around.

The side door opened, and there was another voice. It was Grandpa. "Excuse me, ladies. I'm going to have to ask you either to put out the cigarettes or move all the way out to the designated smoking area in the parking lot."

The ladies mumbled something as they left for the parking lot. Once they were out of sight, Grandpa called my name. "Carl, they're gone. We must hurry. They could finish and be coming back at any time."

I pushed my way through the bushes and ran to the side door of the hospital. Once inside, Grandpa motioned that we shouldn't talk. Then he pointed to the utility closet. Slipping into the closet, I left the door slightly ajar so I could see when it would be clear to come out. Grandpa walked by the closet and gave a light rap on the door to let me know he was heading to the front door to move to the rendezvous spot. I found a pail in the closet to sit on because I had to wait until the smoking ladies came back into work.

It didn't take long until I heard the door open and the sound of two ladies talking. That was a good sound. I waited a little longer to give them time to get down the hall. After a short time I couldn't hear anything, so I slowly pushed the door open and popped out in the hallway. Quickly I moved to the stairs leading up to the third floor. As I ran up the stairs, I could feel my heart pounding from the excitement of what I was about to do.

Each flight of stairs I ran up, I got closer to getting Ernie out of this place where he should never have been. With just a few steps left to climb, I slowed down and listened to what might be happening on the third floor of the hospital. All was quiet. I approached the doorway and peeked around the corner to see if anybody was in the hallway to stop me from getting to the laundry chute that would take me down to Ernie. Up and down the hallway I moved looking for the laundry chute. I thought it was in this hallway that I was in, but it was nowhere to be found. I didn't like to think that I'd have to pass in front of the nurse's station to get to the next wing of the hospital, but I'd have to if I was going to get to Ernie. The nurse at the nurse's station was sitting right there working on the computer. A blue light on the wall started to flash and a voice boomed from all corners of the hospital saying, "We have a code blue in room 312. Code blue in room 312!"

It was like the clouds in the sky broke loose, but instead of rain, there were people all running into one room. The nurse at the nurse's station was the first to leave for the room leaving the hallway clear for me to hunt for my laundry chute.

I didn't know how much time I had before things would get back to normal, so not to look out of place, I ran up and down the hall until I found the chute. The blue light was still flashing, and the hall was clear. I lifted the large door and prepared for a ride down to the basement. Crawling into the chute, I made as little noise as possible. Carefully shutting the door to the chute with only the light sneaking around the edges of the door, I could hardly see my hands in front of my face. Cautiously I removed my feet and hands from the edges of the chute, and I started to slide very slowly, but only for a short time because I was picking up speed. A burst of light flashed in front of me. For a second I did not know what it was. Then it hit me. It must be the second floor laundry chute; someone had made a deposit. Then there was a flash and a thump behind me. Someone up on third floor had made a deposit. I could hear the dirty laundry getting closer. I tried not to touch the walls of the chute because that would slow me down; and that would mean that the dirty laundry would catch up to me, and I know I didn't want that to happen. The first floor chute entrance should be coming up soon, and I seemed to slow down at that spot. If I could stop myself and move far enough off to one side, I could let the dirty laundry go by.

No sooner had I thought those words then I was at the entrance of the first floor. As soon as I spread my hands and fee out, I stopped on a dime. The chute was large enough so that I could move to one side. As the laundry reached me, I gave the bag a push to get it on by me. I listened until it hit the door down in the laundry room. Once again I let go of the walls of the chute and continued my ride downward. I could not let myself crash through the door at the end of the chute just in case there were people in the laundry room. To slow myself down I placed my feet on the walls until I stopped at the door. Just like at the top, light was shining in around the edges of the door. I pressed my face to the door looking for a crack big enough so that I could see what was happening on the other side. I couldn't see anything, and I couldn't hear their machines running, so I pushed the door open just a little and looked. No one was in the room that I could see, but I could only see a small part of the room through the space that I was looking through. I had to go because I had wasted too much time already. I had to get to Ernie, and I would have to deal with what or who was on the other side of the door.

Lifting the door of the chute, I dropped out into a laundry cart with the dirty clothes that I had tried to avoid running into. Now I was standing in them. Quietly shutting the chute door in case the workers were nearby, I hopped out of the cart and moved to the door that I knew would lead to the hallway.

The door I opened just enough to poke my head out and look around. Again all was clear to move to the next stage to free Ernie. I dashed for the stairs that would lead me into the ward that Ernie was living in. The stairs I took two at a time, but I could hear voices, so I had to retreat and find a place to hide. As fast as I climbed the stairs, I was now running down them. Where to hide was going through my head. The back side of the stairs was open, so if I crawled back in there and hid in the shadow until they passed, I'd be okay. The voices I heard were now only feet from me. They must be the workers from the laundry room complaining about the amount of work they had to do yet tonight. The door closed behind them, and it was my chance to head up to Ernie's.

Crawling out from under the stairs, I dashed for the staircase, ascending the stairs as fast as I could. It seemed like my feet weren't even touching the steps. The big double doors were closed this time; this could be a problem. I remembered from dad's story of when he was in the information center that the back door had an alarm at the top of the door. I looked all around the edges of the door and couldn't see anything unusual about it. There were no posted signs warning that an alarm would sound. Through the doors I would go, because I had no back-up plan. This was the only way into the ward without having to check in at the front desk, and that was not an option. As I opened the door, a wave of many voices flooded my ears. Many people were moving about considering it was so late at night. I had hoped all would be quiet and that I could slip in and get Ernie and slip back out. Up next to the wall there was a cart with glasses of water, juices and cookies. This must be the time that they brought around a late night snack to the night owls on the ward. I grabbed the cart and headed towards Ernie's room.

"Hey you!" I'd been caught. Do I run and leave Ernie behind, or do I try to come up with a story? "You with the snack cart. Do you have any extra cookies?"

I turned the cart around and said, "I sure do. How many would you like?" The somewhat large man hurried over to my cart.

"Three of these; no four of these will do just fine. Thank you." He must have felt a little guilty because he said, "They're not all for me; they're for the other guys too."

"That's fine. They would just go to waste if I didn't deliver them all tonight."

"Okay. Seeing that you put it that way, I could take a few more for our second break of the night."

"Why, of course; that is a good idea."

"Say, you're new here aren't you?"

"Yes, Sir, it is my second day here."

"So how do you like the job so far?"

"I like it."

"That's great. I've got to get back to my job. I'll see you around. Say, kid, what is your name anyway?"

"Carl is my name."

"Nice meeting you, Carl, and thanks again for the cookies."

"You're welcome."

With cookie man leaving, I wasted no time pushing my cart to the doorway of Ernie's room. I looked in to see Ernie sitting in front of the window looking out. He didn't hear me come into the room.

"Would you like a late night snack, Sir?"

Ernie hurried to his feet, looked at me and said, "No snacks for me tonight, but I'm ready to take a long walk if you would be so kind as to help me."

Ernie covered his mouth and chuckled to himself quietly. Then he took off the robe he was wearing. He was already dressed in dark clothing to make the run for freedom. Just then Ernie's face changed from happy to worried. I didn't have to ask what was wrong; I could see a blurry reflection in the window that someone was standing in the doorway. I turned my cart around to see who was blocking our way out. It wasn't any of the workers; it was Bear.

"Hello, Bear. Are you looking for a late night snack?"

"No, I've had mine from the real snack person."

"So, Bear, if you don't want a snack and you know that I'm not the real snack person, what is it that you want?"

"I need you to look for my kids when you leave here."

"Why don't you have the state police look for them?"

"They are looking for them, but the police want them so they can put them in jail."

"Bear, where do you think your kids are?"

"We had moved to the very outskirts of town in a heavily wooded area until the police found us. I told the kids to run while I stood my ground. I threw rocks at the police to give the kids enough time to run away. My rocks were no match for their guns. I was hit in the leg, and over the years I ended up here in this ward of the hospital."

"What makes you think that I can find your kids when the state police can't find them?"

"Carl, I know that you are not from here. You, I believe, are from the place that only a few dare talk about and even fewer dream about going to find." I stood there saying nothing. "Carl, your silence tells me that what I have said is true."

"You are right, Bear. I'm from the freedom settlement, and I'm going back soon so I will not have time to look for your kids."

"If by chance, Carl, you would see them, tell them that their father is alive. Take them with you if you can; and if there is anything I can do for you someday, I will forever be in your debt."

"Bear, I'll do what I can, but there is only the slimmest of chances that the kids and my path will cross. I will not be back this way again, because I have no reason to return to the city."

"I understand, Carl."

Bear hung his head and began to leave the room. I felt so bad for the man. "Bear, I will still look for your kids, and I will take them with me; but I can't tell you where I'm going. Why don't you come with me now?"

"No, I can't."

"What do you mean? Why not?"

"If I was to go with you and the kids would come here and find that I had left them behind, what kind of a father would I be?"

"I understand what you are saying, Bear. I do have a request for you."

"What is that, Carl?"

"The escape route that I had planned has a few workers in our way that will need clearing for a little time. Then there is the problem of locking a door to make it look like we left the building by another way. Would you be willing to help Ernie and me?"

"Sure. I'll help!"

"You will?"

"Sure! If you don't get out of here, you can't look for my kids. Tell me what you want me to do, and I'll do it."

"I'll tell you on the way. Ernie, grab your things and let's go."

Ernie grabbed his pillow from his bed, cradled it in one arm and said, "Lead on, Carl."

"Ernie, is that all you're bringing is just your pillow?"

"No, Carl. Look inside."

I looked in the pillowcase, and there he had all kinds of things: clothes, medicine, scissors, food and a small bottle of water. "Ernie, it looks like you have everything but the sink."

Ernie reached into his pocket and pulled out bars of soap. "Carl, I may not have the sink, but I did get the soap!"

"Bear, look out in the hallway to see if it is okay to go."

Bear walked out in the hall like he always did. Then with a quick motion with his right hand, he told us to come out.

Once out in the hallway I said, "Follow me and stay close. Bear, if anybody tries to stop us, we will need you to start a fight to give us a chance to get away."

Bear didn't say a word; he just nodded his head and smiled. We saw no one as we moved down the hallway to the stairs. We pushed our way through the double doors and headed down the stairs to the laundry room. Once at the bottom of the stairs, I motioned for them to hide under the steps.

"So far so good. Now Bear, here is where I'm going to need you to help me. You will wander into the laundry room, grab the workers, put them in the laundry elevator and send it up to the top floor. To keep the workers from coming back down too soon or telling somebody, you will stop the elevator in-between floors so it will take the other workers a while to get them out. Then come out and get us. Once we're gone out the back door, we will need you to lock the door behind us. Then you can go back to your room like nothing ever happened."

"Carl, that sounds good; but what happens to Bear when they find out what he has done?" Ernie asked.

Bear replied, "No need to worry. I'm known to walk in my sleep. The people here have seen me do some crazy things while sleep walking. They will think that I'm sleep walking again and that I didn't know what I was doing like so many times before."

"Are you ready, Bear?"

"I'm ready."

"Then go! We will be waiting for you. If we don't see you in three minutes, we're coming in."

"I'll be back in two minutes," said Bear with the biggest smile I had ever seen on his face.

Ernie and I watched Bear open the door and wander into the laundry room. Then the door shut behind him. It was less than ten seconds and Bear was coming out the door again and walking over to us. "Come on. There is not one in there."

"That's great. Let's go, Ernie, before they come back." We ran to the door and hurried inside. Once inside I turned around and bolted the door shut.

"Bear, once we are gone, you can unbolt the door and go back to your room." Bear had this funny look on his face. "What's wrong, Bear?"

"How are you and Ernie getting out?"

"That's simple, Bear. We are going out into the backyard here."

"Carl, there is no way out. There is a high wall all the way around, and Ernie is much too old to climb it. And you have no ropes."

"We will be climbing down into the storm drain that leads into more tunnels that run all over town like underground streets."

Bear stuck out his large hand to say goodbye. Just as I started to say goodbye, there was someone trying to get in. "We have to go now. May God bless you, Bear."

"And you also, Carl."

We hurried out to the drain and pulled the cover back. While helping Ernie find the ladder, I could hear the workers banging on the steel door to the laundry room. I took one last look at Bear standing in the doorway. He was bolting the door to the backyard. I climbed down the ladder partway and wrapped my legs around it so I could use both hands to pull the cover back into place. As the cover slid into place, it clanged so loud it hurt my ears.

I called out to Ernie, "Ernie, have you reached the floor of the tunnel?"

"Yes, Carl, I have. But I have one question. No, make that two questions."

As I floundered for the floor of the tunnel with my one foot I asked Ernie, "What are you questions?"

Before Ernie could get the first question out, I reached into my pocket and turned on the flashlight that I got from Grandma. "Well, now that you have turned on the light, I only have one question left. Which way are you going?"

"We will be going this way until we see the fifth street tunnel. Then we will go down two manhole covers before we climb back up on the street. We will hopefully not have to wait too long to get picked up by my Grandpa in his car."

"Carl, how will we know that we are at the fifth street tunnel?"

"The city has made it easy for us by writing the names of the streets at each intersection of the tunnel. They intended it to help their workers know where they were when working in the tunnels. Now we will use them to help us escape the city. Look here, Ernie. Do you see where it says Second Street? We have only three more blocks to go."

"I hope I can walk that far. I'm not in as good of shape as I was back when I knew your dad. We don't get a lot of exercise there in the hospital."

"I'm sure you will do just fine; but if you need to rest, you just let me know. We can stop as many times as you need to."

I walked beside Ernie down the tunnel. I could see that his pace was slowing down, but he was not asking for a rest. There was another street intersection coming up. This should be Fourth Street. I'd stop there, and if Ernie asked why I was stopping, I'd tell him that I needed a rest because it was only the beginning of a very long night. I shined the light up on the wall of the tunnel where the city had written Fourth Street, so I slowed down and came to a stop.

Ernie took a few more steps and then turned around and looked at me. "Carl, why are you stopping? That only said Fourth Street. We still have one more street to go."

"I know, Ernie, but I need to rest a little. It has been a long day, and it is only the beginning of a very long night. Come over here and sit with me while we rest for just a few minutes. Then we will get going again."

"If I sit down, I might not get back up with these old bones of mine."

"Sit down and I will help you back up when it is time to go." I reached out my hand and helped him down to the floor of the tunnel. Ernie gave a big sigh when he leaned back up against the wall. "Ernie," I said, "Did you think that the day would ever come that you would leave the city and head to the settlement that you had helped so many people get to?"

"To tell you the truth, Carl, I had always hoped that someday they would send someone back to get me. I gave up hoping when people from the settlement stopped coming back go get more people. You are the first person back from the settlement in many years. It has been so long that I'm not sure how long it has really been."

"I wouldn't have thought about looking you up if it wasn't for my dad saying something. You see when I left the settlement, I left late at night; and it was not until morning that the people of the settlement noticed that I was gone and they came after me. I had gotten to a point of no return you might say. They could not make the journey any further because they did not have the right equipment. That is when my dad said, hoping I could hear him, 'Look for Ernie, and bring him back if you can.'"

"I had thought that maybe one day Mark would come back to get me. I had never ever given any thought to the idea that his son would find me."

"I found you, and now we are heading home. Speaking of heading home, it is time for us to get going so we can meet up with Grandpa." I jumped to my feet and reached out my hands to Ernie.

"Ernie, take hold of my hands, and I will help you up." Carefully I pulled Ernie up off the floor to his feet. He teetered back and forth a little, but then he steadied himself by reaching out for my arm.

"Carl, if you don't mind, I'd like to hang onto your arm a while until the stiffness gets worked out of my knees."

"That's fine, Ernie. You hang on me as much and as long as you need to." We took off walking, and I could feel Ernie swaying a little, but he got better the longer we walked.

"Carl, what was that noise?"

"What noise?"

"Listen!" We stopped walking and then I heard it. There was someone else in the tunnel walking toward us. "What do we do, Carl?"

"We need to get to the fifth street intersection and turn up there hoping that we don't run into the person or persons that are in the tunnel. We need to pick up the pace if you can, because we do not want to get caught down here. There would be no way of talking our way out of why we are down here."

We walked as fast as Ernie's legs could go. We had no idea where these people were, or if they had stopped to listen and they knew that we were down here. I shined my light on the wall looking for the words "Fifth Street" and there they were. I tapped Ernie on the shoulder and pointed to the sign. He smiled. As we turned up the fifth street tunnel, I stopped.

"I'm going to listen and try to hear if the people are getting closer or farther away." I cupped my hands behind my ears trying to hear even the slightest of sounds.

Ernie tapped me on my shoulder and whispered, "Do you hear anything?"

"No, not yet; but I want to listen a little bit longer before we move on." Again I cupped my hands around my ears and strained to listen. Then I heard it as plain as day. Two voices were talking to each other, and I could hear footsteps. They were coming this way and they weren't that far away.

I took Ernie by the arm and whispered in his ear, "We need to move further down the tunnel and hope that they don't come our way."

We moved down the tunnel as quietly as possible passing a ladder that lead up to the street. Ernie stopped and pointed up. I shook my head no and motioned for him to keep walking. The voices were getting louder and clearer. We came to a second ladder heading up to the street.

Ernie stopped and whispered in my ear, "This is where we get out, you said."

"I know, Ernie, but we have to wait until these voices move past us to that when we climb the ladder, they don't hear us and come back and catch us. Plus pushing the manhole cover off will make a lot of noise. They will come running when they hear that, but I hope that we are long gone before they reach this tunnel. We are far enough away from the main tunnel that if they start to come this way, we will rush up the ladder and get out on the street above and hope the Grandpa will be there to help us get away." Ernie nodded his head agreeing with the plan. Then he pointed to his ear and then pointed down the tunnel. I cupped my hands around my ears. I could hear the voices. They must be very close to the fifth street tunnel entrance. They were talking about the tunnel.

"Do we really need to check each tunnel?"

"Hey! You know that's what the captain said we had to do, so that's what I'm going to do."

"Now wait a minute here. How is the captain going to know it we went up each tunnel?"

"He might ask."

"Wow, let me take a wild guess here. We tell him that we did, and he'll be happy."

"Okay. I'll follow your lead." I looked Ernie in the face and made the motion of wiping sweat off my forehead.

Ernie pulled on my arm to bring my ear down to him and whispered, "The Lord was watching out for us on this one."

"Yes he was."

"Carl, what do we do now?"

"We just have to wait a little longer, and then climb to the street and meet up with Grandpa."

"How long is a little longer?"

"Why? What's wrong?"

"Carl, I'm old and this cold, damp air down here is making me very chilled."

"Okay, we'll climb up to the street now. I'll climb up first and push the cover off. Then I'll come down and help you up. There is one thing you have to do when you get to the street; look both ways before you stick your head out too far. It is very early in the morning, but there are still people out there driving around. Here I go! Oh, and Ernie, if those guys come back, don't wait for me to come down and get you. Start climbing and don't stop."

I grabbed onto the rungs of the ladder and pulled myself up to the manhole cover. As I wrapped my legs around the ladder, I listened to see if there were any cars coming down the street.

"Carl, are you down there?" The sound of a voice on the other side of the manhole cover frightened me, and I almost lost my grip with my legs. Then I realized it was Grandpa.

"Grandpa, don't do that! I almost fell." Just then I felt Ernie grabbing the ladder.

"Carl, the men are coming back!"

"Grandpa, help me get the cover off. There are two men down here in the tunnel, and Ernie says they are coming this way. They are not that far away."

I could hear grandpa struggling to help me get the cover off. At the same time I could feel Ernie climbing up the ladder, and it wouldn't be long and he would be at my feet. Pushing with all my strength, I could feel the cover start to move. Grandpa's finger curled around the edge of the cover, and with a big growl Grandpa pulled the cover back. I could feel the rush of fresh air come over me. Then I felt Ernie's hands hit my feet.

"Don't just stand there, Carl. Get moving. They are in the fifth street tunnel and I can see the light from their flashlights."

I scrambled out onto the street. Grandpa and I both reached down into the hole each taking a hold of one of Ernie's arms, and we pulled him out of the tunnel.

We could hear the men's voices saying, "Is there anyone down there? We are with the state police."

Grandpa motioned for Ernie and me to run to the car. As I turned to run for the car, Grandpa grabbed my arm and pulled me close. "Nice work, Carl. Now get in the back seat of the car and stay down low."

"What are you going to do?"

"I have to put the cover back on or the state will know something is fishy."

"Grandpa, they will see you."

"That's okay. I'll just say that I noticed the cover off and that I was just putting it back on so no one would get hurt. Now go!"

As I ran away, I could hear the voices say, "Who is up there?"

Grandpa replied back, "I'm Captain Wilson of the state police. Who are you?"

"I'm Patrolman Jay Sherman, Sir. My partner and I are on tunnel patrol."

"I haven't been told of any such thing."

"Our desk sergeant read the new directive to us tonight at role call. The state has ordered all cities with tunnels like ours to be patrolled randomly to crack down on illegal activities."

"That sounds like a great idea."

"Sir, may I ask you a question?"

"Yes, you may."

"Why are you removing the manhole cover?"

"Well, Patrolman Sherman, I'm not removing it; I'm placing it on the hole. I was driving down the road, and when my headlights shined in front of me, I noticed that the cover was off. I didn't want anyone to drive over it and cause and accident and have someone get hurt. Does that answer your question?"

"Yes, Sir!"

"Now I'm going to finish putting this cover back in its rightful place, and you two can continue your patrol of the tunnel. I will have to check your report out when I get into the office next time and see what you found."

"Yes, Sir! Have a good night, Sir."

"I will. I'm going home."

I could hear Grandpa's footsteps coming closer to the car. I raised my head slightly to make sure it was Grandpa, and it was. Grandpa looked into my eyes but showed no emotion.

He opened the car door, slid into the seat and reached for the key to start the car.

Grandpa looked forward and said, "You two stay low. There are two people looking out their windows, and I don't know how much they might have seen. We will need to get out of here fast but not raise any suspicions."

The car started and we were moving. Ernie and I felt every turn and bump in the road. It reminded me of my first ride in the police car to the hospital with the doctor. Maybe all policemen drive like this.

"You two can sit up now. We are almost out of town, and there are no more houses out this way until we get to our house. That will be about five minutes." Both Ernie and I struggled to get up in the back seat, because we had been squished down low for so long. I saw Ernie rubbing his knees; he was in pain.

"Ernie, are you going to be okay?"

"Yes, I'm fine. It's just that I have not done so much running and hiding since . . . . Ummm . . . ."

"Since you helped my dad get out of the city."

"Yes, Carl. It has been that long, but I do have to tell you I did not help your dad all that much to get out of the city. Most of it was clues left by his grandpa. I was there just to encourage him to keep searching and not give up."

"Alright you two, listen up. There is a car following us. It may be nothing; but then again, the people that were looking out their windows may have called it in. I'll pull into the garage and close the door. Carl, I'll need you to take Ernie into the house through the tunnel. I'll go in the back door of the house and wait until the car either drives by, or if it does stop, I'll talk to them outside, since the house will be hopefully full of kids. Any questions?"

Ernie mumbled something. "What did you say, Ernie?"

"I said another tunnel!"

"Yes, Ernie, I'm sorry, but we must go this way. You'll have to get used to it. There will be more tunnels yet today."

"Great!"

"I'll see you two inside in just a few minutes." Grandpa shut off the car and the garage door was shutting automatically.

"Okay, Ernie, let's move to the tunnel."

"Is this a long tunnel?"

"No, the tunnel will lead into the basement of the house, so it is a short tunnel."

"Carl, where is the tunnel?"

"You're standing on the door."

"Sorry! I didn't know."

"It is okay, Ernie. If it was obvious, the police would have found it and me a long time ago. You'll go first, and then me. Once you get down in the tunnel, I'll shut the door and climb down. We will be in the house in no time flat."

"Good. It will be good to rest, because you said we weren't done for the day, right?"

"You are correct, Ernie. We have to get to a safe place before we can stop for the night. Ernie, there is a ladder with about nine or ten rungs that you will climb down until you reach the floor of the tunnel. I'll shine my flashlight on the ladder so you can see where you have to put your feet, okay?"

"That will be great. Thank you, Carl."

"Alright Ernie, can you see the first rung?"

"Yes, I can. Thank you. The light really helps. I feel much better when we have a light on."

What Ernie just said must be true for him. He was climbing down the ladder as if he was a kid. When we got to the bottom, I said, "I'll shut the door and then I'll be down."

As I grabbed the door and started to move it into place, the garage door opened. I heard voices-angry voices-and they were not happy with Grandpa. I finished putting the door in place and descended to the floor of the tunnel and said to Ernie, "Grandpa was right. There was someone following, and they sound mad. As much as I would like to hear what they are saying, I think it is best if we move toward the house and get inside to let them know what is going on, if they don't know already."

"Carl, if it is okay, could I keep the flashlight?"

"Yes, if that is what helps you, then you can have it. You get to lead then."

I handed him the flashlight. We moved through the tunnel like water through a pipe, and we were at the trap door leading into the house in no time.

"Now Ernie, before we get too far into the house, we will have to listen to make sure there are no police in the house already. What I will do is climb up a secret set of stairs that Great Grandpa Roy put in. There I can listen better."

"What if there are police in the house? Then what do we do?"

"Let's hope the house is safe, because I really don't know what to do then."

I opened the door into the basement and climbed out. Then I grabbed Ernie's hand and helped him out. I put my finger up to my mouth, and he nodded his head. I motioned for him to follow me to the secret stairs, and then motioned for him to sit on the bottom step and rest. I made my way up the stairs and popped open the trap door at the top and listened. There was Grandma's voice, and there was the doctor's voice. I pressed my ear to the door leading to the hallway to listen for any other voices and possibly hear what they were saying. I strained to hear something. Just then someone walked by the closet where I was hiding. It was Grandma.

"What is Russell doing out there with those policemen? Doesn't he know that we have things to do yet? And where are Carl and Ernie? He better not have gotten Carl captured by the police because of one of his crazy ideas."

To ease Grandma's mind, I gently knocked on the closet door. Grandma stopped rambling on about Grandpa. I opened the door and our faces met.

"Carl, it's you," she said.

I quickly answered, "SHHH! I'm okay, and Ernie is in the basement. Is the house safe?"

"Yes, but what is happening with Russell?"

"Some people saw Ernie and I come up out of the tunnel under the street, and Grandpa thinks they may have called it in. He is out there trying to get rid of the policemen. Where are the kids? Did you get them all? Where is Amber?"

"I'm right here, Carl."

The door opened a little farther, and there she was. "What are you smiling so big for, Carl?"

"I'm not smiling, Grandma . . . . Am I?"

"Yes, you are."

"I must be happy to see you, Grandma."

"Carl, you did not start smiling until you saw Amber."

"Let's get on with more important stuff. Is it okay for Ernie and me to come up out of the basement?"

"Yes, it is safe enough."

"Good. We'll go to the basement stairs and meet you in the kitchen. I think Ernie might be hungry."

"Carl, I think it is more likely that you are hungry. You eat just like your dad."

"How is that?"

"Your dad always seemed to be eating something."

"I'll see you in a minute, and you can meet Ernie."

Grandma closed the closet door and I turned to head back downstairs. The door popped open again. Grandma said, "Russell got the policemen to leave."

"Good. The sooner the better."

"Carl."

"Yes, Grandma."

"Amber is very pretty. If you play your cards right . . . ."

"Grandma, enough already!"

Grandma closed the door once again. I better get Ernie and head to the kitchen and get some food. Then maybe I could find out what the police said to Grandpa.

"Ernie, get ready to go. The house is safe, and we will be going up to the kitchen. You can meet the rest of the crew that will be going with us and get something to eat."

"Great! Food! I did miss my snack you know. I heard you ask about Amber. Is she your girlfriend?"

"No! She's not my girlfriend. She is the girl that is the leader of the kids that we are taking back with us."

"Carl, what is this lever for?"

"Ernie, don't touch that!"

I was too late. The stairs folded into the slide and down I came, crashing my head into the wall with a thump. "I'm sorry, Carl. I didn't know that it would do that."

"It's okay, Ernie. I'll be alright. Let's just go upstairs and meet the crew. Follow me."

I opened the door to the kitchen. There was Grandma with this big smile on her face and Amber standing next to her. A smile started forming on my face, so I had to fight it off. Otherwise Grandma would never let me hear the end of it. Beyond Grandma and Amber was a sea of faces, both old and young. There were kids everywhere. Some were sitting at the table eating, and others were on the floor with small plates of food. Every kid had a smile on his face. I looked for my little buddy, Karl, with a K; but I did not see him.

"Amber, where is my little buddy, Karl?"

I felt a tug on my arm. I turned my head to see who it was. There was Karl, smiling with a cookie crumb falling out of his mouth. He was holding a handful of Grandma's cookies tightly in his hand.

"There's my little buddy."

"Hi, Carl." I could hardly make out the words because he had so many cookies in his mouth. I just had to laugh.

Grandpa spoke, "Now that we are all here, let us pray to God and thank Him for this day." The kitchen went silent for only a few seconds, and then all the kids started to pray, and the adults joined in. It sounded like a thousand bees swarming around. I tried to listen, but all the prayers blurred together. I'm sure God was smiling hearing all these prayers of thankfulness. I took my turn thanking God for all that he had done for me and this group.

"God, you know we have only just begun our journey to the settlement. Give us all the strength to make the journey. Amen!"

I opened my eyes and looked around. Most had finished giving thanks to God. There were many red and wet eyes looking at me. I didn't want to stop the moment, but we adults needed to talk so we could get ready to move out.

"If I could have all the adults meet in the living room; we will need you kids to stay in here. We need to talk a little, and then we will be on our way. Stan, could you stand in the doorway and keep the kids in here? But I want you to be able to hear what we are saying, because you are going to be a leader of a group also."

"Okay, Carl. I can do that."

"Thank you, Stan."

I worked my way through the sea of kids and down the hallway to the living room. All eyes were on me when I looked around the room. "Today is the day that I have been waiting for. Many years ago I had a dream that someday I would go to the city to get my grandparents and bring them home. Little did I know that I was dreaming too small in comparison to how awesome my God is. Look at all of you, and look at all the kids. Isn't our God awesome!?"

Ernie shouted out, "Tell it like it is, Carl!"

Out of the corner of my eye, I could see Grandma and Grandpa hugging each other and crying tears of joy. Then I felt tears starting to well up in my eyes.

"Now that I got that said, here are your assignments until we get to the settlement. Each one of you will be in charge of a small group of kids. Amber, do you have a count on the number of kids we have? And remember, don't count you and Stan."

"We have 55 kids."

"We have nine adult leaders. That would mean that we . . . ."

"Carl, would it be okay if I was not in charge of any of the kids? At my age I don't know if I'll be much help."

"Okay, Ernie. We can do that. Now we have eight leaders. Yes, Doctor, do you have a question?"

"Well, I was wondering if it would be a good idea to put Ernie in my group. That way I could make sure he is getting the things that he needs for a man of his age."

"What do you think, Ernie?"

"That is a great idea."

"Now we have 56 kids. We will want a good mix in the groups. I don't want all boys in one group, nor do I want all the wee ones in one group. These groups are what we will use to keep track of each other. We will eat in our groups and sleep in our groups until we are home. Are there any questions on anything so far? Good. Here is what we have to do. We will walk along the river toward the old mill, or what is left of it. Once we are all there, I will climb up the wall where the water wheel was and open up a small door. We will then have Kevin, Doc and Grandpa come up next. They will take turns pulling the kids up the wall and into the tunnel using ropes. Those adults that are not up in the tunnel will be down below tying the ropes onto the kids and keeping them calm and very quiet. Once we are all up in the tunnel, I will give you the next set of instructions. Now do we have any questions?"

"What if the kids are afraid to go up the wall?"

"Well, Nurse Glover, you will have to get very creative to make it look fun."

"What if there is an adult that is afraid to go up that wall?"

"Then I will have to get creative and make it fun for that person." I got the hint that Nurse Glover may not like the climbing of the wall. I couldn't tell her what she was in for once we got in the tunnel. "Are there any other questions?"

Kevin raised his hand, "When do we leave?"

"We will leave as soon as we divide up the kids. I would like each leader to find a room in the house. Amber and Stan will bring you your kids and introduce them to you. Get their supplies that they have. Divide up the weight so all have some but not too much. When you are done, send one person from your group to the kitchen to report that your group is ready. Once we are all ready, I will leave out the back door to see if all is clear. Grandpa, I think it would be good to go to the attic and look out the windows up there to see if there are any police in the area of the old mill or the path along the river. If there are no other questions, let's find a room, get our kids and get ready to move out." It was quiet as the adults left the room. "Amber, can you wait up a minute? Can you make sure Karl is in my group?"

"I was planning on doing that. I thought you might want him with you."

"Thank you, Amber." Stan was busy splitting up the kids in eight groups. "The groups look good to me. What do you think Amber?"

"Stan knows the kids really well. I'd say what he has done here should work."

"Well, Stan, we will go with your groupings, and if we need to make changes down the road, we can do that. But for now let's get the kids to their leaders. Have them bring their stuff with them. They may have to repack." I was surprised at how quiet the kids were. No one was crying, complaining or fighting. Let's hope it lasted. "All right, kids that are in my group, why don't you bring your stuff over to the table and see if we need to repack anything." I asked one of the boys, "What is your name?"

"Jeremy."

"Do you have a last name?"

"McNeal is what they tell me it is. I was very small when they say the police came and took my Mom and Dad away. Amber found me crying one day on my front porch. When she found out that my mom and dad went to jail, she said I could come and live with her because her mom and dad went to jail, too."

"Well, Jeremy, your family just got bigger. Okay kids, I need you to dump out your things and let's see what you are bringing with." I looked through the things the kids had gathered. The amount that they had gathered in such a short period of time was amazing. "You kids did a great job of collecting things to bring to the settlement. How did you get all this stuff?"

"Mr. Wilson, we know a lot of nice people that give us things sometimes. We told them that we were going to move to another city, and would they like to help by giving us some supplies for the long trip."

"That was a good idea. One thing I will need you kids to do is call me Carl, not Mr. Wilson. Save that name for my Grandpa, okay?"

"Okay, Carl."

"And what is your name?"

"Molly Swanson. But my Mom and Dad would call me Sweet Pea."

"Are your mom and dad in jail too?"

"No, they died last year when they were in jail."

"May I call you Sweet Pea?"

"Yes, you can, Carl."

"Sweet Pea, how old are you?"

"I'm four and a half."

"Carl, there are some kids here."

"Thank you, Jeremy, for telling me that. I need you kids to pack your stuff up again, and then sit over there in the corner. As soon as we are ready, we will go."

The kids from the other groups were streaming into the kitchen reporting that their groups were ready. Grandpa's group reported that all was clear and that we could move out any time, the sooner the better. I stood up on a chair and counted to make sure I had seven kids and that they were all there.

"Okay, kids, what I would like you to do is go back to your leader and tell them to line up outside in the backyard. Be very quiet and bring all you stuff. We are moving out now. Now go!" Each kid turned and ran to their leader. It wasn't long until I heard footsteps from every direction.

I told my group, "Kids, it is time for us to get our things and go outside in the backyard." When I walked out on the back porch, I could not believe my eyes. The kids and leaders were all in a row like the corn behind them.

"Listen up. From now on we cannot have any talking unless you see the police coming; then tell your leader. My group will go first. Grandpa, I would like your group to go last. If at any time we have to hide, group leaders, it will be your responsibility to keep your kids together. Let's move out."

I gathered my kids and we started walking along the corn-field toward the river. The groups moved along so quietly it was as if they had pillows on their feet. When my group reached the path, I whispered in Jeremy's ear, "I need you to follow the path. I have to talk to another leader."

Jeremy nodded his head and went down the path to the old mill. As each leader passed by I asked if everything was all right, and each one said yes. Then I ran back up to the front of the line and took the lead again.

The light of the moon lit the path nicely. I could see some of the places I stayed the first night when I came to the city. I got so carried away remembering my first days that I almost forgot to stop and make sure that the area was safe. With the construction of the new state prison, they had cleared the land of trees and there were no hiding spots.

I told my group of kids to sit down. As each group caught up with us, I had them sit down. After everyone arrived, I pulled the leaders together to talk about how we were going to get to the old mill and the wall. Before I could say anything, I heard a car coming down the road from the direction of the city. I told the kids to be absolutely quiet. I was thinking that we needed him to quickly pass by or turn around and go back to the city, because we would be running out of darkness soon. Inside my head I was yelling at the car to get moving; but the more I yelled, the slower the car moved. Then the car stopped. The engine was turned off and the policeman inside got out and began to walk around the construction site.

Grandpa made his way over to me. "Carl, I think we have some trouble here. One of the last things I heard at the station was that the construction site had been losing equipment during the night and that they might put a patrolman out on the site to stop the loss of equipment."

"Grandpa, why didn't we see the policeman when we first got here? This policeman just showed up now."

Just then Ernie tapped me on the shoulder and pointed at a policeman coming out of the construction site to meet with the policeman that just drove up. We were too far away to hear what they were saying. They didn't talk long, and the policeman that was on duty got in the car and turned it around to head back to town leaving the new patrolman all alone at the site.

I told the leaders, "We need to come up with a plan to get the policeman out of our way so we can move on. What do we have for ideas?"

No one said anything. They took turns looking at each other hoping that someone else had an idea. We needed an idea, and we needed it fast, and no one was saying anything.

Grandpa said, "I could go up and talk to him to see when he would be making a trip into the construction site. That would give us time to get into the tunnel."

"Grandpa, you don't sound real sure that it would work."

"No, I'm not sure he would make a trip into the construction site, because where he's standing you can see almost the entire site without moving."

"What else do we have for ideas?"

Amber leaned forward and said, "Someone needs to let himself be seen and start running hoping the patrolman will chase."

"I have a few problems with that idea. First, whoever sacrifices himself would not be able to make it back here without bringing the policeman back with him; so he would not be able to go to the settlement. That brings up my second problem. The person knows too much that if caught could be forced to talk and tell what he knows, and that would then put everyone in jeopardy."

"Can I say something?"

"What is it, Doc?"

"Who would volunteer for the job knowing that they would be left behind, and would face being arrested and beaten until they told what they knew or die keeping the secret? As a doctor I have seen what the police can do to a person. I hate to say it, but I would not volunteer for the job."

"That is okay, Doc. No one will be left behind. We will have to come up with another plan."

357

"Why?" Amber asked as she pulled my arm to spin me toward her. I could see the anger in her face. "I'm volunteering. I can run fast, and I know the city better than anyone. I know of a million places to hide, and there are many people that will help me hide until things cool down. I can do it!"

"No, Amber, you're not going. The kids need you."

"So what are we going to do? Just sit in the dirt until daylight and get caught doing nothing? Not me! I'd rather get caught trying to get away than get caught doing nothing."

"My answer is still no! We still have time to think of something."

"Fine! Let me know when you come up with something. I'm going back to be with my group of kids."

Amber got up and walked past me. I reached out and grabbed her by the arm and said, "Amber, let me talk to you for a minute."

"No. You have said enough."

"Please, Amber. Stop and let's talk."

She pulled her arm from my hand and walked away. I turned to the rest of the leaders, "I'll be back in just a minute. Have a few ideas ready."

I followed Amber back to her group. "Amber, stop. Listen to me."

"Why, Carl? Did you really listen to me?"

"Yes, I did listen to you."

"Carl, I know I can do this. I want to do this. You say the kids need me. You're right. They need me to pull the policeman from his post long enough for you to get them into the tunnel."

"And what if you get caught? I couldn't stand the thought of what the police would do to you to get you to talk."

"Who said I'm going to get caught? And if I did by the remotest chance get caught, I would die before I said anything. My kids need the chance to live in a community of love, and that is what they will get when you get them to the settlement."

I knew what she was saying was true. Her plan was the best. I looked back at the group and they weren't talking; they were too busy watching Amber and me. I turned back to Amber, and she was ready to say more in the defense of her plan, but I didn't need to hear anymore.

I clamped my hand over her mouth and looked her in the face and said, "You're right! Get ready to run."

"Really?"

"Yes, Amber. It is the only way we can move on."

"I can do this!"

"I know. I want you to run like you have never run before, because I'm coming back to get you after I get the rest of these people to the settlement."

"No, Carl, don't come. Stay at the settlement. I'll be fine. I have lived on the run from the state for most of my life."

"I'm coming back. I promise I will be back to get you and bring you home. There are some things in the house that you may need. Grandma and Grandpa won't be back, so take them. Take whatever food is left. Do whatever you can to keep the police away from here for at least 30 to 45 minutes. That way we can get everybody and the supplies in the tunnel."

"Carl, you don't need to come back and get me. I'll be okay. My mother talked about an aunt that lives in a town not far from here. I'll make my way there and start over."

"No! Stay here and I'll be back as soon as I can. I give you my word; I promise. I will be back to get you! Now let's go tell the rest what you are going to do." We walked back to the rest of the leaders. As we weaved our way through the sea of kids, I found my hand in Amber's hand. It was strange but nice.

"Has anybody come up with a different idea on how to get the police out of here?" I looked at the leaders. "Don't all speak at once."

Grandpa came up to me and said, "We talked about it, but we came up with nothing new."

"Amber and I talked about her idea, and we decided that since she is willing to have the police chase her, then that is what she is going to do."

"No, Carl, you can't let her do that!"

"Grandma, it will be okay. Amber is very smart, and she knows the streets. She will be able to hide. I have given her a promise that I'll come back and get her as soon as I get you folks to the settlement. She will not have to be here that long."

Grandma had tears in her eyes as she came up to give Amber a hug. The rest of the leaders hugged Amber and thanked her for the sacrifice that she was going to make. "Stan, can you divide Amber's group and help them get into their new groups? The rest of you leaders get your kids ready. Once Amber has gotten the police to move from his post, we don't have a lot of time to waste; we don't know how long she will keep him away. The state might call in more police, so we will have to move quickly. Get ready for my signal, and run to the old mill wall that you can see right there in front of us."

The leaders walked by Amber one more time to say words of encouragement. I walked up to Amber, took her hands in mine and looked into her face. "Amber, I'd like to pray with you before you make your run."

In a voice so quiet you almost couldn't hear her, she said, "That would be nice."

We prayed and held hands for what seemed like forever. When we had run out of words, we stopped and just looked into each other's eyes. It was then I realized what Grandma had been trying to tell me for the longest time.

"Amber, I would like to tell you something. I love you."

"I know, Carl. Your Grandma told me that the first time we had a chance to talk. I love you too, Carl."

"You do?"

"Yes, I do. I had to get used to you at first, but after awhile you kind of grow on a person."

"Then you're going to wait here in the city for me to come back and get you, right?"

"I'll be waiting."

I could see the leaders had the kids ready. Grandpa walked by us and gave me a push in the back and said, "Kiss her already. We don't have forever."

I was about to say something to Grandpa when Amber's hands clamped onto my face and she kissed me. "Now Carl, if you want a second kiss, I'll give you one when you come back to get me."

"You know I'll be back. I promise you that!"

"It is time for me to go."

"Amber, what do you plan on doing to get the attention of the policeman?"

She leaned forward and whispered in my ear. Then she walked past all the kids telling them to be good and that she would see them soon. She said she had to do something very important, and that they should listen to the adult leaders. As she jogged back down the trail, she stopped to wave goodbye.

As she darted into the woods and headed for the road, we all lost sight of her for almost five minutes. Then we hear her shouting from the road about a hundred yards away from the policeman. I was amazed; the policeman did nothing. She started walking toward him still yelling to try to get him to chase her, but nothing was happening.

I told the leaders as I ran by them, "Stay here!"

I ran down the path and then cut up through the woods until I came to the ditch alongside the road just 20 feet from Amber. "Carl, she yelled, "What are you doing?"

"I'm here to help you get the policeman's attention."

I pulled out my slingshot and loaded it up with the small rocks from the side of the road. I drew the slingshot back and gave it a high arch to make the rocks rain down on the policeman. I didn't want to hurt him; I just wanted to get his attention. Quickly I launched the rocks and reloaded to get a second shot off before the first wave of rocks hopefully landed all around him.

The second wave of rocks were launched through the air. The first wave reached my target, and with the second wave soon to be on target, that is when I would head back into the woods. With the policeman ducking for cover, he wouldn't see me run from the ditch back into the woods. He would only think one thing, and that was that Amber had launched the attack on him, and he would give chase. As I ran through the woods, I could hear the anger in the policeman's voice as the rocks rained down on him. I did not stop running until I got back to the group.

Grandpa told me what had happened. "Carl, I don't know for sure what you did; but after some yelling by the policeman, he took off running, and Amber stayed there and did not run."

"What? She was supposed to run and stay as far away as she could and not get caught. What was she thinking?"

"It's okay, Carl. She took off running when he got closer."

Amber's brother jumped in the conversation. "Amber is a very fast runner. When she did start running, she was at only half speed. She was toying with the policeman to make sure that he would not quit but continue to chase her. And he is still chasing her."

"Can anyone see Amber now?"

I only heard people muttering, but no one said anything. It was killing me not knowing what was going on, but I needed to get the people moving. "Okay people, it is time to go. Doc, I want your group to go first. Once you get to the wall, get the ropes out and climb up the wall. The old stone wall is very easy to climb. Open the door to the tunnel, send the rope down and start hauling kids up. Then when Kevin and Grandpa get there, get up the wall and help pull up the kids. Any questions?"

"Yes, Doc, what is it?"

"When we talked about the plan, you said that you would go up the wall first."

"True. But since I ran to the road and back, I need a little time to rest and catch my breath. I know you can do this. Take your group now and go!"

Doc turned to his group and said, "Follow me and don't stop."

We all watched the doc climb the wall, open the door and crawl in. That is when I sent the next group with Kevin. Then Grandpa's group went next. The three men were up in the tunnel pulling kids up the wall as fast as they could. Sometimes the kids looked like spiders hanging from a thread with their legs and arms kicking around.

"Are you ready?" I asked the rest of the groups.

We took off running. About halfway to the wall I heard a loud explosion behind me. I turned around and looked in the direction of Grandma and Grandpa's house, and there in the sky was a huge fireball lighting up the pre-dawn sky. I didn't know what to do. Part of me said run to the wall, and another part of m e said run to the house and see if Amber was alright. I stood there motionless until Grandpa yelled for me to keep moving. I ran to the wall, and Grandpa threw down a rope. Quickly I tied the rope around my waist, and then gave the rope a tug to let them know that I was about to climb the wall. I was the last of our group to climb the wall. Halfway up I tried to look over my shoulder to see what was happening back at the house when I saw another fireball. I lost my footing and began to fall. The rope around my waist had stopped me from falling to the ground but not without cost, because the rope had slid from my waist to under my armpits. The pain I felt now I'm sure was less than what I would have felt if I had fallen to the ground. Once again I grabbed onto the wall and finished the climb; this time thinking only about finding each foot and hand hold until I reached the tunnel door.

The excitement of looking into the tunnel that I had come out of a few days back and thinking of going home helped me finish the climb and set my feet on the floor of the tunnel to look out over the city. It was then that I could see that it <u>was</u> Grandpa and Grandma's house that was burning. The smoke was drifting towards the city, and I could hear the crackling of the old timbers of the house that had been in the Wilson family for many years. I looked at my Grandparent's faces, but they didn't seem sad at all.

"Grandma, aren't you sad about seeing your house burning?"

"No, Carl, knowing that it helped draw the police away so we could escape was worth it. Besides, we aren't going to need it anymore. We will be making a new life at the settlement."

"I'd rather see our house burn to the ground than to let the state get a hold of it," Grandpa jumped in.

"I guess you're right, Grandpa. We better shut the door, and I'll tell you what will happen next now that we are in the tunnel."

Chapter 12

Homeward Bound

"**E**veryone sit down and rest awhile. I will tell you what we are going to be doing next on our journey home."

For the next 20 minutes or so I told them all that we had to do and what dangers we could run into. As always I asked if there were any questions, and there was none. Were there really no questions, or were they too tired to ask or too afraid of the answer they might get?

"Grab your things and leave nothing behind for the state to find. Stan, remember to drag the ladder over the floor to cover our footprints."

"Yes, Carl. I'll do that."

"Stan!"

"Carl, I know. As soon as I'm done with the ladder, get it up to you because you will need it."

"From now on we will only talk when we need to, and only use your flashlight when you absolutely have to so we can save on batteries. We'll try to move as quickly as possible; but if we need to rest, let me know, and we can stop if possible. Here we go!"

My flashlight was the only light on as I lead the way. I could hear the kids whispering as we walked deeper into the tunnel. Doc said to someone further back in the group that this was not so bad. I knew that in a short while he would be telling a different story when we got to the wet, slippery slope in the tunnel. You could feel the tunnel floor was starting to head down, and the walls were getting wet. I began to slide along the floor, and it wouldn't be long before we would have to get the ropes out. I heard Stan coming with the ladder.

"Make way for the ladder!" Stan called out.

"Stan, you're just in time. Put the ladder down here; and as you head back to the end of the line, tell all those with the long ropes to come up front. And have the rest of the people find a place to rest out of the way of the people coming with the ropes."

"Okay, Carl. I'll send them your way."

I grabbed the ladder and turned it so it would stretch from wall to wall. The rope I had in my backpack I dug out and tied around my waist. As each person came with their rope, I tied them together end to end.

"I need all the leaders to make sure your kids hang onto the rope with both hands and walk backwards. The leaders need to go first just in case someone slips. That way you can catch them before they fall too far and get hurt. My group will go first. Kevin and Stan, I'll need you to man the rope. I have wrapped it around the one leg of the ladder to help you lower me down."

"Are you guys ready?"

"Yes, we are ready."

"Kids from my group, grab onto the rope. Where is Sweet Pea? I need her here next to me so I can keep an eye on her. As soon as we get to the bottom, I will give two big tugs on the rope; that is when you can tie the rope off and send down the next group. Stan, I'll need you to go last; but before you get started, you will need to send the ladder down to us controlling its descent by hanging onto the rope. Once we have the ladder, let the rope go and we will coil it up for later. You, Stan, will have the fun of sliding down without the aid of the rope to slow you down just like my dad did many years ago. He said the important thing is not to get going too fast. Stop if you have to; but if you fall, try to keep your feet out in front of you and cover your head. Here we go; start lowering us down."

I shut my flashlight off to save on the batteries. The kids in my group didn't seem to be scared; they were laughing and giggling for now. When the tunnel floor got wet and slippery and they started to fall down, then I thought the giggling would stop.

"Carl."

"Yes, Sweet Pea. What is it?"

"How long do we have to do this?"

"What do you mean, Sweet Pea?"

"How long do we have to be in the dark like this?"

"Well, there will be times when we will be in the dark; and then there will be times where we will have our flashlight on, or we will use candles to light our way. Are you afraid of the dark?"

"Sometimes."

"I have been in this tunnel before, and there is nothing really to be afraid of. I'll be right here, and all the other kids are here."

"Amber's not here."

"I know, Sweet Pea. Amber had to do something very important."

"Will she be coming soon?"

Great. Now what do I tell her? I can't tell her that in a few days I would go back and try to find her, and then maybe bring her back. I needed to say something. "Amber will be with us as soon as she is done doing the very important thing."

"That's good; I miss her very much."

"So do I, Sweet Pea. So do I."

I had been noticing that the floor was getting steeper and wetter. I felt a tug on the rope. "Help! I'm falling!"

I stopped walking backwards and spread my feet and bent my knees hoping that I could catch whoever was falling. I could hear somebody coming closer. A small body crashed into my leg. With my right hand I reached out into the darkness to help this person to their feet and to have them grab a hold of the rope again. "Who do I have a hold of?"

"It's me. Karl."

"Well, Karl, it is very nice of you to drop in. Are you alright?"

"I think so."

"Let me get my flashlight and look to make sure that you are not hurt."

I shined the flashlight on Karl, but it was almost impossible to see if he was hurt or bleeding for all the dirt that he had picked up sliding down the tunnel floor. "Karl, you look alright. What I need you to do is to hang onto the rope, and we will try to go slower. We should be nearing the end of the steep part of the tunnel. Then we can sit down and rest and wait for the others."

"Alright kids, here we go; not much longer."

I shut the flashlight off, put it in my pocket and began walking backwards again for what seemed like a short time. I wasn't sure if it was my imagination or if we were really that close to the spot where the tunnel flattens out. Digging the flashlight out of my pocket, I turned on the light and shined it around. I untied the rope from around my waist and let it drop to the floor.

"I need you kids to stay hanging onto the rope because I need to look around."

I had the kids stay up along the wall, because I didn't want them to go down the tunnel and find the shaft. When I walked back to the kids after looking around, I could see that they were tired. They were still hanging onto the rope, but some were sitting and some were lying down.

"Alright kids, you can let go of the rope now. Come with me and sit over here and rest."

As the kids dropped the rope, I gave it two big tugs. I didn't want to yell in the tunnel just in case someone on the outside could hear us and come after us.

"Jeremy, I want you to make sure the kids stay next to the wall just in case someone would happen to kick loose a rock; you will all be out of the way."

"Carl."

"What is it, Sweet Pea?"

"Can we have your flashlight?"

"No, I'm going to need that; but what I can do is light a candle, and that will light a lot more than just my flashlight."

"Oh goody! We're going to have light."

I looked for a place to put the candle that it would give the most light. There, on a ledge just above the kids, would be a good spot for the candle. I lit the candle, dripped wax onto the rock, and placed the end of the candle into the wax. It didn't take long for it to cool down and harden to hold the candle up.

"How is that, kids?"

"Yea!" The kids shouted and clapped.

"Okay, good! Now we need to be very quiet again."

Silence fell over the tunnel once again. I walked down the tunnel toward the shaft trying to think of an idea on how to get everybody down the shaft, and there we would rest for as long as we could. As I entered the large room, I shined the light across the floor looking for the shaft entrance, but I wasn't seeing it. There were so many more rocks on the floor than when I first came through. All of the states' blasting and digging had loosened the rocks. As I walked around the many rocks, I looked for the entrance to the shaft. There it was, but it was partially blocked by some big boulders. I placed my hands on one of the rocks and tested to see if the rock could be moved. I placed my shoulder up against one of the boulders and pushed with all my might, but it didn't even wiggle. Shining the light on the hole, I saw that there was enough space for us to slip by the boulders blocking the entrance.

I heard the volume of voices picking up. I needed to get back to the group and get them to quiet down. On my way back to the group there was a loud boom, and the ground shook and dirt fell from the ceiling of the tunnel. The kids were screaming. I ran as fast as I could to get to the kids to calm them down.

"It's okay, kids. The state is just working on the prison above ground; we should be okay."

Grandma and her group of kids arrived. "Grandma, how many more groups are there left to come down?"

"Just three more."

"They are going to have to hurry. With the blasting up there, I'm not sure how long the tunnel will last."

"They are going as fast as they can, Carl."

"I know, Grandma. It's just that I fear for the safety of the kids. I have gone down the tunnel further, and there are some big boulders in the tunnel that were not there the first time I came through. The state has knocked them loose with all their blasting."

"Carl, you'll have to be patient."

"I know, but it is not easy."

"Why don't you go rest awhile, Carl. I'll let you know when Stan gets down here."

"All right. I'll work on how I'm going to get everybody down the shaft."

Grandma asked, "Carl, don't you think we can rest for a few hours?"

"I'm sorry to say we can't rest until we get past the shaft. We will be safer from the state police and the blasting."

The state let another blast go. It knocked Grandma to the ground, and I rushed toward her to help her up. "Grandma, are you okay?"

"I'm fine. I think you're right, Carl. There is no way we could get any rest with all that blasting going on."

Another group had made it down; two more and we could move on. I found a spot away from the kids so I could think of a way to lower people down the shaft. Sitting off to the side, I racked my brain to think of some way to get the people down; but no ideas were popping into my head. I was coming up blank. With each blast of dynamite, more and more dirt and rocks were falling. It was getting harder and harder to think, because I could hear the kids whimper with each blast.

A small hand touched me, so I looked up; it was Sweet Pea. "Carl, your Grandma said I should tell you that Sticks is coming down the tunnel now."

"Thank you, Sweet Pea, for telling me that. That is good news." I rose to my feet, and Sweet Pea and I joined the group. "Untie the ropes and store them. The two longest ropes we'll need to get down the shaft."

"How far is this shaft from here?"

"About 20 yards, Doc. Once we get down through the shaft, we will all sleep for a while."

"That's good. Ernie is getting very tired, and some of the kids are falling asleep each time we stop," Doc replied.

We could hear Stan coming down the tunnel. Clunk, clunk, clunk. Then he came into the room where we were all resting.

"Stan, you made it. Take a few minutes to rest."

"I'm going to take a few hours to rest. That took a lot out of me; I'm tired."

"I'm sorry to say, Stan, that we don't have a few hours for you to rest. We have to keep moving. Kevin, Doc and Grandpa, I need you to come with me to where the shaft is. We need to move this boulder over here if possible." The four of us grabbed onto the boulder. To our surprise, it moved easily into place. "Good work, men. Now we will take the ladder apart and place two or maybe three legs of the ladder and span the rocks. If we put our ropes over these legs of the ladder, we can lower the ones that need help. Some of the kids are old enough that they will be able to climb down the rope by themselves. I want a leader to go down the shaft first to help them get down and get settled once they reach the bottom. What leader would like to go first?"

Doc spoke, "I'll go."

"Great! When you get down there, I want you to find a place to put a candle for light so we have something to work by as we bring the kids down the shaft. Have them spread out around the room. That is where we will sleep for a few hours."

"Carl, should we start now?" Doc asked.

"The sooner the better. As soon as you get down there, I'll send my backpack down. I have candles and matches in there. As soon as you have the candle in place and lit, then we can start sending the kids down. I'll need at least one more leader down there when it comes time to lower those that need help. Off you go, Doc."

"Wait! I have one more question. How are you going to get the little kids to hang onto the rope tight enough so they don't fall?"

"We are going to take four rungs of the ladder and lash them together to make a seat like on a swing. All kids know that they have to hang on tight when they are on a swing."

"That answers my question."

Doc grabbed the rope in both hands. Sitting on the edge of the shaft, he slid himself off and swung into the opening of the shaft. In just seconds he disappeared into the dark. We could only hear him breathing as he climbed down the rope.

"I made it! I'm down. Send down your backpack." Grandpa tied my backpack to another rope and lowered it down. "Thank you. Now give me a few minutes and I'll have the candle in place."

We could hear all kinds of noise, but we weren't seeing any light. "Doc, what's going on down there? Where is the light?"

"I dropped the matches. Can you shine your flashlight down here? Maybe I can find them faster than me searching for them in the dark." I went to get my flashlight; but before I got to it, I heard a voice from below say, "I found the matches." Soon there was light shining up from the shaft.

"I'm ready. Send down the kids."

Stan helped line up the kids that he thought could climb down the rope by themselves. It sounded like they had stopped blasting rock. That was good for us. While the other leaders helped the kids get down, I went over to Grandpa to see how he was doing lashing the swing seat together.

"Grandpa, are you almost done with the seat?"

"Look for yourself, Carl."

"That is exactly what I was thinking. Now tie the rope onto it, and we can test it out with Sweet Pea. She is the lightest. If it wouldn't work or it breaks, Doc would be able to catch her."

We were down to the last few people to go down the shaft. "Grandpa, bring the swing seat over. We are ready for it now." Grandpa and I worked together to get the seat ready for the trial run.

"Sweet Pea, where are you? We need you to take a ride on the swing seat."

I heard her voice from the other side of the room. "Here I am, Carl."

"Are you ready to take a ride down the hole?"

"Yes, it looks like fun."

Grandpa and I placed Sweet Pea onto the swing and then pushed her out over the shaft opening. "Okay, guys, lower her down. Take it slow."

She was down in what seemed to be only seconds, and then we were hauling the seat back up. "Next!" yelled Doc and the other men up the shaft. We loaded the kids on the seat one at a time and got them down safely. Now we were ready to lower Ernie.

"Alright guys, you have had it easy with the kids. Now we are going to send you Ernie." Ernie looked very scared. "Ernie, are you okay?"

"Yes, Carl, I'm fine. I'm just a little scared about going deeper into the earth."

"Well, to ease your mind, once you get down the shaft, we don't go much deeper. What you need to do now is sit down here on the edge of the shaft, and we will put the swing seat under your seat. Is everything alright, Ernie?"

"Yes, I'm good. I can do this."

"All right men, get ready." They pulled all the slack out of the rope and almost lifted Ernie off the floor of the tunnel, and it frightened him.

"Oh my!" Ernie grabbed for me.

"It's okay, Ernie. The guys just got a little carried away when they pulled the slack out of the rope. As you can see, they are more than capable to get you down. If you're ready to go, I'll give them the signal and you will be on your way." Ernie didn't say anything. He just sat there on the edge of the shaft. "Ernie, did you hear me?"

"Yes, I heard you. I was praying that I would make it down in one piece."

"You'll be fine. Are you ready then?"

"Ready as I'll ever be."

"Okay men, he is all yours. Let's lift him up and get him in the center of the shaft. I'll reach out and stop him from swinging, and then you bring him on down. On the count of three. One, two and three."

I could hear the men grunting to lift Ernie into the center of the shaft. He was swinging back and forth like a pendulum on a clock. I reached out with my hand and stopped him from swinging. Ernie looked up at me and said, "Thank you. I was wondering if I was ever going to stop swinging."

"Hang on tight, Ernie. I'll see you in a few minutes." They began to lower him.

I was the last one that had yet to go down the shaft. It was my job to make sure we did not leave any evidence for the state to find if they happened to stumble onto the tunnel. I took one rung of the ladder and dragged the floor trying to erase our footprints from the dirt.

Then I stood at the edge of the shaft and yelled down to the men, "Send up another rope. I need to tie it to the end of the ladder so we can pull it off of the boulders and bring it down to us and not leave anything for anybody to find."

The extra rope I tied to the one end of the ladder legs. The state had started blasting again, and dirt and rocks were falling in the tunnel that we had just come down. Suddenly I felt extreme pain in my left leg and I couldn't move. I turned on the flashlight fearful of what I might see. The light shining on my leg showed I was in deep trouble. A rock had slammed into my leg and had pinned it up against another boulder. I tried to move it myself; but the way that I was pinned, I could not get any leverage to move it. I could feel blood running down my leg. The men were going to have to come back up the shaft and get this rock off my leg, and then Doc would have to fix me up.

Before I could call out to them for help, Grandpa yelled up to me. "Carl, are you coming?"

"Well . . . Grandpa, I have a bit of a problem up here."

"Like what kind of problem?"

"That last blast loosened up some rocks, and one has pinned my left leg up against the boulder here next to the shaft. I'm going to need you men to come up here and free me. Doc may have some work up here to do too."

"Carl, how bad is it?" yelled Doc.

"Doc, I feel blood running down my leg; and if I try to move any, the pain is really intense."

"Carl, don't try to move anymore. Just stay put."

"Say Doc, I'm pinned up against the boulder. I'm not going anywhere."

"You know what I mean, Carl."

I shined the light over the shaft opening and there was Stan's head popping up out of the hole. "Thanks for coming."

"The others are coming. They are right behind me." There was Doc, Grandpa and Kevin popping up out of the opening.

"Well, guys, what do you think?"

Kevin spoke up, "It looks like you did a fine job on your leg."

Doc came over and started poking around on my leg. "Where is most of the pain, Carl?"

"In the lower part of the leg."

"Men, we need to remove this rock without causing anymore damage to Carl's leg. Russell, I would like you to hold onto Carl just in case when we lift the rock off his leg, there may be a rush of pain; and we can't have him put any weight on that leg until I can take a good look at it."

"I don't think we are going to have to move it very far, and we should be able to get his leg out," Stan said.

Doc replied, "I think you're right, Stan. Let's all get a hold of the rock. When I say go, pull. Give it all you got. Ready? Go!"

The men must have gotten the strength of about ten men because the rock moved easily. I was so happy to be free, and then the rush of pain that the doctor warned me about hit me harder than the rock. I fell backwards up against Grandpa and another boulder. The pain was so bad I couldn't speak to tell anyone. My mouth was moving but no words came out.

Doc yelled out, "Lay him down quickly. We don't want him to go into shock. We can't have that."

Then I felt many hands helping me to the ground. Grandpa yelled down to Grandma, "Send up a blanket as fast as you can."

"Russell, what is going on up there?"

"Carl is hurt; but the doctor is looking after him, and he will be okay."

"I have the blanket, Russell."

"Tie it to the rope and I'll pull it up."

I felt kind of funny and a little dizzy, and I could feel the doctor working on my leg. "So, Doctor, how bad is my leg?"

"Carl, I'll tell it to you straight. You have broken your leg. You have a few good size lacerations, and there will be a lot of bruising. I will need to set the leg now. I'll tell you, it is going to hurt, and hurt a lot."

"Let's do it and get it over with."

"Guys, you'll need to hold him down while I set the leg. Carl, I need you to try to relax your leg muscle so it is easier to set your leg. I'm going to count to three, and then I'll set it. Is everybody ready?"

"Yes!"

"Here we go. One, two." The good doctor grabbed my leg and set it. "And three."

"I'll look at those cuts and we'll get a splint on your leg. Then we'll have to lower you down the shaft. You will not be able to put any weight on that leg. Russell."

"Yes, Doctor."

"I'm going to need two rungs from the ladder to make a splint and the leather straps to tie it to Carl's leg."

As the doc continued to work on me, I was hoping that the state would not start blasting again. The other guys prepared the ropes to lower me down. They would not be able to use the swing seat since two of the rungs from the ladder were now tied to my leg.

"Carl, are you feeling better?"

"Yes, Doc, thank you for all you have done. Am I ready to go? We need to get going. I can rest more when I get down with the others."

"Carl, you can go any time now. Just don't put any pressure on that leg, or I will have to re-set it. I don't think you want me to do that again."

"I hear you loud and clear-no pressure on the leg. Okay, guys, the doctor said I'm ready to go. Let's get me down the shaft."

"I'll stay up here to help you get started down the shaft, and then I'll climb down once you get cleared."

"Thanks, Kevin, for doing that."

The other men slipped down the shaft as fast as they came up it seemed. Kevin made a loop in the rope for me to put my right foot in. I would stand up instead of sit like the rest. I scooted along the tunnel floor to the shaft and slipped my foot into the loop.

"I'm ready whenever you say go."

"Go ahead, Carl. We got you," Grandpa yelled.

I slipped off the edge and swung back and forth. Kevin reached out, grabbed my arm and stopped me from swinging so much. Then I descended to the room below. Grandma was there asking so many questions they all blurred together.

I said the only thing I could say, "Grandma, I'm okay. It's just a broken leg. The doctor said I'll live."

Grandpa and the doctor grabbed me under each arm and carried me over to a spot and laid me down. I looked around the room at all the faces of the kids. None of them were smiling anymore.

Sweet Pea came up to me and looked long at my leg. "Carl."

"What is it, Sweet Pea? Why are you crying?"

"My doll broke her leg, and we could not put it back on."

Sweet Pea cried harder and wrapped her arm around my neck. "Sweet Pea, listen to me. My leg is going to be fine. The doctor fixed it, and I'll be walking in no time; you'll see."

"Are you sure?"

"I'm sure."

Kevin came down the rope just in time. The state started blasting more, and we all could hear the rocks falling in the tunnel. "Everyone needs to stay away from the opening in case rocks would fall in the shaft. Kevin, have you pulled down the ladder legs yet?"

"I'm going to do that right now." Kevin pulled on the rope tied around the one end of the ladder legs, and they came crashing to the floor kicking up a lot of dust and dirt.

"Let's turn out the lights and get a few hours of rest. We still have a long way to go before we get to the settlement."

One by one the leaders put their kids to bed and blew out their candle. Quiet fell over the tunnel; even the state stopped their blasting. I fell asleep with Sweet Pea curled up next to me on one side and Karl on the other. Grandma had made sure all my kids were taken care of along with me. She had put a blanket over the three of us. I slept like a baby until Grandpa came over and woke me up.

"Carl, wake up. We have been sleeping for what seems like forever. Some of the kids are awake already, and they are hungry."

"Let's feed them. And make sure they get enough, because they will need the strength and energy to help them stay warm. Grandpa, tell Grandma no cooking. We don't want to fill up the room with smoke. We'll have to eat our food cold. Have Grandma set up a makeshift kitchen. Have the leaders come and get the food for their group of kids."

We all ate a hearty meal and drank water to make sure we were ready for the day. "Everyone listen up. We will be taking the small tunnel on the far right. The space is very small at first but it will get bigger. We will take our time. Don't rush the person in front of you. After a while, the tunnel will start to climb up. You'll have to use the sides of the tunnel walls to help you move along. We will then reach an area my dad called the upper room. There we will see daylight. If the sun is out, we will wait until almost sunset. We have been in the dark too long, and our eyes will not be able to withstand the bright light of the sun. Any questions?"

"Carl, who do you want to lead since you are hurt?"

"Kevin, are you asking or volunteering?"

"Maybe a little of both."

"If you would like to lead, Kevin, lead on. You can't make a wrong turn because there is only one way out now."

"I'll lead then, Carl."

"One more thing. Make sure you have everything; don't leave anything behind. I'm going to go last since I will be the slowest of all crawling through the tunnel with my broken leg."

I watched as each person crawled into the tunnel again. It made me laugh as I thought how it looked. It reminded me of Kayla when she was young how she would suck the peas off her fork one at a time until her plate was clean. It would be good to see her again. Soon it was my turn to get swallowed up by the tunnel. I dragged myself to the small tunnel entrance, but before entering I looked around with the flashlight to make sure we didn't leave anything behind. I looked up at the bottom of the shaft and said, "Amber, I will be back to get you. I promise." Then I turned off my light and entered the tunnel dragging my leg. The pain in my leg had lessened from yesterday. The long rest that we took must have helped.

I could hear the ones ahead of me moving through the tunnel; no one was saying much. Everyone pushed themselves to keep moving because they wanted to get out of the tunnel. It was wise for me not to tell the people what they were in for before we started our journey, or there may not have been as many that would have taken me up on my offer to bring them to the settlement. The person in front of me was getting further away, and I could not hear them as well.

I put all my thoughts and energy into moving forward. One nice thing about traveling in the dark was that you lost track of how far you had gone, and time wasn't that important. We may have been crawling for miles or just a hundred yards, and we may have been traveling for hours or minutes. There was a rumble coming from the front of the pack, and I couldn't tell if it was good or bad.

"Carl! Can you hear me?"

It was Grandma's voice. It was her feet that were in front of me. "Yes, I can hear you, Grandma."

"The first group made it to the upper room and it is very bright; it hurts their eyes. What should they do?"

"Tell them to sit along the wall with their back toward the light and rest." I could hear them pass my message from one group to another until they got too far away.

Grandma called back to me, "Carl, is your leg okay?"

"My leg is doing very well." Grandma had stopped and waited for me. I could tell because her voice sounded closer. "Grandma, why have you stopped? Is the group in front of you stopped?"

"No, I just wanted to make sure you are okay and not left all alone in the tunnel."

"That is very nice of you. I think you can start again. I must only be a few feet behind you now."

"Carl, can you hear the kids' voices? They sound very happy."

"Do you think the kids will want to eat something when we get there?"

"Kids always want something to eat."

"We may have to wait awhile until the sun begins to set before we leave the cave. It may be hard to keep the kids quiet and out of the water."

"What water?"

"There is a pool of water below the upper room, and there is a waterfall also."

"Carl, this place sounds wonderful."

"We can have the kids read the writings on the walls the earlier travelers wrote as they made their way to the settlement. That could keep them busy for awhile."

I felt the floor of the tunnel getting steeper, and the sound of the kids was getting louder. Knowing that, it gave me energy to crawl a little faster so I could enjoy the happiness of the group.

Grandma was talking to somebody, but I couldn't tell what they were saying. Someone had turned on their flashlight.

"There you are. What took you so long?" It was Kevin and Stan.

"What are you doing back here? Who is watching the kids?"

"Your Grandpa. He has them all sitting down, and he is reading the writings on the wall and telling the kids how he knows the writers of the words. As you can hear, or should I say what you can't hear, are the kids talking. They are listening to every word your Grandpa says. He is a great storyteller," Stan answered.

"Back to my first question. What are you two doing back here?"

"We thought we would come back and give you a hand and drag you the rest of the way out to give your leg a rest."

"That sounds good to me. How do you want to do this?"

Kevin said, "I think if we just take a hold under your arms and just start walking, that should work. If we get tired, we'll rest a bit and then do it again until we get you up to the upper room." They placed their arms under my armpits.

"Carl, you can help us by folding your hands across your chest. That way we don't have to grab tight, and we can move along faster."

"Like this?"

"Yes, exactly! Are you ready?"

"Start dragging." I felt like I was being dragged by two work horses. "You can slow down a little."

"That's okay. We're doing just fine."

"What is the hurry? We can't leave the cave until sunset."

"Your Grandma said that when we all get together, then we can eat. I don't know about you, but I'm starving."

I could see that these two were not going to slow down one bit, so I saved my breath and let them drag me. Besides, it was faster than me crawling. It seemed like no time at all and I was entering the upper room with the rest of the group. To my surprise the kids cheered and applauded my entrance to the room. The guys dragged me over to my group of kids, and they flocked around me and wanted to look at my leg to see if it was still there and it didn't fall off. I showed them by moving my foot.

Grandma and Nurse Glover had been busy working up some food for us all. Grandpa got a break from his story-telling when the kids saw me enter the room. I looked toward the waterfall. The sun went under some clouds making it possible to look at the faces of the people in the room. But when that sun came back out, we all had to look away because it hurt our eyes.

Nurse Glover came over to me with a plate of food. "Here, Carl. I made you up a plate of food."

"Thank you, Nurse Glover. That is very kind of you."

"It is the least I can do for you. After all, you have set us all free from the state. By the way, Carl, you don't have to call me Nurse Glover. You can call me Lisa."

Grandma got into the center of the room and said, "Kids, here is what we are going to do. First we will pray in our group and thank God for all He has done, and thank Him for this food we are about to eat. Then one group at a time will come by and pick up their food, and then go back to your group area to sit down and eat. When we are done eating, we will all take a short nap. No matter whether you are tired or not, you will lie down and rest. Carl said we still have a ways to travel before we get to the settlement. Isn't that right, Carl?"

"Grandma is right. Once we leave the cave here, we have about a 1 ½ to 2 mile walk through the woods and meadows before we reach the settlement, so eat up and rest up."

My kids got closer to me and waited for me to pray, but I asked, "Who here would like to pray for the food today?" Some of the kids looked down at the floor, and some just shook their head.

"Karl, would you like to say a short prayer?"

"I'm not real good at praying."

"Karl, you don't need to be fancy. All you need to do is say what is on your heart. God will be pleased with that."

"Okay, I'll pray. 'Dear God, We kids and Carl would like to say thank you for the food we are going to eat. Thank you for getting us all out of the city and bringing us to this new, fun place to live with Carl. Oh! God? Can you fix Carl's leg? He broke it. He didn't mean to break it. It just happened, so don't be mad at him. Amen!'"

"That was a very nice prayer, Karl. Thank you for praying for my leg. Now when my grandma calls our group, I don't want you to run; walk nicely. Get your food, come back, and we will eat together."

I no sooner got the words out of my mouth and Grandma came over to say that it was time for my kids to get their food. Amber had them trained well. They walked in a single file line with no pushing or fighting. I wondered if someday when I had kids, they would be as well behaved as these kids. I only hoped so. There was no way of telling what time it was, because no one had a watch anymore. Most of the leaders traded them off to people to get more supplies without the state seeing a big drop in their credit account. With no watches, we had no clue as to how long a wait we would have before the sun set.

One by one the kids came back and sat down next to me. We ate, and I talked with each of them to see how they were feeling. Some were sad, and some were happy. When we had finished eating, I had Jeremy gather our plates.

I told the kids, "We all need to take a short nap so we will be ready to go when the sun is not as bright."

The kids said nothing. They just nodded their little heads and lay down. I lay back and put my head on my backpack using it as a pillow. I wasn't tired, but I closed my eyes to think on what we would do next.

"Carl, wake up. The sun is setting." When I opened my eyes, there were Grandma and Grandpa looking down at me. Grandpa was always trying to be funny. "Carl, are you going to get up, or are you going to lay there and rot?"

"I'm getting up." I began to rise to my feet when I was reminded by a very sharp pain in my leg that said, "I'm broken, remember?" That is when doc came over dragging some parts of the ladder.

"Hey, Doc, what is that?"

"Carl, this is how we are going to get you to the settlement."

"What is it?"

"It is a travois. The Native American Indians would use them to pull their women and children when moving from place to place."

"How does it work?"

"There will be two of us guys strapped into this harness made with ropes, and we will pull you along while you sit here."

"Have you seen this work before, Doc?"

"No, but if it worked for them, why wouldn't it work for us?"

"Well, help me in. I'll lead us out of the cave. Make sure we forget nothing. Grandma, can you make sure my kids are lined up right behind me?"

"I surely can do that for you, Carl."

"Is everyone ready?" There was a collective roar of yeses from the kids and leaders. "Are you ready to pull me?"

"We're all strapped in," said Stan.

"We will have to go through a tunnel for just a short distance. I hope this travois fits through the tunnel or I'll have to get off and crawl."

"Carl, you didn't say it was going to be this steep."

"Sorry. I forgot you haven't been here before. I spent many hours in this part of the cave when I was getting things ready for the journey to the city."

The guys pulled me up the tunnel, fighting to get me and the travois through the narrow passage. "Carl, we made it. We're at the mouth of the cave." The guys pulling me headed out of the cave.

"Stop! We need to wait until the rest of the groups make it out before we go. Kevin and Stan, can you see the trail that runs alongside the creek?"

"Yes, we do," they both replied at the same time.

"You will follow it until you see where it forks off. Take the right fork. That will take us into a small wooded area and then into a meadow. We'll cross the meadow and head back into the woods for a short distance. We will come in on the far end of the settlement. We will stop every so often to make sure we are not leaving anyone behind."

"Carl, what kind of greeting will we receive when we enter the settlement?"

"Kevin, that is hard to say. I have been trying to think of the best way to enter. We still have some time before we get there. I will have to ponder that for a while."

"There is the last group. Can we go now?"

"Yes, Stan. We can go now."

As we moved along the trail next to the creek, I tingled all over. It was good to be back home where we didn't always have to look over our shoulders to see if the police were coming, or if someone was telling the police what we were doing.

"Carl, you said to take the fork to the right, right?"

"Yes, we want to go to the right. Stan, I need to ask you a question. Did you and Amber ever teach the kids to sing?"

"Oh yes. We would sing a lot. When the kids were afraid or hungry because the police were looking for us so much that we couldn't get out to find food, we would have the kids sing. It didn't stop the hunger pain, but we did feel a little better when we got done."

"Did the kids ever learn the song, 'Jesus Loves Me'?"

"That was their favorite song. Why do you ask?"

"I think I have figured out what to do to let the people in the settlement know that we are coming, that we are the good guys, and not the state police. We will sing 'Jesus Loves Me' as we enter the woods after the meadow. The sound will enter the settlement gently without alarming them. They will all gather in the center of the settlement to see what is happening. They might send out a scouting team to make sure we are friendly people."

"I like that plan. It has been many years since I sang that song."

"Well, Kevin, you will be able to sing it anytime you want now and not have to worry about the police. Stop here.

I would like to send a message to all the leaders to have the kids be ready to sing at the right time."

The travois stopped. I called out, "Jeremy, come here. I want you to do something for me."

"What is it you want me to do?"

"Jeremy, I want you to go to each of the leaders and tell them to have their group ready to sing 'Jesus Loves Me' as nicely as they can when I tell them to, and don't stop until I tell them to. Do you got it?"

"Yes, I got it."

"After you tell them all, come back and join your group. Now go!" Jeremy took off down the path stopping to talk to each leader.

"If you guys are ready, we can go again."

By the time we got through the small wooded area, Jeremy had finished his mission and was ready to give his report. "Carl, all the leaders think that is a great idea. They said that as soon as you and our group start singing, they will join in."

"Well done, Jeremy."

Jeremy was just beaming; he was so happy to be of help. The time it took to cross the meadow seemed to be but an instant, and we were about to enter the wooded area before the settlement.

"Carl, do you want us to stop and wait for the groups to catch up?"

"Yes, stop and rest. You have been dragging me for such a long way; you must be tired." All the groups gathered together around me. "We are only a few hundred yards from the settlement. I want you all to stay in your groups. I do not want anybody running into the settlement before I have let them know that we are here and we have not been followed. We will start singing when we enter the woods. We will walk to the edge of the settlement, and the guys here will drag me in. I will meet with the leaders at the settlement, and then I will come back and get you. Some of the leaders may come back with us. Do not be afraid; they may ask you questions. They may want to know your names or ages. These are good people, so don't be afraid to talk with them."

They all stood in silence, some looking at me, and some looking around still amazed at the place that I had brought them to. "Grandpa, will you bring up the rear to make sure we don't lose anybody going through the woods?"

"Yes, Carl, I'll do that."

"Carl?"

"Yes, Grandma, what is it?"

"If it is okay with you, I would like to stay back with Russell."

"Grandma, you sound a little afraid. Are you?"

"Just a little."

"Why?"

"Your Grandpa and I were very mean to many of the people that are possibly at this settlement, and they may not like us here."

"Well, that is just too bad for them! They will have to work on their forgiveness now, won't they? All you have to do is ask them to forgive you for what you have done to them."

Grandma leaned over and gave me a hug. I could feel tears rolling off her cheeks onto mine. Grandpa was right behind her with a hug and a word. "Carl, I'm so glad to say that you are my grandson. You did a fine job leading us home-even with a broken leg. Now let's finish the journey."

"Amen to that, Grandpa. Okay people, let's move out."

We headed down the path weaving our way in-between the trees. I could feel the excitement building in me. It seemed as if it had been forever since I left. I wasn't sure what kind of reception we would receive. Dad would be proud, but mom would struggle between wanting to kill me for what I put her through or hug me until she squeezed the life out of me.

Stan turned around and asked, "Carl, when should the kids start singing?"

"They should start now. Stan, get them started."

"I can't sing! Amber is the singer."

I yelled out, "Who can start the singing?"

Lisa yelled back, "I'll start then."

She started her group singing first, and then the next group started and then another growing in volume as each group joined in. The song never sounded as sweet as it did now being sung by all these little voices. Their voices filled the woods with sweet melody. The birds hushed their singing to listen to the children sing from their hearts. We were getting closer to the settlement, and I was sure the people had to be hearing the singing. Would they send people out, or would they wait until we entered the settlement? It had been a long time since my dad showed up on their doorstep. Would they be ready for this many at one time?

"Carl! We can see buildings and there are people running about back and forth. Should we stop here?" Stan asked.

"No! We'll get closer. Jeremy, tell the kids and leaders to stop singing. Tell them it was wonderful and thank them for doing that."

Jeremy ran down the path to tell each group thank you and that they could stop singing. Then he reported back, "Carl, everybody is eager to see their new home. They are asking how much longer."

"They will not have much longer to wait. Let's go in and let them know that their prodigal son is home."

We headed into the center of the settlement. I could hear people talking, but I could only imagine what they might be saying.

"Kevin, Stan, get a little closer and then make a sharp u-turn so I will be facing the crowd. Is there a man in the group that looks like he could be my dad?"

"Yes, there is."

"Good. Stop in front of him."

"Carl, there is a lady standing next to him; she is crying," Kevin said.

"That would be my mom."

"Hang on, Carl. We are going to do the u-turn now," Kevin announced.

As the travois did a u-turn, I closed my eyes slightly. I kept them open just enough to see the faces of the people I missed so much. When the people saw who was lying in the travois, many covered their eyes, and many more pointed. Even before I came to a stop, I could see dad and mom running toward me and reaching down to touch me.

I opened my eyes and said, "I'm back. Did you miss me?" The crowd cheered when they saw I was okay.

Dad answered, "I knew you'd come back, Son."

"Carl Wilson, what is the big idea running off like that?"

Mom hugged me, and dad patted me on the back and tried not to cry. Once mom let me out of the headlock that she had on me, I could see that Great Grandpa Roy and Great Grandma Frieda were next in line to hug me; and there was no mistaking the screaming and crying of my little sister, Kayla.

"Mom, Dad, Everybody," I said pointing to each one. "I would like to introduce you to two of my friends. This is Stan and this is Kevin Zabling. Dad, you might remember the Zablings."

"I sure do." Dad reached out and shook Kevin's hand, and then reached for Stan's hand and shook it also.

"There are a few more friends of mine waiting to meet you all if you would like to meet them."

"Son, how many of your friends did you bring back with you?"

"I'm not really sure, but I think it's less than 65."

"You're joking, right Carl?"

"No, Sir. He's not joking. There are more than 50 some kids and 6 adults I think." Kevin piped up.

I replied, "Why don't we just have them come into the settlement, and you can meet the kids whose parents are in jail or have died at the hands of the state. Stan, please go tell the groups to come in, form a line and have them sit down."

Stan unstrapped himself from the travois and ran a short ways into the woods. He led out the first group and showed them where to line up. The people of the settlement watched as the kids kept coming, group after group lining up in front of the people who would become their new families. Dad came close to me and said, "Carl, you went back to find your grandparents. Did you not find them? Would they not come, or are they dead?"

"None of the above, Dad. They asked to come out last. They are a little afraid of how some of the people will treat them, since they were with the state police and may have had something to do with putting their family members in jail."

Dad took off running towards the woods yelling, "Mom! Dad! Come out! Welcome home!"

I motioned for the guys to turn me around so I could see. I got turned around just in time to see Grandpa and Grandma run out of the woods and embrace dad. Tears ran down my face as I watched my dad reunited with his parents, something he had dreamed of. Dad was so happy to see his mom and dad that he did not see his old friend, Ernie, sneak up behind him.

Ernie surprised dad when he asked, "Do you have a hug for your old friend, Ernie?"

Dad yelled so loud it echoed, "Ernie! You made it."

"Hey, Mom, is it okay that I brought home a few friends for dinner?"

"It's more than okay, Carl. You did a great job." I could see that the people of the settlement were inching forward wanting to meet their new friends but not sure if they should. "Go ahead, people. Make them feel welcome. They are not going anywhere." The people walked forward and mingled, asking names and ages. The whole place was a buzz.

"Mom, where are my friends going to stay until we find a permanent place for them to live? There are a lot of kids that will need to be taken into families, because they need the love and care of parents."

"Carl, don't worry. We will call a meeting and talk about what to do with all your new friends. But for now just enjoy your homecoming. We can talk later when we get you home. I see by the splint on your leg that you had a little trouble. When did that happen?"

"I was about ready to drop down the shaft. The state was blasting to build a new prison over the tunnel, and some of the rocks let loose. One pinned me up against a boulder and broke my leg."

"A broken leg is a very bad thing to have out here in the wilderness. There is no way to set the break. You could limp the rest of your life, and it may not be as strong as it was."

"It will be okay, Mom."

"Carl, I don't think you realize how serious a broken leg is."

"I do, Mom. Do you see that guy there next to Ernie, the older guy?"

"Yes, I see him. What about him? Are you going to say you talked a doctor into coming back with you?"

"Yes, not only a doctor, but two nurses also. The doc already set my leg."

"Carl, I think that rock that hit you in the leg must have hit you in the head also."

"No, really Mom. He is a doctor. Hey, Doc! Can you come over here? I would like you to meet my mom."

The doctor walked toward us, and I could see on mom's face that she was having second thoughts. "Hello, Mrs. Wilson. I would like to first say what a wonderful young man Carl is. I should introduce myself. I'm Doctor Kittleson."

Mom reached out her hand to shake the doctor's hand. "Carl said that you set his leg. How bad of a break is it?"

"Nothing to worry about. It set back into place very well, and it should heal nicely if he stays off of it for the next few weeks. Isn't that right, Carl?"

"Yes, Doctor, but as soon as I can, I've got to go back."

"What? Carl, you are not going back to the city!"

"Mom, you don't understand. I have to! I promised her I would come back."

"Who is this 'her'?"

"Her name is Amber. She is like the mother to all these kids. She took them in and made sure that they got fed and had a warm, dry place to sleep each night. Tell her, Doc!"

"He is right, Mrs. Wilson. Amber is a pretty incredible young lady for her age. Now I have said enough. I'll let mother and son work this out."

"Carl, tell me one thing. If this girl . . . ."

"Mom, her name is Amber."

"Okay. If Amber is so incredible like the doctor said, where is she now? Why is she not here?"

Grandpa could see I was in need of some help and came to my rescue. "I can answer that question for you. Oh, by the way, I'm Mark's dad and this is my wife, Ramona, Mark's mom. It's nice to meet you. Now about Amber, she gave up the opportunity to find freedom. She knew that if someone did not draw the police away from the tunnel, we would all be caught and sent to prison. That would be a very slow death both physically and emotionally. We don't know what has happened to Amber. We pray that she made it to a safe house somewhere in the city. If I could have had a daughter, I would have liked to have a daughter that is as compassionate as Amber. I know as a mother you don't want to let him go, but I also know he'll go back because he is a man of his word; and I'm proud to say he is my grandson."

"Thanks, Grandpa."

"Now Mom, do you see why I have to go back?"

"We'll talk about it tomorrow. For now let's enjoy the homecoming."

"Hey, Grandpa Edwards, come meet my other Grandpa."

For the next few hours the whole settlement ate together and talked. It was great to see each family of the settlement had taken in a couple of kids. Ernie was sitting at our table along with Great Grandma and Great Grandpa Wilson, Grandma and Grandpa Wilson, Mom, Dad, Kayla, me, and two more that we will add to our family, Karl and Sweet Pea. As I leaned back in my chair at the table and listened to everybody talk and laugh, I could now say that everybody in my family was in one place for the first time in many years. There were four generations of Wilsons at one table. This was a miracle. Thinking back to when dad first told me about his mom and dad, I thought we would never be together at one table. Yet here we were.

The reunion of Great Grandpa Roy and Great Grandma Frieda and Grandpa Russell and Grandma Ramona after all these years and heartache was great to see. They were talking and laughing as if they never missed a day. I think Kayla was as excited as I was to meet her Grandma and Grandpa Wilson for the first time. She would not stop hanging onto Grandma Ramona's arm. The best part was that no one had to leave. We were all home now.

I felt a tug on my shirt sleeve; it was Sweet Pea. "What do you need, Sweet Pea?"

"I need Amber, but she's not here. I miss her hugs."

"Would it be okay if I gave you a hug in Amber's place?" Sweet Pea stood there a few seconds and thought about what I had just asked.

"Okay!" Sweet Pea jumped into my arms and gave me a big hug.

"Sweet Pea, I thought I was going to give you a hug; but instead you are hugging me."

"Carl, it looked like you needed a hug too."

"You're right, Sweet Pea. I do need a hug."

"Carl, when will you be going back to get Amber?"

"As soon as my leg heals and the doctor says it is okay."

"When will your leg be better?"

"Soon. But not soon enough for me."

Grandpa Edwards stood up and motioned for all of us to quiet down. "The first thing that I would like to do is welcome our new friends to the settlement. I myself like seeing the smiling faces on these young children. Carl, I would ask you to come over here; but with your leg all broken up, I'll come over to you."

As Grandpa Edwards made his way over to the table where I was sitting, I looked at my family's faces. The men were all smiling and the ladies were all crying. Mom mouthed the words, "I'm so proud of you, Son."

"Carl, when I first got word that you left the settlement, I was afraid that you wouldn't make it back. I prayed that night for your safety. That night when I went to sleep, I had a dream about you. To make a long story short, in this dream I saw you coming back with many people following you. First I dismissed the dream thinking it was caused by something I ate for supper. I told your Grandma, and she hit me in the arm for saying what I ate caused me to have a weird dream. Then she told me that she had the same dream. We, as a settlement family, prayed for you daily and trusted in God to bring you home. Welcome home, Carl." The settlement erupted in applause and cheers. Mom and Dad were the loudest, and Kayla was whistling and jumping up and down.

"Thank you, Grandpa, for all your prayers. I needed every one of them."

"Now that you are home with your whole family and there are no missing pieces to the Wilson family, we will not have to worry about you."

Sweet Pea hopped off my lap and went running over to Grandpa Edwards. I reached out to stop her, but she was gone in a flash. She tugged on the pants leg of Grandpa Edwards. With her hands on her hips, Sweet Pea loudly said, "You're wrong. Carl is going back to get my friend, Amber. He promised her he would." Sweet Pea spun around and looked me in the eyes and said, "Didn't you, Carl?"

The whole settlement gasped. "Yes, Sweet Pea, you're right. I did promise Amber I would go back to get her, and that is what I will do as soon as I'm strong enough. Sorry to say, Grandpa Edwards, you're not done praying for me yet!"

Printed in the United States
93047LV00005B/1-15/A